# **Blood of Winterhold**

## Stephen Almekinder

Hard Shell Word Factory

For Mom and Dad, very special parents.

© 2000 Stephen Almekinder

Trade Paperback
ISBN: 0-7599-0090-6
Published October 2001

Ebook ISBN: 1-58200-547-8
Published April 2000

Hard Shell Word Factory
PO Box 161
Amherst Jct. WI 54407
books@hardshell.com
http://www.hardshell.com
Cover art © 2000 Dirk A. Wolf
All electronic rights reserved.

*All characters in this book have no existence outside the imagination of the author, and have no relation whatever to anyone bearing the same name or names. These characters are not even distantly inspired by any individual known or unknown to the author, and all incidents are pure invention.*

I

HE SPIRALED out of the trance and his fingers spiraled up the familiar curve of the prayer horn. He passed through one layer. His thumb and forefinger caressed the *S* shaped curve which represented eternity. He emerged from another layer. The tight button of truth slid beneath his ring finger and little finger. He broke through the last layer and his palm brushed the symbols of beauty and despair and love in rapid succession.

The prayer horn slipped from his hands and settled between his crossed legs. He opened his eyes, but just barely. The sun off the endless snow slashed through the slits, fuzzed by his eyelashes. As a matter of discipline, he did not close his eyes but held them half open. The cold burning light filled his eyes and seemed to penetrate deeper and deeper into his skull. He let it dig in.

Even as the hard edge of the light off the Waste drove a wedge up into his sight, he became acutely aware of the uneven surface of the frozen snow beneath him. It tilted him to one side and he discovered the muscles on the left side of his body were pulled taut to keep him from tipping over. He shifted his buttocks, which only served to reveal a new set of ridges in the snow beneath him. He forced himself to sit still in the new position.

The conspiracy of sensations was completed by the dead weight of his breather mask tugging at his neck. He had pulled it down and off his face just before he entered the trance. He needed to breathe unimpeded and, since he was in a shallow cave out of the wind, he did not need to circulate the frigid air through the baffles of the breather mask to keep his lungs from icing over.

Trys myr Lyn pyr Drun sat in a cave in the Northern Range and faced south. Using the techniques learned from his training to be an Interpreter of the Caynruhl clan, he had entered his trance in an attempt to lay to rest some of the doubts which had plagued him of late. The breaking of the trance by what he considered to be minor irritations only intensified the doubts. All of his life he had wanted to be an Interpreter; one who read, comprehended, and interpreted the words of the Chronicles of Blood through the Rituals, and by means of ceremonies helped to fulfill the spiritual aspirations of his clan. But was he meant to be an Interpreter? His fingers were numb from rubbing his prayer horn over and over in an attempt to answer that one question.

Maintaining his uncomfortable position and forcing his eyes to endure the wedge of bright light, he fumbled in his lap for the prayer horn. It was his favorite one. The carved bryl antler was etched with a series of symbols which were meaningful to both eye and finger. Arranged in a spiral about the horn, they aided the worshipper to flow up one side and down the other in an infinite loop of meaning embedded in sensation.

He touched the finely worn circle of peace and was prepared to glissade up and around the spiritually sensual series of symbols when a sound reached him which once again wrenched him back to the physical world before him. It was the soft crunch of a cautiously placed boot, followed by a dry hiss as the granular snow filled in the cavity around the boot. It was a common enough sound, but never had he heard it so distinctly. His thumb pressed the circle of peace deep into his forefinger. He had to look. He had to open his eyes fully to the world just beyond his rigidly held lids. He used the old Waste trick of slitting open first one eye, adjusting to the glare, and then bringing the other into play.

Below his cave lay a steep and narrow gully. It widened out at the base of the hill and the ridges on either side of it blended slowly into the snow of the Waste. They formed a pocket which was protected from the direct blast of the Waste wind. The inner sides of the ridges were comprised of lichen covered rocks, prime feeding for the bryl, while the configuration of the pocket resulted in a deep cushion of softly drifted snow, perfect hunting conditions for the predator. In this case, the herd of bryl was small, seven animals in all, and the predator was man.

Scramble and pause. A scarf of snow blew from the top of a drift, wrapped about the intent hunter, broke and blew away. Scramble and pause. It was the ancient hunting technique of approaching prey. Vary the pattern and catch the creature off guard. Do not stay too long in one position and do not move too quickly. Scramble and pause. It was slow and painful for both hunter and hunted. But it worked.

With eyes wide open now, Trys watched the hunt. The hunter was faceless behind his breather mask. His hood was up and his singlesuit tightly laced to provide him with the maximum protection from the bitter cold and the sharp ice. He was the anonymous personification of the hunter. And after one final pause, he dashed forward to fulfill his task.

The bryl closest to him leaped straight up, twisted in midair, and hit the snow running. But the soft powder slid beneath its hooves and slowed it down. The hunter lunged forward in an attempt to get in a clean thrust with his light hunting spear. Despite the awkward start, the bryl seemed to be darting out of range as it followed its comrades toward the mouth of the gully and the safety of the Waste beyond. The chase took on a sense of suspension as both pursued and pursuer matched their speeds for the briefest of seconds.

A second spear darted in from the side of the bryl and plunged cleanly through its heart to dissolve the suspension. A second hunter had lain buried in a snow drift near the mouth of the gully. His rise and throw coincided perfectly with the actions of the first hunter. Trys blinked. Even from his vantage point, he had not noticed the second hunter. The maneuver required the two hunters to work in absolute harmony. There was no room for thought, for that would only slow one down. It was all done by reflex and instinct developed over years of hunting together.

The hunters lost no time in securing their kill in the traditional manner. The one who had delivered the killing blow, yanked his glove off his right hand, grasped the haft of his spear with his bare hand, and jerked it free from the body of the bryl. The creature twitched and lay still. The hunter held up his spear and let the blood fully coat the blood metal which formed the spearhead and sheathed half of the spear shaft. The blood metal was heating up. Whenever the metal came in contact with blood, it took the heat from it and magnified it. In the frigid climate which held the entire planet in its grasp, blood metal allowed life to emerge from death. When the man was satisfied that the metal was completely coated, he tipped the point over his shoulder and slid it firmly into its back sheath where the warming metal lay close to his body and would provide him with the precious commodity for hours to come.

He then dipped his hand into the blood which poured from the steaming wound. He first scattered a few drops in an arc upon the snow and then up toward the sky to propitiate Mother Ice and Father Sun. The hunter watched as the drops of deep red blood arced up and out to lay down a trail of pink dots across the snow. And the trail led his eyes up toward the shallow cave where Trys still sat. In a glance he saw and recognized the man on the hillside. He waved and the way in which he twisted his open palm revealed to Trys who he was. He was his younger brother, Gyrs myr Lyn pyr Drun.

The snout of his breather mask dipped toward the other hunter and he spoke one muffled word. The other nodded but did not pause in his task of sewing up the death wound of the bryl. The preservation of blood was the preservation of heat, the commodity most valued in the eternal winter which reigned upon the surface of the planet. The man bent over the bryl, slid the head of his own spear into the blood which soaked the tightly napped fur, and then laid it aside as he set to work on the body. He worked deftly. In a matter of seconds he gave a final tug on the gut string, taken from another bryl some time before, and he was finished. He stood up briskly enough but with a definite catch in the motion of rising. Trys knew that he was his father, Drun pyr Khun myr Jynth.

His father straightened and then arched his back. Like the catch in his stance as he rose, Trys realized that the gesture was uniquely his father's, but that both were performed with more stiffness than Trys ever remembered having seen before. Drun slid his breather mask down to hang about his neck. He glanced up at Trys where he sat. He smiled. His appearance at that moment made Trys wonder when he had gotten so old. Years of squinting against the glare of the sun off the ice, he was notorious for not using goggles to protect his eyes, had deeply lined his face. His nearly closed eyes pulled the rest of the skin on his face toward the two sockets, making the lines more expressive than any of his other features. Like the stiffness in his movements, Trys could not recall noticing the lines on his face and connecting them with the onset of old age.

Drun turned then to help his other son to truss up the bryl to prepare it for the walk back to the clan caves. Trys shook his head once to clear it of the vestiges of the trance and to express to himself his sudden awareness of the age of his father. He had known but not recognized it. A fine Interpreter I will be, he thought. I do not even notice things about those I see every day.

He then scrambled to his feet and tucked the prayer horn into the belt of his singlesuit. Not bothering to slide his breather mask into place, he secured the hem of his Waste cloak to his belt to give his legs freedom of movement and stepped out of his cave. He had used the cave for meditation many times before and he knew the face of the cliff below it well. He dropped lightly from ledge to ledge and slid the last few yards to the floor of the gully, keeping his balance all the way.

His brother rose and looked down on his father who was tightening the last knot on the carrying harness which held the body of the bryl. Gyrs turned to Trys as he strode up and tugged down his own breather mask.

"Well, big brother, finished communing with the gods?" He grinned as he said it, but the usual hint of sarcasm was also detectable. Gyrs respected his brother but was too aware of being the younger one.

Drun glanced up at Gyrs. He looked as if he was about to reprimand him. Instead, he swung up and turned to Trys. "Did we disturb you?"

"No. I had finished. And believe me, Gyrs, I was not communing with gods or anything else. Unless you count the ice I was sitting on or the cold wind in my face. It was not one of my better meditations."

"Too bad. We, on the other hand, had a very good hunt as you can see."

"Yes. In fact, I saw the whole thing. Very neatly done. You two work together brilliantly."

Gyrs snorted at the compliment but was genuinely pleased with the praise from his brother.

Drun nodded. "Your brother has the speed and energy of youth. His reputation in the clan for his skills with both hunting spear and blood blade is deserved. Patience will come with time."

"I timed my thrust perfectly."

"I was not faulting you. You did wait until just the right moment. There have been times when the kill was not so neatly done."

Gyrs nodded agreement. His impetuosity on previous occasions had caused him to waste more blood than was thought proper by a hunter like his father who was versed in the old ways. He also recognized the tempered praise implicit in his father's statement.

"Father is always the perfectionist. Maybe that's where you get it from Trys."

"Perhaps."

"You got the brains and I got the strength and reflexes. A fair distribution, the way I look at it." Gyrs grinned just a bit too widely to be convincing. He was never certain which son his father liked best and for Gyrs it was always a question of who was the best. He weighed a compliment like a skilled hunter weighed his throwing spear, testing it for heft and power.

Trys did not take up his brother's challenge. The soured meditation had left him feeling restless and unfocussed. Instead, he chose to agree with Gyrs since he knew that even shallow flattery usually deflected his brother's escalating competitive spirit. "Yes, I'm sure it is. I was never as good as you with the blade or the spear. I kept too close to the Rituals for that."

Drun grunted and shook his head. "You are both my sons. I always try to treat you as equals. You, Gyrs, are very good with your hands but you also have an excellent mind. If you did not you would not be as quick and sure as you are on the hunt or in battle. And you, Trys, did keep close to the Rituals, as you put it, and I did not discourage that. It was what you wanted and what you are good at. You do have skill with the blade even though you hide it. You believe an Interpreter does not need such a skill. Well, you are mistaken in that."

"I know, father. I did not mean to sound ungrateful."

"We can't stand here all day and talk. We must get this bryl back to the clan and dress it properly. You are finished, Trys. Come back with us." His father spoke abruptly but his command was couched in a gentle tone of voice.

"Of course. I've finished for today."

Gyrs opened his mouth to make another biting comment but shut it when he saw his father's face. He would brook no more barbs. Instead, Gyrs yanked his breather mask up onto his face, tugged the hood of his singlesuit over his head, and grabbed one end of the trussed bryl. He remained poised over the carcass, waiting for someone else to take up the other end. Trys recognized the gesture. He pulled up his own breather mask, meticulously settled it in place, and then slowly tied his hood, taking care to prolong the process to aggravate his brother.

Gyrs jerked on the back legs of the bryl as Trys tried to secure his grip on the front legs. The two glanced up and even through the narrow slits of their masks, they could tell the sparring had gone far enough. Trys nodded to his brother. The snout of Gyrs's mask dipped in acknowledgement. They might compete but they still loved and trusted one another.

"Let's go." Drun slid his bloodied spear into his back sheath. He pulled his shoulders blades back as if to cup the rod of warmth which settled between them.

With long resilient strides, Drun led the way back up the gully. Trys settled his share of the weight of the dead bryl upon his shoulder and set out after his father. Instinctively, he matched his stride to his father's and Gyrs followed suit. The carcass required that they match their pace and they swung into the familiar pattern.

The crunch of boots upon snow filled the space between the narrowing sides of the gully. Drun bent slightly as he attacked the steeper angle of the gully and his ankles twisted to plant as much of the wide soles of his boots upon the snow as he could to give him traction for the climb. The low spikes upon his boot soles bit cleanly into the hardened snow and his legs pulled him steadily up the slope. Trys ducked his head and followed his father. He watched for the spike holes and placed his own feet squarely within their outline, in that way his father broke trail for him and made his own climb somewhat easier.

Drun topped the slope and without pausing set out along the narrow ridge which ran up to join the rising foothills of the Northern Range. In his turn Trys reached the top and swung onto the trail broken by his father. He spared a quick glance backward as he felt Gyrs scramble to the same level and shift the weight on his shoulder. Gyrs sketched a salute and bobbed his breather mask to indicate to his brother he was doing just fine. Trys raised his own hand and set out in earnest after his father who was moving slowly but steadily up the narrow ridge.

To either side, the snow sloped away gently when compared to the jagged thrusts of ice and rock above them. The Northern Range surged abruptly from the Waste and soared to close to one thousand feet in its initial elevation. Range built upon range to take the upper peaks thousands of feet high until the tops were lost in the frequent blizzards which roared through the atmosphere.

The facade of the Range was a study in contrasts between the pure white of the ice and snow and the deep black of the obsidian rock. Trys looked up to see the curved back of his father silhouetted against the towering piles of stone and ice. It was a sight which Trys loved but also respected. The mountains and the Waste were his home. Vertical grandeur and horizontal immensity, neither could be taken for granted for a moment, for that was the moment in which they could take your life.

The three negotiated the slope of the ridge with ease and paused as they reached the lowest tier of the Range. Here the snow, which had provided relatively secure footing, gave way to ice slicked rock. Drun unwound a length of rope from about his waist, secured one end to the harness on his singlesuit which secured his weapons, and passed the other end back to Trys. Trys balanced the stiffened leg of the bryl on his shoulder to free both his hands and with a few deft movements tightly knotted the rope about his own harness. The free end then went back to Gyrs who performed the same operation. The three were then prepared to ascend the slopes above them with some sense of security. If one fell the others knew how to break that fall and prevent themselves from following.

The wind died down and Drun slid up his breather mask to test the temperature. The light from the afternoon sun fell full upon the slopes they had to climb and warmed the air to a bearable level. He snorted and pushed his mask up on his head to free his face from the close embrace. Trys followed suit. The air bit deep but cleanly into his lungs. There was no chance of its freezing them. In the Waste the breather mask was the only reliable barrier between the subzero air and the warm and delicate lining of the lungs. Lose the integrity of the mask or remove it entirely and the lungs could be frozen in a matter of minutes.

Trys looked at the landscape which vaulted far overhead and stretched away beneath him. Winterhold was harsh. Relax your guard for a moment and it would take advantage of that weakness to break or kill. Winterhold was beautiful. The harshness which killed also allowed for a type of life which filled the senses to the brim and even over. Follow the rules and you survived. Disobey or even mock them and you had to suffer the consequences. There was little room for compromise. Those were the simple yet inexorable rules.

Perpetual winter held all of the globe in its grip, except for a narrow band at the very equator, and made certain demands upon the people who inhabited its snowy vastness. They lived a largely nomadic existence as they followed the herds of migrating bryl, an antelope like creature whose flesh and bones and hide provided most of the necessities of life. The bryl moved with the seasons to find the lichen on which they lived and the clans followed the bryl. It was one of the simple and inexorable rules.

Those rules were written down. They were also studied, dissected, and put back together in different combinations. The rules were contained in the Chronicles of Blood and embodied in the Rituals. The Chronicles of Blood were the written record of how past generations had dealt with the struggle against the raw elements as well as a history of the struggles amongst the clans. They told the clans how to survive but also how to do more than simply survive. From them emerged the Rituals which were religion and survival training in one. Certain members of the clan were chosen to read and interpret passages from the Chronicles and shape them into the Rituals which guided every aspect of their lives. Those interpretations directed the clans to the best wintering grounds where the bryl were likely to be plentiful as well as tutoring them in the best way to commune with the gods.

In a clan each member had a task to perform. No one was allowed the luxury of living off of the others. Where death was only the thickness of a breather mask membrane away from life, everyone had to play his or her part. Gyrs had chosen to become a hunter for the Caynruhl clan. In fact, due to his youth, unending zeal, and excellent teacher, he had become the premier hunter. He had learned the myriad skills required in the hunt from his father who still held the position of High Hunter within the clan.

Trys had taken a different path and had also been helped along it by his father. Trys studied the Chronicles, performed the Rituals, and became a novice Interpreter of the Chronicles. His role was different but no less important, for survival on Winterhold did not consist merely of feeding the body. In the savage climate it also meant feeding the soul so that it might thrive amidst the hardships which beset it from every side.

The harshness of the land was reflected in the harshness of the Rituals by which each clan lived. The Rituals mirrored and personified the land. The mirroring and personification helped one to survive. If the Rituals required much from the participants it was only because they were a training ground for survival in the Waste. Better to endure a Ritual and learn how to deal with the fickle and unforgiving climate in a controlled process than to learn a lesson in the real thing but not live to put it into practice. Everyone participated in the Rituals, but Trys had learned how to enter into their actual development. In that sense he dealt with the spirit of the land even more directly than Gyrs who went out into it every day.

The three stood there with their masks raised and stared at the wild landscape they knew as home. Drun snorted in his characteristic way to indicate his awe of the sight and at the same time their need to be moving on so that darkness did not catch them still on the trail. Both Gyrs and Trys understood all of that from the one sound. They knew their father well.

The brothers shouldered their burden again and fell into an easy lope which covered ground without taxing their strength or making them sweat. Excess moisture upon the body was to be avoided at all costs. Too much and it froze, and that killed. Drun fell back and matched his stride to theirs. The trail was wide and open as it ran in a slowly descending curve toward the lower hills where the winter caves of the Caynruhl were located. Each clan spent the winter, a time when storms ravaged the Waste daily and the temperature dropped to close to a hundred degrees below zero, in their own set of caves. They followed the migratory wanderings of the bryl during the milder seasons.

Trys glanced over at his father who walked just behind him and to his left. He caught Drun looking at him. The concern he saw there puzzled him. Like any father he was concerned about both his sons, but usually it revealed itself in less obvious ways. Drun realized that Trys had seen him. He snorted and tugged at his breather mask unnecessarily.

"Cyln myr Callyn pyr Jod awaits you in the clan caves."

Trys nodded. That was more like his father. He had something to say and had made a start. However, the pause which followed was longer than Trys expected.

"Yes, I know. She is on a visit from the Hold. She often visits at this time of the year before the storms of winter make travel impossible."

"So, your special guardian wants to see her favorite one. Maybe she has some special trinket for the new Interpreter." Gyrs's resentment of Trys's special relationship with the warrior who was bodyguard to the Queen/Lady of Winterhold was thinly disguised. It was an area in which he could not compete with his older brother.

"Gyrs, enough." The edge in their father's voice silenced Gyrs faster than his words did. Through the stiff body of the bryl, Trys felt a catch in Gyrs's stride as if he had been dealt a physical blow.

Trys's earliest memories contained the presence of Cyln myr Callyn pyr Jod. She was a member of the Caynruhl clan who had been chosen to serve as a bodyguard to the Queen/Lady Alisande who ruled her half of the kingdom from the heights of the Hold.

Cyln was a warrior with few equals among men or women. For reasons which Trys had never understood, she had taken him under her special protection. Every time she visited the clan she came to the cave of his family and taught him things about weapons and honor and politics, the things which occupied her life within the Hold.

The Hold lay far away to the south. It was a warren of buildings perched upon the slopes of a periodically active volcano. It was the seat of half of the power within the kingdom. Queen/Lady Alisande sat upon her throne high above the Waste while King/Lord Nordseth sat upon his throne at the foot of the mountain of the Hold.

Generations ago a schism had occurred which broke apart the kingdom. For reasons still unknown, the King/Lord left to lay siege to the Hold. The conflict had raged and subsided and raged again until it finally settled into an uneasy but consistent state of siege which endured to the present day. Neither side won and neither side lost. Commerce with the rich trading centers of the south was allowed within certain strict guidelines. The splintered society adapted to the new configurations of power and both King/Lord and Queen/Lady ruled, each had half of the kingdom and each maintained their part of the siege which seemed to be eternal.

The Rituals had gone with the people into the Hold. But on the slopes of the mountain with the fiery heart, a place to be revered but which also managed to debase the cold, clean lines along which the true nomad's mind traveled, the Rituals had changed. The presence of warmth in a consistent quantity had altered the way the original nomads who climbed the throbbing sides of the mountain looked at the world. It meant that the Rituals altered to match the new outlook. Where they had been a means to an end, the end being survival upon the frozen Waste, they became an end in themselves. They became embellished and stylized. The original purpose still resided within each Ritual, but it nestled like a seed deep within a hard shell. The Rituals came to serve different purposes as the Interpreters strove to draw power to themselves and keep it. They were used to bolster and justify the existence of the royalty and the subluminaries who circled about the binary star of the King/Lord and the Queen/Lady.

On every trip she made back to the caves of her clan, Cyln talked to Trys and explained to him just how the Hold operated. The explanations had been simple when he was young, but they had grown in complexity as he had grown, until he now felt he knew the inner machinations of power in the Hold almost better than the relatively straightforward struggles for control in the clans about him. In the Waste, the blood blade settled most arguments; in the

Hold, poisoned words did more damage, and the blade was used only to finish off the near moribund bodies.

For a long time Trys had been fascinated with the stories and viewed them as a sort of fiction, far removed from his own sphere within the clan. But after Cyln's last visit, he began to feel the fiction rapidly gaining reality. Cyln had been grim as she discussed the latest maneuvers within the power structure of the Hold and Camp. His mentor talked in general terms but with an intensity she generally reserved for battle plans. Trys had forgotten it in her absence. The fact that she awaited him brought it all back and that, coupled with his unsatisfactory meditation, troubled him more than he expected.

Trys turned to his father. "Do you know what she wants?" He asked it in the vain hope that his father would minimize the importance of her presence. The hope was in vain.

"I do not know. I only know it is of the utmost importance."

"Did she put it that way?"

Drun smiled a brief smile. "As you well know, she would never put it that way. No, it was the tightness at the corners of her mouth that put it that way."

Trys nodded. He understood. A curious sinking sensation hit him in the pit of his stomach. It had nothing to do with the fact that just then they were making their way along a razor sharp ridge where sheer drops of several hundred feet plummeted away on either side of them.

They negotiated the ridge and reached a series of natural terraces which allowed them to drop by degrees down to the level where the caves of the Caynruhl were located. Drun loosened the rope which bound them together and quickened his pace as they neared home. He had delivered his message and seemed disinclined to elaborate further.

Trys hopped down the familiar stones of the terraces but was preoccupied by the anticipation of what awaited him. Gyrs noted his pensive mood and began to jump just a second before Trys jumped. The body of the bryl slammed into Trys's shoulder. Only after the third slam did Trys snap his head around to catch Gyrs grinning. He wanted to reach back and slap the grin off his face.

But even as he began to turn he realized he might be leaving the clan soon and not returning for a long time. He had no real evidence of that, but it seemed the likely course. Cyln would not have come so late in the season for an insignificant reason. Instead of a slap, Trys grinned back at his brother. That disconcerted him more than a blow ever would have and he looked warily at his older brother, wondering what maneuver was being used.

With both brothers in a state of puzzlement for different

reasons, they reached the open area before the entrance to the caves of the Caynruhl. Drun looked back once before he entered the tall opening where two warriors always stood guard against an unexpected attack from creatures either wild or civilized. Both of his sons were grinning foolishly. He shook his head for he knew neither one had cause to smile.

## II

THE AIR IN THE chamber of the Seer throbbed with the heat from the roaring fireplace. Even though a sharp wind blew down Steelstain Alley from the distant Waste and kept the nighttime temperature far below zero, water ran in rivulets down the outside of the windows. Nyls pyr Fytrys myr Wynt stood near a window, watched the water run, and wiped his fingertips through the unfamiliar sweat which trickled down his near naked body. He loved the cold and would often venture forth in the streets of the Lower Hold with his singlesuit open at the neck just to feel the icy wind wrap around his throat. He flicked away the warm drops distastefully as the heat in the chamber of the Seer continued to bludgeon him.

He turned toward the fireplace and squinted against the red glow. With an effort he moved closer to the fire and the figure which lay close to it. The ex-First Seer Sebaste lay motionless, bundled up tightly, already like a corpse in his winding furs. But he was a corpse who spoke. For hour upon hour, the voice of the Seer had filled the stifling air of the chamber and pressed word after word into the heat dulled mind of his young protege. Even now he spoke, although his voice rasped as the power which Nyls had come to rely upon ebbed away.

"From the window in the final tower, one looks down upon the buttresses which arc up and in to come to rest just beneath the window. They seem to barely touch the massive wall and yet their sure support can be felt through the very stones. Within the edifice of memory, the buttresses are the basic tools of memory recall: sight, smell, taste, hearing, and touch. They support all the rest and help to connect memory to memory, just as a physical buttress helps to hold up the walls of an actual building. We have been over them again and again. And from the window, which corresponds to the memory of my service to the King/Lord Nordseth, one can see them and use them to delve deeper into the ten year period when I was First Seer in the Camp. I just want to give you signposts now. It is all I have the strength or time to do."

Nyls approached the hearth. A chunk of coal cracked and settled into the deepening ashes. Nyls winced as the puff of heat rolled across him. "Yes, Sebaste, I know. Do not worry. I am getting it all. You taught me well. I can visualize the edifice of memories and could tell you the entire history of all of the Sebastes from the first one down to you. It's just a matter of walking through the building and recalling memory after memory as the mind's eye travels across the surfaces of the building."

"Yes. We have been over it again and again. Practice is the only sure way to build the edifice, to organize and be able to recall all of the memories. All of the thousands of memories. All of them there like solid blocks of masonry. All of them."

Sebaste's head rolled away from the fire and toward Nyls. His eyes were glazed in the pale face framed by the ice white hair. His skin was cold to the touch despite the savage heat which baked it. Nyls had wrapped him in the furs hours or days ago, he had lost track of time, as he followed his mentor in his wanderings through the rambling building of his memories, and at that time his skin had been dry and cold. With an effort of will, Nyls moved in closer to the fire and touched the Seer's cheek. It felt like it was glazed with ice. Sebaste stirred at the touch and focussed his eyes upon the young face above him.

"Ah, Nyls, there is so much to pass on to you."

"You can do it. You have done it. I have nearly everything. There is only the final tower to mount."

"The final tower is my own. It represents my own personal memories. The memories of my own life which is yet subsumed in all of the others who came before me." His head jerked up and he struggled against the bonds of the furs. "Are you sure you want this? Are you sure?"

Nyls pressed down upon the taut shoulders of the dying man and felt the strength which still remained in the shivering body. Even racked as he was by the wasting disease of the blood which stole the heat from his body, he still had power.

"Yes, I am sure."

"You must give up both patronymic and matronymic. You will no longer be Nyls pyr Fytrys myr Wynt. Instead, you will be merely, Sebaste. Just Sebaste, and not even First Seer for I gave up that position years ago when I left the service of the King/Lord. I gave up the traditional post. No, I was forced to give it up. You remember. I have told you, haven't I?"

"Yes, I remember. King/Lord Nordseth pyr Nystrin myr Olda feared the power your memories gave you. He did not want you to know what he might do based on what his ancestors had done. He wanted, and still wants, absolute power over his subjects and himself."

"You do remember. But are you sure?"

"I am sure. I willingly renounce my claim to both my father's and my mother's heritage."

"On Winterhold, blood is all. It is heat and so life. It is

measured carefully and determines who and what each becomes. You are incredibly brave to give that up."

Sebaste relaxed. His shoulders slumped and his head rolled back as if it had come loose from his neck. Nyls studied the old face for signs of life. He saw the nostrils flare and knew Sebaste was still there. He also knew he was holding on to life by sheer will power. The Seer had to pass on his final set of memories before he could let go and lose all memory.

Instructed in the rigorous technique of memory recall, Nyls had absorbed all of the memories of the Sebastes who had come before. Just like himself, Sebaste had crouched at the death bed of his predecessor and listened to the final words which would remain embedded in his mind to be passed on to the next heir. The Seers had acted as advisors to the royal family since the first nomads had crawled up the slopes of the mountain and reveled in the heat found there. Their special talent for recall had made them a useful tool in ruling, for a review of how past situations had been handled gave the monarch the opportunity to avoid making the same mistake again. Sometimes it worked, more often than not it failed. Rulers do not like to listen to cautionary tales.

Sebaste turned his face toward Nyls. "Listen, for we are at the final tower in the edifice of my memory. It contains my own personal memories, my contribution to the pile. You will know some of the later ones for you were present when the events occurred, but you must listen closely so that you can recall them as I remember them, not as you do, for you are not yet Sebaste. Do you understand?"

"Yes, Sebaste, I understand." Nyls held the Seer's head in his lap and watched the concentration of will gathering there. Sebaste nodded and began the ascent of the final tower.

"Shallow steps lead up to the raised entrance of the tower. In that way I moved from the previous Sebaste's memories to my own. The shallow steps are worn in a trough in the center, so many feet stepping on the stones so many times. The last step takes you across the threshold and into an antechamber, small and roughly finished off. No comfort, strictly utilitarian. You know this chamber, don't you?"

Nyls nodded and added, "Yes, very well."

"Good. For I must skip over this chamber and three others beyond it. You know them and can recall the memories they represent with no difficulty. I have tested you often on these early memories. It is the later ones, the ones close to the top of the tower which I need to review once more, perhaps more for my sake than for yours, for you are an excellent heir. You will serve well, if you can discover who you can serve and in what way. But that is part and parcel of the memories.

"You stride quickly through the next three chambers after the antechamber. The architectural styles vary widely. I was trying out different methods of memory storage and recall, my own designs. It is for you to decide how successful I was. But there is one noticeable improvement, the chambers are more finished, polished if you will, as you progress. I did learn as I went. Three rooms here are equal to about three decades of time. A long time but relatively uneventful if you don't count the embellishments around the windows and the ceiling designs. Perhaps I was bored, perhaps that is why it took so long to complete only three chambers of memory."

Sebaste heaved a sigh then. Nyls bent lower to search for a continued breath. It was there. Nyls offered an observation to nudge him onward. "There might have only been three chambers but the memories are concentrated. Each embrasure, every tile carries a wealth of memory. I noticed that right away. It is well constructed."

"Thank you for saying so. Flattery, even now, perhaps particularly now, is much appreciated. But we must continue. Leaving the third chamber you enter a large hall of unusual proportions. It swells from the low entrance, builds in grandeur and scope and is then terminated abruptly by a brutally simple wall. It is this chamber and the memories it represents which I must talk about.

"The low entrance is where I emerged from the relative obscurity within the court of the Camp and took on the full scope of my duties. I served well, the straightforward architecture of the swelling hall speaks to that. The blank wall is much more problematical. Quite simply put, I was dismissed from the service of King/Lord Nordseth due to that monarch's obsession with control. He could not stand to have anyone else privy to his plans and he perceived my power of extrapolation of future events based on familiarity with past ones as an invasion of his privacy, and so a diminution of his power. It was a slap in the face. I did my job well and was extremely circumspect. Many was the time I was approached to 'alter' recalled memories in favor of a particular Lord or Lady. They believed that by bribing me they could somehow alter history. My belief in what was and the way in which it had been handed over to me was strong enough to withstand these temptations. I had all of posterity to think of. If I altered one memory it would somehow compromise history as I knew it. I could never pass that sort of legacy on to my heir. So I was much more truthful than any of the King/Lord's other counselors. Perhaps that is why I was so much more dangerous to him.

"Provided with these chambers on Steelstain Alley in the Lower Hold, I still retained my connections with the various sources of information which served to fill my storehouse of memories. Nordseth did not negate my existence then, he merely sidetracked it. Due to my illness, which made itself evident nearly two decades ago, I was placed in the relative warmth of the town which surrounds the base of the Hold. There I continued to receive pupils from among the First Lords and Ladies and, in fact, was able to tutor youths from both Hold and Camp. At the time of the schism, the King/Lord had taken the First Seer with him and so traditionally those duties had been restricted to the Camp. You can trace all of those lines clearly in the architecture which leads one's eyes down the hall. The moldings, the wall panels, and the fluctuating yet symmetrical pattern of the floor tiles all point in that direction; the direction in which I believed I was going. I designed it to do that, to direct the vision forward and upward. But the lines are cut off abruptly by that wall, that simple, blank wall."

A sigh shuddered the length of the old Seer. Nyls squeezed his shoulders and he nodded ever so slightly.

"That wall is this place. And yet there is more beyond it. Small chambers and narrow halls. Nothing on the scale of that grand arching space. But I have learned that the spectacular, either in architecture or memory, does not assure one of immortality. It is the small things, the details which count. You know that, don't you, Nyls?"

"Yes, Sebaste, I know that. It was one of the first things I learned from you and it is one of the things you keep teaching me."

"Yes, the wall and then the details. The first room beyond the wall is a modest one, simply designed and finished. It is a lot like this chamber; the memories which make it up bridge the gap between the walls and support the floor above. Serviceable and solid. From the comfort of Steelstain Alley, I watched the professional and amateur plots for power grow and collapse both above and below me. You and I were even involved in one which served to establish the tenor of the present Queen/Lady's reign. It is there in the long, thin slabs of stone which run parallel across the floor and which are mirrored by the finely wrought beams overhead. Look at those slabs and beams and you can recall all of the essential memories and many of the embellishing details.

"You see, it begins there just within the threshold. For his own nefarious purposes, Nordseth had chosen a young and potent First Son to become Consort. His name was Gerred pyr Nordseth myr Phylla. At first it was thought he was merely one more in a long line of ineffectual Consorts and Concubines which shuttled back and forth between King/Lord and Queen/Lady. The entire system of Consorts and Concubines had been established by the Interpreters of the Rituals within the Hold. It was designed to maintain the purity of the blood lines for both halves of the crown. Since the King/Lord and the Queen/Lady never actually met one another after the schism, proxies were carefully chosen to represent the monarchs. Concubines who possessed certain strains of blood belonging to the Queen/Lady were sent to the King/Lord, while Consorts in whose veins ran the blood of King/Lords were dispatched periodically to the Hold. Offspring were produced frequently enough to insure that the lines would continue, but not so often that clear lines of power would be threatened. It is all there, clear for you to see. Slabs and beams, solid and sure.

"The next room is connected to the last by an unadorned door. You walk through it into a space similar to the last one in concept but executed with more fervor. The memories congeal thickly here. The straightforward parallel lines of the previous room are crossed again and again and not always in a consistent way. It might seem to verge on chaos, but a very real intent is there. Sometimes you will find it is the only way to arrange memories within the edifice.

"In the choice of Gerred as Consort, King/Lord Nordseth underestimated the potency of his First Son. Gerred and the Queen/Lady Alisande fell in love, an emotion strictly prohibited to the monarchy and one which had disastrous results for all concerned. They went through the Ceremony of Mating, the Ritual which provides the thin trickle of heirs for both of the thrones, and Alisande, primed by a variety of Ritual drugs, became pregnant. After the Ceremony, and still under the influence of his own battery of Ritual drugs, Gerred visited Alisande in her garden at the top of the Hold. I recall it that way, but perhaps the act was one of reckless love. Memories must be interpreted. I leave you both possibilities. You must decide whenever you come upon it which one to relate.

"Love or drugs, Gerred was caught in the garden of the Queen/Lady by the disguised henchman of the King/Lord, Lord Kysel myr Ryuth pyr Zor. Disguised as a purveyor of Ritual drugs to the Hold Interpreters, Kysel was scheming to take over both of the thrones and he would stop at nothing. After a fierce fight, Gerred escaped from the garden and the Hold. Battered and weary he stopped at my chambers on his way out of the Hold and in flight to the south. Once a favorite pupil of mine, I provided him with a blood blade and a way out of the Hold. You and a merchant in hides smuggled him out of the Lower Hold and down to the merchant's barge. From there it was an easy, albeit smelly, trip to the trading centers of the south. You recall all of that quite easily, don't you? It comes within the ambit of your own direct memory."

"I recall it very vividly. I also recall that the situation in both Hold and Camp deteriorated even further and you sent me south to try to find Gerred and bring him back to the North. You hoped his presence, as disastrous as it had proved before, might act as a catalyst for the change which was heavy in the air."

Sebaste nodded and Nyls continued. "I found the former Consort. He was acting in a third rate theater with a couple of his actor friends, the only ones who had stayed by him. He had nearly hit bottom by that time. It was not the poor wages of the actor which had brought him to that pass, rather it was the sommess which he consumed in large quantities. Lord Kysel had bribed an Interpreter to introduce an addictive dose in with the Ritual drugs he had to take for the Ceremony of Mating. His skin was already deeply tinged with silver when I saw him. It meant that he was far advanced in his addiction. It meant there was no going back. He did use one of the side effects of the narcotic, the numbing of the nerve endings and the reduction of the amount of pain experienced, to help keep in him sommess. He had become a paid dueler in the pits, those places where disputes of all kinds are settled by mercenaries hired by the opposing parties. His skill with the blood blade had vastly improved and he was a formidable champion, for a price.

"However, his career, both on stage and in the pit, was cut short by the appearance of Lord Kysel who had been sent by King/Lord Nordseth to kill him. Kysel declined to do so in a moment of uncharacteristic weakness, or perhaps it was overelaborate cunning on his part. Perhaps he believed he could use Gerred somehow to unseat both King/Lord and Queen/Lady. His schemes tended to be too complex for their own good. He did tell Gerred of how the Queen/Lady had disappeared from the Hold and of how she had been pursued Northward by his men as well as those from Hold and Camp. They had lost her in a snow storm. Months later she emerged from the North ostensibly at the head of an army composed of the fractious clans of the North. It's true leader was Brys pyr Prys myr Edya. He had forged a formidable force from the warring clans and placed the weakened Alisande at its head. She was weakened because she had given birth to a supposedly stillborn boy child, although no one ever did see the body since Cyln, Alisande's loyal bodyguard, said she had consigned it to the Waste as was her right and duty. Brys kept the death of the infant a secret and used the bogus child as a claim to the throne of Winterhold, a united throne. It was that which broke Gerred free from his self-destructive round and sent him back North. He still loved Alisande and felt he had to do something to save her. He knew he would die anyway since he was so far gone on sommess. He wanted to sell his life dearly."

"Good." The sound was a whisper from between Sebaste's blued lips. "You recall well. And you recall that Gerred came here to Steelstain Alley upon his arrival in the Hold?"

"Yes, of course."

"He came back. And so we enter the final chamber. Straight lines break down here. The dying curve replaces the precise horizontal line. But that is as it should be. It is how things are. The decisive path bends and meanders and becomes little more than an abstraction. But truth clings even to such meanderings. It is the truth of history; it is the truth which you must absorb and recall for someone, even if it is just for yourself."

"I understand. It will not be lost."

"Not lost. Never must be. Keep it well. Keep it the way I kept the blood blade I then passed on to Gerred when he was headed south. I like to believe it helped him to stay alive long enough for him to return for the final conflict with Kysel and Nordseth and himself. The blade had been mine. That is, mine and not Sebaste's. It was the only object I claimed as my own. The forces of the army of the North were involved in a pitched battle with those from both Hold and Camp. The blood blade got him back to the Hold, but he would not take it up the mountain with him. He returned it to me and asked that I pass it on to his son, the son whom he believed existed. And so he left the blood blade I had given him, although he did possess an inferior one which would serve him for the job ahead, and he went back up the mountain, through the battle which raged all around, and into the garden. There he faced Kysel for the final time. He killed him and most of his men, but was mortally wounded in the process. Since he was so filled with sommess and his nerve endings so numbed, nearly all of his vital organs had to be damaged before he could actually be brought down. But he did fall. She held him as he died and told him that indeed their child had lived. She could not bear to tell him what she believed to be the truth then. He died and things were never the same, in either Hold or Camp. Things changed and continue to do so. Things change and pass away and return."

Nyls slid his hand gently down to Sebaste's chest. The faint beat of his heart could still be felt.

"And return. Just like old Sebaste. Sebaste is dead, long live Sebaste, eh? It is not just royalty of which they can say that. Eh?"

"Yes, Sebaste, not just royalty."

"The last room I described was my own. My own last room. I need now to break through a wall and give you a portal through which to walk and from which you can begin to build your first room. I will put it in the center of the final wall, the one which lacks embellishments of any sort. You know the current situation in Hold and Camp as well as I do just now, perhaps better since you have not been wrapped up like a bundle of dry bones for the past few weeks. You tell me what you see and I will fill in what I surmise."

Nyls breathed deeply of the hot air which swirled so tightly about his head. He shook his head to clear it and frowned down at his dying mentor. Sebaste did not look at him. He seemed to be staring fiercely at the mantel above the hearth, as if by concentrating on that one solid piece of masonry he could hold on to the ragged ends of his life.

"The current situation. It has...degenerated." He paused.

"Yes, degenerated. A good word for what has happened since the death of Gerred in that garden far above us. Degenerated."

"It has degenerated in the sense that communication between the two half thrones has nearly ceased altogether. The Interpreters talk to one another and try to force both King/Lord and Queen/Lady into accepting another Concubine or Consort, but both seem intent upon defeating such a purpose. Delaying tactics have become an art and the tension between Hold and Camp has been solidified into a tangible thing. Nordseth gets closer to death by inches each day. His consumption eats away at him from the inside. And as he dies he grows more cruel. He holds power but with an unsteady hand now. Kysel did more damage than he imagined when he stepped in and tried to wrest power from both monarchs. Nordseth loses power and to keep up the illusion that he still retains an unlimited source, he orders acts which cause more and more blood to flow. He believes the violence is a manifestation of an active and powerful will when in truth it is the beginning of the final stage of dissolution. He is dangerous; the situation is dangerous."

"Well put. Suspicion and fear rule the Camp now. And what of the Hold? What is the situation there?"

"That is more problematical. Queen/Lady Alisande has taken her disgust with anything connected with the Interpreters to an extreme. She suppresses them whenever she can, although her control there is limited since their power base is not directly under her dominion. She focusses so much of her attention on the Interpreters that other areas of her domain have been largely ignored. A barely contained chaos buzzes at the highest levels of the Hold. Certain military leaders have been able to take over some of the neglected areas and so gain power for themselves. In many ways, Alisande is stronger and more determined than she was before Gerred, but she has not directed her strength and determination and so she slowly weakens."

"And the people. The ones below all of the power struggles. What of them?"

"They have always grabbed the crumbs which have fallen from the high tables. Now entire dishes are being swept off those tables and the people eat their fill and gather their own form of strength. The classless have become the biggest threat to both Hold and

Camp. They have nothing to lose and something, even if it is mere subsistence, to gain. The classless can no longer be ignored. A few leaders are emerging. If they can direct the bursting energies caged there, even in the most basic way, they might be able to sweep away much of the old order. It is an uncomfortable time for all."

"An understatement to end it, eh? That is like you, Nyls. I can still call you Nyls, for until I die I remain Sebaste. There is one other item I must give you my opinion on, although the final decision will certainly be yours to make. You know Alisande has formally requested that I, that is Sebaste, ascend to the heights of the Hold and serve her as First Seer. That goes against all tradition. The King/Lord took the First Seer into the Waste with him at the time of the schism. Ancient loyalties are being questioned here. I have put her off since I have known for some time that I was dying. Strangely enough, I did it out of loyalty to my original oath. I swore to the King/Lord to serve only him. I would like to keep that oath. And it looks as though I shall. But you are a different matter. You will become Sebaste, but Sebaste in your own right. You have sworn nothing to anyone, except me. You will have to decide who to serve, if anyone. You will have to decide."

His last words faded and a spasm twisted his face. Nyls bent lower and a drop of sweat splashed on Sebaste's icy cheek. Sebaste spoke in a thin dry voice which threatened to break at any second.

"You decide. I have given you the portal. I trust you to make a fine edifice beyond the rude opening. There is one thing I cannot tell you outright but concerning which I can leave a hint. It has to do with the schism, that seminal event which altered history and set us all on the path we now walk. All I can say is, listen. Memories are recalled through all of the senses, but not as often through sound. Listen. That is all I can say. The rest is for you to find."

"I will, Sebaste. I will find it, whatever it is. I will make you proud of me. Sebaste? Sebaste."

The question turned into a hushed cry. Another drop of water hit Sebaste's cheek. Nyls had ceased sweating.

"Sebaste is dead, long live Sebaste. And you will live long. You will live forever within me and beyond me. You were Sebaste and now I am. Motherless and fatherless, I must claim my inheritance of memories and they will long outlive an inheritance of blood."

Sebaste straightened the quickly cooling body before the hearth. He smoothed the tightly bound fur across its chest. And then he curled up in the relative coolness behind it. He closed his eyes and slept and fantastic buildings rose up in his dreams. He walked through them and knew he would be able to recall every cornice and turret for the buildings were his as he was theirs.

## III

THE LIGHT OF early evening made its contorted way into the chamber through an absurdly expansive window. Its diffusion did consign the corners to blessed obscurity, for one had the feeling that what lay there did not deserve close contemplation. The light did reveal a fine vein of quartz which ran diagonally down the side of the mountain which loomed a few feet from the large window. The tavern, of which the chamber was a part, had been built close up against the mountainside of the Hold as if for added support, which indeed it had need of after so many years. As with the corners of the chamber, not much of the tavern deserved close contemplation. It was the perfect place to hold the furtive plottings of a nascent revolution. Like all of Hold Gate it was close and squalid, yet redolent of a certain type of vital and violent life, the kind which swept people up and delivered them sooner than later to a violent and colorful death.

It was to this chamber of contorted light that Lyrdahl pyr Ryx myr Lyndahl, the mastermind of the beginning of a revolution, made his way. He opened the door with great care, partly out of habit, for he had entered many rooms like it with similar caution born in the thickly suspicious atmosphere of plots and counterplots, and partly to keep the door from tumbling off its nearly rusted through hinges. He glanced about. The filth in the corners held no menace and the simple table and three battered chairs hid no one. The panoramic view of the vein of quartz which ran like a crystalline stream down the side of the mountain drew a snort from him. Both the view and the boldness of the window appealed to his appreciation of the absurd.

Lyrdahl pyr Ryx myr Lyndahl had a well developed sense of the absurd. His family tree had sprung from it and been twisted and stunted by it. Over three centuries ago one of his ancestors had befriended someone he had believed was an itinerant warrior. The simple hospitality of his tent and his fare had made a lasting impression upon the hungry man. But his hunger had encompassed more than dried bryl meat for it had finally driven him to seize the throne of the King/Lord. That and only that would satisfy his hunger. And well satisfied it was. The man had been the first ancestor of the current King/Lord Nordseth to sit upon the throne. It had been a whole throne then, large enough for King/Lord and Queen/Lady with room to spare for their numerous offspring.

For the bestowal of a single frugal meal, Lyrdahl's ancestor was elevated to the position of a First Lord. He stood upon the right side of the throne and it was he who passed the steaming bowl of food up to his King/Lord and Queen/Lady. A Lord of the Bowl; even now it made Lyrdahl grin wryly. Raised by the bowl and brought down by the bowl. It was that simple and that absurd.

It was Lyrdahl's grandfather who had managed to reverse the absurd good fortune of the family. Displeased by the way in which Nordseth's father was ruling his half of the kingdom but not politically wise enough to bring about change through official channels, Lyrdahl's grandfather had fallen in with a group of dissatisfied First Lords and Ladies which concocted absurd schemes against the life of the King/Lord. The schemes were absurd because none could be carried out without resources which the group did not possess. Lyrdahl had always been told by his father, who related the story with a great deal of pride in his voice, that it was his grandfather himself who came up with the brilliant scheme which could have brought down the King/Lord. Instead, Lyrdahl's father admitted grudgingly, it brought down their family.

It was startlingly simple. As Lord of the Bowl, Lyrdahl's grandfather was the last one to have access to the food of the King/Lord before he ate it. It went through various tasters before reaching his grandfather's hands and so no one would ever suspect his grandfather of poisoning the food. After all he was Lord of the Bowl and as such a bit of a joke. He secreted a leather packet of dried snow spider's blood in his sleeve. A simple twitch of his arm as his hand passed over the Bowl and the poison was broadcast over the entire dish.

It was simple and yet it failed. After one hand had distributed the poison, the other one shook so that the Bowl caught on the arm of the throne and spilled down and across the right foot of the King/Lord. The combination of the snow spider's blood and the gravy thick with herbs had created an acid which splashed and burned the foot of the King/Lord. And so ended the illustrious reign of the Lord of the Bowl and with it went the fortunes of the family.

Their genealogy had been eradicated from the Chronicles of Blood and the family exiled from the Camp. Lyrdahl's grandfather had been summarily executed and, if the attempt had been less absurd, the rest of the family might have shared the same fate. Instead the King/Lord glowered down at the family gathered together before the throne, twitched back the long robe which hid his foot and showed them the still painful scar left by the acid dish, and then burst into laughter. He recognized the absurdity of it and that alone saved the family from complete extinction. They were spared but scattered, forbidden to gather together again as a family for a full century.

A century was a long time and Lyrdahl had no intention of waiting that long to regain his class, although he was not so certain he wanted the family which came along with it. But he was a product of his family, which meant he had ambitions. Where his grandfather had been content to clumsily try to poison the King/Lord, Lyrdahl was working to topple the entire system which placed King/Lord and Queen/Lady at its pinnacle. He had ambitions and he did not view those as absurd.

He had left the family's tent six long years ago. Not allowed to be officially connected with any one clan, his family had developed a system of attaching itself to one clan as it wandered the Waste and then switching to another one which it met during its travels, hopefully before their welcome wore out, a period of time which grew to be very short indeed. In an attempt to legitimize this form of sponging, his father referred to it as "selective attachment" and puffed himself up as some aristocrat in exile simply taking what belonged to him by right.

A fierce argument about the manner in which they lived finally drove Lyrdahl away from the remnant of his family. One day when his father had been pontificating about his glorious "selective attachment," Lyrdahl had stood up, spit to clear his mouth of the food they had just begged from the lowest class within the clan they were currently following, and called it "parasitic and blood sucking." He had walked away and not looked back.

And, like every other classless man, woman, and child he knew, he finally found himself in Hold Gate. It was the refuge and the bastion of the classless. None of the other classes wanted the tottering edifice and so the squatters ruled. The once impressive structure still held together, although floors deep in the interior were known to give way with a groan and crash into the floor beneath and, depending on the strength of that floor, might or might not come to an uneasy rest for a time. It was a structure imbued with a certain chaotic life which was slowly and surely clearing away its inner supports to leave a clean open space which vaulted higher and higher as the floors moved lower and lower.

Lyrdahl had been fascinated by the structure of Hold Gate. As the ancient bastion which had once guarded the major entrance into the Hold, Lyrdahl saw it as a connection to the past which contained hope for the future. He coined phrases like that while studying the architecture of both the building and the society which swarmed through it and seemed to thrive on its rotting interior.

Phrase had led to phrase until one day he realized he had a philosophy at least as sound as Hold Gate itself, and the people he talked to about it listened to him as if they truly believed in what he said. From there it was a small step for him to make himself believe in what he said. From those simple phrases, and he realized with a twinge of shame his father would be proud of them, had grown the beginning of a revolution.

While he had begun the movement with cogent phrases, he was not content to allow it to drift onward, producing only rhetoric but no substantial results. Just as he designed phrases to fit the occasion and fire the imagination, so too he set out to design an organization for the revolution which would ensure the results he desired.

His aim was not to oust King/Lord and Queen/Lady and take their places, but rather to overthrow the entire class system and to replace it with one of his own devising. He had felt its repression and the bitterness of exile from its safe structures. And while he modified his ultimate goals as he met with either success, or more often failure, he had settled upon a method of organizing his adherents whose ranks swelled and shrank, but never completely ran dry, in order to ensure that the revolution would go on despite the numerous setbacks. To this end he established a system of cells so that no one person, if captured, could betray too many of his fellow conspirators. It had worked better than he had imagined at first and the revolution had begun to take on a life of its own.

Lyrdahl moved to the table and selected the sturdiest chair. He placed it behind the table and with his back to the window he sat down. He glanced over at the arrangement of the other two chairs. Not satisfied with their positions relative to his own, he jumped up and slid the one on the left closer to the other one, thus placing the two next to one another but not quite facing him directly. He had come to meet with the other two members of his cell and he needed to be in control of the dynamics around the ramshackle table.

Finally content with the arrangements, he sat back down. He placed his elbows on the table, which groaned slightly until he shifted some of his weight back off his arms, and rested his chin upon his joined fingertips. He knew from experience it was an imposing stance, contemplative yet indicative of power. While he waited he contemplated his revolution, for he did think of it in those terms, although he did not refer to it like that when dealing with his lieutenants.

The revolution was necessary, but not yet inevitable. It was his job to make it inevitable. The conflict did not arise so much from the struggle of class against class but more from the sparks which flew when an old established system came in contact with a new way of thought. The traditional class system was deeply entrenched in everyone's mind and way of thinking. What was not so firm was the idea that the ways established in the Hold must be kept simply because they were now the old ways. It had become a conflict between the old ways, those set up when the Hold was established, and the ancient ways, those which the clans of the open Waste still practiced and lived by.

The Interpreters told the people this even as they were the catalyst for change, since it was they who had altered the essence of what the ancient Rituals had been when all of the clans lived in the Waste. They had altered them, and so had altered the way in which people thought about them and also changed the fabric of the society in which they were embedded. Lyrdahl admired the Interpreters for that. Their system of manipulation had been set up slowly but carefully, and it worked in the same fashion. The Interpreters themselves were inevitable. It was that sort of inevitability which he desired for the revolution.

However, Lyrdahl firmly believed the Interpreters had pushed the Hold Rituals just a bit too far down the throats of all the classes, but mostly the lower classes whom they viewed as a superstitious lot who could be controlled by mumbo-jumbo. They had grown complacent in their power and tended to underestimate those whom they believed they controlled. Increasing inequities were perceived by the lower classes and the classless and sentiment began to rise against the perceived source of those inequities, the Interpreters.

It was upon this that Lyrdahl based his revolution. The classless had nothing to lose and everything to gain, since they hoped to gain recognition and status as a class through the revolution. A primary part of his plan was to use the lowest classes and the classless, those who were not allowed to own weapons, a permanent abode, or to marry above their level, the list of things which the lowest classes are not allowed to own or do went on and on, as the core of the revolution. They were the perfect material with which to start the conflagration for they truly had nothing to lose and everything to gain. In fact, that was one of the slogans which he used again and again when trying to win over converts.

For the time being, Lyrdahl could work only with the lower classes and the classless, for even though the middle and upper classes were just as beset by the Rituals, they did partake of the spoils. Lyrdahl knew once he broke the barrier between the highest of the lower classes and the lowest of the higher classes, then his revolution would be inevitable.

Lyrdahl heard a rapid knock on the door which faded almost as soon as it began. He was about to speak in a quiet yet commanding tone when the door swung open. A man slipped through and closed it behind him. Lyrdahl maintained his position at the table and acknowledged the new arrival with a gracious nod of his head.

"It is good to see you once again, Lon myr Pyta pyr Ghyn. I do appreciate your coming on such short notice. I want you to update my two lieutenants on the situation on the other side of the Hold."

Lon myr Pyta pyr Ghyn continued to stand just inside the door with his hands behind him resting on the warped panels, not so much to assure himself that the door remained closed, but as if to keep in contact with the corridor outside and anyone who might be approaching. He was a well fed man who had attempted to disguise the fact. His clothes were shabby but in a self-conscious way. The patches and worn spots did not appear to have been put on or worn through by the man currently wearing the clothes since they did not quite match up with his physique. He raised one hand to smooth the front of his singlesuit and his elbow poked into the leather several inches below the patch on the sleeve. His eyes were too bright and his stance too erect for him to be one of the classless in whose costume he now stood.

"No trouble, Lyrdahl pyr Ryx myr Lyndahl."

"Ah, about the name. To my two trusted lieutenants I am known as simply 'Syrn.' I know it sounds a bit absurd but that's the way they like it. Much more conspiratorial."

Lon nodded in a way which indicated he knew that the love of the conspiratorial posturings could not be ascribed entirely to the lieutenants. "I understand. Is this not a risk in any case? Having me break in upon your little 'cell?'" He pronounced the word as if it too were part of the conspiratorial trappings.

"A calculated risk. I need the information you can provide and I wanted my two lieutenants to realize that Hold Gate is the not the only bastion of revolution."

"It sounds like a sound business decision to me."

"I accept the compliment." Both smiled.

Lon was a merchant of some repute on the other side of the Hold in the enclave which sheltered the main docks of the Hold. From there the boats went up and down the River Ice, connecting the Hold to the North and the south and acting as a conduit for the riches pouring in both directions. It was often said if you could not find what you were looking for among the docks of the Hold, then you could be assured it did not exist.

Lyrdahl waved Lon to the chair on his right and he sat down, but not until he had taken a surreptitious swipe at the seat of the chair to clear it of the thickest layers of dirt. Before either could say another word, they heard a complicated series of raps at the door to the chamber. The raps ended and a deep and protracted silence began.

Lyrdahl was just about to tell the person outside that it was all right to enter, when the door swung open so little that the ancient hinges made no protest at all and a small, thin man stepped through in a fluid sideways movement. His narrowed eyes swept the room and, not finding any other object upon which to rest their nervous, suspicious gaze, they ended up scrutinizing the stranger in the room. The man's face was thin but with a pinched quality which was not simply genetic. He was one of the classless. Poor food and little of it, along with lodgings which kept out only the most bitter blasts of winter, had conspired to produce the small, thin man.

"Jhon, it's good to see you. This is, ah, Lon." Among the conspirators the patronymic and matronymic were invariably dropped. It smacked of the system which they strove so mightily to overthrow, and the less known about any person was the better for all concerned.

Jhon darted his head down and up to acknowledge the stranger and fingered the battered hilt of a long knife of blood metal he had tucked into the belt of his singlesuit. He then sidled along the wall until he was in a spot as close to the table as he could get without actually leaving the reassuring solidity of the wall. His dark eyes, beneath an uneven line of hair stuck tight to his head by an unwholesome combination of grease and dirt, sized up the seating arrangements. He knew one member of the cell had not yet arrived.

Without seeming to look, he reached down and yanked a low stool, made of the porous volcanic stone commonly used to make furniture on Winterhold, out of the tangle of garbage in the corner near him. Instead of lifting the stool to carry it closer to the table, he dragged it along the floor and kept watching the other two. He stopped once, made a quick calculation with his darting eyes as to acceptable distances and positions, and moved the stool a couple of inches more before he sat down upon it. One leg was missing and it tilted abruptly as he settled his weight onto it. He hopped back up as if stung, yanked the stool about so that the three legs would provide him with the best possible support, and sat once more. Both Lyrdahl and Lon breathed a small sigh of relief when he was finally settled.

Lyrdahl smiled. "Jhon here is a merchant of sorts also, aren't you, Jhon?"

Jhon snorted and dipped his head. "Merchant of the classless. Provide goods which people who have no money can't afford. Merchant."

All of them knew just what a merchant of the classless meant. Jhon was a small time thief and smuggler who managed to procure by illegal means, the only ones open to one with no recognized class, goods which had been substandard to begin with and sold them at mildly exorbitant prices to other classless people who could not really afford them. Jhon's revolutionary leanings meant he made even less profit than even the most incompetent of his fellow smugglers. He had been a prime recruit for Lyrdahl, easy to convince to join the revolution and a living example of what the oppressive system was capable of producing.

Lyrdahl liked to show him off and Jhon usually obliged. He had so little self-esteem that being touted as the example of the common man, the one for whom and by whom the revolution was built, gave him a chance to feel important.

"Jhon, and hundreds of others like him, is the backbone of the revolution. He is the disaffected man who has been crushed beneath the weight of the monumental system of class for generations. He is the target for the mumbo-jumbo of the Interpreters who are the prime agents of the oppression. Over the centuries the Interpreters have developed their system of Rituals here in the Hold and have established what they refer to as the 'new tradition.' What they mean by that is a system of Rituals in contrast to the ones still found in the Waste among the nomadic clans. The Hold Rituals are bloated and rotting, elaborate travesties of what the Rituals once were. And, of course, the Interpreters want to maintain this 'new tradition.' But this tradition is merely a veneer. It is insubstantial and unconvincing. The once ascetic life of the Interpreters is a thing of the past. They demand more and more from the lower classes, and the classless in particular, because they are easy targets as they scratch a bare existence from the edges of society. Hand in glove with the higher classes, they demand more and more spoils, which consist of increasingly larger donations from the participants of a Ritual. Well, the 'new tradition' is not a tradition so much as it is a style of living, and styles change. We will make it change."

During his speech, Lyrdahl had risen to his feet, as if the power of his own words pulled him upward. He lowered his head to make the last statement in a low and penetrating tone of voice. He then sat back down.

Jhon looked up at him from his rickety stool with a glaze of awe across his face. Lon sat at ease in his chair and, glancing at Jhon from the corner of his eye, made sure to keep a look of respect and agreement on his face. Lyrdahl passed his hand across his brow and looked at each of his comrades as if he were bringing himself back to the squalid room and the current situation with a decided effort. He bestowed a smile on each and sat back down.

"Now, since the last member of our little cell has not yet made her appearance, perhaps you could give us a brief update on your activities since we last met."

"Certainly, Syrn, certainly." Jhon stopped and cleared his throat and as he spoke he kept his eyes directed at the table top as if reading his report from its scarred surface. "I live along the River front. I work along the River front. Progress of the revolution has been good. Several new recruits from among the classless who live in the shacks which cling to the piles out over the River Ice. Quite a community now. Quite a few classless and more every day. Born into it. Not much else we are allowed to produce, except children. Quite a few now and all for the revolution. For freedom and the right to work and earn our own food. That's all. That's everything."

Lyrdahl nodded and turned to Lon. "Jhon's territory is along the River Ice. His community is that of the classless who have built homes and existences for themselves from the refuse which washes up along the River. They inhabit particularly mean dwellings which cling like barnacles to the pilings among the ancient series of docks which are no longer in use due to the danger of collapse. Jhon recruits quite openly there since it is an entire community apart; no one bothers with them. Like the rals which scurry through their houses, they are the scavengers and pests which the authorities of the Hold must tolerate since they cannot eradicate them. A sad case, is it not? An eloquent case for revolution."

Lon nodded, while Jhon bobbed his head up and down enthusiastically. Lyrdahl opened his hands and sighed. He then brought his hands together, the fingertips joined once more in his favorite pose.

A bang on the table startled both Lon and Lyrdahl. Jhon banged it once more and, with an obvious effort, stared up and into Lyrdahl's face. "I have lived all my life as classless. My mother lived all of her short life as classless. My grandmother knew what it was to have a lowly class. I must try to regain class or abolish it altogether. Not sure which is better. I am sure the revolution must occur for either to happen. I will live to see it or die in support of it. Die for it. Die for something other than a hovel on a pile in the River Ice. But I hope to live." He added the last almost apologetically as his enthusiasm waned and he realized how he had been carried away.

Lyrdahl suppressed a smile and instead put on an intent look of fellow feeling. He was genuinely proud of the feeling which his revolution could produce in people.

"Yes, we will all live to see the revolution come to fruition. We will live to see you and your fellows swarm up from the River like the rals which infest your houses and take the Hold for all of the classless. I do not intend the comparison to be demeaning, in fact, I feel it is vibrant with life. The oppressed are like rals, hunted and despised but surviving and even flourishing. Their time will come. Our time will come."

A rapid and yet light footfall sounded outside in the corridor. The three men looked up at the door as it opened and a young woman stepped into the chamber. She entered boldly and let the door swing wide. It hit the wall with a thump. She turned to close it after poking her head out into the corridor to make sure no one was out there. After hauling the reluctant door into its jamb, she turned and strode across to the remaining chair.

"Sorry I'm late, Syrn. Customers at the apothecary shop kept me. We've had a real run on herbs to loosen the bowels of late. Mostly from the lower echelons of the lower classes. Now there is something to use in a revolutionary slogan." She grinned and her eyebrows tilted with mischief. On her face, which possessed a beauty compounded of fine and interesting lines as well as a vibrant life behind those lines, the mischief was playful and somewhat self-deprecating.

"You are late, Roxyna." Lyrdahl spoke as if he had not heard her explanation and quip. His fervent attitude, so evident a moment before her arrival, had changed. He was now the official in charge of a great undertaking which brooked no delay. She ceased grinning, but left her eyebrows tilted at their lively angle. Lyrdahl looked long and hard at her face and his attitude changed yet again. It softened into something resembling love.

Roxyna myr Roxyna pyr Khyn had once been the lover of Lyrdahl pyr Ryx myr Lyndahl. She had broken it off. But Lyrdahl had twisted the severance about so he believed he was the one who had ended the relationship. She let him believe what he liked, for she still admired him, even though she knew most of his weaknesses. That was a part of her survival instinct. Do not harm someone intentionally for he or she might be in a position to harm you at some point. She had lived in Hold Gate all of her life and so possessed both her beauty and a sure knowledge of herself which had developed and matured in the rough environment of the Low Hold and Hold Gate in particular.

Her hair was cut short like Jhon's and in the same style, "revolutionary crop," a fashion shocking to many but worn proudly by those committed to the cause as well as those who simply wanted to be in style. The latter served as an excellent screen for the true revolutionaries. The Ice Guards could not arrest every person in Low Hold who sported a short haircut.

But there the resemblance ended for her hair was clean and a deep burnished red. Both the cut and the color suited her long face. It was a face which mirrored a surprising depth of sensuality but remained inviolable, much like a frozen well whose clear depths were protected by a thick but transparent coating of ice. Roxyna possessed qualities which made her desirable and erotic, but not easy. Lyrdahl had learned that to his continuing dismay.

"I told you why. Was I supposed to shove the customers out of the shop and tell them I had a meeting of my revolutionary cell to attend?"

"No, of course not. You know what I mean. We have a limited amount of time here. We should not be seen together too frequently or for too long."

"The frequency or length of our time together never used to bother you."

Lyrdahl twitched his lips and narrowed his eyes. Roxyna grinned at his discomfort and explained to the others. "When I first joined the cause, Syrn and I would often meet to discuss underlying philosophical causes for the revolution. Those sessions were most illuminating."

Jhon nodded eagerly as if the contemplation of something so sublime was natural, while Lon nodded in a much more knowing manner. Lyrdahl twitched once more and then tapped his fingers smartly on the table in an attempt to regain control of the meeting.

"We are here to discuss the progress of the revolution. We have already had a report from Jhon. Things progress nicely along the River front under his sure guidance. Roxyna, perhaps you would be so good as to give us some idea of how you have spent your time and then we shall hear from our guest here."

"I have spent my time, as you put it, selling herbs and drugs to those who venture into the apothecary shop where I work and at the same time dispensing small doses of revolutionary philosophy. No new recruits this time. But then I've had no new customers and the old ones have heard my thoughts upon the inequality of power too often to want to swallow more."

"That's fine. We strive not merely to recruit new members to our cause but to spread the seeds of doubt among those who would never officially join us. However, it is they, the vast multitude of the lower classes, who must support us, if only by their silence and inaction at the correct moment, if, no, when this revolution assumes its final and true shape. You have done well then in consolidating our gains."

Roxyna nodded to Lyrdahl. She was genuinely pleased by his approval for she did still believe in the concept of the revolution, although her intimate knowledge concerning its leader left her hesitant at times about the forces driving it forward. They seemed too self-serving too often and the residue of idealism left in her still wanted to believe that the revolution would come about for only the most noble of reasons.

"Good. And now we will have a report from our guest. I will call him Jhym for reasons of security." Lyrdahl turned to Lon who eased himself toward the table to bring them all in closer as he began to speak in a low voice.

"I operate on the other side of the Hold, among the Hold Docks. As I'm sure you know, the Docks attract a diverse mixture of people from all over Winterhold. We have sailors who man the boats which travel up and down the River Ice and longshoremen who load and unload those boats and a sample from every other race and class throughout the world. It is true that if you cannot find what you are looking for or news about someone you are looking for among the docks of the Hold, then you can be assured it or they do not exist.

"It is because of this mix that the revolution has taken hold, but it is also the reason it has not flourished. Let me explain. With so much temporary work and cheap labor available, the lower classes and the classless predominate, for chandlers tend to be blind to a person's class when a boat loaded with bryl hides anchors and the master of the Docks has given them only six hours to unload and clear that particular anchorage. The economy of the Docks is to be found largely under the table. The ground is there in which to plant the seeds of revolution but its fertility tends to be uneven. Dissatisfaction among the classless is not as intense nor as uniform as it is here in Hold Gate. Among the Docks a classless man can work and earn a living wage. The restrictions of class are blinked at there so the economy may flourish.

"I have planted what seeds I could and have seen some results. There is a small coterie of the perpetually disaffected who have rallied about the banner of revolution quite willingly, almost too willingly to my way of thinking, and they form the nucleus for an organization of sorts. But they tend to make speeches more frequently than they make a revolution."

Lyrdahl interrupted. "If open insurrection broke out here, would the Docks follow? Could you lead them to it?"

Lon paused before he answered. "I cannot be certain of that right now. I believe violence would flare up in sympathy to what might happen here, but I don't think it has enough fuel to sustain a prolonged conflagration. Also, the distance between Hold Gate and the Docks makes any news which gets to us old enough to be anticlimactic."

"Work for it. Keep at it. We all must. It is our duty and our need." Lyrdahl swept his hands up and out to include all of them sitting around the table as well as the world beyond.

"I will. I do." Lon's reply was intense enough but studied. Like Roxyna he believed in the revolution but still threw a jaundiced eye upon some of its means and the forces behind it. He was a pragmatist as well as an opportunist. "The work continues, of that you may be certain."

"Good. That's all we can ask."

A confused rush of booted feet from somewhere below sent a shiver through the floor of the room. All three froze and glanced at the door. As if not to disappoint them, a loud bang threatened to topple the door from its hinges. Two words only were spoken, but only two were needed. "Ice Guards."

Lyrdahl was on his feet and moving toward the window. "The landlord. He and I have an understanding. He refuses to join in the revolution, but he does have enough sympathy for it to help us out in matters like this. For a price, of course."

Lyrdahl shook his head and forced open the shutters which groaned and threatened to fall off their hinges.

"This is the way out. The outside of this fine old establishment is uneven enough to provide easy handholds for most of the descent. Our host will delay them as long as he can, or at least as long as he deems practical for the amount of money I last gave him. Hurry now. We have no time to lose."

Lon and Roxyna were right behindCed Jhon stayed near the table and kept watching the door. The long knife which had been tucked into his belt, for lack of a sheath, was now poised in his hand. Its scarred curve glowed in the dimming light reflected from the vein of quartz just outside the window.

Lyrdahl helped Roxyna up to the sill. She shook off his hand and slid over the edge by herself. The ancient edifice of the tavern was buckled and swayed in many places so that as Lyrdahl had said, it was easy to find handholds, although not all were solid. She clambered down to the roof of a dormer which seemed to be designed to help to hold the building away from the cliff at the same time it used the cliff for support.

Lon was on his way down when Lyrdahl called out. "Wait there. The Ice Guards might have the alleys covered. There are ways to reach the alleys at some distance from here without going all the way to the ground. I'll show you."

Lyrdahl turned to Jhon. "You're next. Come on."

"No. You. Go." Jhon kept his knife pointed toward the door and spoke over his shoulder. Lyrdahl could see the determination in his face and nodded.

He had just slipped over the sill and let himself down by his hands to reach the first solid ledge below the window when the door burst open. The hinges gave way first and it swung inward on its lock for a moment before tumbling to the floor of the chamber. Instead of letting go of the sill and climbing down to join Lon and Roxyna, Lyrdahl pulled himself up and peeked over the edge of the sill.

Jhon still stood by the table with his long knife in his hand. Four fully armored Ice Guards had already entered the room and taken up positions on either side of him. Their blood blades glowed long and thin in the strange light which filled the room.

A warrior entered the room. He was older, his silver hair bright against his dark armor. He was also a First Lord since his shoulder armor glittered with the convoluted blood metal markings that indicated his status. Lyrdahl recognized him as Lord Grendyl pyr Tal myr Joryth, a particular enemy of the revolution. He stopped in front of Jhon but did not draw his blood blade. Instead he placed his fists on his hips and surveyed first the room and then the man before him.

"Rebel." It was a statement, not a question. "Conspiring in filthy back rooms. Well, it is typical, I must say. Where are the others?"

Jhon was silent. The blade of his long knife held steady.

"Where are the others?" Lord Grendyl repeated the question in a weary tone of voice. "We know there are others. Where are they? Out the window, I suppose. Well, we have all of the alleys covered around this hovel that the landlord calls an inn. Unless they can fly, they won't get away. Let's have a look out of the window now. Maybe the scum is still clinging to the wall outside." He gestured to his men to take care of Jhon as he took a step toward the window.

The Ice Guards were closing in when Jhon moved. He kicked the table over to his left and followed it with an abrupt lunge. The two Guards were taken by surprise as first the table and then the small man flew at them. His long knife flashed. One went down with a gash across his face and blood flowing into his eyes to blind him. The other tried to get around the table. His full armor would not allow him to step over it easily.

Like a whirling snow devil, Jhon slashed and cut and spun and nearly gained the door. The First Lord fell back at the onset, drew his blood blade, and watched the frantic movements of the small man. Anticipating him, he made a dash in the direction of the door and got there just before him. For a moment it was long knife against blood blade. Jhon was an alley fighter and his knife was deadly in close quarters, but Lord Grendyl was an experienced warrior who kept his own blade close to his body and utilized the edge rather than the tip.

Grendyl waved the unwounded warriors back and they formed a semi-circle about the two combatants. He stepped back and parried the thrusts and cuts of the small man. "Give up. Drop the knife and we'll let you live. We want information, not your life. We're out to crush a rebellion, not to kill individuals."

Jhon looked straight at the First Lord. "You don't understand, do you? I am the revolution."

"Nonsense..." Lord Grendyl barely had time to finish the word before Jhon threw himself at his opponent. His knife streaked toward the heart. The Lord turned his armored arm to him, let the knife blade slide in front of his chest, and then snapped his forearm and upper arm tightly together to clench the blade between them. With a sudden twist, he wrenched the blade from Jhon's hand and swung the hilt of his blood blade around to smack him in the face.

Jhon staggered back, blood running across his left eye. Instead of surrendering, he fumbled in his singlesuit and lunged yet again. He never reached his opponent. A blood blade entered his right side, passed through his body, and pinned him to the wall. The tip of the blade screamed as it hit the stone of the wall and Jhon slid down and off it. He was dead before his body finished crumbling.

"Stupid. Both him and you." Lord Grendyl scowled at the Ice Guard who had dealt the killing blow.

"But he pulled a blade." The Ice Guard pointed to a thin blade clutched in his hand.

"I knew that. I can defend myself. We need information about the rebellion, not any more potential martyrs, although even they would be hard pressed to make a martyr out of this one. Just another ral from the River front."

He poked at Jhon's body with his boot. "All right, let's get out of here. Leave him for the landlord to clean up. Perhaps the Guards outside have had better luck, although I doubt it. This one was simply begging for a martyr's death. The others are too clever to be caught easily."

Lord Grendyl and his warriors left the room. Lyrdahl took one last look at the crumpled body of Jhon against the wall before he let himself down to join the others in their flight across the uneven rooftops of Low Hold.

He spoke softly to himself. "He was right. You can't be a truly useful martyr, Jhon, but you won't be forgotten. Perhaps you were right. Perhaps you are the revolution. Perhaps."

## IV

IN THE CAVES of the Caynruhl, illumination was balanced against the ability to breathe and the temperature was kept at a level which was adequate but not luxurious. The clan inhabited a series of caves within the Northern Range whose full extent no one had ever determined. Each clan had its own caves and no one infringed upon another clan's property unless extreme need dictated. The caves provided shelter from the worst blasts off the Waste in the dead of Winter and were only used during that severe season. The other seasons were spent in following the herds of bryl along their migratory routes.

A continual draft of cold air surged through the caves. It kept the temperature down but did provide enough fresh air to allow one to breathe in the atmosphere thickened by the black smoke from the coal fires which burned continually in each family's own cave. Torches composed of tough bryl hide tempered with just the right amount of bryl fat added to the thickness of the air, but did give off enough light to allow the clan members to go about their daily routines. As with everything about life in the Waste, it was a balancing act between light and darkness, cold and warmth.

Trys left his mother, father, and brother by the family hearth and climbed the short, steep slope to the cave which he called his own. He reached the narrow opening and paused. Below him Gyrs bent over the body of the bryl and worked his knife up and down, back and forth as he cut away the hide and dressed the meat. His father prepared the salt which would be used to preserve the flesh and his mother stirred the stew to which she had just added chunks of the fresh meat. The shadow of each one wavered on the walls behind them even as their faces glowed redly from the firelight in front of them.

She awaited him. His mother had given him her familiar smile when he had entered the cave, but that expression had been jarred by a fleeting sadness. Trys knew Cyln myr Callyn pyr Jod would not have travelled North from the Hold quite this late in the season unless the reason was compelling. He turned from the radiant circle below him. A single torch guttered in his cave. The light pulsed through the opening and then settled down as it was trimmed to burn properly.

Trys ducked his head, pushed his left shoulder through the gap in the stone, and entered his cave. He stood just inside the entrance.

He was tall but his cave was taller. He could stand upright and move about in most of it without having to stoop.

Sparsely furnished, his cave reflected his chosen vocation. An Interpreter of a clan possessed few objects and those were dedicated to the study and interpretation of the Rituals. A modest pile of sleeping furs, a couple of low bryl bone stools, and an unadorned chest constructed from brum hides stretched over bryl bones were the only items of any size in the cave. The chest contained his three singlesuits and his simple Interpreter garb, a collection of prayer horns, his blood blade given to him by Cyln herself and which was well cared for but seldom used, and a set of hide pouches made for him by his mother and in which he kept his few treasured objects.

Cyln myr Callyn pyr Jod stood in the center of the cave. She turned from trimming the twisted hide torch jammed into a crack in the wall of the cave over the brum hide chest. The fire flared up and died down as it slowly ate its way along the fat saturated length. It illuminated only part of the left side of Cyln's face and Trys could not tell upon first entering just what expression lay there.

Trys bowed to Cyln. She returned the salute and then reached out to grasp his hand and forearm. Close to her he could see she appeared to be more intent than usual as her eyes scanned his face minutely.

"Trys myr Lyn pyr Drun, it is good to see you once again. The Waste has been kind."

Trys nodded at this traditional greeting and knew Cyln uttered it with real feeling, something unusual in and of itself, since her stoicism was renowned in the clan. He gave the response.

"And to you, Cyln myr Callyn pyr Jod. I pray it shall always be so."

"Well might you pray that."

"I beg your pardon?"

"Nothing. Nothing but the mutterings of an old warrior."

"Hardly old."

"Perhaps not in years but there are other ways to age, and to do it quickly. Living in the Hold seems to be one of them."

Trys motioned to Cyln to be seated on a stool as he moved to the one next to his brum hide chest. He sat and opened the lid of the chest.

"Excuse me, but I have a Ritual to perform in a short time and I need to prepare a few things."

Cyln stared hard at the stool he had indicated as if she were seeing it for the first time, but she remained standing.

"What Ritual?" Cyln asked as if she was not really interested but needed to say something.

"The Ritual of Acknowledgement of Birth. The child was born

yesterday and it appears he will survive. In fact, he is healthy and quite vocal. You can hear him crying throughout the caves." Trys smiled. "I must admit it is one of my favorite Rituals. It is so simple and meaningful."

As Trys glanced up with the smile still on his lips, he was struck by Cyln's pose. He had often faced her in the duelling pit of the clan where she had trained him to use his blood blade. She had begun to pull herself down into a familiar defensive posture when she made a conscious effort to straighten up and relax.

"Yes, simple and meaningful. Of course, it is that."

"Yes. Yes. Anyway, I'm just going to pull out a few things here. We can talk as I do it."

"Yes, talk. Of course."

Trys pulled the prayer horn out of his belt and slid it into a large hide pouch. He tugged the drawstring tight and dropped it back into the chest. He scooped up another smaller pouch and opened it. It contained a jumble of objects and he could not remember if the one he wanted was in this pouch or another one.

He turned from the chest and dumped the contents of the pouch out upon the floor in front of him. A hodge-podge of bone needles, casting stones with rune-like figures carved upon them, and other small objects carved in bone spilled out. A medallion, without its leather thong, rolled from the pile and toward Cyln. She started, but Trys was too busy searching through the pile in front of him to notice the momentary twitch.

"I'm looking for a small drinking horn. I use it to give the child his first Ritual taste of water made from melted snow. I thought it was in this pouch but I don't see it."

Cyln stepped forward and picked up the medallion. Her hand shook slightly. "This...this medallion. It is the one I gave you, is it not?"

Trys glanced up. "Yes. It is."

"What happened to the thong?"

"Oh, it broke a long time ago. I just never bothered to put on a new one."

"You don't wear it then?"

"Not for a long time. Why do you ask?"

"Don't you remember?"

"Remember? Remember what?" Trys was puzzled by Cyln's agitation. He had seen her agitated on a hunt when nothing went well, but this was altogether different. It was almost as though she had a secret.

"Of course, there is no reason for you to remember. I probably only told you about the medallion once and that was a long time ago."

"Told me what about the medallion? Tell me again and I'll probably remember."

Cyln took a deep breath and looked hard at Trys for a second. "Yes. Very well. The story of the medallion. The medallion was mine. Look at it carefully. It has the Queen/Lady's seal on it, the image of Mother Ice. It was given to me by Queen/Lady Alisande herself. I wore it proudly as a badge of my office."

"How did I end up with it then?"

"I gave it to you only seconds after you were born. Your mother went into labor with you and, in the Waste tradition, I took her outside of the caves to give birth. Two warriors began a duel close by and ended up nearly falling over your mother. I fought them off and managed to dispatch both of them, but not until you had been born. It was the dead of Winter and the cold was savage that day. The medallion, which I always wore about my neck and secured to my singlesuit with leather thongs so it would not bounce around and hinder me, had been thoroughly splashed with the blood of the two warriors. It was hot with the life from the blood. I wrapped you up in a hide along with the medallion and got both you and your mother back into the caves. The medallion might have saved your life since the cold was so severe. That is the story of the medallion."

"I guess you did tell me once a long time ago. It seemed like a legend, something that only happens to the sons of King/Lords and Queen/Ladies."

Cyln stiffened as if she had been slapped. "No, it happened just the way I told it. Just that way. Believe me, it was no legend."

"I believe you." Trys spoke soothingly in an attempt to calm the obviously distraught Cyln. He did believe the story but thought the manner in which she told it was curious. She had told it as if it were a legend, or at least as if it had happened to someone else. And yet, he had had the medallion as long as he could remember.

"I am here to ask something of you." Cyln paused in her headlong plunge. "I am here to ask something of you and I am not sure how to do it. I want you to take the medallion with you but not wear it until I ask you to."

"Take it with me? Where am I going?"

"I have come North to ask you to return with me to the Hold."

"The Hold." Trys had known that such a request was coming but it still caught him off guard and now, coupled as it was with the request concerning the medallion, puzzled him. "Why?"

"Why do you need to go to the Hold." It lacked all intonation associated with a question. Rather it sounded like the classic way in which the answer to an examination question was couched. Then, instead of continuing on, Cyln paused yet again.

"Yes, why? I know your attitude toward the Hold. You have told me countless times the only reason you stay is out of loyalty to your Queen/Lady. You despise the way in which the inhabitants live there; you cannot stomach the political infighting; you believe the Interpreters of the Hold have twisted and debased the ideals of the Rituals." Trys could see that Cyln was growing more anxious by the moment. "I do believe you want me to go with you. I just need to know why?"

"It is because of the Queen/Lady Alisande that I must ask you to come with me. As you say, my loyalty to her motivates me now. The Queen/Lady's prejudices against the Interpreters are pushing her further and further toward total suppression without realizing what that means. As you well know, I have no love for the Interpreters of the Hold. But I do know they can make the difference in the balance of power between the two half thrones. Nordseth uses them often and skillfully to further his own interests. And he has become more cruel of late, seeming to stop at nothing to impose his will upon people and events. That frightens people, and frightened people will do almost anything."

"Have you told your Queen/Lady this?"

"Yes, and she says she understands. But she does not act upon that understanding. A fourth potential node of power has also developed of late. A revolutionary group has sprung up. They descry the policies and actions of both the monarchs and the Interpreters. More people seem to be flocking to their way of thinking. By people I mean the lowest of the lower classes and the classless. The lower classes tend to look to the Interpreters for guidance since they seem to provide an alternative to the traditional methods of the monarchs, while the classless gravitate toward the revolution since it is outside of all systems as are the classless themselves. The Interpreters recognize the dynamics of the power struggle as does Nordseth. My Queen/Lady says she does, but does nothing to consolidate her position. She has even managed to bully the Interpreters of the Hold into suppressing the practice of sending Consorts and Concubines between Queen/Lady and King/Lord. The practice was barbaric but its suppression irks the Interpreters, the aristocracy, and even the lower classes, who still believe it is the duty of Queen/Lady and King/Lord to propagate in their own special way."

"You talk like an old warrior of the political battles in the Hold."

"I have my scars, earned in trying to protect my Queen/Lady. But the fight is not a clean one and there never seems to be an end to it. One battle simply leads into the next one."

"Why me?"

"I don't know, precisely." Cyln looked long and hard at Trys. Her mouth worked once or twice as if she were about to speak but no words came out. Finally, just as Trys was about to tell her she really did not need to tell him precisely, she slammed her right fist into her left hand. The smack seemed to loosen her.

"You need to come back with me because of old secrets, which I cannot yet tell you about, and new situations, which I know nothing about. I cannot give you good solid reasons. That bothers me as much as it does you, perhaps more. You know I like to be able to grasp the hilt of a blood blade before I wield it. But right now, I have little choice. To be honest, I do not really know what I expect you to accomplish. I am like a hunter who stalks her prey but cannot say exactly how she will take it when the moment comes. The situation will determine the 'how.'"

Trys believed all she said. He knew her intentions were good and her determination firm. But he also felt there was an undercurrent to the entire affair which she was not telling him about. At first he had been hurt and suspicious, but after seeing her agony of indecision, he knew the secret would have to remain for the time being.

"I trust you, Cyln myr Callyn pyr Jod. You do not need to tell me any more. I will go with you."

"I knew you would, Trys myr Lyn pyr Drun. We will leave at first light. I have already talked to your mother and she agrees. I will now explain things to your father."

"Yes. Fine." And then Cyln was gone, as if anxious to move and begin the familiar and comfortable preparations for a long journey.

Trys stood in his cave and took a deep breath. A vagary of the circulating air puffed a thick cloud of coal smoke about his head. He coughed and ducked his head into the clearer air close to the floor of the cave. There lay his things, the few objects which belonged to him. On top of the pile lay the medallion. The image upon its face was in shadow but its edge caught the ruddy light from the torch. The red crescent burned like a sharp blade which cut him off from everything he had ever known.

He shook his head. Sometimes he felt there was so much he did not know. Even something as fundamental as why Cyln myr Callyn pyr Jod had ever picked him to show special favor to. At times, he had even toyed with the idea that they were related in some obscure way. That was one of the things he would have to ask her as they journeyed south. It would be a long trip. There would be plenty of time for explanations and revelations.

He shook his head again. He had just remembered where he had left the drinking horn which he needed for the Ritual of

Acceptance. He took two long strides and reached up to a high shelf and felt about for the slim length of the horn. His fingers closed about the familiar object.

When he brought it out into the light from the torch, he was puzzled for just a second. The shape was familiar, but did it always have the image of a bryl leaping in just such a manner carved on it? The familiar and the unfamiliar, the known and the unknown seemed to be blending just then. All he could do was to hold on to what he did know and not be thrown off balance by what he did not know. Trys ducked his head and left his cave without looking back.

## V

DAWN SMUDGED the sky off to the east as Torkild myr Rhynth pyr Jyrs approached the royal Tent. He stopped and glanced up at the battlements of the Hold whose grim prominences were gilded by the gathering light. He had slept little during the night and the majestic spectacle of the Hold, in all of its early morning glory, oppressed him more than usual. He threw a muttered curse in its direction from the side of his face not frozen in a perpetual grin, and then turned to the royal Tent. The tail end of his curse was still on his twisted lips when he did so and in his tiredness he felt like extending it to include that structure as well.

As First Servant to the King/Lord Nordseth pyr Nystrin myr Olda, he had numerous responsibilities, the chief of which was keeping his King/Lord informed of the latest news in both Camp and Hold. That task had kept him up most of the night, meeting with smugglers from the Hold and cutthroats from the Camp. The status of the reliable informants had dropped off markedly of late, but Torkild knew it was due to the fact that the ground swell of dissatisfaction which glorified itself with the name "revolution" was based solidly on the lower classes and the classless.

While Torkild's own origins were humble in the extreme, he felt no sympathy for the aspirations of the revolutionaries. He had been taken in by the King/Lord many years ago and given his position of trust. The King/Lord had surprised many of his loyal followers who had expected the honor of First Servant to be bestowed upon them. Instead, Nordseth had chosen a man twisted in body and face to stand at his side and respond to his most immediate and personal needs.

Torkild had been cast out by his clan when very young due an inherent weakness of his body. But rather than lying down to die upon the Waste in the time honored tradition, he had followed his clan, eking out an existence from the scraps of bryl bone and hide thrown away by them as they moved along their nomadic path. A faulty breather mask and a threadbare singlesuit combined with a bitterly cold blast of wind to permanently cripple Torkild by partially freezing his left side. His limp and the frozen and twisted left side of his face were reminders of the desperate walk. He had survived and by that survival won the admiration of his clan. He had been allowed the rejoin them. But he could not stand to remain there.

Migratory patterns of the bryl had brought the clan close to the Camp and Hold where Torkild had been dazzled by the richness and variety of life. What had convinced him to stay behind when the clan wandered off had been the presence of others like himself. In the Waste there was no room for the marred. The survival of the clan could not be tied to someone who might not be able to perform his function at a critical time. In Hold and Camp, where the environment was held somewhat at bay, people who did not possess all of their faculties could survive and even flourish. He had been noticed by Nordseth and taken into his personal service.

Torkild believed Nordseth had taken him up, not because he felt Torkild would prove to be a capable servant, there was no way for him to know that at the time, but because of his obvious and dramatic flaw. The King/Lord himself suffered from a dramatic but not so obvious flaw. He had contracted a form of tuberculosis many years ago which often threw him into bouts of coughing during which he spit up blood and which generally weakened him.

But rather than growing more virulent, the disease settled down to debilitate over the long term. Nordseth coughed out his life in small amounts, but had not yet reached the end of the reservoir. Nordseth understood Torkild's flaws and appreciated them for what they were, debilitating but not deadly. Trust had sprung up between the two upon first meeting when each saw himself mirrored in the other. And finally, Torkild had nothing to gain from his position except the favor of Nordseth. Without Nordseth, Torkild might well be dead in the Waste. Theirs was a wonderfully balanced symbiotic relationship.

Torkild tugged back the flap on the royal Tent and hitched his stiff left leg forward into the opening. Immediately inside the Tent, night still held sway. The long narrow approach to the sleeping quarters of the King/Lord was lit at uneven intervals by torches. The first one was at some distance. The King/Lord liked to keep those who approached him at a disadvantage.

Torkild limped along the corridor and looked keenly to either side, especially in the intervals between the torches. He had traversed about half of the length of the corridor when a movement in the deep shadows to his right caused him to stop.

"It's me. It's..." He shook his head as if at his own stupidity. "Why do I insist on talking to them? They are perfectly deaf and yet I talk to them."

A warrior separated himself from the shadows. Every part of his singlesuit was dull black and his hood was pulled up. Even the short throwing spear which he carried was black from the butt to the tip of the head. He was one of a dozen guards who stood watch over King/Lord Nordseth every time he slept. Carefully selected for their prowess with spear and short blade, each one was also deaf.

The King/Lord would never have anyone near him during his unguarded moments of repose who might overhear anything of any consequence. Torkild had never heard him talk to himself and he assumed that the King/Lord was sufficiently cautious even in his sleep to never talk, but his paranoia demanded he ring himself with a silent company of warriors who could never hear anything, even if there had been anything to hear.

Torkild hastily gave his own personal sign of recognition. The large eyes of the warrior gleamed keenly from his hooded face. He nodded and his spear slid back the few inches which indicated he was at rest once again. Torkild limped on at a rapid pace, and yet he made it appear as stately as he could with his stiff leg.

"The flawed attending the flawed, watched over by the flawed. Our King/Lord has a macabre sense of humor. Very few realize that, and even fewer appreciate it." Torkild muttered to himself as he hurried forward.

The end of the tent corridor was a well of darkness. No torches burned within fifteen yards of it. It was the King/Lord's final attempt to put anyone who approached him at a disadvantage. Torkild knew the entrance to the sleeping quarters intimately, but he always hesitated before plunging into the shadows which gathered there. A final tug and brush at his singlesuit to make sure it hung upon his rangy frame with some semblance of distinction, and Torkild limped the last few yards.

A curtain of soft white bryl hide was the final barrier to the sleeping quarters. Torkild reached out cautiously for the extreme left hand corner of the hanging, even though the folds were draped so one would assume one was intended to enter from the right hand side. In actuality, most visitors were supposed to enter from the right for there lay the King/Lord's final defense. A cascade of blood metal tubes was stitched onto the hanging. Any disturbance to the hanging resulted in a waterfall of sound, musical and imperative. Nordseth did not want anyone to get close to him without his knowledge.

Torkild's fingers brushed the edge of the bryl hide in the dark and caught a familiar fold. He lifted it barely an inch. There was silence. The blood metal tubes, concentrated on the right hand side of the hanging, swayed but did not clash together. He lifted it another inch and another until he could peer in.

This cautious approach was part of Torkild's own system of defense. He needed to determine what sort of mood his King/Lord was in before he faced him. He had learned that lesson early on. A severe bout of depression and an attack of paranoia had coincided when Torkild first entered the employ of the King/Lord. He had walked in unthinking and had received a brutal attack. Although it had only been an onslaught of words, the King/Lord always had a weapon of some sort concealed nearby and the attack could have easily taken on a much harder edge. Since then he did everything he could to prepare himself for the interview beforehand for both his sake and his King/Lord's. Nordseth did not suffer fools at all.

The illness of the King/Lord required that he have fresh, cold air and so his sleeping chamber was open to the sky. The couch itself occupied the center of the chamber and was raised on a low dias. When Torkild looked in, he first saw the sleeping couch. The furs were kicked into a pile at one end and tumbled down and across the dias to the floor. This evidence of a restless night was reinforced by the actions of the King/Lord himself. He paced the length of the chamber with long jerky strides. Torkild watched him reach one end, halt, spin about, and lurch off for the other end. His thin lips moved as he did and his eyes flickered here and there.

Torkild was supposed to be the personal servant of the King/Lord. Ostensibly, that entailed arriving when the King/Lord rose and helping him in his toilet and to dress him. Nordseth was fully dressed and had probably splashed some water onto his face. Even though Torkild arrived earlier and earlier, thinking to catch his King/Lord upon first arising, he had not yet succeeded in the attempt. The one thing which Nordseth did still rely upon him for was information on any important event, or unimportant one for that matter, which might have occurred in the Camp or Hold during the few hours he had slept fitfully in his chamber.

While Torkild did fulfill his duty in that regard he had grown more cautious of late about providing every detail of every ongoing situation. Only last week, Nordseth had ordered the summary eviction of a group of Interpreters who he said he had reason to believe were plotting with the revolutionaries to usurp his power. That decision was based on the slim evidence which Torkild had provided concerning dissatisfaction with the way in which certain Rituals were being performed in the Camp. The group of Interpreters in question had felt there were not enough First Lords and Ladies present at the Ritual.

Nordseth had perceived it as a subtle plot to surround him with more enemies and to do him in. He had been all for executing them out of hand, but Torkild had managed to coax him into simple exile. The evidence of guilt was slim, even by the King/Lord's own standards, and the outcry was immediate and loud from the High Interpreters of the Camp. The King/Lord had stuck to his decision and the Interpreters had left the Camp, fuming but alive.

The light in the well, which was the sleeping chamber of the King/Lord, suddenly increased and Torkild knew the sun had broken free from the icy mists of the horizon. The light, falling as it did from above, reduced shadows to a minimum and gave each object a pallor and intensity which fascinated Torkild. It was while he was contemplating the leveling effect of the light that Nordseth suddenly stopped in his pacing and spoke without looking toward the curtain where Torkild was concealed.

"You can come in now, Torkild. You have watched me in my restless pacing long enough."

Torkild started. The King/Lord often performed this little trick of seeming omniscience but it always caught Torkild off guard. He grabbed the edge of the hanging and rattled the blood metal tubes rather more than necessary as he swung himself through it. The jingling accompanied him to the center of the chamber where it died out like the final whisper of a departing snowfall.

"I did not mean..."

"To intrude, yes, I know. If it were someone else, it would be intrusion. As it is you, it is merely your duty." Torkild recognized this as praise and, even though faint, it was welcome.

Torkild noticed Nordseth was dressed for the day except for one article. The half crown, half of its circumference wrought in fine gold and the other half composed of a band of plain blood metal, lay half buried among the sleeping furs on the corner of the dias. Torkild also noticed that the deep blue of the King/Lord's gown contrasted starkly with the pallor of his face. It had been a rough night. Even now he clutched a balled up piece of cloth and worried it between his long, thin fingers. The cloth was dull red, the color of dried blood, and it concealed a decahedron of blood metal.

When the King/Lord coughed, he coughed up blood in small amounts. The decahedron of blood metal wrapped in the cloth moved closer to his face and away. A look of dissatisfaction passed over the features of the King/Lord. Both he and Torkild knew he was about go into another fit of coughing.

Torkild set his mouth in a grim line. Nordseth did not appreciate pity and Torkild had grown inured to the sight of his monarch coughing out his life slowly and painfully, but his servant still felt a pang every time it began, for the beginning was the worst. The surge from deep within which could not be stopped or even slowed caused the King/Lord the most pain, both physically and emotionally. It had come to seem inevitable, if not eternal, but the onset only intensified Nordseth's feeling of powerlessness. His body betrayed him. From there it was a small step to the feeling that the entire world conspired against him.

He coughed once. It was low and guttural, almost as if it might not develop into anything worse. Nordseth paused and held his breath. His fever bright eyes fixed themselves upon Torkild's ruined face and the muscles along his jaw clenched. He coughed again. And again. The fit had begun.

His eyes dulled and he moved the dull red cloth up before his face. He bent and swayed as the paroxysms racked his body. He caught the small drops of blood in the cloth where they covered the decahedron with a fine sheen of red. The blood metal began to warm and even as he continued to cough, the King/Lord bathed his ice cold hands in the heat generated by his own blood. The surges slowed. One last cough to clear his throat and it was over. He lowered the cloth bound decahedron but only to the level of his chest where he clutched it to him and let the heat radiate through his thinning flesh and brittle bones.

Torkild waited silently. He did not ask his monarch if he needed anything. He knew the ritual. Do not ask if he needed anything and never, never ask after his health.

Nordseth took a deep but cautious breath and moved toward the dias where he sat down slowly on the corner after pushing the half crown away and further into the tangle of furs. He nursed the decahedron in its nest of red cloth and looked up sharply at Torkild.

"Very well. What has happened during the few hours I was stretched out here like a corpse?"

Torkild cleared his own throat. "Of course, the Interpreters are upset at the expulsion."

"Let them be. I have a kingdom, or at least half of a kingdom, to manage here. I cannot be concerned about the feelings of a small group within that kingdom."

"Small but powerful."

Nordseth raised one eyebrow at the seeming impertinence but let it go. He did trust his servant to tell him the truth and encouraged Torkild to speak frankly, within limits. Both knew where those limits lay.

"Granted then. What about my counterpart in the Hold? How does the Queen/Lady Alisande deal with her problems?"

"In her usual way."

"Ah."

"I am reliably informed that the Interpreters within the Hold are growing more and more frustrated with her repressive tactics. She follows her customary pattern of quelling them since she knows she cannot quash them."

"Ah, yes, so predictable in so many ways."

"However, my King/Lord, it is not the Queen/Lady who polarizes the situation in the Hold; it is the revolutionaries. Their influence in the Hold, and Low Hold in particular, far exceeds that in the Camp, due to your campaign of suppression. They agitate and plot and cause enough trouble to allow First Lord Grendyl pyr Tal myr Joryth to step forward into a position of strength. He draws more power to himself every day and he distrusts the Interpreters as much as he despises the revolutionaries."

"A man after my own heart."

Torkild looked at him cautiously from his good eye. "But not a man after your throne?"

Nordseth raised his head and took a deep breath. "Perhaps, but I doubt it. And even if he does covet it, I can admire him for that. He would not succeed. He is too much the old soldier to want to sit upon a throne which would sap his strength and kill him by degrees."

"Nevertheless, he does act boldly within the Hold and has gathered more support from all levels of the aristocracy even as he hounds the revolutionaries and outrages the Interpreters. The Queen/Lady is balanced very precariously upon the top of an unsteady heap of warring factions at this moment. Soon it will take only a very small nudge to send it all into chaos."

"Chaos. I used to fight desperately to ward it off. Now I am not so sure. Not sure at all."

Torkild studied the face of his King/Lord. He saw there the remnants of the pinched pain from the bout of coughing, an explicable and familiar expression. But burning through the pain was a desperation and cruelty which had become only too persistent of late. Nordseth had always been resolute in his purpose and had commanded that acts of cruelty be done before in the name of stability, that all encompassing term which justified almost anything to further secure his half throne, but never to such an extreme. Where once he would have ordered selected assassinations to take place to maintain the status quo as he defined it, now he broadcast murder across the social spectrum. Orders for "corrective" assassinations could never be traced directly back to the King/Lord, he made sure to shuffle enough middlemen between him and his target to obliterate any trail, but he did not discourage the popularly held belief that he was ultimately responsible for the deaths. Fear of that sort was a sword which he wielded with vigor and skill.

"Am I a monster?"

"What?" Torkild narrowed his good eye while he calculated what his response to the question should be.

"A monster. A creature who craves destruction above all else? You think that at times, I know. And at times, you are right. But I am a monster of their creation." Nordseth waved his hand at the world outside the cloth walls of his narrow enclosure.

"Then it's their fault."

"Yes. And no." The King/Lord rose from the corner of the dias and stepped down to the ground where he began to pace slowly and precisely back and forth in the same path. Torkild noted his sovereign placed his feet in the same way and almost in his own footprints each time. The precision of movement helped him with his precision of thought.

Torkild had seen just such a movement many times and he knew the King/Lord was simply waiting to be prompted before he began to speak. He gave him a few more moments and then uttered a simple and seemingly straightforward question. "Then whose fault is it?"

Nordseth glanced over as he continued to pace and something resembling a smile passed across his thin, arched lips. "Whose fault? Theirs and mine. But I suppose mostly mine. I'm aware of what I am doing. Never forget that. Even when I do not want to be reminded of it, I know it. I have set my feet, our feet I should say, on a bloody path. But it is the only one which I could follow. Blood runs along it and across it and under it. And it has gotten worse of late. I know, yes, I know."

"But, my King/Lord, you are a victim..." Torkild made a feeble attempt at murmuring a rebuttal and was silenced by a cold look and the tight line of the lips which had almost smiled a moment before.

"No. One thing I am not is a victim. But it was one who could be called a victim of mine who set me upon this path and kept me there. One of my victims. Do you know which one? Can you guess which assassination set the blood to flowing so freely?"

"The elimination of High Interpreter Setros? He was assassinated while at a Ritual."

"No. He was sent to the gods with their praises upon his lips, that is if he really did believe in the gods and I have my doubts. No, not him. It was Cym myr Jyn pyr Ton."

Torkild frowned. The name was not familiar to him. She was not a First Lady, that much he knew. But he could not think who she was.

"Pardon my ignorance, my King/Lord, but I do not know..."

"You do, but you forget. That in itself makes the act even more heinous. That is why it is the act which set the blood to flowing fast and furious. Cym myr Jyn pyr Ton was a woman without a class. She eked out a living, if it can be called that, as a prostitute. She spent most of her time on the fringes of the Camp but made occasional forays into Low Hold. The one advantage of the classless is that they can move freely between Hold and Camp. Who cares what they do? Well, I came to care. You reported to me she had been seen leaving the tent of a certain First Lord here in the Camp, about whom we had our doubts as far as loyalty went, and going directly into the Low Hold on several occasions. And always shortly after that, certain of our minor plots underway in the Hold were confounded. I can't even remember which ones now so they must have been very minor. You perceived a pattern. I agreed. I had her brought to me in the middle of the night. You were sleeping. It was a whim really. But a whim which has cost me and others dearly. She was terrified, but even through the fear I could tell she was too simple to be a spy. If she was carrying messages it was in relative innocence. I do not believe anyone is completely innocent. I questioned her but did not really listen to her answers. They were meaningless. She was important. She represented every threat I felt pressing on me then. She was actually no threat at all. And I had her killed. I felt her last breath upon me. That was the first step down the path which has become steeped in blood, pointless or otherwise. That is true cruelty. And the fact remains that I would do it again. I would have to do it again."

"But she was a minor player in a much bigger game."

"Yes, decidedly minor, but she represents a flashpoint. Her actions occurring when they did and my reaction to them, which resulted in her death, took me past a barrier which I cannot recross. And my share of the agony is that I must be aware of what I am doing. I know I have been tempted by an easy way out, which is to yield to what seems to be my destiny, and to sublimate my dissolution in a bath of blood. I am not certain if my will is active anymore or if the violence has merely become seductive because it makes me think I still retain that active will to control and rule. I will continue to be cruel and continue to spill blood. It is all I have left."

Torkild was about to protest once again, thinking that as a loyal retainer it was his duty, when he stopped. His King/Lord had always demanded the truth from him and he suddenly realized if he protested he would be lying. He knew Nordseth had been drained of his former vitality and it was that very loss which the King/Lord tried to make up for by his increased cruelty and orders for more deaths than were necessary. The engine which he had set in motion could no longer be stopped and perhaps its course could not even be deflected. That frightened Torkild who knew his personal loyalty to his King/Lord would keep him at his side to the end of the path, wherever it lay.

"You hesitate. As well you should. I know what I have become but I need you to remind me of it. I will delude myself. I must to retain my sanity. I need your presence to remind me of the truth of it all."

"My King/Lord, I am at your service."

"Yes, you are. I just give you fair warning; watch me, for I might take it into my head that you represent a threat."

"The warning is taken, my King/Lord."

The faint smile returned and was gone in an instant. Nordseth then straightened himself, swept his long fingers along the front of his robes, and marched purposefully to the sleeping dias where he pulled the half crown from the tangle of sleeping furs. He glanced at it, pursed his lips, and rammed it onto his head where the band pressed a white line into the flesh of his forehead.

"Let's go to see what awaits us today."

"The Ritual of Renewal of the Defense of the Camp is the first order of business today, followed by..."

Nordseth interrupted him. "Tell me as we go."

Torkild limped ahead of his monarch to sweep back the curtain and bow deeply but unevenly. The hem of the King/Lord's robe hissed against his cheek and neck in passing. Torkild drew back from the contact with the icy cloth. He paused to shake his head to clear it and to throw off the tingle which still ran along his neck. He then had to lurch quickly to catch up with his striding monarch.

## VI

A RISE AND a fall, a rise and a fall; the loping gait of Trys myr Lun pyr Drun fell into the pattern dictated by the undulating landscape he ran through. He glanced over at his companion, Cyln myr Callyn pyr Jod, and that brief alteration of his rhythm nearly caused him to trip as his outstretched foot did not meet the next rise evenly. He caught the handle of the sled and stepped onto the extension of the runner. The team of a dozen cayns plunged on steadily and tugged both him and the sled effortlessly over the low drift. The sled yawed as it hit the softer snow at the base of the rise and Trys stepped off into a swirl of sharply driven snow particles which forced him to duck his head but did not prevent him from regaining his loping rhythm.

Trys and Cyln had set out several hours ago from the home caves of the Caynruhl. Trys had said farewell to his mother and father and brother as if he were just going for a jaunt into the Waste. Everyone knew it was more than that. No one said anything other than the standard things, and somehow Trys took comfort in that. He had left with no regrets and at least the illusion that he would return soon. That illusion sustained him for a couple of hours as he and Cyln yanked and pulled the sled and the team of cayns down the steep slopes of the foothills of the Northern Range on their way to the open Waste.

The foothills were behind them now. Trys glanced back, careful not to break stride. They had left at first light and the sun was now climbing toward zenith. The high peaks stood out white against the pure blue of the nearly cloudless sky. Trys knew every fold and crevice in the vast pile of stone behind them. By comparing relative distances between two of the major valleys leading out of the Northern Range, he could tell they were headed south and slightly west. He then checked the map he kept in his mind, a trick which every inhabitant of Winterhold had to learn to avoid getting lost in the vast uncharted spaces between landmarks, and told himself that by going south and slightly west they would reach the Hold in approximately eight days.

Trys turned from the Northern Range and lowered his head as he increased the length of his stride which took him deeper into the Waste. Cyln never looked back. She called insistently to the cayns, urging them to put on more speed. Her voice was low and guttural and the ears of the cayns pricked up as they listened to her grunting chant. They ran faster than Trys could ever remember. The powdery snow in the undulating area at the base of the foothills rose in puffs as the churning feet of the cayns and the long runners of the sled moved along.

The granules of snow rasped against his breather mask, filling his ears with the familiar shushing sound. Picking up his pace, he moved ahead of the sled and the plunging cayns. He swung along, trying not to think of anything in particular, and watched the texture and pattern of the snow before him. He had just completed one step and was beginning another when he recognized the roiling of the snow before him. He stopped, his left foot poised in midair. Before he could speak he heard one muffled word from Cyln. "Quicksnow."

She tugged the sled over and yanked up her breather mask to yell at the cayns who had already noticed the treacherous patch ahead and adjusted their course. The sled gouged a deep cut in a low hillock of snow as it swung wide of the depression at its base. Quicksnow was very loosely packed snow which collected in the low areas near dunes. It supported very little weight and shifts within the pocket created currents which sucked in the unwary traveler. Only its surface, which roiled and twisted in slow vortices, gave any indication it was a quicksnow pit and not just another area of safe snow.

"Quicksnow." Cyln repeated her warning in a clear voice with her breather mask still up.

Trys raised his own mask. "I know."

The cayns slowed as they pulled the sled up the slope of the next dune. Trys stood at the edge of the quicksnow and let them run by. Through the toes of his boots, he could feel the tug of the deep currents within the snow. As the sled moved past, he reached out and grabbed a side bar and let it pull him up and over the rise of the dune.

Before them lay a gentle downward slope which led to the Waste plain, stretching for mile upon mile ahead in unbroken flatness. Trys continued to hold on to the side bar and stepped onto the wide outer flange of the runner to ride the sled down the slope. He knew Cyln would not mind him riding the sled on the downward run, although she was very particular about tiring the cayns unnecessarily. He was a bit surprised when he found her next to him on the sled. She grunted to the cayns and leaned to the right to compensate for their added weight as they slid past a dip in the snow.

The cayns pulled the sled smoothly and steadily out on to the flat, not seeming to lose any speed after leaving the slope. Trys was about to let go of the sled and step off to begin running alongside when Cyln spoke up.

"Stay on. It's easy for them to pull here. No need to tire ourselves just yet."

Cyln continued to ride on her side of the sled. She watched the land ahead and grunted an occasional word of encouragement to the cayns.

The sun was warm on their faces and Trys pulled his breather mask up to the top of his head when Cyln did the same. He knew this was his opportunity to ask about what awaited him in the Hold, and yet he held back as if to prolong the moment when everything would change. Right now they were still simply Trys and Cyln, novice Interpreter and older mentor. After he asked his question and received his answer, he knew things would never be the same.

"What can I expect in the Hold?"

Cyln dipped her head to acknowledge that the question had been asked and that she was now free to begin the process of educating him in the ways of the Hold.

"You can expect much and get little."

Trys was surprised and a little amused at the ambiguity of her answer. "That seems like something someone in the Hold would say."

Cyln gave him a wry look. "It is something someone 'of' the Hold would say. And I suppose I am that someone now. I didn't use to be."

Trys could hear the pained regret in her voice as she said it.

"You are Cyln myr Callyn pyr Jod, a member of the Caynruhl clan first and bodyguard to the Queen/Lady Alisande second. That is the way I have always seen you."

"Once I was that person. Now, no longer. I have lost, no, suppressed the core of my being in order to survive in the Hold and carry out my duties to my Queen/Lady. Survival in the Hold differs vastly from survival in the Waste."

"What will I have to do to survive?"

"You will have to learn to walk numerous thin lines. Those lines separate truth from lies. You must walk on the truth side of the line, but not too far into the truth. It is madness at times for one who grew up in the clean, hard Waste."

"You have done well. You are still the Cyln myr Callyn pyr Jod I knew as a child."

"Are you sure? Or have I gotten so good as dissembling that I still seem to be that person to you?"

"You are that person, I know it."

"Ah, the certainty of youth."

"No, the certainty of my convictions. I trained as an Interpreter. It has helped me to form my own opinions and establish who I am."

"That is a luxury in the Hold."

Trys shifted his weight to compensate for the tilting of the sled as it hit a patch of wind ripped snow. "What do you mean? Pardon me for saying so, but you have always made out the Interpreters of the Hold to be a gang of dissolutes. Even if their training varies wildly from what I received in the Waste, there must be a core of truth which they would have to strive for."

Cyln leaned in the same direction as Trys and grunted twice to the cayns to settle them back down to running evenly after the runners of the sled bounced over the last of the twisted snow. She glanced over at Trys and nodded.

"Yes, I must give you a clearer picture of how things stand in the Hold. That knowledge might be more useful to you than a fine blood blade. Get into the sled and sit on the bundles at the end. I will stand on the end of the runners. We need to balance the load for the cayns."

As the cayns slackened their speed, aware that some change was occurring behind them, Trys scrambled up onto a bundle of heavy weather furs which crowned the top of the well packed sled. Cyln swung around and placed one foot on the end of each runner which projected out beyond the frame of the sled. Both looked straight ahead and Trys knew Cyln felt more inclined to talk freely while performing some task.

"An Interpreter in the Hold is not like one in the Waste. In the Waste he or she is an integral part of the clan, one part of the whole. In the Hold, the Interpreter is set apart and given a special place of honor. The dissolution that you mentioned can become a characteristic of the Hold Interpreter. Since there is no work, other than officiating at Rituals, the Interpreters have established another path to follow, that of spiritual exploration. However, the term covers a multitude of sins and allows them great license. Drugs are used by Interpreters in the clans, but on a very limited and specialized basis. You use them to aid in the interpretation and only use them when you see fit. In the Hold, drugs have become essential and, even worse, fashionable. Standing aside as they do, they had to find some other function. They try to make themselves our conscience. I will never have a sommess besotted skeleton as my conscience."

"So the truth is clouded by drugs."

"And politics. Sometimes I think the politics is much worse than the drugs. Drugs are indulged in by the individual and affect only the individual; politics affects everyone."

"What do you mean by politics?"

Cyln sighed. "Politics is as much a part of the air of the Hold as the cold is a part of the air of the Waste. The Interpreters have established their own agenda. They know as a group what they wish to attain and that is more power for themselves. They would like to be able to rule both the sacred and the profane. And authority in one sphere makes it easier for them to gain influence in the other. Many of those in the secular ruling class listen very carefully to the Interpreters, hoping to advance their own aims by using the Interpreters, only to find themselves being used in turn. They are clever and insidious. However, there is one who blocks them whenever and wherever she can; Queen/Lady Alisande."

"You have told me how much she despises the Interpreters. Why?"

Cyln was silent for a moment. The moment grew longer and Trys looked back. Cyln's face beneath the overhang of the breather mask was grim.

"The Queen/Lady sees fit to obstruct the Interpreters in various ways. The precise causes are known only to her, but I can give you a sense of why she does what she does. Yes, I can give you that much."

Each word of her last sentence was spoken heavily but Trys thought he detected slightly more emphasis on the "you" than on any other. Cyln had spoken of this often enough before but always cautiously, as if she were weighing each phrase before uttering it. Trys had the sense that at least some of the caution was now gone. The bodyguard allowed more to come through, although she still scrutinized each piece as she continued, careful not to let too much slip through.

"Back around the time of your birth..." Cyln paused. "You do know some of what happened then, don't you? You have been told?"

"Yes. You mean the attempted conquest of the Hold by the loose federation of Northern clans led by Brys pyr Prys myr Edya and its subsequent defeat?"

"Yes. It was a trying time for the Queen/Lady. It greatly disturbed her sense of who she was and what she should do."

"You mean she questioned whether or not she should be the Queen/Lady?"

"Well, yes, in a way. She knew she had to continue on as ruler of the Hold and so the half kingdom that was hers. It was a matter of duty. But it was the manner in which to do it that she agonized over. The events of the period affected her in a very personal way. She was not simply the Queen/Lady reacting to threats to the half throne, but a woman struggling with issues which shook her to the very core of her being."

"What issues?" Trys felt Cyln was struggling herself to find words which hinted at but did not reveal too much.

"I am the bodyguard of the Queen/Lady Alisande myr Rystarte pyr Grendyl. As such I guard not only her physical body but her thoughts and emotions as well. I cannot answer you directly." Cyln made her statement in a voice which was formal and brooked no further questioning.

Trys nodded and adjusted himself on his perch. "I understand."

"She retreated to her garden high up on the side of the Hold. There, amid the hot and steamy atmosphere of her flowers and the hot water spring which bubbles forth from the side of the mountain, she rested and recuperated for some time. Long enough, in fact, that delegations from both the Interpreters and the aristocracy were sent to her to find out when she would emerge from her solitude. Both groups had first reveled in her withdrawal from the dynamics of the situation in the Hold. They sniped at each other with words and finally with blood blades, and only then realized that neither one was powerful enough to overcome the other in open combat. It was an anxious time for everyone in the Hold. The defenses of the Hold were under repair following the fierce battle with the Northern clans. The threat from the Camp loomed large, although King/Lord Nordseth pyr Nystrin myr Olda seemed disinclined to press his advantage and invade the Hold itself. His firm belief in maintaining the status quo kept him from sending in a force. As I was in direct control of the defense of the Hold at the time, I can tell you it would not have taken much of a force to have swept our warriors from the battlements. It was a most anxious time indeed.

"The delegations, sent at different times, both asked the same question. When would the Queen/Lady emerge and rule directly once more? Nearly two months after she entered the garden, she left it to appear on her throne. She donned her garments of office with undisguised disgust. She had never liked the robes of state before but now, after spending her days in only a simple shift of light fabric in the pervasive heat of the garden, her skin crawled when it first came in contact with the stiff brocade. Her skin was like milky ice as she sat upon the half throne and her voice trembled at times, but she had returned. She was the Queen/Lady once again and as such she ruled with a firmness which I had never seen before. I had conversed with her in the garden. I was the only person she saw regularly. And I did know what she had been through, but even I was surprised by some of the edicts which she issued upon reascending the throne.

"She commanded the Interpreters to pore over the Chronicles of Blood and to find a way to stop the exchange of Consorts and Concubines between Camp and Hold. Of course, they resisted. But they had to give in because of the support given the Queen/Lady by certain First Lords and Ladies. In essence, she pitted the aristocracy against the Interpreters and, for the time being anyway, the Lords and Ladies have prevailed."

"They might be dissolute but they are still Interpreters. I must admit I do not agree with the decision of the Queen/Lady Alisande."

"You have not had to go through what she went through at their hands. You have not had to become an object which they dress up and parade through the Hold. You have not had to lose..." Cyln trailed off. She yanked on the sled unnecessarily and the cayns leaped ahead.

"I ask your forgiveness, Cyln myr Callyn pyr Jod. I did not think before I spoke."

"No, no. In a way you are right. It's just there are secrets which threaten to tear out your heart sometimes. Secrets which must be kept. It is my duty. My duty. And I admit I do not agree with all of the methods of the Queen/Lady. She has suppressed a group which can well afford to bide its time and one which will never forget even the slightest insult. Her policy is much more dangerous than a frontal attack. The King/Lord manipulates them and uses the Interpreters, while the Queen/Lady alienates and antagonizes them. Dangerous, very dangerous."

"And where do I fit into all of this?"

"You are the outsider, an unknown element. I take you to the Hold and ask you step into the midst of the warring factions. I put you in danger. Do you think you can handle it?"

Trys held on tightly as they hit a patch of snow covered ice and the sled bounced up and down. When the runners slid cleanly through granular snow once again, Trys relaxed his hold on the side of the sled but discovered that his neck and shoulders were still tightly clenched. He had assumed he was being taken south for a purpose, but he had hoped Cyln would give him more direction.

"I am to merely step in. And what? See what happens?"

"Yes. Think of it as meditation. You enter the meditative state not certain where you are headed and you let the act of meditation take you where you will go. Let it unfold."

"It does not sound quite so refreshing as meditation."

"True. I would not ask you to do this if there was any other way."

"Any other way to do what?"

"I do not know. I must admit I am trusting in the gods on this one. Like any old hunter I have a feeling about how I should proceed, and this is it."

Trys sighed. "I see. Well, I am here and I will trust you. I always have. You have been my benefactor and like an aunt to me. Even though blood does not tie us together in the same way I am tied to my parents, I have many of the same feelings for you which I do for them."

"Your parents are good people, very good people." Cyln stopped with what Trys thought was an emotional catch in her voice. He glanced casually backward but could not see her face.

"Yes, I know."

"Let us just say I was there at your birth and that blood is not always the final determining factor in the matter of relationships. Not always. Spirit is more enduring than blood. Does it not say that somewhere in the Chronicles?"

"Well, yes. 'Blood cascades from generation to generation and endures as long as the flesh of man and woman shall, but the origin of the spirit is in eternity and to eternity shall it return.' That's in the Twelfth Chronicle, the one often called Grym's Book for the Interpreter who wrote it down several centuries before the Hold. It's rather obscure. Grym was a simple clan Interpreter and chose to remain so even when offered the office of High Interpreter. It was not fashionable then to be obscure and is certainly less so now."

"And yet you know it and sound like you revere his words."

"Yes. There is a refreshing simplicity there even for a modern Interpreter like myself."

"Keep his words in mind. They may be a shield and comfort to you in the times ahead."

"What does that mean?"

Cyln was about to reply when she was interrupted by the dying flight of a spear. The timing of its throw had not matched the forward surge of the sled and its trajectory did not carry it far enough. It plowed into the snow three feet from the moving right runner of the sled and spattered Trys with snow. He twisted around to see three snow skimmers off to their right. They rode the wind down toward them. Cyln did not even glance away but instead began grunting in earnest to the cayns to put on more speed.

Two warriors rode upon each skimmer. The large sail on each skimmer was taut with the steady wind which had picked up from the northwest. Both warriors crouched low on the light framework composed of bryl bone and hide as one steered the craft using the rudimentary rudder and the lines which controlled the sail, while the other one stretched out across the bow and waited with throwing spear poised.

"Brylkyn!" Trys shouted.

Cyln spared a glance backward and nodded as she recognized the device of the bryl horn worked upon the sails of the skimmers and stitched into the shoulders of the singlesuits of the warriors. Brylkyn and Caynruhl were ancient enemies, vying for the same hunting grounds and fighting over the same caverns for generations.

Cyln smiled grimly and shouted to Trys. "It is good to know that battles are not only waged in the halls of the Hold. The wind is in their favor just now. The cayns can only maintain this speed for a short time. There are spears lashed to the sled on either side down near the runners."

Trys nodded and leaned over the left side of the sled to yank free a spear. He was glad he chose that side for a spear thunked into the frame on the right hand side and made it waver in its course. By levering himself up on his knees and tucking his feet through the lashings which held on the rest of their equipment, he was able to get himself in position for a throw of his own.

He watched the smooth flow of the skimmer closest to them and, waiting until it slid into a low depression, he threw. His timing was almost perfect. The skimmer rode up and out of the depression and into the path of his spear. The long head of the spear smashed the leading tackle of the sail as the velocities of the spear and skimmer combined. The sail tore from its frame and the skimmer slid to a stop.

The two remaining skimmers zipped past the damaged vehicle and put more distance between themselves as they closed on the sled. Even as Cyln urged the cayns into a last spurt of speed, one skimmer tacked about and approached the sled from the other side. Trys grabbed up another spear and waited to see which one of the skimmers would come closest first.

The warriors were obviously experts at this type of warfare for they matched speeds and completed their bracketing movement flawlessly. Still on his knees on the sled, Trys swayed from side to side in order to keep his balance and to allow him to throw to either right or left depending on which side presented the best opportunity.

"Left!" Cyln shouted this and tugged the cayns to the left just as the warriors on both skimmers threw their spears. The two arched up and out. The one to the right fell harmlessly into the snow while the one from the left whistled close over Trys's head as the sled lurched under its arc.

The sled hit a bump in the mixture of ice and snow and popped up in the air. At the top of the its rise, Trys threw his spear at the sled on their left. The throw completed, Trys fell forward onto the furs and clung tightly as the Cyln slewed the sled to the right.

When he next looked up he saw the sled on their left catch a ridge of hard snow and flip over, even as the warrior working the rudder fell backwards off the skimmer with a spear protruding from his chest. The frame cracked as the skimmer turned over and over. The warrior on the bow was tangled in the wreckage as the broken skimmer plowed deeply into the snow.

The final skimmer held its distance but continued to match

their speed. Trys righted himself and watched their pursuer. A gust of wind struck the sled and Trys had to grab for a thong on the bundle of furs to keep himself from going over. Off to their left a squall of snow sprang up and moved inexorably toward them. It extended for several hundred yards in either direction and resembled a moving wall.

"Snow wall!" Cyln yelled this above the noise of the rising wind and then yanked her breather mask down and into place. Trys did the same after he checked the progress of the remaining skimmer. It seemed to be slowing as the two warriors saw the snow wall and tried to decide if further pursuit was warranted.

In seconds the snow wall had reached them and they were moving through a world which had neither left nor right, up nor down. Encased in a sphere of whiteness the cayns plunged on, dragging Trys and Cyln with them.

"Lost them! Won't follow! Well done!" Cyln yelled the words into the snow storm. Trys shoved the last spear he had picked up back into the furs and made sure he was secured to the sled. His heart pounded from the action of just a second ago and he made a conscious effort to slow down his body and mind.

Just before the attack, he had felt that Cyln might have revealed a little bit more about what he was supposed to be doing in the Hold. He also wanted to find out more about her air of mystery regarding her relationship to him. But all that would have to wait. A snow wall was not one of the worst phenomenons of the Waste, but then nothing could be ignored with impunity where the Waste was concerned.

Trys hung on to the furs and shut his eyes. In the blackness which was tinged by the utter whiteness outside his lids, he tried to meditate but found the state of trance slipped away again and again. Finally, he gave up and merely slept, that final refuge where many questions found answers but were never brought back to the waking state.

## VII

FROM HER HALF throne upon its dias, Queen/Lady Alisande myr Rystarte pyr Grendyl watched the slow yet persistent progress of the broad bands of sunlight across the immense floor of the Hall of the Throne. The Hall was on the southern side of the Hold and all day its tall windows admitted the light which fell from a cloudless sky. All day the bands moved across the gathered throng of petitioners comprised of First Lords and Ladies, Interpreters of every rank, merchants of spices and metals, workers in stone, hunters and warriors from the near Waste, and that anonymous multitude whose place in society one could never easily label. The impartial bands of light fell across high and low alike, glittering on jewels here and dulled by dark and simple garments there. And Alisande watched the sunlight, nearly stupefied by the drone directed at her all day long. It was a day of open court, a day which the Queen/Lady hated.

The slow progress of the light had been attended by a slow alteration of its hue. It had started out as rich gold; it was now a harsh yellow. It was the type of light which allowed for no illusions. It neither softened nor flattered. And it perfectly matched Alisande's mood.

She glanced to her right where a strong bar of light fell close by. The light should have illuminated her bodyguard, Cyln myr Callyn pyr Jod. Instead, it lit up a patch of the dias where clumps of dust stirred fitfully in the air warmed by the sun.

With an effort, Alisande brought her attention back to the supplicant before the throne. It was near the end of the day and Alisande checked the priority list at her left hand to make sure he was the last scheduled petitioner. According to the scribbled notes, something Cyln would not have allowed the scribe to get away with normally, it did appear he was the last one, although there was a totally illegible scrawl at the bottom which was not in the same hand. A last minute addition? Alisande fervently hoped not.

According to those notes then, the man who stood before her was called Byrn myr Ghyn pyr Kod. His class was simply given as "low" and his occupation as tanner of hides. That fact was corroborated by the odor of tanning fluids and old hides which hung about the throne.

The Queen/Lady raised her fingers to her nose and breathed deeply through her mouth as Byrn myr Ghyn pyr Kod's monotonous voice droned on. He was nervous and instead of making his voice quake or go higher it seemed to drop it deeper into a persistent boom where individual words emerged every now and then, like a bit of hide rising to the surface in one of his vats. Alisande nearly laughed at the image as she thought of it, and once again raised her fingers to her face to take a breath through her mouth as well as to cover her suppressed smile.

His complaint centered around an injustice done him by a vendor who supplied him with the chemicals which he used to tan the hides. Normally such a case would not have been brought before the Queen/Lady herself but taken care of by an army of minor officials who occupied the Hold for no other purpose. However, the vendor in question was one who had been granted a royal charter. Needless to say, it was not the first time this complaint had been lodged. It seemed the quality of the fluids was not satisfactory and was certainly not that agreed upon at the time of the purchase of the fluids. The tanner kept introducing large words in cumbersome phrases as if to show the Queen/Lady that he had some education. She did not doubt he had some education, but she felt he might have gotten cheated in that transaction also as the quality of the product seemed substandard.

He finished with his specific complaint and was moving on to more general topics, which threatened to severely tax his supply of large words as well as to lead them both into a morass of unsubstantiated charges as yielding and treacherous as quicksnow, when the Queen/Lady leaned forward and raised one hand. The tanner stopped with his mouth open.

"Your complaint is registered and I will see that you get full restitution for your losses."

The tanner blinked and, recalling that his mouth was open, shut it and bowed extremely low before his monarch.

"You are kind and wise. Wise and kind, my most glorious Queen/Lady Alisande myr Rystarte pyr Grendyl, most wise and kind. Kind and wise." He clung to the two words which he had managed to come up with and continued to say them as he bowed his way backward away from the throne.

Alisande watched and listened to him go. "Kind and wise" seemed to hang above the drone of the crowd in the Hall of the Throne. The people still in the Hall had no further business with the Queen/Lady but merely stayed on to gossip with friends and soak up some of the royal atmosphere. Of all the cases she had listened to and passed judgement on that day, the tanner's case gave her the most satisfaction.

She had listened to the First Lords and Ladies who complained about subtle and no doubt non-existent infractions of their titled rights, such as which scrap of the limitless Waste could one clan hunt on but another must avoid. She had been subjected to harangues by prosperous merchants who felt they had been cheated out of a few coins by rivals in dealings which were shady from the very beginning. And so, the tanner's tale, which dealt with what was obviously an injustice and one which was easily remedied, was refreshing and pleasingly human in scale. Alisande felt good about her judgement.

"Kind indeed, but I would submit that the wisdom was somewhat precipitous."

Alisande took a deep breath, not bothering to raise her hand to her nose this time, although the impulse did return but for different reasons. The voice, and its tone of admonishment, was all too familiar. High Interpreter Dwilkon glided forward. He was on the same level as the throne, not having bothered to take his place like other petitioners at the base of the dias. His hands were concealed within his robes of office, consisting of a heavy brocade overwrought with thick swirling designs which accentuated his already impressive stature. The concealment made Alisande uneasy and she checked an instinctive glance to the side to see if Cyln was there and prepared to protect her from any hidden danger.

In her own defense, she held up her hand and was somewhat surprised when the High Interpreter did stop. "I have one further matter to attend to, High Interpreter Dwilkon. It is scrawled here at the bottom of my petition list."

"And it please your Queen/Lady, I am that scrawl. I had your clerk enter my name thus since it was not entered earlier, even though I was certain I had requested the usual audience. An oversight on my part, I am sure."

Alisande refrained from any comment. The unctuousness of the remark angered her but she knew it was intended to do just that. "So many details seem to be missed in Cyln's absence. She is quite extraordinary in that respect."

"And in many others. When is she expected back?"

"Oh, soon. Quite soon." The Queen/Lady knew it was best to not reveal too much about the duration of her weakened defenses. The Ice Guards were adequate to keep the armies of the King/Lord at bay but could not save her from a single insistent Interpreter like Cyln could.

He began to murmur something about her incisive presence when Alisande cut him off. "You have a petition?"

Dwilkon nodded and dipped his head to one side in a gesture designed to be self-effacing and yet an affront at the same time. His hands, filled with various scrolls which rasped together drily, emerged from his robes. "Yes, one or two, and it please my Queen/Lady."

Pleasure has very little to do with it, thought Alisande and pulled herself up on the throne to endure the oily, purposeful voice of the High Interpreter.

"Very well, let us hear them. It is late in the day."

"Indeed, my Queen/Lady, it is that. I am here in my official capacity as High Interpreter. The Interpreters of the Hold are troubled." Dwilkon paused and rolled the scrolls together to produce a rustling which caused Alisande to grip the arms of the throne. "I have here a variety of written testimony alluding to shocking treatment of Interpreters within the Hold town and even within the Hold proper."

"Shocking treatment? What is the precise form of this shocking treatment?"

Dwilkon glanced down at the bundle of scrolls and then back up. "I will not subject my Queen/Lady to all of the details, even though it is in the details that the truly shocking qualities are manifested, but rather I will summarize the problem." One more pause to refer to the unopened scrolls and he then drew himself up to his full height and thrust the papers toward the Queen/Lady as if he were threatening her with a blood blade. "Disrespect for the Rituals and, by extension, the Interpreters."

Alisande slightly loosened her grip on the throne but still remained tense and cautious. "I see."

"No, you do not see." Dwilkon came as close to spitting this out as his oily voice allowed. "I humbly beg the pardon of my most exalted Queen/Lady, but I can only assume you do not see what goes on, for if you did I can only assume you would do something about it."

She tightened her grip once again and watched the face of the High Interpreter. His eyes blazed and his lips twitched ever so slightly. He was in a fine fury and she knew it. But she could meet fury with fury; it was the acid politeness which frustrated her.

"Interpreters are left waiting by the primary participants at the sites of important Rituals. They are given inferior positions in royal processions, often behind the ranks of Second Lords and Ladies. Their counsel is not heeded even when it is asked for, which has become more infrequent. Privileges relating to trade in such things as Ritual drugs and paraphernalia are held in abeyance or revoked altogether for no significant reason. In sum, Interpreters lack the respect they need to perform their functions."

The High Interpreter had wrought himself into such a fury that his final statement was spoken in a high pitched tone, making him sound almost hysterical. Alisande waited for him to finish and watched for him to begin to settle down before she spoke. She was surprised at the violence of his feelings and the way in which he expressed them. In her experience, it was unusual for an Interpreter, and especially a High Interpreter, to show so much emotion. A lugubrious monotone was the standard means of expression.

"Let me say, High Interpreter Dwilkon, that in my official capacity I respect the Interpreters. My own observation leads me to believe their influence has not diminished of late but rather has grown. The loss of respect of a few Lords and Ladies has been more than compensated by the influx of the lower classes to the public Rituals. Those people who possess, shall we say, less education than the inhabitants of the highest levels of the Hold seem to trust implicitly in what the Interpreters say. That to me is power of a singular nature. And I must admit it makes me cautious and even distrustful. I have never made any secret of my dislike for the Interpreters. I will not dissemble to you in the way which you, and others like you, creatively rearrange interpretations to suit your own needs."

"Too diplomatic. They're liars, plain and simple."

"Who speaks like that before the Queen/Lady?" Alisande turned from the sour look on Dwilkon's face to discover who dared to interrupt in such a manner. A warrior in full battle regalia mounted the last two steps of the dias and stopped near the throne. His shoulder armor was well used but immaculately maintained as was his breather mask which hung from his empty sword belt, weapons being prohibited in the presence of the Queen/Lady.

"Lord Grendyl pyr Tal myr Joryth, I had not expected you."

"I know. And you must be bored to listen to the blatherings of this one." Grendyl pointed at Dwilkon with his bearded chin as if it was the most effort the High Interpreter warranted. Dwilkon did not speak or change his expression but a crinkling sound emanated from the rolls of paper he still held as his fingers tightened about them. "I have a petition..."

"Which must wait to be voiced until I am finished with mine." This was inserted like the thrust of a blood blade and it stopped Grendyl.

Before her stood her two strongest enemies who happened to also be her two strongest agents. As Dwilkon ruled and led the Interpreters, so did Grendyl influence the aristocracy, or at least that more militant segment of it concerned with strength through military prowess. Lord Grendyl pyr Tal myr Joryth had grown old in the service of the Queen/Ladies. He had served under Alisande's mother and grandmother. His patronymic indicated he had blood ties to the half throne and that fact alone made him a power to contend with. He bore the scars of many hard campaigns both out in the Waste and within the Hold. His brutality was tempered by fairness, for the power of his convictions did give him strength and assurance of purpose.

As she was growing up, Alisande had seen Grendyl every day and had come to regard him as a father figure. It was only when she had taken on the responsibilities of the half throne that she had come to realize the old warrior was a fervent guardian of the throne but not necessarily the person who sat in it. To him the idea of the throne meant more than the person sitting in it. After all he had seen other Queen/Ladies come and go, and only the throne remained constant. His loyalty was true but his methods were his own.

"Enough. Dwilkon, leave your written petition with me and I will review it and give you a decision later. Grendyl, what brings you here? Be brief. This session of open court has already lasted long enough."

"The rebellion, my Queen/Lady." The First Lord did not consider the movement which aimed at the overthrow of the aristocracy and the Interpreters as anything more than an uprising by rabble. To him it never deserved to be called a revolution. "The rabble continues to stir up trouble, mostly in the Low Hold but disruptions have occurred in the area near the Docks. I can't really say it's spreading. But it is getting more people stirred up, and when people get stirred up they cause problems. You ordered me to deal with the rebellion. Well, I can't."

Dwilkon, who had not moved from his place near the throne, smiled and interjected. "So, the great warrior fails to fulfill his charge."

"Damn you, Dwilkon, shut your thin lipped mouth."

"Stop! What do you mean, you can't?"

"I can't because my troops have had their hands tied. I have provided all of the warriors who are currently in active opposition to the rebels. They are my men. But you, my Queen/Lady, have imposed restrictions upon their activities. They may not search a place or a person without just cause. They may not disrupt the regular flow of traffic in an area. They may not take into custody anyone without sufficient grounds for suspicion. What does that allow us to do? Nothing effective."

"I do not want unnecessary bloodshed."

"Blood is shed and will be shed. This might not be a revolution but it is a rebellion. It will never end unless its leaders and their followers are dealt with harshly."

Alisande watched the man before her and felt sorry for him. He was a preeminent First Lord, a hardened warrior of many campaigns, and in his own way, a staunch supporter of the half throne. But Alisande felt sorry for this man because he had lost a son to the revolution. Of course, he had many sons but one by a favorite concubine had grown straight and tall and true, much like his father, and had joined the Ice Guards. Ambushed in a narrow back alley in Low Hold, he and his company had been massacred, not even given a chance to draw their blood blades and die like warriors. The son had not been legitimate and would never have inherited any of his father's titles or positions, but he had been possessed of his father's courage and convictions.

"I understand, my Lord Grendyl. I know what it is to lose a child."

Grendyl's head snapped up and his fists clenched. "Lose a child? You think it's about that? I am a warrior of the Queen/Lady. I am a defender of the half throne. That is cause enough for me to desire to eradicate the rebels. My personal history does not enter into it."

"As I say, I understand..."

"No. You do not." Grendyl roared this out. Dwilkon took a step backward and Alisande shrank back on the throne. "I do not ask for understanding. I ask only to be allowed to do my job. Grant me that and I will go away."

Pressed into her throne, Alisande felt the full weight of her responsibilities upon her. Hemmed in by Interpreters and yelled at by First Lords, she was suddenly overcome with the desperate need to break free from the tightening circle. She glanced once more to her right. There was no Cyln there to protect her. Kicking at the long robes which hindered her movement, she pushed herself up and out from the throne. She gained her feet even though she had to waver for a moment in order to get her foot off a fold of her robe of state and onto the solid surface of the dias.

"I am Queen/Lady Alisande myr Rystarte pyr Grendyl. I rule in the Hold. I command both Interpreters and warriors alike. Dissatisfaction exists within the Hold. I will determine how it should be handled. You will listen to my orders and carry them out as they are delivered. I have had enough. This session of open court is ended. Clear the Hall."

Both Dwilkon and Grendyl were caught off guard by this show of determination on the part of their Queen/Lady. They had grown so used to cajoling her or yelling at her that they had forgotten she was a force in her own right. She was the Queen/Lady and they were her subjects. Involuntarily, both bowed before the display of force.

Alisande was never certain that anyone would have obeyed her. Both Dwilkon and Grendyl did actually bow before her as she stood trembling with anger and frustration, but the events which occurred next did not allow the session of open court to end the way she would have desired. Even as their heads were going down and Alisande was swaying at her full height on the dias, she became aware of a disturbance on the periphery of her vision. Six individuals began to push their way through the thinning throng toward the throne. They came from different directions but all moved in lines which centered on the throne.

In the pause which followed her order to clear the hall, the Queen/Lady saw, without looking directly at them, the six individuals make for the throne in earnest. Where at first they had turned their shoulders to slip between two people, they now used their hands to push people aside. Protests were voiced among the crowd but no one did anything to stop their progress. No one was certain just what their purpose was and it was generally assumed they were petitioners who were concerned they would not be heard.

As the momentarily contrite heads of the High Interpreter and the First Lord rose and Alisande searched for something to say to keep her hard won advantage, the six individuals struck. Who they struck and the manner in which they did so, surprised and overwhelmed their targets.

Six Ice Guards were stationed at the foot of the dias. Six had always been an adequate number since Cyln had always been present as a final line of defense, and Cyln had never relied upon their abilities in a crisis. Her doubts were fully vindicated in this instance.

The six went down even as they were about to draw their blood blades. But to give them their due, they were attacked in an unusual manner, in a manner which a true warrior would have frowned upon. Short, sharp blows to stomach and throat and all six were writhing on the steps of the dias, gasping for breath which they could not draw in through their damaged throats.

Six Ice Guards went down and six assassins rose up, armed with blood blades. They did have to pause to draw the blades and in that pause Grendyl leaped forward and shouted.

"Behind me, my Queen/Lady! Get behind the throne!"

He did not leap forward empty handed. He swung the heavy rod of a sconce torn from the wall behind the throne over his head. The wickedly sharp decorative ironwork at its end whistled as it spun. Alisande remained before the throne and drew forth from the sleeve of her robe a long thin blood dagger. She rolled back the hanging sleeve on her right arm, the one which held the blood blade, and gathered up the drooping folds of the left sleeve to use as a shield against the blades of the assassins. Planting her feet she stood ready to defend herself.

The six assassins consisted of four men and two women. Three of them, two men and a woman, dropped into a crouch and headed for Lord Grendyl, watching the deadly arc of the sconces's end. He charged them and they backed off just enough to draw him away from the throne. As he turned to go back toward the throne they lunged in and forced him to swing the sconce and follow it with a quick charge. Their blades flickered against the heavy iron of the rod just enough to turn it and allow them to dance backward out of its range.

While the three engaged Grendyl, the others closed in on the throne. Alisande moved the tip of her blade in a figure eight and watched the approach of the assassins. The woman approached the Queen/Lady and held her blood blade to guard herself and not in an offensive position.

The two men advanced with blades swinging to force Dwilkon out and away from the throne. He glided backward with his hands concealed in the wide sleeves of his robes. A nod from one attacker to the other and they split up in an attempt to flank the High Interpreter.

His glide continued and the assassins stepped forward more quickly. They concentrated on Dwilkon's movement and did not pay attention to their own relative positions. They ended up circling beyond Dwilkon and leaving him an open avenue back to the throne. He threw up his hands. They jerked back and Dwilkon glided back in the other direction. Cursing each other they swung their swords and closed in on him, frustration replacing caution.

High Interpreter Dwilkon watched the faces of his two opponents and when he realized that simple anger had taken over, he acted. First his left hand and then his right flicked out from the voluminous sleeves of his robes. The two assassins stopped.

One man looked stupidly at the small dart which protruded from his chest while the other clawed at the one which impaled his throat. The darts were no longer than four inches and looked harmless. And while the darts themselves could not inflict significant injury, the poison which coated them was deadly. The man with the one lodged in his throat went down first. Every muscle in his body stiffened and he tumbled over. The other one followed in a couple of moments, still staring at the dart as if he could not figure out what had happened to him.

While Dwilkon dispatched his opponents, the three blades encircled Grendyl and he had to continue to swing the heavy rod and turn to face at least two of them to keep them all at bay. He charged and stopped, charged and stopped, but they drifted off, keeping their distance and keeping him within the circle of blood metal.

Suddenly, he stopped and dropped the end of the sconce to the floor. It hit with a dull crash. The three assassins stopped also and observed him. His head sank along with the rod. Assuming that he had tired, he was an old man after all, and could now be finished off with some ease, one of the men who stood just to Grendyl's left gathered himself and lunged with his blade straight at the First Lord's heart.

The end of the heavy sconce rose as if it were the lightest of rapiers in Grendyl's hands and smashed into the approaching blade. The decorative metal work at the end slid around the blade and a quick twist of the rod snapped it. The man staggered forward and within the crushing arc of the sconce. The same decorative work which snapped his blade smashed his head and he went down. Grendyl spun about but the other two moved off even as they maintained their positions on either side of him.

During all of this, Alisande stood before the throne and faced the woman who she supposed had come to kill her. But the woman did not advance to attack the Queen/Lady. She merely stood before her and watched her and the struggles of her comrades. As they fell she became more nervous and finally she dropped the point of the blood blade which she held. Alisande stopped the circling movement of her own blade and spoke to the woman.

"Stop this and give yourselves up now. You are deep in the Hold. You can't expect to escape. Give up now and I will spare your lives."

The woman turned to the Queen/Lady. She was young but her face was coarsened by exposure to the elements and to the vissicitudes of a life lived on the edge of poverty and starvation. Her singlesuit was meticulously patched but still coming apart at elbows and knees. The hands which held the blade were red and broken at the knuckles.

"Long live the..." Her voice cracked and she had to clear her throat before she could continue. "Long live the revolution. We do not expect to escape. We only hope that our actions will help others to escape from the lives they live. Remove the High Interpreter and the First Lord. We want...justice. Give us that, my Queen/Lady. Just give us that."

Alisande could tell that the first part of her speech had been well rehearsed, the usual slogans drummed into her again and again. But the final plea was all her own and, as such, truthful.

"I can give nothing to those who kill for what they want."

"I do not want to kill. I do not want to die. But I cannot live as I have. You have left us no other way. The law of the Waste applies here, kill or be killed."

"No, it does not. This is the Hold. It is different."

The woman stared hard at the Queen/Lady then to see if she really believed what she had just said. "It is not different. It is..."

She was cut short by a jerk of her body. She staggered forward with the tip of a short throwing spear protruding from between her breasts. The red and broken hands dropped the blood blade and rose to touch the point of the spear. One last accusing and yet sad look crossed her face before she sank to her knees and toppled over on her side.

The Ice Guards swarmed up the steps of the dias even as Grendyl charged and dispatched the final assassin with an unstoppable blow to the chest. For a few moments the Queen/Lady was jostled by the crowd about the throne until the Captain of the watch shouted to his men to stand back.

Grendyl and Dwilkon made their way to the Queen/Lady. Dwilkon looked as unperturbable as ever with his hands tucked into the sleeves of his robe. Alisande wondered whether he had any other poisoned darts concealed there. Grendyl leaned on the bent rod of the sconce while its crushed end rested in a pool of blood on the dias.

"You did well, both of you."

"We only did our duty. Do you believe me now that this rabble is dangerous and needs to be crushed? They nearly killed you."

"They were not after me. They wanted to assassinate you and the High Interpreter."

Grendyl snorted. "I suppose I'm not surprised."

Dwilkon nodded as if he expected something of the sort. "The dissidents see us as the primary cause of their troubles. Of course, it's utter nonsense. The Interpreters serve the people."

"After you have served yourselves, you mean. Gods, man, they may be fanatical but they aren't stupid. I want to find out how they got this far. Someone should have known this was going to happen." Grendyl put emphasis on the 'someone' since he knew the Interpreters had a pervasive intelligence gathering network in place throughout the Hold.

The High Interpreter merely sniffed and glided up to Alisande. "With your permission, my Queen/Lady, I wish to retire to recuperate from this ordeal."

"That's it. Run off and take some drugs to restore your nerves, if you have any left."

"Lord Grendyl, I believe it would be best if we all retired, as the High Interpreter phrased it. I declared this session of open court ended some time ago. I would truly like it to be over."

As the Ice Guards gathered up the bodies from the dias and the people filed out of the Hall, Alisande sat down on the throne and watched them. They were her people. They were people who hated and distrusted her key advisors. They were people who suffered and died for what they believed in. And they did not all believe in her. At that moment, with the sun nearly gone from the high windows of the Hall, Alisande was not certain what she believed in herself anymore.

## VIII

BEYOND THE crest of a snow dune the sky suddenly cleared. Trys and Cyln had driven hard all day through the edges of a snowstorm. Surging now to envelope them and then falling away to let them ride through crystalline clear air, the snow had bedeviled them all day. They and the team of cayns had had a hard time maintaining a steady pace, but Cyln knew they were close to the Hold and wanted to reach the mountain before the day was over. Cyln grunted encouragement to the cayns and they leaped against the traces to pull the sled up the slope of the snow dune. They too knew they were close to home.

The lead cayn broke the knife edge of the top of the dune and disappeared over it in a flurry of snow. The rest of the team followed and the sled tipped over the top and jerked down the other side. Cayns and sled careened down the dune, throwing up a miniature snowstorm of their own. They reached the bottom and Cyln tugged back on the guide lines to make them pause. The jolt awoke Trys who had been dozing on the sled. With his eyes still half shut behind the slits of his breather mask, he struggled to free himself from the cocoon of hides.

"I'll take over for a while, Cyln. You rest now." He spoke from beneath his mask and when he got no response from his companion, he pulled up the mask to repeat his offer, thinking she had not heard. The cold air slapped his face and he was completely awake.

"That won't be necessary. We're almost there."

"There? You mean, the Hold?"

"Look there. Ahead of us."

The snow kicked up by the tumble down the dune blew away in a light breeze and Trys looked up. Involuntarily, he took a sharp breath of icy air. Before him lay a plain from which rose a mountain of glittering gold. A halo of golden light exploded about the jagged peak of the mountain as the setting sun dipped toward the horizon. Bursts of light ran from the very top down the steep sides. As they stood and watched, the sun moved slightly lower and the light flickered and danced on the slopes.

"The light on the mountain is dazzling." Trys was awed by the brilliant display.

"It's called tuff. Volcanic eruptions in ice create chips of glass. You wouldn't see something like this in the Northern Ranges since there is very little volcanic activity there. Yes, it is impressive, especially at sun rise or set. I suppose the Hold does have a beauty all its own."

They sat silently for a few moments and Trys drank in the sight. As the light ran farther down the sides and the hues deepened, the cayns stood and began to fidget. Cyln clucked to them and straightened the traces.

"They know. We are close to home and we must get going before the light fails. Approaching as we are from behind the Hold like this, we will lose light faster. One good run and we'll be there."

A snap on the traces and the cayns were off. They pulled hard and with little guidance from Cyln headed for what appeared to be a channel in the snow which extended out from the side of the Hold, across the River Ice and onto the plain. As the sled reached the indistinct end of the channel, which merged with the snow of the plain itself, Cyln stretched her neck to look to both left and right. After tugging on the harness to send the lead cayn slightly to the left and then straightening him out, she let them run at their own pace, which, despite the long distance they had traveled that day, was a rapid one.

The channel was marked by a regular series of outcroppings of stone on either side of them. While some were completely drifted over, enough were left clear for Trys to see they were all the same size and the same design. Constructed of carefully smoothed stones fitted together so neatly as to make the joints invisible from a distance of more than a few feet, the markers were in the shape of truncated pyramids. Most had a cap of snow to finish them off but some were bare on top and a few even stood revealed to their very base by the shifting wind. They stood about twice as tall as a tall man so that as the sled ran along, Trys had to look up to them. There was a gap of approximately fifty feet between the monuments with the channel itself being about three times that distance in width.

"Is this an old approach to the Hold?"

"Yes. It is the ancient Waste Way. Tradition has it the first inhabitants of the Hold, which was really just a mountain then, walked this way out of the Waste. The monuments were erected to honor the trail and to mark it for posterity. Until the schism, thousands used to come to the Hold along this route. However, after the split occurred the Way was considered too wide and open to defend properly and was no longer used as a primary road. The same thing happened to the terminus at the foot of the Hold. Hold Gate was once the grand entrance to the Hold. During royal processions, say after a successful campaign against an enemy in the Waste, warriors would stand on the top of the pyramids and salute the triumphal return of the King/Lord and Queen/Lady. Now it is no longer used as an entrance to anything other than a world of lost hopes. It is the home now to the growing multitudes of the classless and the lowest classes. The entrance itself is still there and a small door is still in unofficial operation. That's why we're approaching from this direction. The Blood Guards of the King/Lord keep an eye on the Way but generally ignore the trickle of traffic along it. It should be easy for us to slip along this no man's land and into the Hold."

The channel between the monuments was filled with the type of fine granular snow which allowed the runners of a sled to slip through easily. They slid along smoothly on the even surface and soon Trys could make out the details of the massive structure at the base of the mountain which Cyln had called Hold Gate. It was on a scale which impressed with sheer size. Perceived from a great distance, the rough outline of its shape reminded Trys of a mountain of the Northern Range. The lines leaped up, paused at a series of ledges carefully designed to recall mountain paths which teetered on the brinks of precipices, and then leaped yet again to the truncated peak which repeated the design of the monuments between which they moved.

Even if he had not been told that the structure in front of him was a gate or a door, he felt he would have known its original function. Like any door which has not been used in a long time, its function was still obvious but somehow held in abeyance. The hand itched to open it to see the view, since the view from an aperture which was designed as a door but whose use was discontinued is always different than the view from a window. The initial function was different and the difference seemed to cling to the opening, not allowing the eye to merely see the opening as a point from which to view the outside. Trys found himself trying to imagine what it must have been like to pass through that opening.

Hold Gate rose nearly three thousand feet into the air and its base covered approximately ten acres of land. It was constructed in the same manner as the monuments with the flawless joining of smoothed blocks of stone. As they got closer, Trys was able to make out a series of small openings which encircled the Gate beginning at about five hundred feet from the ground. It had obviously been designed for defense since the openings were large enough to allow for a warrior to throw a spear through but not large enough to permit easy access of an attacker, even assuming such a theoretical attacker could reach the height necessary to enter through one of the openings. Near the very top the openings did increase in size and grew more elaborate, being inset into a frieze which depicted well faded glories of past reigns.

The actual gate itself was deeply recessed and the approach was riddled with defensive openings which would have made an assault directly upon the gate a warrior's nightmare. Spears and projectiles would have rained down upon the attackers, crushing them before they could even reach the gate. They were still some distance from the gate and the shadows were deepening quickly, but Trys believed he could make out its general characteristics.

It appeared to be as massively constructed as the overall structure. The gate was not so much one entrance to the Hold but rather a series of entrances. The main gate stood several hundred feet high and could split in half with each side pivoting to reveal an opening several hundred feet in width. Inset into the main gate was a complex arrangement of subsidiary doors, ranging in size from half the size of the main gate to little more than a narrow door through which one would have to turn sideways to slip. Each of the doors was embellished in a different manner and, while there was no attempt at symmetry in the layout of the secondary openings, the overall impression was one of unity with the smallest entrance leading in a natural progression to the largest.

Enchanted by the architectural marvel before him, Trys did not even notice the danger approaching them until Cyln swore under her breath.

"Gods' blood. I've stuck to the channel. They're not supposed to attack. Idiot Blood Guards."

Trys pulled himself up on the sled to see seven light one man sleds moving to intercept their course. They moved in a ragged line beyond the flanking monuments to the left of the sled. Each sled was constructed of bryl bones with hide stretched across them to give the rider a place to sit or stand. In essence they were little more than runners bound together by hide, which made them very light and very fast. A team of only three cayns pulled each sled, which meant they could move at high speeds for short distances but had little staying power, since the cayns were trained to pull with all their strength and did not have others in the team to fall back upon as in a larger team where some might pull while others merely kept pace to recover some of their strength.

"They're not supposed to do this. The unspoken understanding is that individuals or small groups can move freely into and out of the Hold. Either some fanatic First Lord to the King/Lord has ordered otherwise or the captain of this company of Blood Guards has taken it upon himself to try to win points with his superiors. We have to get over the causeway which crosses the River Ice in order to be in the realm of the Queen/Lady. Once there we'll be safe."

"How do we get there? They'll intercept us before we even reach the end of the causeway."

"Yes. They expect us to make a run for it. So, we'll do what they do not expect and carry the fight to them."

"Remember, Cyln, we only have two throwing spears left. We used most of them in the fight back in the Waste."

"Then we have to make each one count. Get ready."

Trys wriggled out of the hides and knelt on the sled, wedging his feet into the framework of the sled to steady himself. He untied the two spears and held one in each hand. Holding the traces with one hand, Cyln reached up over her shoulder with her free hand to where her blood blade was sheathed in its scabbard across her back and freed the bindings on the hilt. She yanked it out and ran its edge along her forearm where a small patch of well scarred flesh was exposed. The blade drew a thin line of blood which coated its keen edge. Activated by the blood, the blood metal began to heat up and made the blade limber enough to not break when brought out into the subzero air. She tugged off her breather mask and swung it back over her shoulder and then held up the blade near her cheek. The glow of warmth given off by the metal satisfied her and she poked the blade over her shoulder and tipped it back into its scabbard.

"Ready?"

"Yes." Trys hefted the spear in his right hand to make sure the center of balance was where he wanted it, while he held onto the other spear and the frame of the sled with his left.

"I'm going to charge them and try to wreck or scatter them. Hang on!"

With her feet secure in the fastenings on the runners, Cyln hauled to the left on the traces and leaned her body into the turn. The cayns suddenly swerved but did not break stride. They shot through an opening between two of the monuments and slowed down only minimally when they hit the rougher snow outside of the channel.

The Blood Guards had closed the gap between them and the first three sleds were just swinging around to begin their run parallel to the channel, thinking they would outdistance the larger sled and then cut into the channel and intercept their prey. For this reason they were not in a position to attack but rather to be bowled over by the greater weight and size of the big sled. Cyln handled the cayns beautifully and they managed to lunge past the teams of the other sleds, thereby avoiding getting tangled with the other cayns.

The solid frame of the big sled rammed hard into one light sled. The driver flew off his sled which was demolished by the impact. He and the cayns rolled here and there across the snow. The cayns all got to their feet but the man lay still.

Two other sleds came up fast at an angle from behind them. Trys glanced around at the terrain over which they would be traveling in the next few seconds. A noticeable rise in the snow lay just ahead. He turned back to the sleds closing on them and waited until he felt their sled begin to mount the rise. Their sled rose and leaped over the crest. Just as he felt them top the crest in the pit of his stomach, he drew back his arm and threw the spear.

The sled went over the crest and sank and Cyln tugged the cayns hard to the left, gave them their head for about four beats, and then slewed back to the right. A light sled with a surprised warrior came barreling down upon them, its runners not even touching the snow.

Cyln reached out and yanked Trys over to the left and both of them clutched the framework as the other side smashed hard into the flying one man sled. The cayns from the light sled tumbled end over end as the traces broke and it cracked up and stopped abruptly. However, the rider did not stop. He described a perfect arc over their heads and hit the snow on the other side of their sled with a dull crunch.

Their cayns did not pause and hauled them up another slight rise in the snow. Both Cyln and Trys righted themselves. Cyln shook out the traces and Trys grabbed up the remaining spear before he looked back. The warrior from the sled they had collided with was a dark tangle on the snow.

Over the rise Trys could see another broken tangle. It was the sled at which he had thrown his spear. The point had hit the frame just above the front runner. That in itself was not enough to disable it, but the end of the spear had then jammed into a clump of snow which the driver had tried to go over instead of around and been rammed up through the frame. The over zealous cayns had then proceeded to tear the sled apart as they lunged and pulled with all their might trying to move forward. The driver had then gotten tangled in the traces and was being dragged at a slowly diminishing pace out into the Waste by the frantic cayns.

They coasted down the gentle slope of the rise and out onto a broad flat area which lay before Hold Gate. The cayns were tiring now. They had run and pulled hard. Trys looked back over Cyln's shoulder. The four remaining sleds were spread out but closing. It appeared they were being cautious and keeping an equal distance between themselves so they all approached the big sled at the same time.

"Four left."

"I know." Cyln said this without looking back. She lightly snapped the traces and cooed to the cayns to coax more speed from them. "After you throw the last spear, we have an extra blood blade strapped to the bundles on the left side of the sled. See what you can do with that. I don't think they'll get close enough for us to ram another one. They know now."

Trys nodded and positioned his right foot more securely against the frame of the sled. A cry reached them across the snow and the four sleds leaped forward as their captain, in one of the outer sleds, called for an attack. They came straight in and Cyln held their sled to a straight course for the Gate. The unequal race was on. Even though they were traveling at approximately the same rate of speed, the two center sleds drew ahead since the snow was smoother in front of them. Cyln spared one glance back.

"Give them three more heartbeats. Then take out the one whose driver is standing straight up on the runners."

Trys nodded, listened to his heart, and rose up and threw in one movement. As soon as Cyln saw the spear leave his hand, she slewed the sled to the right. Three of the pursuing sleds followed. One did not. It plunged straight ahead as its racing cayns pulled on the last course they had been given. There was no one to alter their course now. Their driver lay far back upon the snow. A throwing spear impaled his chest and its end quivered in the quickening wind off the Waste.

Trys stretched forward to uncover and unsheathe the extra blood blade which was wrapped up with the other bundles on the sled. It was an old blade in need of repair. The wrapping of leather on its hilt was nearly gone and its edge was nicked along its entire length. He hefted it and peered back at the last three sleds which were closing fast.

"What do I do with it, Cyln? I don't think I can throw it like a spear and I don't want to waste it."

Cyln grunted roughly. Trys was not sure if the grunt was meant for him or the quickly tiring cayns.

"Here take the reins for a moment and give me the blade."

She thrust the bunched leather thongs into his hand and grabbed the sword from him. He held them awkwardly, sprawled as he was across the pile on the sled. The cayns immediately noticed the difference in drivers and slowed their pace. "Keep them going." A sharp snap on the reins and the cayns surged forward.

Cyln shook herself. She had grown stiff driving the sled; leaning this way and that, now hauling on the traces and then slackening them up. A deft reversal of her feet on the runners of the sled and she was facing their pursuers who had bunched up as they all entered the narrowed channel of the final approach to the causeway which led across the bridge to Hold Gate.

All three drivers had pulled throwing spears from sheaths on their sleds. All three paused to get the proper balance and gauge the shrinking distance between themselves and the large sled, and then all three cast their spears. It was obvious that at least two of the three warriors were veterans of combat in the Waste for while one spear, the one thrown by the persistent captain who occupied the center sled, fell far short of its target, the other two flew high and true.

But the spears were thrown toward another veteran of combat in the Waste and Cyln grinned as she watched the descent of the spears. At the last moment, when the points of the two spears were seemingly about to pierce her, Cyln swept up the old blade and gave it a sharp twist. Both spears plowed deep into the snow off to her left.

Holding tight to the sled with her left hand, Cyln then began to whirl the blood blade about her head with her right. She watched the approaching sleds intently and let the blade fly. It rose up and out, maintained a flat spin, and then descended to slice into the middle sled. It missed cayns and driver but it did cut the reins and bury itself deep in the framework of the sled. The damaged sled swerved and did not go over but did bang against first one sled and then the other, slowing all of them as they tried to avoid a crash.

With a cry of satisfaction, Cyln turned to grab up the reins of her own sled. A sharp snap and the cayns put on yet another burst of speed, probably their last, and they hauled the sled to the end of the causeway and up onto the bridge over the River Ice.

Once onto the bridge they were officially in the realm of the Queen/Lady. Either due to the crossing of that boundary or to the fact the drivers were still trying to prevent a crash, all three sleds slid to an uneven halt and bellowed commands could be heard. The young captain of the detail was not happy and he took out his frustration upon his remaining troops.

"That will be his last command for quite some time," grinned Cyln. "A loss of four men and five sleds to a heavily loaded and much larger sled carrying an old warrior woman and a young man will not sit well with his commanding officer."

Trys nodded and sat back down on the bundles. He realized he was shaking, and it was not simply due to the exertion of the running battle.

"You did well. Good throwing. I guess you have learned something in the Waste other than how to be an Interpreter."

Trys nodded again. He pulled up his breather mask and took a deep breath of clean, cold air. The quivering of his hands began to abate and he looked up at Hold Gate which loomed over them as they slid along the bridge.

Even though the sun still gilded the plain far out beyond the mountain, torches had been lit in the deep recess which led to the Gate itself for it was already thick with shadows. The torches served to cut away some of the shadows but to deepen and define the overall sense of impending darkness. The upper sections of the Gate caught the unsteady light and Trys could make out designs in the stonework which represented many of the legends of the Waste concerned with the major gods and the pantheon of lesser ones.

Father Sun and Mother Ice loomed large and confronted one another across the seam which ran from the top to the bottom of the Gate. Perhaps it was the uncertain torchlight, perhaps the intention of the artist, but Trys had never seen the two primary gods represented in just such a manner. His teaching, and indeed his inclination, was to view the two gods as antagonistic yet fundamentally compatible. One element raged against the other, but ultimately the two did work together for the good of all mankind. The figures upon Hold Gate seemed to be brutal and unrelenting in their opposition to one another. Face was set against face, and fist against fist. Even the rays of the sun clashed dramatically against the spikes of ice and looked to be a obdurate as the stone from which they were carved.

The severely cut folds of their gowns led the eye downward through a motley throng of lesser gods, heroes, villains, and animals who all gambolled or fought according to their nature and story. The lower panels, representing what appeared to be the more obscure depths of the underworld, were lost in darkness and flickering light. However, the same light which served to confuse the eye as concerned the carvings upon the Gate did reveal a different sort of underworld, one which did not rely upon unsteady light to give it the appearance of movement.

Scattered throughout the massive recess which led up to the Gate, and out onto the end of the bridge which spanned the River Ice, was a assortment of people and objects, not represented in the panels above but which did rival the designs with an urgency and bizarreness all its own. Roughly made shops, many consisting of nothing more than a bryl hide thrown on the stones of the causeway and littered with bits and pieces of items which might have been scavenged from some midden heap, occupied both sides of the main channel and spilled over into a series of decaying galleries which ran along the banks of the River Ice for several hundred yards on either side of the Gate.

Trys took all of this in as their sled crossed the bridge. He was still craning his neck to get a better look at the imposing architecture of the Gate when he was enveloped in a mass of humanity such as he had never seen before. The sheer numbers stunned him. In the Waste even a gathering of the entire clan in the main cavern meant the numbers of people were limited and one did know everyone there.

Here he was surrounded by a crowd of people whom he did

not know and who were cheering for him and Cyln. He recoiled from the noise, loud expressions of any sort were not part of the Waste culture, and the smell. His nostrils were assaulted by a tide of scents most of which had to do with unwashed bodies and singlesuits worn too long. In the Waste, one might not wash for days but one kept clean, since dirt and sweat could mean death by freezing. Moisture of any sort was meticulously eradicated; it could freeze in seconds in the subzero temperatures.

Trys looked back at Cyln who was impassive as usual and who continued to try to force a passage through the close throng. The cayns were exhausted and barely able to make headway against the crush of bodies. As the clamor continued, Trys next found himself shrinking back from hands which reached out to him. At first he thought they intended to tear him from the sled and he was about to unsheathe his blade when Cyln's hand on his shoulder stopped him.

"Beggars." Cyln shouted above the din.

"What? What are they doing?"

"Begging. They think we are some sort of rich heroes who have run the gauntlet of the Blood Guards. They want food or money."

"Why do people have to beg for food? Does not their clan take care of them?"

"Most of these are classless and clanless. This is the Hold."

The cayns stopped then; the press of people was just too much for them. Cyln swore and swung up and over the sled. She ran down along the cayns and took the harness of the first cayn and began to tug them through the crowd. Still shaky from the mad ride up to Hold Gate and then bombarded by the overwhelming sights and smells and sounds of his first crowd, Trys scrambled as high as he could go on the sled. But instead of leaving him alone, the crowd took his retreat as a sign he should be importuned even more strongly and they surged forward and onto the sled where they began to pick at the tightly tied bundles.

They had made little progress since they crossed the bridge and were still outside the main recess leading up to Hold Gate. The crowd had forced them off to the left and close to the galleries on that side of the Gate. Trys tried to locate Cyln in the mass of bodies in front of him but he could not make out her form. The press of the bodies pushed him to the edge of panic and the smell from those unwashed bodies made his stomach twist.

He began to gasp for breath and look desperately for a place where he might be able to vomit, if it should come to that he told himself, when he felt a light touch on his arm. He looked down to see a slim hand resting on his forearm. He followed it up to a face which smiled reassuringly beneath a head of closely cropped and deeply red hair.

"Follow me." The voice was low and sweet and cut through the tumult around him. Without hesitation, he slipped off the sled, shoved aside a number of dirt encrusted hands which reached up to his face with palms open, and let himself be led by the slim hand into the nearby gallery. He stumbled across some rubble at the entrance to the gallery and was vaguely aware that his savior stopped the supplicants who had followed them into the gallery by a combination of low muttered words and stiff shoves.

Trys was about to turn around to thank her when he realized his stomach was in complete revolt. He rushed for the edge of the gallery. Kneeling between two broken columns, he retched into the River Ice. When the paroxysm had passed, he wiped his face with his trembling hands and stood up.

At first he did not see his guide for she stood behind a column between him and the crowd which still milled on the causeway. He called out tentatively, thinking perhaps she had already disappeared. "Hello. Are you there?"

"Oh, yes. Right here." She stepped from behind the splintered pillar. The movement was done boldly and she raised her head slightly when she came to face him. The initial stern look melted into the same smile of reassurance he had first seen.

"I do apologize for...this. I don't usually..."

"Vomit out your guts in front of strange women?"

"Well, yes, that. I was just so overwhelmed by the crowd."

She nodded and moved closer. Her step was light across the broken slates of the gallery floor and her body swayed in a manner which struck Trys as very appealing just then. It was as if her shoulders and breasts, hips and legs all performed an impromptu dance which brought her magically closer to him. Her singlesuit was old but neatly kept and it fitted her body snugly. As she moved in, he was struck by the smell of herbs about her, bitter and warm at the same time.

"You are trusting. I could rob you right now quite easily."

"But I trust you."

"That might be a big mistake."

"I have only just arrived at the Hold."

"I know, and with someone as famous as Cyln myr Callyn pyr Jod."

He then realized Cyln was probably famous as the bodyguard to the Queen/Lady. "Cyln is my friend. She and I were coming into the Hold when the crowd rushed us."

"I am not surprised that such a fine young Lord does not know what the classless are like. But then why should you?" Her tone now carried a bitterness more pungent than the smell of the herbs.

Suddenly it was most important he explain to her just who he was, and assure her he was not a fine young Lord. "I am not a..."

"You are..." She cut him off but was in turn cut off.

"There you are! I thought you had been shoved into the River Ice by the crowd." Cyln rushed in from the causeway followed by a contingent of Ice Guards. "I finally got through to the Gate. These Ice Guards said they were not expecting us. Anyway, they managed to clear a path back here and we can now go into the Hold."

"It's good to see you, Cyln. There is someone here who helped me. She pulled me out of the crowd..."

Trys turned to find his savior. The gallery was empty. A cutting wind off the River Ice swept down the gallery to dissipate the rank smell from the crowd on the causeway and to leave behind the trace of a warm and bitter scent.

"Who?"

"Ah, no one. No one in particular."

"Let us get into the Hold. I have had enough of battles today."

"Yes. I too have had enough."

As he followed Cyln up out of the gallery, he turned once more and thought he caught a glimpse of a moving shadow among the broken columns. He raised his arm, the arm she had gripped to pull him from the crowd, and sniffed at it. It smelled bitter and warm.

## IX

HIGH INTERPRETER Dwilkon stood at the window of the reception chamber and tapped the fingernails of his left hand against its cold stonework. A trace of fine powder appeared where he tapped. He noticed it, clicked his tongue, and stopped tapping. Carefully, he moved his hand and blew the granules of powder off the stone. He looked closely to make sure he had gotten all of it before he turned from the window and glided to the center of the chamber.

The chamber was where he received new entrants to the ranks of the Interpreters of the Hold. For this reason it was located in a certain spot in the Hold and decorated in a certain way. Dwilkon knew the importance of first impressions and had designed the place where he greeted the new arrivals with that in mind. The chamber was set in an outer wall and rather low down on the Hold proper. From the single wide window a view was afforded of Low Hold, complete with the hovels at the foot of the mountain and even a glimpse of the shacks which perched on the pilings out over the River Ice. Beyond the squalor lay the uninterrupted Waste, clean and white and dazzling.

Just as a stark contrast was evident outside the chamber, a contrast had also been arranged within. The chamber was ancient, one of the first hacked from the solid stone of the mountain when the first settlers had climbed up from the Waste. Its low ceiling and uneven floor and walls still bore the imprint of the chisel.

The roughness of the chamber was contrasted by a variety of exquisite furniture which served to soften the impression of hardness. A wide, solid stone chest dating from the same period as the chamber, took up nearly one entire wall. A table stood close to the window. It was exotic in both material and design, being made of wood from the distant south which was carved to spiral up from a narrow base. Two low chairs, which allowed one to either sit or recline and which dated from the first period of decadence of the Hold, were placed on either side of the table. A lush carpet of finely woven brum fur covered the entire floor and, in a style reminiscent of an earlier period, climbed nearly halfway up the walls.

Dwilkon looked about. The chamber was prepared and it seemed to await the arrival of the newest Hold Interpreter, just as he did. Dwilkon had risen steadily through the ranks of the Interpreters of the Hold until he now held the position of High Interpreter to the

Queen/Lady. There were many High Interpreters in the Hold but no others who tended to the spiritual needs of the Queen/Lady herself, a task which was in and of itself onerous, to say the least. Everyone knew the Queen/Lady held all Interpreters in contempt and distrusted each and every one. Dwilkon's title meant he held a unique position which granted him wide powers but also required him to coax along the Queen/Lady.

His skeletal fingers rubbed a small lens which hung from a finely wrought chain about his neck. The lens was his badge of office. Each Interpreter wore one, ostensibly to be used to minutely scan the Chronicles of Blood in the quest for the correct interpretation of its ancient and sacred words.

Outwardly he was little changed from the days when he first began his service to his Queen/Lady. He was still gaunt and still carried himself stiffly upright. The one change which was discernible to anyone who had known him back then could be noticed in his face. His face used to be round and puffy and shine with a muted but distinct silver cast. He had been a consistent user of sommess back then, the drug which heightened the higher functions of the brain while it slowly numbed the senses of the body. Sommess removed one from oneself. The Interpreters, and other heavy users, claimed it took one to a different plane, removed the dross of this world, and left one stripped and ready for a leap into another one. If the dosage was heavy enough for long enough it would kill the user, and so there was truth in that claim.

Dwilkon had once believed the search for inner knowledge was the primary mission of an Interpreter and that sommess aided him in the search. The day he had woken from a sommess binge with his hands deeply gashed from clutching the broken shards of his own lens and his sleeping furs soaked with his own blood, he had stopped taking the drug. Even as he had held up his hands, which had not hurt in the least due to the pervasive numbing effect of the sommess, and had looked deep into the cuts, which also did not bleed extensively, again due to the sommess, he had realized his search for inner knowledge would only lead him to face the final knowledge of death.

And he had wanted to live. It was as simple as that. He had wanted to live and to search for knowledge in other ways. From then on, he took small amounts of other Ritual drugs but only as absolutely required by the demands of particular Rituals. He never touched another vial of the silver liquid called sommess.

He experienced a regrowth of his body's senses and through them the use of his mind, which did come through the sommess addiction with a keen edge to it. He advanced quickly to a position of irrefutable power within the Hold. As a former addict he knew just how to control all of the others who used the drugs which were concomitant to the their roles within the Hold. He had made his weakness into a strength and gained the respect and fear of almost all within the Hold.

Dwilkon moved to the table and stood with his back to the window. He glanced down and moved about the objects there. He shifted an incense burner closer to the center and slid the ceremonial lens for the novitiate closer to the edge and within easy reach of his thin fingers. All was in readiness.

A muffled knock and scrape at the door and Dwilkon straightened himself to his full imposing height. He raised his chin to allow him to look down his long thin nose at the opening door. The first impression was an important one and the High Interpreter always made the most of it.

The novitiate, in the form of Trys myr Lyn pyr Drun, stepped through the door. His guide disappeared and the door closed so silently and quickly that he glanced back only to see the solid panel of the door as if it had never been opened to let him through. His entire trip though the labyrinthine corridors of the Hold had been like that, passed from one silent gliding guide to the next, sometimes not even aware they had changed until he turned to ask a question.

He had been separated from Cyln soon after they had entered the Hold. She had shouted she would find him later. Tired from the running battle to the Hold, overwhelmed by the rush of new sensations, and half choked by the clouds of drug laced incense which seemed to fill every room where there was an Interpreter, Trys wondered distantly what "later" meant.

Taken to a small, bare chamber he had been allowed to change from his travel garb into his best singlesuit, the one reserved for special Rituals. But the soft leather and the neatly done laces did not make him feel important here in the Hold. Not even the fact he had put the medallion Cyln had given him into the pocket on the left thigh of his singlesuit and laced it tightly shut, made a difference.

Instead, he felt embarrassed by the clan style of singlesuit as he passed dozens of Interpreters decked out in their Ritual robes, silver threads in swirling designs across the dark, heavy fabrics. The fluid lines seemed to intertwine with the wraiths of smoke from the incense burners which were everywhere. Trys followed his mutable guides as if moving through a barely waking dream until he found himself with his back to the closed door in a chamber which did possess an incense burner but which was not filled to overflowing with the thick scent. Trys took a deep breath of the relatively clean air.

Dwilkon beckoned to him and Trys crossed the room. The

thick pile of the fur reminded him of walking on dust snow, soft and yet resilient underfoot. He stopped a few feet away from the High Interpreter and looked up at him, for he was slightly taller than Trys. He saw a gaunt, impassive face with deeply set eyes which searched him from head to toe with one raking glance. Numbed as he was from his sojourn through the drug laden air of the Hold, he found he could look straight back at the Interpreter with little trepidation. The tall man was impressive but not intimidating, even though his eyes had the potential to be.

"What do you see?" Dwilkon's hand swept up abruptly on the first word to direct Trys's gaze out the window and swung languidly back to his side by the last word.

Trys turned first his eyes and then his body to the window, the one following the other slowly as if in a dream. "I see..." He coughed to clear his throat of the fumes which lay twisted there. "I see the Hold and the River Ice and the Camp and the Waste." He stopped his catalog when his sight reached the unending horizon.

"Most novitiates see only the Waste. You see what is close as well as what is far away. That inclusive vision will stand you in good stead here in the Hold. I am High Interpreter Dwilkon."

"I am Trys myr Lyn pyr Drun of the Caynruhl clan, Second Interpreter and acolyte to the Higher Mysteries."

"That is who you were out there." Once again the hand rose and drooped. "Here you are novitiate Interpreter Trys. Patronymic and matronymic are generally dispensed with."

"Yes, as you say." Trys was bothered by the sudden loss of part of his identity. He took a breath and fixed his attention on the High Interpreter.

"No, continue to look out of the window. There are things there I would have you observe."

Trys nodded, bothered by the preemptory manner in which he was addressed, and moved his gaze back to the panorama spread out below them.

"The Interpreters are agents of the gods. We interpret the holy and profane writings contained in the Chronicles of Blood. It is our duty to mediate between the souls of the people and the spirits of the gods. But it is not easy. The role of the Interpreter is viewed in different ways in different settings, such as the settings which lie before you. You have just come out of the Waste, that vast expanse which occupies the background of the scene below. There the ancient ways of the Interpreter are maintained almost intact. You are part of the clan and yet comment on it, showing them the wisdom or error of their ways; a truly commendable vocation."

Trys listened hard to the inflections with which the words were spoken. They flowed from behind him and seemed to envelope his head. He was not certain whether the residue of the drug laced air still made his head buzz slightly or whether it was the coaxing yet firm manner in which the words of the High Interpreter pushed him on and on. He tried to detect sarcasm but was baffled by the steady and seemingly logical way in which the words impacted him.

"Still upon the Waste but crouched close to the River Ice is the Camp. That enclave belongs body and soul to King/Lord Nordseth. He rules there absolutely and merely suffers the presence of the Interpreters to keep up appearances. However, since they are so important to him, he does allow the Interpreters to carry on their work. But sufferance creates an environment which, while not inimical to growth, certainly curtails it. The Interpreters are used by the King/Lord to his own ends and must carry forth their work within his context. The Interpreters of the Camp show people their wisdom and their errors, but must make one seem like the other at times. Once again, a commendable if tricky vocation.

"In the foreground, so to speak, is the Hold. I consider the Hold to be the bastion of the Interpreters. It is where we develop and refine the Rituals and redefine our position relative to society as a whole. It is the training ground for the Interpreters of the future."

Dwilkon's voice rose and intensified with the last phrase to cut through the buzz which still plagued Trys's head. He turned then to look at the High Interpreter.

"Queen/Lady Alisande myr Rystarte pyr Grendyl rules the Hold." Dwilkon paused. "Her rule differs from that of the King/Lord. Where he is an absolute monarch, she is not absolutely a monarch. She tends to equivocate upon matters of great importance. That is not to say she cannot be firm and even harsh upon occasion, but she does not possess the single-mindedness of the King/Lord. And..." He paused again. "She distrusts, I might almost go so far as to say dislikes, the Interpreters. That is a burden we must bear. It makes it difficult at times to perform our duties. The Queen/Lady does participate in most of the major Rituals but refuses to be part of many of the minor ones, and her attitude throughout can be, well, let's say, trying."

As the High Interpreter paused again, Trys murmured something about how he understood. A hint of a smile curved Dwilkon's thin lips and then vanished. He nodded.

"And that leaves one part of the scene before us to be examined. The Low Hold. It occupies a central position in the landscape out there and it has also taken that position as regards the politics of Hold and Camp. Low Hold is the breeding ground for revolution. Out there in that decrepit structure known as Hold Gate and in the hovels which cling like barnacles to the edge of the River Ice, ideas are stirring which cause men and women to strike out against the established order in violent and profitless ways. The leaders of the so-called revolution believe there is an injustice in society which they must eradicate. But their only goal is to tear down. They have no thoughts as to what to build in place of what is destroyed. Quite frankly, the Interpreters disapprove of the means of the revolution, violence and disaffection on a grand scale, but we do recognize the need for change does exist."

Trys stared out at Low Hold. The crumbling but still magnificent pile of Hold Gate rose out of the jumble of temporary structures which crowded about its base as if for support, both physical and moral. He recalled the jumble of people he had passed through on his way into the Hold and one person in particular. He could not tell who harbored revolutionary thoughts and who did not, but the sheer energy and diversity of the life which swarmed down there struck him as refreshing compared to the staleness of the incense drenched life up here in the High Hold. Dwilkon's recognition of the need for change seemed sincere when it issued from his lips; he put what sounded like real conviction into the words he spoke. But once it was said, it left a false note behind, like the dying ring of a flawed bell.

"Are, um, are you certain their only goal is to tear down? Have you talked to a revolutionary yourself? Have you found out what it is they want?"

The long thin fingers of the High Interpreter left off fondling the lens which hung about his neck and spread wide. He also tilted his head and smiled a patient smile.

"An insightful yet, I fear, a naive observation. I know what their goal is. My informants have left no doubt as to that. They want to tear down the existing edifice, preferably stone by stone, and leave a barren space behind, more barren than the Waste by far. The Interpreters are willing to intercede for them with the aristocracy. We will act as their representative, as we always have, and even aid them in the formation of their demands. It is our duty. It is what we do best. But they will not listen. We cannot even approach them. That is short sighted and tragic. It will only lead to grief greater than any they have known up to this point."

"Perhaps they hope to reach the absolute bottom of grief so they can start back up toward hope again. Perhaps..."

The fingers which had been spread wide in a benign gesture, suddenly clenched to cut off Trys.

"You are a novitiate. You have just arrived in the Hold. Forgive me, but you do not know all that is going on here."

"That is certain," murmured Trys.

"What?"

"Nothing. I was just agreeing with you. Of course, no doubt

you are right."

Dwilkon took up his lens once again and weighed it first in one hand and then in the other. This novitiate would require close observation. He had been brought in from the Waste by Cyln, bodyguard to the Queen/Lady, and that in itself was enough to necessitate the watch. But his attitude also indicated a restless and perhaps contrary spirit. Such things always required a close watch.

Trys turned back to the window. From where he stood he could look down a narrow slot in Low Hold which he supposed must be what passed for a street. He had heard of the periodic volcanic activity of the mountain which shook the Hold and caused the buildings to slide down pre-cut channels in the rock rather than to tumble into ruins. The mutable street might not have existed in its exact configuration a few months ago and was likely to take a different course a few months hence. But for now it ran relatively straight from the Hold to the River Ice.

At the river end stood a person. The slim figure was in sharp silhouette against the sullen waves of the River Ice. The posture of the distant figure made Trys squint to try to bring it into sharper focus. Drug bemused as he was, he could have sworn it was the young woman he had encountered in the gallery along the river.

"As you say, High Interpreter Dwilkon, I have just come from the Waste. But already I have met people who seem to believe in certain things. And their belief appears to be strong. Is it not the duty of the Interpreters to listen to, understand, and foster those beliefs by integrating them into the Rituals?"

Dwilkon's eyes narrowed and he blew a faint thread of breath through his pursed lips. "You must learn what it means to be an Interpreter of the Hold. There are matters here far beyond your current scope. They run like the streams of molten rock deep in the heart of the mountain. No man will ever look upon those streams; few Interpreters will see all there is to see within the Hold. Let that be enough for now."

The incense seemed to prod him onward. It made him fret under the simplistic view he was being forced to acquiesce to, at the same time it robbed him of the energy to force the issue. He swung his head about as if to butt it up against the implacable wall of the High Interpreter, and instead he found himself nodding meekly.

"Yes, I see. Too much, too fast."

"Precisely. Slow down and let yourself be absorbed into the culture which exists here. In that way you will come to understand what is and what is not possible; what is and what is not desirable. It will mold you and make you strong in your convictions."

"Yes."

"Good. In recognition of your new position, I present you with this lens, the symbol and tool of an Interpreter of the Hold."

Dwilkon picked up the lens by the blood red cord from which it hung. The lens was encircled with a flowing design in blood metal. It spun at the end of its cord and flashes of light darted across Dwilkon's gaunt face.

"The cord is the color of blood which is the binding element of Hold society. Interpreters study the Chronicles of Blood and perform the Rituals which grow out of the ancient record. The lens is fixed in a setting of blood metal which represents Sun and Ice, the two gods of Winterhold. The flashing rays of the sun hold one side while the long fingers of ice grip the other. They meet in discord but the sparks from the clash form a bond which cannot be broken."

Without seeming to move, Dwilkon suddenly appeared in front of Trys. Trys's gaze was fixed by the spinning light and without looking he held up his hand and Dwilkon slipped the cord over it. The lens turned slower in front of Trys's face but still captured his attention.

The lens was used by Interpreters of the clans in the Waste, but in a much more utilitarian form. The one Trys had possessed, and which he had used only occasionally when studying the smaller text of the Chronicles, had been a large, coarse hunk of glass which warped the letters at the edges. The elegance of the object he held fascinated him. Its finely wrought design drew his eyes and his mind toward it. The symbol made solid held a power which he could not resist.

At that moment, Trys felt incapable of resisting anything. Utterly exhausted from his journey to and through the Hold, surrounded by a place and culture familiar and yet differing in significant ways from his own, and finally confronted by the High Interpreter whose views he found compelling and frightening at the same time, he stood and let his mind empty of all but the spinning light of the lens.

From a great distance, he heard a knock on the door. He was vaguely aware that a servant entered at Dwilkon's command, crossed the room, and placed a tray upon the table

"You are late."

"A million pardons, High Interpreter, but we ran out of some of the drugs and had to send to the apothecary's chamber for more."

"But I checked...never mind. Set them out. Minor Ritual drugs first, then major Ritual ones, and then those used for personal enlightenment."

Dwilkon watched the man carefully at first and then turned to Trys. Even though all of his attention seemed to be focussed on the novitiate, he still kept a close watch on the servant.

"These are the most commonly used Ritual drugs. Here in the

Hold we differentiate between minor and major Rituals with numerous subdivisions within those two large categories. Each Ritual, no matter how small or brief, has a drug to go along with it. The drugs are used by the Interpreters and sometimes by the participants who may not be Interpreters."

"Why?" Trys broke his gaze away from the lens and slowly lowered his arm, still catching the flicker out of the corner of his eye.

"Why what?"

"Why so many drugs?"

"It has been some time since I have gone among the clans, but have they changed so much they no longer use drugs during Rituals?"

"No. Drugs are used, but only as an accessory. In the Caynruhl clan the High Interpreter does not require any Interpreter to partake of the drugs as long as he is satisfied that the interpretations are true to the spirit of the Chronicles."

"A charming provincial custom, I am sure. In the Hold we do not have the luxury of variation from precise interpretation. Thousands of lives are affected by a single interpretation of a single passage. Spirit has very little to do with it."

"That seems unfortunate. I thought that..."

"Recall our conversation of a few moments ago. The Hold is not the Waste. Things are different here, very different."

"Yes. Different."

"Let me point out the nature of some of the drugs upon the tray." Dwilkon moved to the table and Trys followed. The servant hovered behind them, keeping his distance but placing himself directly in back of the High Interpreter.

"The first row contains those used primarily in minor Rituals, such as the dedication of a new chamber in the Hold or the blessing of the food prepared in the royal kitchens. They are used only by the Interpreter since participants in minor Rituals are not required to be in an anticipatory state."

"By anticipatory state, I take it you mean prepared to interpret?"

"Here is an excellent example of how things are different here in the Hold. Each and every time an Interpreter begins a Ritual he has the chance to transcend this plane, to merge with the larger and more meaningful cosmos. He anticipates that during each Ritual."

"Of course, clan Interpreters are aware of the transcendent state but they do not actively seek it each time they perform a Ritual."

"The quest for transcendence has reached a high degree of refinement here in the Hold."

"Does that not give the person of the Interpreter precedence over the Ritual itself?"

"The Interpreter is the Ritual. It is only through him the truth of the Chronicles can be revealed. Transcendence is devoutly to be wished for. And to accomplish this the primary drug, a foundation drug if you will, is betril. It relaxes and prepares the mind for the reception of truth. Next we use cymcon which allows the Interpreter to focus intently upon the object or the words involved in the Ritual, to see within them in a manner of speaking.

"We then build upon these basic drugs, just as the major Rituals are built from minor ones. Jontspur is one of the primary drugs used in the Ceremony of Mating, a Ritual which is in abeyance just now due to the formidable edicts of the Queen/Lady but one which must return some day soon. Interpretation in the Hold is a feat of diplomacy. Balance one truth against another and judge which serves better.

"But as I was saying, jontspur is used in the Ceremony of Mating. It is the drug administered to the participants and it heightens the need for sexual intercourse while it blunts sexual sensations. The dosage is critical, too much one way or the other and the Ritual can be spoiled."

"By the Ritual, you mean the participants?"

"Ah, yes, in this case the participants are the Ritual. Regrettably, the Interpreter does not enter into the Ritual of Mating and, therefore, controls only the grossest movements from the outside. It is a perfect example of how drugs allow one to enter into the moment of Ritual. Without them one is bereft of that participation."

"This is all very different in the Waste."

"Yes, I know, very different." Dwilkon brushed on past Trys's interjection. "And now we come to the most powerful and seductive of all the drugs, sommess."

Dwilkon picked up the vial of thin glass which contained the sommess. He held it out at arm's length, as if afraid to bring it too close to his lips. The silver liquid which was sommess sloshed back and forth and produced a muted gurgle.

"This is sommess. It is a drug which slowly eradicates most physical sensations but replaces them with a perception of the glory of transcendence. They call it the 'blood of the ice.' It is the essence of so much of what our world is."

"It does kill."

The High Interpreter turned to Trys with a look of pained recognition upon his face. "Yes, it does. Oh, yes, it does."

"You have used it." Wistful and desperate all at once, the expression upon the pinched face before him made Trys aware for the first time of the subtle silver shades on the skin of the High Interpreter. The user of sommess was indelibly marked by the color of the deadly drug.

"Have used it. No more. No more."

He swirled it about in the vial and then set it down on the tray. His fingers moved slowly away from contact with the glass. It was while the High Interpreter was thus absorbed in the retraction of his hand from the once favored drug that Trys caught the beginning of a rapid movement out of the corner of his eye.

Keeping his eyes fixed on the back of the High Interpreter, the servant who had brought in the tray of drugs thrust his hand into the open front of his singlesuit, fumbled there for a brief moment, and then withdrew a needle-like dagger. Trys turned to face the assassin and opened his mouth to shout a warning when he was interrupted by the man himself.

"Death to the Interpreters! Freeze in hell for your crimes against the people!"

The assassin lunged forward and Dwilkon began to turn. The High Interpreter placed his right side against the table and crouched down while bringing up his left hand. In that instant, Trys swung his lens out in a short arc in an attempt to intercept the attacker. The assassin jerked to one side but kept coming, his arm descending for a killing blow.

Trys brought his arm back in preparation for another swing when Dwilkon did the unexpected and stepped in close to the man. The man stabbed clumsily downward and the point of the dagger tore through the robes of the Interpreter.

Instead of throwing up his arms to defend himself, the High Interpreter merely reached up with his left hand and scratched the man's cheek. A puzzled look on the face of the assassin turned to one of excruciating pain. A cry of terror welled up from his throat but burbled and died before it could be heard.

Dwilkon stepped back and away as the man toppled to one side, dead within the second. The body made no noise as it hit the thickly furred floor. The drugs upon the tray rattled as Dwilkon bumped into the table and then regained his balance.

"What...?" Trys managed to get out the one word, but was interrupted by the High Interpreter.

"Poison under my fingernails. Quick acting and always fatal. As you can see, I have enemies everywhere."

"But, why?"

"You heard him. This one was a deluded revolutionary who thought he could rid the Hold of its High Interpreter. Yes, I am a particularly attractive target. I will have to make inquiries to discover who helped him to get this far. He could not have acted alone. Not this deep in the Hold. Others will die because of this." He said the last with a tired voice as if he had been through it many times before and following up on the details quite exhausted him.

"You did me a service. Although I would have killed him before he could have severely injured me, your interception did allow me to walk away unscathed. Thank you."

"It was...nothing. I just struck out when I saw him attacking."

"In any case, it is appreciated." Dwilkon made it sound as if that appreciation went only so far and would only last for a limited time. "You now can see things here in the Hold are different, very different than you were used to in the Waste. Danger comes in many guises and degrees. Watch your back and always watch those around you. This interview is at an end." Dwilkon waved his right hand in dismissal while he held his blood stained left hand stiffly at his side.

Trys nodded mechanically and moved to the door. He opened it and stepped through. His last glimpse of the chamber caught the prone body of the assassin and the tall figure of the Interpreter looming over him in a bizarre tableau. Everything about and within him had changed. Things were assuredly different now.

## X

THE GARDEN of the Queen/Lady Alisande teetered on the edge of the mountain of the Hold as it had for centuries. But now it also teetered on the edge of dissolution. Volcanic activity within the mountain had thrust a tentative finger up near the garden and sent a stream of molten rock down a wall and into the pool where it had hissed and steamed and solidified.

Half of the pool was gone. The other half sat stagnant since the lava flow had plugged up most of the outlet of fresh water. The damage had occurred close to a year ago, but the Queen/Lady had stopped the repairs soon after they had begun. Devastation in other portions of the Hold had required more urgent attention and, like the good Queen/Lady she had become, Alisande put the needs of her subjects before her own.

The once lush vegetation had also suffered from the eruption and succeeding neglect. The plants had withered and shrunk from the area near the parapet which looked out upon the Waste. The frigid air had swirled over the stone wall and pinched back the once luxuriant growth. The larger and hardier plants still grew near the pool but in a untended tangle, the stronger ones choking out the more delicate ones to leave a uniform grayish green jungle. Flowers bloomed infrequently and were smothered in the dense thicket which crowded the edge of the still pool. A fitful maintenance of the garden was carried out, but no improvements were instituted.

The master gardener, a singular position upon the winter planet, fretted about the Queen/Lady's disinterest in the garden. Jyn pyr Modrun myr Synd had been gardener to the Queen/Lady who had had the garden built several reigns ago and as such he was aged but determined. He had seen it fall into disrepair before and he had always been able to bring it back. Even now, the garden was not past saving, but he feared he might be, for his body ached and trembled more each day. By nagging and pleading he had managed to nudge her into allowing him to keep the cold at bay and to keep the inroads of the hardy and most destructive vines to a minimum.

He traced a thick tendril of the archenemy back to where it exited from the rich loam and hacked at it with his pruning tool, an old sword bent to purposes other than the taking of human lives but still possessing the keenest edge that blood metal would hold. The blade severed the vine, but it was too entangled to drop.

He sighed, spit once at the offending tendril, and leaned on the hilt of the sword to help his old bones bend to a kneeling position. Once down he knew it would take a major effort to rise, so he tugged out the cut plant and then poked about in the clump he was working to save. It was composed mostly of a lycandra bush whose violent red blossoms had once cascaded over the verge of the pool. His gnarled fingers, stained dark gray from years of contact with the rich soil mixture of volcanic ash and loam from the banks of the River Ice, grabbed and twisted out sprouting vines.

A tough root gave way after inflicting much anguish to his fingers. It let go suddenly and he wobbled back on his heels. He recovered his balance by jabbing the sword deep into the soil. He then looked into the opening made in the undergrowth.

There lay one perfect lycandra flower. Its redness glowed in the pocket of dark green. He reached in and brought it out reverently in his trembling fingers. Given the scarcity of the blossoms he would never had picked this one, but since it had broken off from somewhere up in the tangle when he pulled out the root, he simply had to hold its delicate petals in his cracked fingers. His skin glowed with the ebbing vitality of the flower.

From where he worked he could just see down to the parapet at the outer edge of the garden. On his way in he had noticed the Queen/Lady on the parapet. He had nodded to her and she had smiled at him briefly and absently. She still came to the garden, but only to stand upon the parapet and gaze out at the River Ice and the Waste beyond. He craned his neck. She still stood there with her back to the garden.

"My Queen/Lady." His voice croaked. He coughed and spat. "My Queen/Lady, look at what I found. Look at what still grows here."

Queen/Lady Alisande myr Rystarte pyr Grendyl turned slowly from her contemplation of the Waste. Most days her gaze was outward, away from the garden and the Hold and toward the River Ice and the sprawling Waste beyond. She still retreated to the garden, but not to revel in the luxuriant heat as she once did. She tended to wrap herself in a Waste cloak and crouch on the parapet to let the frigid air from beyond the wall lave her face while humid heat stroked her back. No longer a place of release for her, the garden had become a sanctuary for contemplation of her own personal thoughts. Like the Waste cloak, she clutched those thoughts closely about her, not even letting Cyln in as she once might have.

Bemused by the interruption, she looked into the garden to where the master gardener stood gesticulating with one hand, while he held the other perfectly still to protect what rested there. She stepped to the edge of the raised platform and hopped down to the sere grass which struggled to live in the coldness near the parapet. The ground was level there but the sudden contact with the soil jarred her and she swayed to regain her balance.

She took a step into the garden and loosened the clasp of her cloak since the heat, while dramatically diminished from its former levels, was still a palpable force. When the lava flow had reduced the size of the pool, it had also cut off a portion of the raw heat which used to issue from the walls of the garden itself. But since she so seldom walked into the depths of the garden, entering it now made her uncomfortable. She had adjusted to the cold and the heat now seemed oppressive.

"Over here, my Queen/Lady. It's a small miracle. Yes, a small one."

Alisande mounted the gentle slope toward the pool. The warm air pressed closely about her Waste cloaked body. She tugged at the edges of it trying to pull it from her completely, but it was secured to her arms by thongs which prevented it from being easily shed.

Step by step she approached the pool, and each step seemed to take her further back into her memories. She had walked the path thousands of times when the garden had been in full bloom. Out of habit, her left hand swung out to ruffle the lacy leaves of a josdryn plant. Dry twigs scratched her fingers. She glanced to the right where the vivid gold flowers of a zephron vine used to climb up the wall which formed one side of the pool. A dull gray line like a dead shadow ran in a jagged pattern up the volcanic blocks. She shook her head and looked down as she mounted the last few yards in order to keep the memories from hurting any more.

"What do you have, Jyn?"

"My Queen/Lady, just look."

The old man held out his cupped hand to her and opened his dirty fingers. The vibrant red of the lycandra blossom filled his palm to overflowing. She blinked. The color seemed to run and blur. She blinked again and realized it was merely a few tears.

"A lycandra. I thought those had all died long ago."

"So had I, my Queen/Lady, so had I. But this one was growing in the middle of that clump of vines. Like it was hiding to save itself."

"A wise flower."

"Pardon, my Queen/Lady?"

"Nothing. It was nothing. It's beautiful and so unexpected."

"Indeed. I've scoured the larger clumps of weeds here to try to save the true flowers many times. But I'm old and getting older and I must not have looked at this clump for many months. It's hard for me to handle the entire garden, especially in the shape it's in."

"You do a good job."

"I'm only doing what I love to do, my Queen/Lady."

"Would that more of us could say that."

Jyn shuffled his feet and yanked the point of his pruning sword out of the soil. He held out the flower to Alisande.

"It's yours, my Queen/Lady."

"Yes, I suppose it is."

The gardener tipped his hand and the blossom dropped into Alisande's outstretched hands. It nestled soft and red against her skin.

"I'm sorry." Jyn said this as if to comfort her for all of the sorrows and worries he knew lay upon her shoulders. "I mean, I'm sorry but I need to get back to work. Much work to be done. Much work."

"Yes. Thank you." Alisande smiled at him. He ducked his head and swung his sword about and began to poke industriously but clumsily at the clump of vines next to him.

Alisande turned toward the parapet. She paused. The path lay clear before her. The old landmarks were still there, if a bit seedy and overgrown. She began to walk back to the parapet, but not back in time as she had on her way up. Everything stayed in its place and retained its proper perspective. The garden had once been beautiful and luxuriant, but now it was going to seed. And she allowed it to go there. She alone was responsible. That too had to be faced.

Just as she reached the low steps leading up to the walkway behind the low wall of the parapet, her fingers twitched and the petals in her hand stirred. She glanced down. The single red blossom confounded her. It was a part of the past and should not have been there. Her fingers began to tighten to crush it. The flower stirred again with the increased pressure. She stopped. Its destruction was pointless. It was better to wait and study it and think about how it fitted in now.

A flower so rare seemed out of place in the wilderness which the garden had become. Alisande shook her head at the heavy-handed symbolism. But for all of that, it was a throwback to happier times. The old memories came crowding in and her throat tightened.

She leaned upon the wall of the parapet and turned to look back up at the pool. The clump of weeds where Jyn had found the lycandra blossom was very near the spot where she and Gerred had made love so many years ago. It was even closer to where Gerred had gone down under the slashing blades of Kysel's men. Immediately after those wonderful and horrific events had occurred, and when the Hold still reeled from being stormed by forces from the North, she had buried herself in the garden. For weeks she had not left its pulsing heat.

The Interpreters had predicted the end of her reign. It was all there in the Chronicles of Blood, they had said. She would never forget their precise words. A Queen/Lady lost, a realm left to return to the wilderness. Those words saved her half of the realm. They sounded again and again in her head while she lay half immersed in the blood warm water of the pool, until she forced herself up on quivering arms and stood knee deep in the pool.

She had vowed to herself then that while the Queen/Lady might indeed be lost, her half of the realm, the Hold and the mountain it stood upon, would not return to a wilderness. All of the deaths would not be for nought. As Queen/Lady she owed that to her people; as a lover she owed that to her love.

She abandoned the garden then. It grew more and more wild, and she knew the Interpreters had been right in the spirit but not the letter of their prediction. A realm, her own personal realm, had returned to wilderness and she made that sacrifice so the larger realm might survive. And survive it did. In fact, it thrived.

Alisande became a firm and knowledgeable ruler, rivaling King/Lord Nordseth in his ability to manipulate Interpreters and ministers alike, but without his often casual cruelty. However, her prejudices did show, for she suppressed the Interpreters whenever she could. Rituals were stripped down to the essentials. She decided to obey the spirit but not the letter of the Rituals. The Interpreters grumbled mightily about it but they acquiesced, or at least seemed to, for she knew their power lay in subtle shiftings behind the more flamboyant scenes she was required to perform.

The realm survived but the Queen/Lady was lost. Not completely and irrevocably lost, but sufficiently for all and sundry to remark upon the severe austerity of their monarch after the battle of the Hold. Alisande administered her realm well. Laws were well thought out, security of its nearly perpendicular borders was maintained, and corruption was kept to a minimum. All was well without. Little was well within the mind of the Queen/Lady herself.

She had mourned the loss of her love in private. Since it had been carried out away from the eyes of the world, no one but her bodyguard was aware of the depth or breadth of the emotion which had been awakened within the garden. She could not share the expression of her grief with any but Cyln. Except for Cyln, Alisande trusted no one completely among the crowds of Interpreters and ministers, generals and servants who milled about her day after day. Cyln helped her to recognize the sycophants and the true servants for who they were, and to then follow the torturous threads of plots which might harm or help the half realm, scotching one and nurturing the other.

But Cyln had left to go North. That in itself was not uncommon. Cyln needed to fill her lungs with the clean frigidity of the Waste. It was what maintained her edge. But even before she had set out to cover the vast distances of the Waste on her most recent journey, she had seemed especially distant. Alisande had blamed herself at first. Her own mood tended to be sour and the wranglings of High Interpreter Dwilkon and Lord Grendyl only intensified her pessimism.

But with Cyln gone, Alisande had retreated to the shattered garden, instinctively searching for a place of safety. She had spent long hours at the wall of the parapet, trying to ignore the tangled ruin behind her or rather to recall it in all of its former vibrancy, and had realized Cyln was preoccupied with something she would not or could not share with her monarch. It was very unlike Cyln. That scared and then angered Alisande. Her bodyguard was there to protect more than simply her body from the blades of assassins. What secret did she have which caused her to withdraw from her Queen/Lady? What right did she have to such a secret?

As she stood at the wall with the lycandra flower still cupped in her hands, Alisande recalled that Cyln had mentioned in passing she had to journey to the clans of the North to bring back an Interpreter. That in and of itself was enough to infuriate Alisande just now. Another Interpreter, another silently gliding skeleton to shadow her and murmur she really should not carry the Ritual chalice in that manner or that she must genuflect three times, not just twice, before consecrating a new royal barge upon the River Ice. Her fingers closed upon the flower and the petals were squeezed out in scraps of crimson. What was she doing? What had happened to her friend?

The familiar sound of the hilt of a blood blade scraping upon stone checked her anger. Her fingers loosened about the petals. Alisande did not turn to the low doorway to the garden through which she knew Cyln had just entered.

As many times as Cyln had tried to prevent the hilt of her blood blade, which was strapped across her back in the preferred manner, from scraping on the low lintel of the door, that many times had she failed. The Queen/Lady waited on the parapet and stared closely at the petals in her hands. She knew Cyln stood just inside the door. She also knew that she fingered the scraped hilt just to make sure that no permanent damage had been done. That was the ritual of the bodyguard's entry into the garden.

Alisande could visualize her bodyguard's movement along the outer wall of the garden where she walked in the cold draft as much as she could. Even though its output of heat was vastly reduced, the garden was still too hot for Cyln. However, Alisande still jumped when Cyln spoke immediately behind her.

"My Queen/Lady Alisande, I have returned." This was said in

her best official voice. "I have missed you." This came from the Cyln who was the old friend and confidant.

Alisande waited a full six heartbeats before she deposited the lycandra petals on the wall of the parapet and turned slowly to face her bodyguard. "Your return is noted, Cyln myr Callyn pyr Jod." She kept her voice couched in her best royal tone. She did not add anything to the statement.

Cyln nodded, as if in recognition of the official welcome and of the fact that she deserved no more. The melting ice on the shoulders of the singlesuit which Alisande knew she always wore when traveling was testimony to the fact that Cyln had come directly to her upon arriving back in the Hold. Cyln remained silent and upright before her Queen/Lady.

"You have been away some time."

"Yes, my Queen/Lady, and I do apologize. The return to the Hold was not as smooth as usual. We were attacked by overzealous Blood Guards. We acquitted ourselves well and repulsed their attack. They sustained numerous injuries and we none."

Alisande blinked and frowned at the report for two reasons. The news of the attack was unexpected since the tacit understanding was that limited travel was allowed through the domain of the King/Lord which surrounded the Hold. But she was also somewhat surprised that the person Cyln had brought back should have taken an active role in the running battle. In her experience, Interpreters tended to be contemplative to the point of near catatonia.

"We? That would be your Interpreter?" Alisande was not going to make it easy for her bodyguard.

"With all due respect, my Queen/Lady, he is not mine. Nor do I think he belongs to anyone but himself."

"Admirable, I'm sure."

"My Queen/Lady..."

"However, in your absence I have had to deal with a myriad of details and the wrangling between High Interpreter Dwilkon and Lord Grendyl. And an attack at the very base of the throne itself."

Cyln stiffened and her hand went to the hilt of her blood blade. "Oh, my Queen/Lady, I did not know. I came directly here and did not even stop to check with the captain of the Ice Guards. Alisande, are you all right?"

"Yes. I'm fine. It was quite a spectacle. I fought side by side with Dwilkon and Grendyl. Both of them acquitted themselves well."

"Who were they? How many of them? Are they all dead?"

"A half dozen revolutionaries who are now quite dead. Dwilkon had come to complain about the treatment his Interpreters received from me and he was interrupted by Grendyl who complained about the treatment he has received of late. He feels his hands are tied and that he cannot suppress the rebels as he sees fit. I managed to put both of them off with the usual litany about how this is my half kingdom and I will rule it as I see fit, when the would-be assassins attacked. I drew my dagger while Grendyl resorted to a wall sconce. Dwilkon used some particularly deadly darts he had concealed in the sleeves of his robes. Watch that in future. We did quite well, and then the Ice Guards finally arrived to finish them off."

"The rebels are gaining in strength and boldness. Perhaps we should let Grendyl have his way in this."

"Perhaps, but I need to make sure he will not create a blood bath, catching up the innocent with the guilty. A precise discrimination in these matters has never been one of his strong points. The people grumble enough now about the aristocracy. I don't want to give more of them good reason to create a true and lasting revolution. As before, and for evermore it seems, I will continue to juggle the inclinations of both Grendyl and Dwilkon and try to keep them from destroying more than is necessary to keep the half kingdom upon a stable base."

"My Queen/Lady, I am so sorry." A genuine expression of anguish twisted Cyln's face.

"Cyln, do not fear. It was not that bad. I was strangely calm during the entire incident. And it did bring Dwilkon and Grendyl together, even if for a few moments, in a concerted effort to preserve their Queen/Lady. I suppose they would rather deal with me than with an unknown successor to the half throne. It also showed me the depth of hatred inherent in some of my subjects. In fact, it seems the attack was not directed at me but rather at the High Interpreter and the First Lord. Perhaps the people still love their Queen/Lady, eh?"

"I will never leave your side again."

"Don't make such a statement. You need to return to the North now and then. However, I am not so certain I fully approve of your reason for going this time. Another Interpreter for Dwilkon to twist to his own purposes? Doesn't that smack of treason?"

"My Queen/Lady, please do not suspect my motives. You know I live only to protect you. I will plunge my blade into my heart this very minute if you feel I have failed you or will fail you."

"Calm down, Cyln, calm down. And for the sake of the gods, keep your blade sheathed. You might do something rash. I need your strong arm and blade to protect me. You can't do that by killing yourself."

"My Queen, my Queen. I am so sorry."

"Stop. I do wish to know more of this Northern Interpreter.

What can you tell me about him?"

Cyln took a deep breath and shuddered. Her failure to protect her Queen/Lady wounded her more than the head of a brum pike ever could. The pike would merely tear the flesh, her failure ripped deep into her honor and her confidence in her abilities. But like the good warrior she was, she accepted the blow and swung to counteract its influence. Her Queen/Lady needed her from that point onward. She must never let her vigilance waver again. It was that simple. However, it did make her task of informing Alisande about the new Interpreter that much more difficult. It would have been much easier to face a half dozen pike wielding warriors.

"His name is Trys myr Lyn pyr Drun." Cyln stumbled on the matronymic and glanced at Alisande to see if she noticed. If she had, it did not disturb her, for she looked at Cyln with the same steadiness of gaze which implied she would listen to all Cyln might have to say but that an initial prejudice was already in place. "And he shows promise." Cyln ended lamely.

She was certain Alisande was displeased. But Cyln, still off balance from the revelations concerning her threatened safety, did not know how to present her charge in his best light. She had hoped for inspiration of some sort to get her through an explanation of her motives, but such aid was not forthcoming.

"Promise of what?"

"He is different. He might be able to bring about change. Change of some sort."

A gust of icy wind broke over the parapet. It sent three of the red petals spinning down and about the feet of the Queen/Lady. She gathered up the edge of her Waste cloak and pulled it about her chest. The petals were swept within the cloak. Alisande took one step forward and felt a soft squish as her booted foot came down on one of the pulpy petals.

"Cyln, you are my trusted bodyguard and you are my trusted friend. I have lived too long within the secret plots which clog the very air of the Hold not to know you too harbor a secret."

Cyln winced and then gritted her teeth in anticipation of a coming blow.

"I don't know what takes precedence in my life. I have tried to become the best Queen/Lady I could possibly be since the loss of Gerred and...of other hopes. I believe I have succeeded, at least in part. You do have a right to your secrets. I guess I had hoped they would not be necessary. I will ask you again, who is this Interpreter who you bring down from the North?"

The pain in Cyln's head caused by the surge of guilt due to her absence at a dangerous time combined with the desperate need for her to maintain the fiction she had built up about Trys, and she shut her eyes tightly for a moment. The surge passed but the pain remained as a dull ache. Her duty to her Queen/Lady required that she continue to conceal Trys's true identity.

"He is the son of clan members who befriended my father years before he died. I owe them blood fealty." She wondered if Alisande could detect the flatness of the statement. At that moment she knew it was the shabbiest of masks and one at which she hoped her Queen/Lady would not look too closely.

"Blood can certainly demand fealty, but in my experience it can seldom get it."

"Pardon, my Queen/Lady, that is the Hold. In the North things are different. The old ways do survive."

"Yes, I know, the wonderful old North. Excuse my cynicism, Cyln, but it seems that the past crowds in upon me today and my sacrifice weighs heavily upon me. You know I feel as if I have betrayed what I once believed in for the good of the half kingdom. I had no choice. I am the Queen/Lady and as such I am the half kingdom. It is all so large and oppressive."

Cyln murmured assent. At that moment she knew precisely what her Queen/Lady meant about sacrificing for the good of the kingdom. She had to betray a trust, or at least conceal a truth from her liege. It gave her exquisite pain, not only because of the concealment but because she was not at all certain what the presence of Trys could accomplish. He was an untried blade which could end up killing the one who held it. And she was like a hunter who stalks her prey but cannot say exactly how she will take it when the moment comes. The situation would determine the how.

The two women stood silently then. Pressures from within and without drew both of them up taut. Alisande could not talk to Cyln the way she once had. Her suspicions concerning the Interpreter from the North ran just deep enough to cause her to stop short of blurting out her anguished uncertainty about the trustworthiness of her bodyguard. She feared too she had lost a good friend once and for all, and she was not willing to put that to a test just yet. She would pretend to trust Cyln and hope that her misgivings were unfounded. She sent up a silent prayer to the gods they were.

Cyln writhed inwardly while her stoic demeanor remained unchanged. Holding back the truth went so against her grain that she had to clamp her teeth tightly together to prevent a scream from escaping. Duty to the realm and duty to people she cared deeply about commingled and tortured her by obstinately remaining inseparable. No clear path led forward. The mire of lies and half truths stretched before her like an impassable swamp of quicksnow. She gritted her teeth and held it all in.

But the next instant she drew her blood blade, spun about, and growled viciously through her clenched teeth as the point of her blade hung steadily an inch from the scrawny throat of an Interpreter. The unexpected rustle of his robe upon the stone just behind Cyln had caused the violent reaction. He appeared to be neither surprised nor threatened by the hovering tip. His eyes possessed a glaze and his skin a silvery pallor which denoted a recent ingestion of a quantity of sommess, the drug used by the Interpreters to approach nirvana.

He cleared his throat of what might have been the remaining droplets of the silver liquid and directed his gaze toward the Queen/Lady. This took some exertion and wrinkles furrowed his brow.

"Queen/Lady Alisande myr Rystarte pyr Grendyl, I come to remind you of the Ceremony of Opening which will soon take place and which you are required to attend. As you no doubt know, it concerns the blessing of a new storeroom for the royal accouterments."

"Damn your silvered eyes, get out! I will see the Queen/Lady attends your Ritual. That is my duty." Cyln spat this out.

"Cyln, calm down. He is only a messenger. Offensive as he might appear, he poses no threat."

"I know. I know. It's just that..."

"Yes, duty has the annoying habit of interrupting our lives. Only I am not sure that duty has not become my life now. Interpreter, you may go now. Tell the High Interpreter I will be along shortly. I will not disappoint him."

The Interpreter began to bow in acknowledgement just as Cyln began to slowly withdraw the point of her blade. The tip of the blade touched the right side of his face at the jaw and ran in a thin line all the way up his cheek.

Cyln watched fascinated and held the blade steady. He did not break off the bow but rather continued and completed it. As he straightened, the gash upon his skin was visible. The sharp point had opened up the flesh but only a small amount of silvered blood oozed forth and the Interpreter seemed to take no notice of his wound. He turned and left the garden with the rustle of robes upon stone.

Cyln dropped the point of her blade and shook her head. "Bloodless beings. I often wonder if their souls are as vitiated."

"And yet you brought another one to the Hold. Is he far gone in sommess or a mere initiate?"

"My Queen/Lady, I told you things are different in the North. He is a true son of...the North." Cyln voice trailed off.

"Of course, of course. Aren't they all. At first. I just hope you have brought in someone who will be a friend rather than a foe."

"I do too, my Queen/Lady. I do too."

Alisande laughed sharply and then swept to the steps leading down off the parapet. A whirl of wind twisted over the wall and sent the red lycandra petals circling upward. Cyln glanced back at them wonderingly as she resheathed her blood blade in its back scabbard and followed her Queen/Lady to the low doorway leading out of the garden. Except for the two petals which had been crushed beneath Alisande's boot, all of the petals were sucked up and out of the garden to dance and fall down the precipice and out toward the limitless Waste.

## XI

MURMURS SNAKED back and forth about the throne within the Royal Tent like the susurration of powdery snow across an open flat. They fell indistinctly upon the ears of King/Lord Nordseth pyr Nystrin myr Olda which were filled with the bark of his own cough. With an effort of will, he stopped his cough for a moment and strained to sort out the murmurs, to discover if treason or mere banality lurked out there in the shadows beyond his throne.

The Royal Tent was a clever contrivance of baffle flaps and hangings designed to capture every sound within its circumference and send it drifting down about the ears of the person seated in the throne. Nordseth strained to hold back the cough which slowly drained him of life for another moment. Nothing but banalities today. The continued insubordination of servants, the sorry cut of bryl meat served up at the last banquet to an indignant Second Lord, the assignation of a quiet corner for a tryst later, the speculations about the eternal ill health of the King/Lord and how it affected his already ill temper; all these and more Nordseth listened to before he released the muscles of his chest and let the cough rip up toward his throat once again.

The open court of King/Lord Nordseth had been drawing to a close when the fit of coughing had struck. It was late morning and outside the Royal Tent the distant sun blazed down from a cloudless sky, giving at least the illusion of beneficent warmth. Within the Tent, it was twilight. Cold shadows were relieved only by occasional pockets of warmth where braziers flared. The supplicants to the throne gathered about the fires, kept burning brightly as much for the heat as for the light, and reviewed their written petitions, making sure that everything was in order before approaching the dread King/Lord. Sloppy petitions were frowned upon and had even been known to get the petitioner exiled or, in a few extreme cases, executed due to misunderstandings about the exact nature of the request. The King/Lord did have his little whims.

At the first sign of the coughing fit, the King/Lord's principal servant had herded the chilled crowds back from the throne. Torkild myr Rhynth pyr Jyrs lurched his way back to the first step of the dias and paused before attempting to swing his withered left leg up and onto the marble step.

Nordseth hacked once more and then sank back in the throne. Torkild glanced up at his King/Lord from his good right eye and, satisfied that his monarch would not begin coughing immediately, for he knew all of the subtle signs of the malady, he began the painful climb to the throne.

Time was when the King/Lord would have never allowed anyone upon the dias let alone approach the throne as Torkild now did. But the debilitating malady had taken its toll over the years and Nordseth now needed assistance, even though he distrusted it and despised himself for needing it.

Torkild had learned to approach his monarch in his unique sidling manner, required by his deformity but put to good use in this instance. The lurch and halt approach, with the right side of his body always toward his monarch, seemed to appease the King/Lord's continued vanity about his sacrosanct person. It was a small, natural ritual which seemed to both monarch and servant the only proper way for the one to come to the other. For his part, Torkild still feared his King/Lord, but that fear was tempered by enough understanding to allow him to care about the man who was the monarch. Whether he knew it or not, Nordseth could not ask for a better servant.

Torkild balanced on his crippled left leg for the second needed to get his fit right leg up to the top level of the dias where the throne rested. And then, by leaning far over to the right and tugging with all of the well developed muscles on his right side, Torkild drew himself up next to the throne. The King/Lord's face was turned to the down draft of cool air and his brow was faintly knit as he appeared to listen to the passing breeze.

Torkild ducked his head once, waved his right hand upward, and cocked his head to one side, as he asked for absolution for what he was about to do. Nordseth kept his face up but let his bleary eyes slide toward his servant. The lids closed and opened to give permission for him to proceed.

With a deft movement, Torkild slid his arm behind the back of his King/Lord and gently but quickly raised him to a sitting position. Nordseth let his chin fall toward his chest as he watched his servant's hand smooth out his robes. A final touch set the half crown firmly upon the still wrinkled brow and Torkild stepped back.

Nordseth nodded his thanks and fumbled with the dull red cloth which held his decahedron of blood metal. The blood from his lips had fallen upon the metal and it was warming up. His gaunt fingers stroked the heat and the joints snapped.

"More inane than usual, it seems."

Torkild leaned a fraction closer. "My King/Lord, I'm sorry. What did you say?"

Nordseth cleared his throat carefully. "I said, more inane than usual. The petitions, that is. They tire me."

"Of course. That is to be expected. I believe you have said upon more than one occasion that the affairs of state are, for the most part, petty."

"Petty but necessary, for in the details lie matters of importance."

"Yes, my King/Lord."

"You have been out." He used the word as if his servant had just returned from a circuit of the known world.

"Yes, I have."

"And?"

"I would not want to interrupt the session of open court."

"You have not. I have interrupted it." Nordseth then glared down into the twilight below the throne and croaked out a command. "This session is in abeyance. I will listen to the final petitions in a short while."

A chorus of "Very good, your Exalted King/Lord" drifted up from below. Nordseth smiled, since he knew that many of those who raised their voices loudest were the most put out by the delay.

He turned to his servant. "That is taken care of. Let's hear what transpires outside."

"Second Captain Kyth pyr Gotyn myr Lyn and his platoon tried to prevent Cyln and a new Interpreter from entering the Hold, as you had ordered. They failed."

"Of course. I expected that. How many did they dispatch?"

"Fully half the platoon."

"Kyth is spirited and ambitious. He is more than willing to lose men to please his King/Lord. I admire that even though he is foolish for trying to please me in that fashion."

"Pardon me, my King/Lord, but it does seem to be a waste."

"Not really. In a sense it was very economical. A few men lost their lives, it is true, but look at the knowledge which I gained. I know Cyln is still as competent a warrior as ever. I know she believes this new Interpreter is important. I know Kyth will do whatever I ask him to do, and even try to go a little further than the actual orders require. That is all useful to me, very useful."

"And what do you make of the fact that Cyln has returned from the North with a new Interpreter?"

"An Interpreter for the Queen/Lady or for the High Interpreter?"

"My sources in the Hold say he was turned over to Dwilkon as required by Ritual."

"So, for Dwilkon and not for Alisande. Why? Any conjectures?"

"He is a youth of the Caynruhl clan. Since he is a member of

Cyln's own clan I thought perhaps she was attempting to infiltrate the ranks of the Hold Interpreters with one loyal to her and, so by extension, to her Queen/Lady."

Nordseth sat up straighter upon his throne. Here was the type of puzzle he loved to ponder and one which also could have consequences for his own reign.

"By turning him over to Dwilkon she chances losing all contact with him. Cyln is direct above all else. I cannot believe she expects to receive secret messages from the youth which would incriminate the Interpreters. After all, Alisande needs no enticement whatever to suppress them and their Rituals. I think Cyln might not know herself exactly how to use the new Interpreter but hopes, like the true hunter which she still is, to intuit that at some later date."

"Pardon me, my King/Lord, but that seems simply foolish."

"Simple perhaps but not necessarily foolish. If she brings him in, turns him over, and seemingly loses all interest in him, the Interpreters have little reason to suspect him of being anything other than he seems. She has thus placed a weapon of sorts close to the heart of Dwilkon. It can be used later and perhaps to mortal effect. Simple but potentially effective. The type of ploy that the convoluted mind of someone like Dwilkon might overlook while searching for complex reasons to explain the presence of the new Interpreter.

"Alisande despises all Interpreters. She undercuts their authority and power wherever and however she can. Since I control the Camp Interpreters and support the Hold Interpreters by covert means, I have the most to lose by upheavals within their ranks. That also means I am in the best position to take advantage of any loss of their power to reinforce my own. It is really just more of the old game; maintain the status quo so that it remains tilted in my favor."

The murmurs from other parts of the Royal Tent faded away and in the silence Torkild could hear the rasp of air through the diseased lungs of his King/Lord. His eyes closed and he seemed to be drifting off to sleep. Only the continued flickering of his eyes behind the closed lids told Torkild that he was contemplating the situation as only Nordseth could. He was weighing the forces moving here and there within Camp and Hold and working out potential moves weeks in advance in the deadly game of power which he played from his isolated throne.

Torkild shuffled his good foot and leaned in closer to his monarch. "My King/Lord, the open session of court is still waiting."

"Let them wait."

"Very good, my King/Lord."

Without opening his eyes, Nordseth spoke. "Watch him. Watch him closely."

Torkild nodded and spoke, simply to verify what he knew to be the order. "You want me to monitor the activities of the new Interpreter."

"Yes. And press those informants within the Hold to give you more complete information. I feel they have been reticent of late. Perhaps holding back, trying to sell to higher bidders. Tell them I give them their lives. The price gets no higher than that. Do you understand?"

"Yes, my King/Lord."

Nordseth's left hand moved up from his lap where it had been clutching the heated decahedron of blood metal. He touched his left temple and fluttered his fingers about his cheek. Torkild knew the hot flesh of the fingers was trying to warm up the cold flesh of the cheek.

"Watch him. I have had many killed of late. I will not stop at one more. He might be important. He might be insignificant. Even that does not matter. Watch him and kill him if I say so."

"My king/Lord is wise..."

"But? What is the rest?" Nordseth's voice was sharp, belying his languid appearance and closed eyes.

"But is it wise to continue to spill blood so...so widely?"

"I will spill blood from the top of the Hold to the foot of my dias. It will wash about my feet if it serves my purpose. Blood is all on Winterhold. Blood is life and blood is death, and I need to control both. Do the Interpreters or the revolutionaries quibble about a life more or less? From this throne, I watch all of the threads run up and down and back and forth, and those of the Interpreters and those of the revolutionaries cross each other again and again. Perhaps there is a conspiracy there, perhaps none. It really does not matter. I matter. What I think and what I decide is best for the half kingdom, which is the whole kingdom, is what matters."

The King/Lord's eyes snapped open. Torkild lurched back a step despite being steeled to the fanaticism he had seen growing in those eyes of late. They were wild with pain and brimming over with anger.

"I will bring it all down in blood, rivers of blood, rains of blood, if I believe it is necessary. I am King/Lord. I must be King/Lord. King/Lord of...this bloody mess...this madness which kills me inch by inch...this death..."

Without warning the cough erupted. It lifted him up on the throne, shook him about, and slammed him down. He coughed and he coughed and the trickle of red down his chin became a solid stream. His feeble hands dragged up the blood red cloth with its decahedron of blood metal. But the cloth could not catch it all.

Torkild leaped forward. He tore loose the sash of white cloth which encircled his left shoulder. It was the simple badge of his office. He held it firmly but gently up to his King/Lord's face to staunch the flow of blood. The moment the cloth touched his wet chin, the cough subsided. It sank back down into his aching lungs much as the blood sank into the fibers of the cloth and dyed it deep red.

"My King/Lord!"

"It is over."

"What? No, you will live."

"No, not that. Open court. It is over."

Torkild almost laughed hysterically at the absurdity of the statement coming from a man with his life blood flowing so freely out of him.

"Do not worry."

"But I do. I am King/Lord. They must not see me so weak. Get them out of here." Nordseth gripped Torkild's arm so tightly that it made him winch. "I am King/Lord. I am strong. I am in control."

"Certainly. Certainly. It will be done. Hold this cloth up to catch the..."

"The blood. Yes, my blood." He glanced down at the cloth and then up at Torkild. "This is yours. Your sash. It is quite ruined now. You will have to get another one."

"I will."

Nordseth squeezed his servant's arm again. The pressure was firmly applied and then released.

After assuring himself that the King/Lord was over the worst, Torkild turned to the assembled crowd and announced that the session of open court was at an end. A few moved forward, importuning as they went. The cordon of Blood Guards swept them back and out into the deepening twilight within the Tent.

When he turned back to the throne, Torkild saw that Nordseth had fallen asleep. He checked his breathing but it was regular if a bit ragged now and then. He adjusted the cloth about him to hide the worst of the blood stains and then sat down at the foot of the throne to wait. The murmurs of the departing petitioners fell about them with the cool breeze from overheard. It reminded Torkild of the clean sound of snow blowing across snow out in the depths of the Waste.

## XII

THE PERMAFROST yielded to the heat on the sill of the doorway into the garden of the Queen/Lady, and a slick smear made the footing treacherous. Dwilkon glided over it without hesitation, but Trys skidded and saved himself only with an awkward grab for the door frame. He skated himself forward, scanning the floor for slippery spots, and stepped stiff-leggedly up and through the door.

A puff of warm, humid air, unlike any he had ever felt before, snapped his attention back to the garden which lay before him. The heat, the colors, and the scents washed over him and his snow and ice dulled senses quivered in the blast. He brushed a hand over his face. It came away covered with a sheen of sweat. Sweat from too much heat was an oddity, to say the least, upon Winterhold.

He breathed in the deep smell of living and rotting vegetable matter. It clung to his nostrils and choked his lungs with its vibrancy. In the first moments, his eyes ached from the unparalleled spectrum of greens and browns which swirled before him. Plants thrust green leaves high above his head and pushed thick roots into the rich soil beneath his feet. The sensory display was all around and all encompassing. He gasped and stood still just within the garden.

The High Interpreter of the Hold continued his glide but did glance back and motioned peremptorily for his novice to move quickly to his place at his side. After several increasingly violent hand wavings on Dwilkon's part, Trys noticed the command and stepped forward, only to nearly stop as his booted feet sank into the resilient carpet of grass. Trys shook his head to clear it. He was stunned by the rush of sensations but eager to take part in the Ritual at hand. A swipe of his sweaty hands across the leather of his singlesuit and he moved into the place reserved for him as acolyte to the High Interpreter; to his right and several feet behind him.

Without turning, Dwilkon spoke to Trys. "The Queen/Lady and her bodyguard will be here in a moment. You are prepared for this Ritual, are you not? You have all of the accouterments?"

"Yes, certainly. I'm ready. I have all of the things here in the bag." Trys swung the large leather bag, made of the hide of an entire bryl, around in front of him. The clatter of the Ritual bones and stones earned him a sharp look from the High Interpreter.

"Be careful with the sacred objects. You are not some scavenger rattling your collected bones about."

"Yes. I'm sorry."

"Compose yourself for the Ritual. Settle your mind and soul so that you may aid in guiding us through the beauties of the Ritual patterns."

"Yes, compose myself. Certainly."

With that Dwilkon straightened his shoulders, only to have them slump as he put himself into a half trance in preparation for the Ritual.

Trys tried to follow his example but his first deep breath, which he used to begin his preparation, drew into his lungs the warm, sticky air of the garden. The foreign atmosphere drew him instead to an examination of his surroundings.

They stood quite near the door back into the Hold in an area paved with large slabs of stone which did an inadequate job of holding the rich vegetation at bay. The slabs were cracked and tilted where the hardy grass shoved up green fingers. The slabs did keep the large plants, those with trunks or creepers, from choking the area but it was still overarched by a partial canopy of green leaves.

The paving ran to the outer wall of the garden. A low parapet crouched beneath the wall and beyond it Trys could just make out an expanse of the Waste through the mist which swirled now thick and now thin about the niche of the garden. A gust of wind sent a wave of mist rolling over the stones but it dissipated before it could reach their feet, smothered by the warmth.

While Trys had never seen a garden before, he sensed the wild growth before him was not quite what it should be. Individual plants were bent over with their burdens of leaves and fruit. Vines ran unchecked across stones and curled constrictively about the trunks of the larger plants. It lacked order. Individual plants should have been cut back relentlessly to help the garden as a whole.

His sense of wonder, tinged with sadness at the plight of the garden, was diverted by the sudden appearance of two figures from the depths of the garden. He heard them before he saw them as they made their way along a narrow path through the tangle of leaves. They spoke in low tones so that Trys could not hear the words just the sounds of speech. He gripped the strap of the bryl hide bag tighter and waited for them to step free of the lush green growth.

Cyln was first. She took one long stride which brought her completely clear of the vegetation. At the sight of the intruders, she tensed and grabbed the hilt of her blood blade. Upon recognizing who they were, she relaxed, although she did press her lips tightly together when she saw Trys. She nodded grudgingly to the High Interpreter. She then stepped to one side and indicated by a sweep of her hand that her companion should join her.

The Queen/Lady Alisande myr Rystarte pyr Grendyl stepped

forth. Her Ritual robes completely encased her from neck to toe, leaving only her hands and face free. The robes were a mixture of severe lines and wild colors. The vertical line predominated giving the impression of tallness while it obscured the actual human form within. The colors leaked from one into another, oozing in a rainbow down from the stylized headpiece where it began with a shocking red.

Her face impressed and fascinated Trys. The overall impression was one of stern command, the expression assumed by a monarch toward her subjects. But the individual features intrigued him with their familiarity. While he had never studied his own face closely, he knew the shape and character of his prominent features. A curious sense of parallelism came over him when he first saw the face of the Queen/Lady. The high cheekbones, the angle of the eyes, and the set of the mouth struck him as being strangely like his own.

The Queen/Lady took in the pair before her and a brief frown wrinkled her brow. But before the expression led to a question, Dwilkon stepped forward. He swept the air with his thin hands and the grass with his long robes as he bowed his head stiffly.

"My Queen/Lady Alisande myr Rystarte pyr Grendyl, we await your presence within the Hold for the Ritual of Blessing. We must, ah, move on. Timing is important for this Ritual. As I know you are aware, the sun must be at just the correct angle for the Blessing of the Northern side of the Hold."

"I am aware the Ritual must be performed. The timing I leave to you, High Interpreter Dwilkon."

"Then, my Queen/Lady, with your permission, may I lead you into the Hold?"

"You may precede me into the Hold."

Dwilkon glided deftly in front of the Queen/Lady who pushed after him, hard on his heels. Cyln followed next, pausing to give Trys a small smile meant to be reassuring, even though he was not certain whom it was meant to reassure. Trys fell into place behind her.

As he put his foot upon the sill of the doorway, he glanced back at the garden and took a deep breath of the warm air. A gust of frigid air from beyond the wall had circled up and over the garden and blew through the plants. By the time it reached his face it was humid and heavy with the smells of growing vegetation and soft earth. He held his breath as he ducked through the doorway.

He moved cautiously through the low, narrow corridor which led from the garden into the Hold. A fall now would have been humiliating. He stepped out and into the subdued bustle of the preparations for The Ritual of Blessing.

A crowd of Interpreters and First Lords and Ladies milled

about in the large chamber as a coterie of officious Interpreters tried to get everyone into something resembling a straight line in the order dictated by the Ritual. They darted here and there, pausing only to check their parchments which contained the order of march. Trys shook his head at the ludicrous proceedings. Nothing like this would ever happen in the North.

"Do not condemn it. It all serves a purpose. Our purpose." Dwilkon murmured at Trys's elbow.

"I do not doubt it, High Interpreter."

"Krenlyf has been waiting for you. He needs the sacred objects within the sack you carry."

"Here is the..." Trys swung the bryl hide sack over his shoulder and, before it touched the floor of the chamber, it was open and a narrow faced Interpreter was rummaging among the sacred objects in a most unsanctified manner.

"Prayer horns, prayer horns. I need the large prayer horns with the embossed figures of Sun and Ice upon them. I do not need this or this." Two prayer horns, which obviously did not suit the purpose, clattered into a corner.

He dug about in the sack to the accompaniment of much rattling as stones and bones rolled over and about each other. Trys had filled the sack himself and had been astonished at the conglomeration of odd bits which passed as sacred objects in the Hold. A prayer horn was certainly a staple of the Interpreter's art but generally one used in the solitude of a trance. The fingers were supposed to run up and around and down the carved horn in a never ending loop to aid in the contemplation of the eternity of the universe. To carry them at the head of an ostentatious procession seemed the height of hubris if not absurdity. But then things were different in the Hold.

"Aha!" Krenlyf's exclamation was muffled since he had shoved most of his upper body into the sack in his search for the perfect prayer horns. "Got them!" This was shouted as he emerged suddenly from the confines of the leather skin.

He waved two prayer horns over his head. While they were large and embossed, their condition was not precisely impressive. The tip of one had broken off, perhaps quite recently as it had rattled about in the sack with numerous hard objects, and the embossing on both was tarnished and dull. Krenlyf paid no attention to their condition but waved them victoriously over his head. He motioned to Trys to pick up the sack now that he was done with it, and then dashed off to the head of the line of procession.

"Now that Krenlyf has what he was looking for, the procession will soon begin. I advise you to take the bryl sack and get to your place." With that, Dwilkon moved smoothly but quickly away to take his own place at the head of the line.

"Yes, High Interpreter, as you wish." Trys muttered under his breath, interjecting as sarcastic a tone as he could into the acknowledgement, and then shouldered the heavy bag.

"Don't let the Interpreters hear you talk that way."

Trys jerked his head up. There at his side stood Cyln. He had not heard her approach. "Where did you come from?"

"I try to be everywhere at once. It's not easy. Do you know where your place in line is?"

"Somewhere up near the Queen/Lady, I guess. This sack is supposedly important. Someone has to pull something out of it along the way."

"Once again, watch your tone." Cyln smiled. "I know it's tempting to belittle the Hold Rituals but it's dangerous to be overheard by those who perform them."

"Yes, I know. I will behave. It's just I have been hauling this sack around all day. It's getting heavy."

"No heavier than the Ritual robes which the Queen/Lady must endure. I will show you just where to go. You are on the right hand of the Queen/Lady." Cyln gave him a significant and somewhat expectant look as she said this. Trys was puzzled and hitched the strap of the sack higher on his shoulder to avoid looking directly at the bodyguard. When he looked again she had moved off and was scanning the line, checking it for any potential dangers to her Queen/Lady.

He settled the strap and hurried after her. She strode briskly down the line and paused only to point out where the Queen/Lady stood before she moved on to reconnoiter further.

Queen/Lady Alisande myr Rystarte pyr Grendyl stood immobile at the center of the forming line. Her posture was stiffly upright, more a function of the Ritual robes than her regal attitude. She stared straight ahead with her eyelids drooping a bit as if she were half in a trance.

Trys took up his post to her right and slightly behind her. The bones in the sack clashed together as he set it down once again.

"You are the new Interpreter in the Hold."

He glanced over at her. She continued to look ahead. "Yes, my Queen/Lady, I am new. New to the Hold anyway."

"Implying you are not an Interpreter?"

"Pardon me, my Queen/Lady, but I am an Interpreter of the clans. I believe there is a distinction there."

"Indeed. It is a distinction which demands to be made." She turned her head as far as her ornate headdress would allow her. "You are young. Youth can often be easily molded in the image of others."

"Once again, pardon me, my Queen/Lady, but I did say I was an Interpreter of the clans. I retain my independence."

"For now." It was said wearily.

"For ever. I hope." Trys added the last not certain how much offense the Queen/Lady might take at his impetuous stand.

"I sincerely hope it may be forever. For your sake."

"You do not care much for Interpreters, my Queen/Lady."

Alisande smiled broadly and indeed would have thrown back her head to laugh but was stopped by the rigidity of her headdress. "I do not care for the Interpreters at all. They have done much to harm..."

A long, low wail from the front of the line interrupted her. In an instant the crowd became a procession as each one stepped into his or her proper place and became silent. Even the Queen/Lady fell silent, though she maintained a sullen look.

The wail ascended the scale again and stopped at a certain note. The note was sustained while at intervals along the procession differently pitched wails were sounded. They were produced by air being blown through hollowed out bryl horns. Since ancient times the horns were blown to imitate the sound of the wind moving across the Waste. The low piercing sounds along the line began to waver, rolling up and down the scale, but the original note still held at the head of the line. Trys noted with some admiration the lung control of the player of the lead horn. He could not detect any break in its purity.

Then, in juxtaposition to the high clear sounds of the horns, came a pulsing beat. Thump and click, thump and click, the pattern established itself and swayed back and forth. The thump was the sound produced by the beating of a thin cylinder of stone against the center of a hollowed out stone. The click was made by the striking of the cylinder on the edge of the stone.

A breathy shout could be heard from the head of the line and, with a smoothness which seemed instinctive, everyone stepped forward with their left foot. The Ritual procession had begun.

Motion became as rhythmic as the rising and falling, the thumping and clicking of the music. Trys fell into step and maintained it easily as he monitored his position in relationship to the Queen/Lady. She kept her face forward and her head up, allowing him only a glimpse of her high cheekbone.

A cool breeze blew steadily in Trys's face as he emerged from the quarters of the Queen/Lady into one of the main halls of the Hold. The hall was wide and high, and the wind, brought deep into the interior of the Hold through a series of shafts cut through hundreds of feet of solid rock, never stopped moving though it.

The air stirred the lavishly wrought wall hangings which

reached from the ceiling to about six feet off the floor to give them an eerie life of their own. The twice life size figures, which depicted Queen/Ladies and King/Lords long dead, shifted and bunched and lived out their static but beautiful lives upon the walls. Trys tried to see as much of them as he could, but the pace of the procession and the requirement to keep precisely to his place limited his view.

Down at floor level, light was provided by rows of torches which were continually replenished. Even as they entered the hall a small crew of servants were in the process of trimming and relighting torches. They paused and bowed low as the Queen/Lady swept by.

"They have developed the task into a minor Ritual in its own right." Alisande spoke without turning or pausing.

Trys hesitated, but then decided she had addressed him and that he should answer. "It is like a Ritual in the old sense, where one acknowledges the origin and purpose of a particular act."

"Perhaps you are right. Perhaps it is one of the few pure Rituals left since I don't believe the Interpreters have gotten their thin hands upon it."

Trys thought he heard a sharp laugh from the Queen/Lady but he could not be sure. The sound of the horns and stones was persistent and pervasive.

Ahead of them the line snaked through a triangular opening in the wall which marked the end of the mammoth hall. The rhythmic music was blown into Trys's face by the steady draft from the peaked corridor as their section of the procession moved onward. Trys expected to be deafened in the reduced space of the corridor but found the acoustics dampened the loudness of the music without reducing its clarity.

Sensing rather than seeing the change, Trys was aware that the corridor dipped and turned to the left in ever so gradual increments. The direction was sustained and both the slope and the curve increased as they descended. The corridor was lit by torches set in niches high up near the peak of the ceiling. The same ingenious system of ventilation which kept the grand hall filled with fresh air operated in the corridor as the smoke was sucked into holes cut just above each torch to keep the air fresh and moving.

The approach to the first chamber was marked by a brightening ahead of them. While Trys was on the side of the procession away from where the corridor entered the chamber, he still could see the bizarre relationship of corridor to room. The corridor literally sliced through an upper corner of the chamber. The left hand wall of the corridor ended to reveal the ceiling of the chamber just inches above the corridor's own peak, while the floor of the room lay twenty feet below the floor of the corridor. It continued on down along the length of the chamber and when it reentered the solid rock the ceiling of the room was about three farther away and the floor three feet closer.

The triangular corridor continued to turn and descend and to cut through a number of chambers. From the way in which the corridor sliced through them at different angles and in different locations within the chambers, sometimes near the ceiling and at other times almost below the level of the floor, it appeared that the corridor had been constructed according to some architectural edict of its own long after the chambers had been made.

The corridor plowed deeply into a dimly lit chamber which appeared to be used as a storeroom judging by the piles of moldering hides and tarnished torch holders stacked in the corners. Nearly all of the left hand wall of the corridor and a sizeable portion of the floor dissolved into the open space of the room. The procession had to squeeze to the right to avoid tumbling out of the corridor and into the room, the floor of which lay about six feet down. Trys held back to let the Queen/Lady sweep past him along the diminished floor.

"Practicality certainly gave way to design in the Grand Spiral," said Alisande.

"That's the name of this corridor, the Grand Spiral?"

"Yes. As you can tell it was constructed long after the original chambers were cut out of the rock. It was designed by a High Interpreter who felt the need for linking most of the central chambers of the Hold to aid in the performance of the Rituals. It spirals down seven levels and ends up at a point on the lowest level precisely beneath the starting point on the highest level. As with all Interpreters he cared more for the end than for the means. I have nearly fallen into that dingy pit numerous times. My robes today allow a little more freedom for my legs than others do. Being a Queen/Lady can be hazardous."

Trys wished he could see her face when she said it. He felt sure a small smile must have brushed her lips.

The descent of the triangular corridor ended in an octagonal chamber whose ceiling was lost in darkness where the lights of the torches could not reach. A doorway occupied the center of each of the eight walls. Three had doors to fill them, three had curtains to cover them, while two were simply openings, the corridor they exited and the one immediately across from it. The ones with the doors were square, the ones with the curtains round, and the open ones were triangular.

Upon entering the chamber, the procession took a sharp turn to the left and encircled the space, continuing the spiral inward when the head of the line came around to the triangular corridor from which the procession still issued. As the last celebrant stepped into the chamber, High Interpreter Dwilkon stopped and with him stopped the music. He raised his hands, cupped them above his head, and then nodded.

At this signal, the procession broke up and a different order emerged. Now groups with specific tasks formed and set about the business of preparing for the ceremony proper. Trys found himself moved brusquely along with the Queen/Lady toward one of the openings which possessed a door. It swung back to reveal a small, overdecorated room filled with a thin cloud of incense into which the Queen/Lady was ushered with some pomp and much speed. Trys gathered that timing was critical and that the procession had lagged a bit despite the steady beating of the stones.

Trys slipped his arm out of the strap and let the sack crumble to the floor thickly covered with brum hides. He knew he had to stand by and hand out what was requested from the sack. To prepare for this, he bent down and opened it up. When he glanced back up servants had just taken off the headdress of the Queen/Lady and allowed her hair to spill down about her shoulders. Alisande's hair was mostly gray but still shot with lines of black, a color very unusual upon Winterhold.

Krenlyf was in charge of the final preparations of the Queen/Lady before the Ritual and he lurched here and there about the chamber as he gathered the required objects and urged others to hurry.

"The obsidian brooch with the figure of Mother Ice upon it. I need it now, Interpreter Trys." Krenlyf snapped his fingers and Trys scratched about in the sack. He held out the brooch. It was snatched up and affixed to the Queen/Lady's robes at the shoulder with a stabbing motion. Trys winced for her.

"He missed the skin. He might be impatient but he is skillful."

"My most Exalted Queen/Lady honors me," said Krenlyf.

Alisande stood still as servants buzzed about her. She looked down upon Trys who still knelt by the sack and handed up various objects as they were called for.

"My hair was once as black as this obsidian brooch. A dangerous color. A passionate color according to the old sayings."

"It must have been...I mean, still is lovely."

"I'm not sure anything is permanent. It is now closer to the color of this damned incense. Silver, no, gray. Gray is the color. Silver is brighter, much brighter and sharper. Like sommess. Do you indulge, Interpreter Trys?"

"No."

"Do you intend to?"

"No," said Trys with no hesitation.

"You sound very certain for a novitiate. What do you think of the use of Ritual drugs?"

Trys hesitated then. Servants continued to move here and there about the room as they prepared her for the Ritual. Krenlyf sped back and forth from the Queen/Lady to the door opposite to the one by which they had entered, and which appeared to lead out into the thin air high above the Waste. He was not sure how much honesty was being demanded.

"The High Interpreter is out there upon the ledge where the Ritual will take place. The Ritual of Blessing for the Northern side of the Hold. I never could figure out what would happen to the Northern side of the Hold if it did not receive its periodic blessing. And Krenlyf here will certainly report to the High Interpreter what is said, but he will also report your Queen/Lady demanded an honest answer. Am I right, Krenlyf?"

Krenlyf paused in his careening about the room to make a moue of disapproval. "Of course, my Most Exalted Queen/Lady. I know your inclinations well enough by now. Trust me to be discreet. Just stand still so I can get this train arranged in the proper Ritual manner."

He tugged at the long, complex arrangement of soft leather which trailed down from the shoulders of the Queen/Lady and across the floor. She smiled as she braced herself against the tug. "You see. Go on."

"I have only recently arrived from the North. While I have seen much use of Ritual drugs, I cannot condemn their use categorically."

"A diplomatic Interpreter. Keep your eye on him, my Queen/Lady. Either he will go far or end up dead in a short time." Krenlyf spoke over Alisande's shoulder.

"Pay no attention to him, Interpreter Trys. He succumbed long ago to the lure of the drugs. And look what it has done to him."

Krenlyf snorted and gave the train one last vicious tug.

Alisande continued. "I am impressed with your strength of will. It is nearly impossible to escape the drugs here within the Hold." She then nodded to the censers which occupied the four corners of the room and which emitted clouds of incense obviously laden with drugs designed to heighten the senses while dulling the intellect. "In so many chambers like this one, I feel sensations more acutely. Heightened senses are alluring, but then I realize that that acuity means I lose a degree of intellectual comprehension. For instance, I cannot fully comprehend the political situation which I was just involved with before we began our little walk. But then, I don't really care. You see how dangerous it all is?"

Trys found himself fascinated with the Queen/Lady. That, in

conjunction with the drug laced clouds of incense which seemed to fill the room to overflowing, caused him to lose sight of Krenlyf for the moment. He no longer cared what the Interpreter might report back to Dwilkon and he began to talk of his aspirations.

"I care nothing for Ritual drugs. I care for the Rituals. In the North they are still pure in form and purpose. I would like to bring that sense of purity here, to the Hold. And not just to the aristocrats but to all the people of the Hold, the ones who have a true need for an Interpreter to lead them into and through the Rituals so they can discover who they really are. The Interpreter is vital to the process. I want to be a true Interpreter."

"It sounds like the naive ramblings of a fool. Or the carefully prepared words of a spy. Do you truly believe it?"

Trys took a step back and stumbled over a low stool. He went down on one knee. Closer to the floor the incense was not so thick and as his head cleared he realized how euphoric the drugs had made him. He had been babbling both foolishly and dangerously.

"I...I do believe it, my Queen/Lady. It's just..."

"It's just you now realize you made a mistake. I don't believe it, and I don't believe you."

"But...but, my Queen/Lady, I..."

"A stripling, my most Exalted Queen/Lady," murmured Krenlyf. "He is raw from the North and even the most ordinary of drugs unbalances him. You are right not to believe him."

Trys started up from where he knelt. His hand went to his shoulder and only when it closed on emptiness did he remember he was not allowed to wear a blood blade in the presence of the Queen/Lady.

At that moment, the door to the outside of the Hold opened and Dwilkon glided in. He was followed by Cyln, whose litheness contrasted with the oily motion of the High Interpreter.

"All is prepared, my Queen/Lady." Dwilkon paused, arrested by the tableau before him. Alisande scowled, Trys gaped, and Krenlyf smiled subtly and nodded his head ever so slightly. "And I see everything is going according to plan in here also."

"Let's get this over with, High Interpreter Dwilkon. I need a breath of fresh air. This room is stifling."

With that she yanked her train about and made for the door. Cyln stepped aside, alert to the anger in her Queen/Lady but not exactly sure of the cause. As Dwilkon and Krenlyf and then the rest of the retinue filed out of the room, Trys remained fixed in one spot.

Trys's frozen expression gave Cyln the clue she needed. He was the cause of the anger. She moved to his side and squeezed his arm. "It's all right. She is under a lot of pressure. She is the Queen/Lady. She means well. She really does." Cyln's apology trailed off, leaving Trys more mystified than ever as to what had just occurred.

He nodded and continued to nod as he followed Cyln to the door and into the blast of icy air which scoured the blessed Northern side of the Hold. The coldness blew away the dregs of incense but could not dissipate the uncertainty about what had just transpired within the room. Once again, things were different in the Hold.

## XIII

TRYS DESCENDED through the Hold. The expansive corridors of the upper Hold contracted as he descended. The vast halls which could accommodate a Ritual procession of ten abreast were replaced by roughly chiseled passageways whose faults and narrowness were cloaked by an ample array of shadows clustered between the infrequent and faltering torches. Trys watched his feet move from light to shadow and back to light over and over again. The monotony of it, in conjunction with the closeness of the walls, was comforting to him.

He had slipped away in the confusion at the end of the Ritual in order to clear his head of the incense which seemed to clot there and to avoid further lessons on the importance of the Rituals from each Interpreter he met. He raised his right hand and ran it along the rough wall. Somewhere far beyond the wall and beyond hundreds of feet of rock lay the frigid Waste. A bracing blast would clear his head and put everything in perspective once again. The wall fell away as the corridor widened for a short distance. His hand fell heavily to his side.

The silence, which seemed such an integral part of the Hold and which oppressed him, coming as he did from the open Waste where the silence was never absolute, was suddenly disturbed. He did not alter his pace but he did listen intently. The disturbance of the silence, for it was more that than an actual identifiable sound, was not repeated. He listened with the trained senses of a hunter not yet dulled by removal from the Waste. No disturbance, only perfect silence.

Abruptly, he stopped. Just as his foot stopped moving and along with the dying sound of the sole upon the rock, he thought he detected the shadow of the disturbance he had heard earlier. He raised his head and opened his mouth as if to drink in any vibrations which might remain within the cold draft as it moved along the floor of the corridor. He heard nothing.

Hunter's instinct, he thought to himself. Just the residue of my not so old habits. In the Hold he was either surrounded by the unnatural commotion of crowds of people or sealed off from all living sounds behind sheets of rock. No predator stalks me here, he thought, or rather none I know about. Predators would be more likely to walk on two feet here and be no less deadly. He reached up to his right shoulder but knew there was no reassuring hilt there.

Blood blades were not allowed in the presence of the Queen/Lady and he had not gone back to his quarters before setting out on his little jaunt.

As abruptly as he had stopped, he started walking again. The corridors of the Hold were crowded with people. Why should this one be any different? There was probably someone behind him, but whether that person wished him ill or not he would have to wait and see. The patient fatalism of the Waste could stand him in good stead, even here.

He negotiated a sharp S curve in the corridor and stepped out into what amounted to a wide hall which drove forward, straight and clean with a slight downward incline. Trys was not aware of it, but he had just reached the border line between the Hold proper and Low Hold.

A few hundred feet along the wide hall and on his right, a blaze of light shot out from a huge arched doorway. Carved on a thin sheet of rock which hung from a massive iron bar above the doorway was a sign which proclaimed the site as the "Royal Arms," in an obvious attempt to offend neither Queen/Lady nor King/Lord.

Beneath the diplomatic sign stood two men. They were dissimilar in stature, choice of clothing, and tone of voice. One was short and stout and clothed in bright colors which were tightly stretched across certain portions of his anatomy. Like his attire, his voice was bright and insistent. He harangued the other man, who stood silently before him, dressed in black from neck to toe and with an expression on his long lean face to match.

Trys could not prevent himself from hearing what the smaller man was saying. It seemed to center around whether or not they were going to enter the inn and the reasons both for and against.

"It's always the same with you, isn't it, Bledsahl?" said the stout man. "Be careful or you just might enjoy yourself. And we couldn't have anything so sloppy as happiness entering your shadowed life, now could we?"

"I choose to err on the side of sobriety, yes. While you, my dissolute friend, charge ahead in your frenetic existence and more than make up for my cautious pessimism," replied the dark man in a low but penetrating tone of voice.

"The inn provides food and drink and companionship. Now what's wrong with that?"

"The food is greasy and overpriced, the drink is alcoholic in nature, and the companionship is less than desirable," observed the man in black.

"The grease makes it stick to your ribs, and the innkeeper has told me many times his inn is slightly higher priced due to its prime location, on the border between the Hold and Low Hold. He caters to the aristocracy, you know. And as for the companionship, his serving girls are among the prettiest I know and his clientele is choice," explained the smaller man.

"But not one I choose to associate with," said the tall man.

"If you had your way, you wouldn't associate with the world at all. Why, you nearly became a recluse after we lost Gerred..."

The darkly dressed man noticed Trys approaching. He reached out and touched the short man on the arm and hissed, "Not that, not here."

The other man stopped talking and turned to look at Trys. He studied his face for a moment and then smiled broadly at him. "My friend, perhaps I can enlist you as an ally. What is your opinion on the drinking of wine?"

Trys entered the bright circle of light before the inn and stopped near the two men. "Well, I would say that wine, taken in moderation, is just fine. Even as an Interpreter, I now and then take a goblet."

"Aha! You see, Bledsahl, I have holy writ to back me up on this one. An Interpreter says it's fine to imbibe."

"Englerth, you are impossible," retorted the man in black.

But Englerth was not listening just then. Instead, he was looking closely at the face of the young Interpreter. Trys glanced to one side, as if to check out how far he had to go and even made a movement in that direction, when the short man stopped him.

"No, don't go. Just a moment, please, friend. I just need to have a brief word with my comrade here."

Trys hesitated while Englerth muttered in a perfectly audible tone of voice. "It's there. The resemblance is there."

Bledsahl coolly appraised Trys who began to back up. "Yes, I do think you are right about that. And you haven't had anything to drink yet, so your sight is not muddled. Yes, there is a similarity."

"Yes," exclaimed the stout man. He turned eagerly to Trys who took several steps back and devoutly wished he had returned to his quarters to pick up his blood blade. "You do look like him."

"Who?" asked Trys cautiously. Englerth was smiling at him so strongly it was hard for him to believe he was in any danger from the small man.

"The him that we used to know. The him that nearly scaled to the heights of both Hold and Camp. The him..."

"That you should stop talking about out here," interjected Bledsahl.

"You're right, Bledsahl. It is a story which deserves to be told over a large goblet of wine."

Bledsahl groaned and smiled wryly. "So, you have outmaneuvered me again."

"Don't I always?" chuckled Englerth. "Let us enter this fine establishment and I will tell you more about the him I mentioned."

Trys looked at the two men and then into the brightly lit interior of the inn. It appeared to be safe enough and he did want to learn more about the ways of the Hold. He nodded and followed them inside.

With Englerth acting as cicerone, they were soon seated in a snug corner of the Royal Arms where they were each brought brimming goblets of snow wine by a servant girl who smiled and blushed at the ardent attentions of the stout man. The impatient call of the innkeeper drew her away from their table. As the girl swayed away, she looked back over her shoulder and ran straight into a round faced man who had just entered. He cursed her fluently but in a low voice.

Trys looked up, attracted by the noise, and noticed that the man made a desperate attempt to keep the serving girl between himself and the table where the three acquaintances sat. With a push, which nearly sent the girl sprawling, the man darted behind a pillar and disappeared.

"Not the type of customer anyone likes," commented Bledsahl who had also watched the little scene.

"No, certainly not," said Trys. "And you know, I feel like I've seen that man somewhere before."

"The Hold is full of that type of man," said Bledsahl. "A paid and petty spy by the look of him."

"A spy. I see." Trys did not elaborate on what he saw, but he shifted his chair to keep an eye on the part of the inn where the man had disappeared.

"He acts too much like a spy to be a very good one," commented Englerth after he drained off half of the contents of his goblet of snow wine. "You see, friend, we are actors. I could play the part of a spy to perfection."

"No one would ever suspect him of having a single important thought anywhere in that head of his," said Bledsahl.

"Exactly. No one would ever suspect me."

"But I would know their suspicions were correct. You have no thoughts worth knowing."

"Bledsahl is forever gloomy, and he likes to try to spread it around. But I stop him," said Englerth cheerfully.

"Again and again," interjected Bledsahl.

"It's my duty. And speaking of duty, that reminds me of our dear departed friend, the one I am going to tell you about," said Englerth.

"Just be careful what you say. If there are spies about, they might find some small bit of what you have to say interesting."

"My story is almost ancient history by now," said Englerth. "I'm not sure anyone is much interested in dead Consorts any longer."

"That's true," intoned Bledsahl in a sepulchral voice.

"But before I begin I must introduce myself and my black clad friend. I am Englerth, actor extraordinaire. And this is Bledsahl, the voice of doom within our little sphere."

Bledsahl nodded to Trys who nodded back, puzzled but intrigued by the odd pair.

"My name is Trys," offered the young Interpreter.

"Ah, from the North then. The shortness of your name belies that," explained Englerth.

"Well, yes, just recently arrived in the Hold as a matter of fact."

"Excellent. Then allow us to act as your guides for further adventures in and around the Hold," said Englerth.

"Don't start, Englerth. You've got an audience of one for a change. Tell your story and don't scare him away," said Bledsahl.

Englerth sniffed and wrinkled his nose as if about to protest, but then thought better of it and grinned. "Very well, my dark friend. I shall do as you say. His name was Gerred. Does it mean anything to you?" asked Englerth turning to Trys.

With a shock, Trys did recognize the name. Cyln had mentioned it in connection with the Queen/Lady. "I believe I have heard something about someone with that name," said Trys cautiously, not certain now who was or was not a spy and for whom.

"See, I told you he was a man of learning. A peruser of the Chronicles should be familiar with history both ancient and modern. I'm sure he is..."

"About to be bored to death," cut in Bledsahl. "Get on with it. I'm not convinced that talking about this in a public place is such a good idea."

"Yes, curt and to the point, as always. Gerred was our friend and a First Son of King/Lord Nordseth. As such he was allowed certain freedoms. He joined our group of actors on the floating stage in the River Ice. The stage, I am afraid, is now defunct, or at least in dry dock. It suffered major damage in the conflict between the Northern invaders and the troops of Camp and Hold. The very conflict in which Gerred died. The three of us were great companions, acting, drinking, eating, and wenching far into the night."

"You may exclude me from your little inventory," said Bledsahl.

"True. Bledsahl sat off to one side most nights. He acts

because he was born into that class. He eats and drinks because he has to live. And it appears he never fraternizes with the women, at least not in front of me."

Englerth grinned and gave Bledsahl a mischievous look. Bledsahl ignored it.

"Anyway, the time came for Gerred to take on his greatest role yet, Consort to the Queen/Lady. I predicted he would be the best one yet, that he would bring glory to himself and bestow rich favors upon us, his friends."

"Wrong on both counts," croaked Bledsahl.

"He almost did. He tried. Was it his fault he fell in love with the Queen/Lady Alisande, that he climbed to her garden at the top of the Hold, and from there had to flee for his life to the south? He played his part brilliantly."

"And yet he ended up addicted to sommess, fighting duels for hire in the dueling pits of the south," said Bledsahl.

"A cruel fate, I grant you," agreed Englerth.

"Crueler still that we joined him in his downward spiral."

"Ah, but Bledsahl, we were the only friends he had left."

Bledsahl nodded in his slow, lugubrious way. "I do not regret that we did it. I am merely saddened by the way it ended."

"It ended in the garden high up on the Hold where it had started. Gerred arrived back as the troops under the command of the Northern chieftain, Brys, stormed the Hold. Gerred slipped in and made his way to the garden of the Queen/Lady, the one place he felt she might be. He was right, she was there. But so was Lord Kysel, whose plots to wrest control from both King/Lord and Queen/Lady had helped bring about the conflict in the Hold. They fought. Kysel was killed and then Kysel's men killed Gerred, who took a lot of killing since so much of his body was saturated with the numbing sommess."

Englerth fell silent. Trys got the sense it was not simply an act but rather that the small actor was truly moved by the memories he had evoked.

"And what do you do now?" asked Trys in a near whisper.

Englerth looked up and smiled in a stagy sort of way. "Why we are still actors. We shall always be actors."

"To be precise, we are performers in a small company which puts on shows, with the emphasis on 'shows,' for the Bloodmetal Guild in Low Hold," said Bledsahl.

"Old Bledsahl here does not consider it acting."

"It is most certainly not acting; it is mere performing."

"Fine, performing. But it does keep us clothed, housed, and fed. The Bloodmetal Guild puts on some great feasts and they also have some lovely serving girls."

"The things of the body yet again. Remember, Englerth, we are of the classless, an even more debased category, if such a thing is possible, than it was before the Interpreters and certain First Lords gained in influence and power."

Trys was anxious to hear more of Low Hold and he asked a question to try to get them headed in that direction. "What is Low Hold like? I passed through it on my way up to the Hold but my impression is pretty vague. It seemed monumental, both in terms of architecture and squalor."

"Ah, a man after your own heart, Bledsahl. He sees the glory that was and the gloom that is," said Englerth. "But Low Hold is much more than that. It's a place which has more than its share of poverty and death, yes, but the life which exists there is more vibrant for it."

"The vibrancy which dear Englerth refers to might be colorful and exciting to the visitor, but it is merely depressing to one trapped within it."

Englerth waved his short fingered hands about as if to wipe away any ill impressions left behind by Bledsahl's gloomy description. "Mere bile on Bledsahl's part, I assure you. Granted, you might say there are two types of repression going on in Low Hold. One is that of Lords, like Lord Grendyl, which is overt and dramatic, while the other is that of the Interpreters, no disrespect intended, which is covert and subtle and often harsher for that very reason. Revolution is rampant and the atmosphere is exciting. No, Low Hold is not a joyous place but it does hold joy."

"And it is our last refuge," said Bledsahl. "We have dropped out of the classes and into Low Hold, isn't that how the saying goes?"

"Ignore him, I have done so for years." Englerth then clapped his hands together as he thought of something. "Come to our next performance. It will be in the large square in front of Hold Gate itself. Yes, you must come and see us perform."

"Yes, perform, not act. Carefully note the word used there," grumbled Bledsahl.

Englerth continued on as if Bledsahl had not said a thing. "It is set for tomorrow, early afternoon. Meet us before the performance in front of the apothecary shop near the main entrance to Hold Gate. That's where we usually gather to prepare for the show."

Trys only hesitated a moment and then agreed. The sharp, pleasant smell of the woman who had rescued him at the entrance to Hold Gate still lingered in his mind. He had some vague notion if he went there, he might actually see her again.

"Excellent," declared Englerth. "And now there is just one other little matter to be taken care of, eh, Bledsahl?"

"If you mean the bill, here, I'll take..." offered Trys.

"No, no, nothing as petty as a bill," said Englerth using his expressive hands to wave off Trys's offer of money. "I mean taking care of a smooth exit from the stage for all of us. Right, Bledsahl?"

"I suppose," sighed Bledsahl. "It will help our friend out here as much as it will us."

"My thought exactly. Now, what will it be? Unforgivable offense to my sister?"

"No, too complicated. Something straightforward and simple."

"Pocket picked."

"Precisely," said Bledsahl, who almost grinned at that point. "Our lack of resources will greatly aid the performance." The dark actor turned to Trys at that. "Note, young man, I said performance. What you are about to see should not be construed as acting. Our acting is on another level altogether."

"What are you talking about?" asked Trys, confused by the turn of conversation.

"Watch and enjoy," said Englerth who then stood up and hurried over to the pillar behind which the would-be spy still lurked.

Trys could hear exclamations of joy and amazement coming from behind the pillar. They were soon followed by Englerth and the man himself. Englerth had the man's arm lovingly but firmly locked in his own and was nearly dragging him toward their table. Once out into the open, the spy apparently thought better of making a scene and went along docilely enough.

Englerth hurried him over to the table. "Look, Myrs, look who I found! It's cousin Jhon. You remember, from mother's side of the family."

Bledsahl stood up and bowed to the man. "A pleasure, I am sure. I do not recall the exact relation, but I'm sure my cousin Kysin here is correct."

"Hug him. It's not often that old cousins meet," urged Englerth as he thrust the man toward Bledsahl.

Bledsahl acted outraged, although Trys surmised that much of it was real repulsion at being in such close contact with the spy, but then warmed up and actually embraced the totally confused man. After he had thumped his back, he stepped back and everyone looked at the man, as if expecting a reaction of some sort.

"I...I...ah, you will have to excuse me. It's been so long. I don't really know. I have an appointment..."

"No," protested Englerth. "You can't go so soon. We've just been reunited after all this time. We must reminisce. We must share old memories."

Meanwhile, Bledsahl was making a great show of checking his pockets. His actions started out calmly enough but soon escalated into full-fledged panic.

"My pouch. My pouch with all of my inheritance money in it. It's gone!"

"What?" cried Englerth. "That can't be. You just showed it to me a few minutes ago. It was the black leather one with the sun design stitched onto it, right?"

"Yes! Gone!"

"But who could have taken it?" cried Englerth in his best borderline melodramatic manner.

"No one I can think of," replied Bledsahl, only slightly less melodramatic.

Even in the midst of the act, Trys wondered how they were getting away with what he perceived as blatant overacting. But the denizens of the inn hung on each word and inflection, and Trys supposed they would believe what transpired on an actual stage was simply real life.

"It must be someone here, in this room, for you had it but scant moments ago," continued Englerth.

"Why, yes, it must be. The only one who has come close to me has been..." Bledsahl stopped and waited a full three beats. "Him!"

A long white finger flashed out of a black sleeve as if to pin the spy to the pillar behind him, and for a moment the man lurched backward as if physically struck.

"Jhon, say it's not true," gasped Englerth.

"I...I did nothing," choked the spy. And then, trying to find something to refute, stammered out, "I'm not...Jhon."

"Aha, he admits to subterfuge. Someone search him. I'm certain you will find my pouch upon his person."

With wide grins, three burly regulars of the inn lunged forward and began to man-handle the ersatz Jhon. He struggled, but only feebly, being too overcome with confusion to know what he should do or not do at that juncture.

After a bit of rough shoving and pawing, one of the men held up a black leather pouch with a sun design stitched onto it. The spy turned green and sank back against the pillar.

"Someone call the Ice Guards," demanded Englerth, "and have this pickpocket taken away." He snatched the pouch out of the man's hand and waved it above his head as proof positive of the man's guilt.

With that the inn erupted into even more turmoil than before, with all of it centering on the small spy. He was pulled this way and that and poked and prodded and called a multitude of uncomplimentary names. Someone ran to call the Ice Guards, while the innkeeper ran to his bar to fill the orders of his guests who were now ravenously thirsty after the performance and who had all sorts of stories to tell each other about what they had seen and what they had done to bring the criminal to justice.

In the midst of the turmoil, Trys found himself being drawn slowly but steadily to the door of the inn and then out into the corridor by his two acquaintances who managed to keep up a steady banter to the people they passed, all of whom urged them stay for a drink. They thanked each and every one and managed to slip by each and every one.

Once outside they moved quickly down along the corridor until they had turned the first corner and the inn was out of sight.

"A good solid performance, that," remarked Englerth.

"Yes, I must admit I played my part well and even you, my dear Englerth, were in top form," responded Bledsahl.

"Why, thank you."

Trys grinned and shook his head. "I've never seen anything like it."

"Of course not. You come from the North, after all. If you stay in and around the Hold for any length of time, you will have the opportunity to see many such performances, and some of them even on a stage," said Englerth.

"I look forward to it," said Trys.

"That is one spy who will not dog your steps for some time to come," spoke up Bledsahl.

"I fear we must head back to Low Hold now, Bledsahl. Will you come with us?" asked Englerth.

Trys shook his head. "Not just now. But I will get down there very soon, if only to see you two perform once again. I do hope I will be a part of the audience next time and not pressed into service upon the stage."

"We shall see, we shall see," chuckled Englerth.

"Let's go, Englerth, before the Ice Guards arrive. We have no desire to answer questions about how much money was actually in the pouch."

"Good by. We shall see you soon, I just know it," sang out Englerth as he and Bledsahl turned and danced away into the shadows which led to Low Hold.

Trys stood and watched them go. He shook his head again and then turned to make his way back to the world of the upper Hold where the acting was not so broadly performed.

## XIV

SEBASTE SLID out of the noisily swirling crowd upon the causeway and into the ruined galleries on the right hand side of Hold Gate. The silence drifted deeper as he moved down the main gallery and a wind off the Waste sliced away the sharp smells of the rancid and perfumed crowd. He slowed his pace, both to enjoy the clean silence and to pick his way with more care among the broken slates of the gallery floor.

It was the first time he had ventured forth from Steelstain Alley since the death of Sebaste, and his own rebirth. He drank in sounds and smells and sights and found a myriad of reflections welling up from his collective memory. He was still dizzy with the collision of memories and the immediacy of sensations on the causeway as he paused in the middle of the main gallery to lean against a pillar which supported nothing.

At one time, the galleries had stretched away on either side of Hold Gate to provide the Lords and Ladies of the Hold with an elegant place to walk and to view the River Ice, and to be viewed by their peers. High vaulting arches framed the view down toward the River Ice and the Waste beyond, while cunningly designed openings in the roof of the gallery let one glance up at the Hold capped mountain far above. The galleries were a sublime example of Hold architecture at its luxurious height.

At the time of the schism, when the King/Lord had left and begun to lay siege to the Hold of the Queen/Lady, Hold Gate had been closed and the galleries abandoned to the ice, snow, and wind. Time and the brutal elements had done their work and the galleries were like a sketch of their former glories. Arches still stood here and there, but gaps interrupted their ambitious lines. The huge slabs of slate which formed the expansive floors were broken and tilted at crazy angles in many places. The roof openings which had been designed to lead the eye upward toward the glory that was the Hold were lost because most of the roof had fallen in. Now the Hold loomed far above, seeming to frown down upon the broken tangle at its foot.

Sebaste looked up at the Hold and, even as he did, a chunk of an ornamental cornice broke off and crashed to the floor about eight feet away from where he leaned as he tried to regain his sense of equilibrium. As difficult as this journey away from Steelstain Alley was, he had had to make it. A message had arrived from Torkild, the closest servant to King/Lord Nordseth. It had made Sebaste decide to meet with him. The message was ambiguous but urgent, and that combination had piqued Sebaste's interest. He had also needed a reason to leave the relative safety of the Alley as the new Sebaste. Sebaste was a creature compounded of memories. He had scant opportunity to gather new memories mewed up in Steelstain Alley.

As the rattle of broken stones died away, Sebaste heard another sound. It was the clatter of more falling stones. These stones were displaced, not by time and slow erosion, but by the feet of a squad of small boys who tumbled into the far end of the gallery. They paused when they reached the uneven floor and stared briefly down toward Sebaste who still leaned against the pillar. Then, deciding he was merely a grownup and one who would not disturb their play, they quickly formed into two teams.

Sebaste clearly heard one group, which consisted of five boys, announce they were the forces from the Camp of the evil King/Lord. The other four boys, numerically outnumbered but noisier for all that, screamed back they would defend the Hold of the Queen/Lady to the last man. And with that the battle began in earnest.

The four Hold defenders scrambled up a crumbling wall which faced the River Ice. Leaping about amongst the broken arches and shattered sills, they managed to stave off the first rush of the attackers by shoving them back down the slope of loose stones which led up to the wall. The five who were repulsed then huddled together to plan the strategy of their next attack, while the four whooped a victory chant and climbed as high as they could up the stubs of the ruined arches.

Sebaste smiled a small smile. He might possess the memories of generations of seers stretching back for centuries, but he still retained the relatively recent memories of his own boyhood. And as he delved into them, he found curious reflections within the repository of previous Sebastes.

For example, he discovered his own mentor had a memory of playing a similar game upon a huge snow drift at the edge of the Waste within the shadow of the Hold. The doubling, tripling, even quadrupling of a single memory was such a new experience for him that he still found it disturbing, but he was learning to select what interested him from the collective memory pool, extract what he could from it, and move on. At first he had been nearly hypnotized by the process of memory recall, to the extent that he had spent hours recalling one incident from the distant past and had forgotten to eat or rest. He had snapped out of the recollective state when his stomach groaned from lack of food and his arm had buckled under him as he leaned upon it. Dip and draw back, that was the pattern he used now.

And as he drew back from the multiple memories of a single childhood game, he heard the scrape of boot on stone behind him. He turned to see a bent figure sidling down the shallow steps which led from the causeway. It was Torkild. He paused at the bottom of the steps and glanced back up at the crowd upon the causeway beneath the frowning facade of Hold Gate. He examined the carved stone of the Gate with a critical eye and then shook his head, as if musing upon the folly of the elemental and eternal conflict between Father Sun and Mother Ice.

He turned to Sebaste who stepped away from his pillar. Ducking his head to keep his left side somewhat averted from the seer, Torkild moved closer. "It's not that simple, as you well know," he said.

"What isn't?" asked Sebaste.

"Conflict. Conflict between Mother Ice and Father Sun; conflict between Hold and Camp; conflict between man and woman. A lot of other emotions get caught up with the simple one of hatred and pulled along."

"Yes, I suppose you're right," replied Sebaste, not certain how to take this philosophizing from the man who had urged him to this meeting.

A shout went up from both sides and echoed down the gallery. Torkild jerked his head around but then lowered it when he realized it was merely a group of boys.

"What are they playing at?" Torkild asked.

"Hold and Camp," said Sebaste. "Didn't you ever play something like it when you were young?"

Torkild squinted hard at the seer with his good eye. "When I was their age, I was struggling for existence in the deep Waste. I lived on the margins of the clan until I was put out for not being strong enough. I followed them clothed only in a threadbare singlesuit and a faulty breather mask. I lived off the scraps they threw away and got my left side twisted about." Here he shifted slightly to give Sebaste a better view of his withered left side. His arm and leg were twisted and nearly useless, while his face was puckered by the scars of having been frozen. "I suppose you could say I did have my games, only I played to live."

"Yes, I do recall that now. Sorry."

"Don't bother to bring up all of the old Sebaste's memories upon that particular topic. It is ancient history and provides few lessons now," mused Torkild.

"I think you may be wrong about that."

"Well, I have been wrong before now and will be again. It's

just I know how to live despite my mistakes. That's the real key to life in either Hold or Camp."

"You are a survivor, Torkild, of that there is no doubt," offered Sebaste.

Torkild smiled a lopsided smile. "I see I hold some small place in the voluminous memories of Sebaste. I guess that's a type of immortality. Oh, and by the way, Sebaste is dead, long live Sebaste."

Sebaste was surprised to hear the phrase. "I thought that was to be said only of King/Lords and Queen/Ladies."

"I believe it applies more to you than to them. Their title stays the same while the person differs. With you, both title and person are virtually one and the same."

"You may be right about that, but my position as advisor keeps me away from the power which both wield," pointed out Sebaste.

"You should be grateful for that distance," countered Torkild.

"Believe me, I am. If the memories of Sebaste have taught me anything it is to beware of power."

Torkild shuffled a few feet away from Sebaste to check on the progress of the game taking place down the gallery. The boys were shouting and running as attack followed attack upon the makeshift bastion of the broken arch.

"You can learn from the memories you have acquired. That's good, and it's why I needed to talk to you," said Torkild as he circled back to the pillar.

A gust of bitter wind swept down the gallery. It caused the boys to scamper for cover for a moment and Torkild to swing stiffly about to place his good right side toward the blast. Sebaste remained standing by the pillar and even lifted his face toward the frigid air to drink in its purity.

The wind died down, the boys came back out and began the battle anew, and Torkild squinted and motioned for Sebaste to step with him around toward the Hold side of the pillar. The two men found themselves in what amounted to a small room. The roof of the gallery still spanned the arches and a wall shut off the space from the main walk. Other than a drift of frozen snow in the corner, the ramshackle chamber was empty.

"I have asked you here for a purpose," began Torkild.

Sebaste nodded.

"I have asked you here in order to ask you to do something," Torkild said as he tilted his head to fix Sebaste with his good eye.

Sebaste nodded again.

"Return to your official duties as Seer to the King/Lord," said Torkild in a low, insistent voice.

Sebaste blinked but did not nod. He had not been sure what

Torkild had needed from him, but his request, while one possibility among the many which he had come up with, had not been at the top of his list.

"Why?" Sebaste asked. He needed time to think and to search his memories for any similar situations. And, he simply wanted to know.

"The King/Lord is dying," said Torkild in a low voice.

"But he has been dying for years and could go on dying for many more. It's the nature of his disease," replied Sebaste.

"Well, he has entered a new phase of dying, then. He is growing more and more unpredictable; his commands cause more blood to flow. I want to prevent that."

"You? Why should you care?" Sebaste sensed it was best to confront Torkild directly about this. His memories of Torkild were of a loyal servant who would always do his master's bidding.

"I have seen rivers of blood in my time. You recall that, surely. I wish to slow or even stop those rivers. Quite frankly, I need someone to help me keep one step ahead of him before he brings on an all out war. The Seer is just the person for the job." Torkild stared hard at him from his one good eye.

Sebaste met the gaze and did not flinch. He was feverishly sorting through scraps of memory concerned with the servant to the King/Lord. Most were superficial, such as images of the limping figure hurrying to and fro on errands for his liege. But there were some which showed his devotion to his monarch was based on more than fear of what might be done to him if he failed. Sebaste suddenly realized that Torkild truly loved Nordseth, the man, not the monarch.

Torkild saw that Sebaste was perplexed. "When I mentioned the name of Sebaste to him, he spit up some blood in the contemptuous sort of way he has. He said the idea was madness and that he had driven away the old man to cease his endless prying into his secrets and his thoughts. He had caught Sebaste once too often telling him what he would do next, even before Nordseth knew himself what he would do. That loss of control necessitated Sebaste's exile. But then, I reminded him that the old Sebaste was dead and that a new Sebaste had taken his place. That interested him."

"Well, it would, wouldn't it? He would like to have yet another person under his control," suggested Sebaste.

"Yes, it's partly that. But I could keep him from overwhelming you, I know I could. And you could help me to reduce his excesses."

"Sounds like a dangerous balancing act."

"As is all life in Camp or Hold," pointed out Torkild.

"But I was put to one side; neither in Hold nor Camp. My current position allows me a certain freedom which Sebaste never used to have," countered Sebaste.

Torkild leaned in, as if expecting something of the sort. "Freedom from what? Freedom from the wellsprings of action which give you your memories. With little contact with the King/Lord or the Queen/Lady and their respective courts, how can you harvest any memories to hand on to the next Sebaste? Are you even a Seer if you have nothing to see?"

The argument struck Sebaste as uncomfortably reasonable. He was young, but invested with the responsibility of centuries of memories. Did his investiture as Seer allow him to merely act as caretaker for what was already in the repository, or did it demand he add to the treasure? That would require some deep dredging of the collective memories and, standing as he was in the ruined gallery with the afternoon waning and the air now suddenly still and damp with the promise of a heavy fall of snow, he was not prepared at the moment to begin the descent.

"I must think about it," said Sebaste.

"Think fast then. Things are changing. The ground is shifting underfoot," responded Torkild.

"What do you mean?" Sebaste was becoming exasperated by this man who irritated him with his logic one moment and then piqued his curiosity the next. It was obvious he was a long time resident of the labyrinthine ways of Camp and Hold.

"The new Interpreter brought in from the North. He is presently the focus of much of the King/Lord's attention. He seems to be just what his appearance indicates; a young recruit which Dwilkon can pervert to his own nasty ways. But things are seldom what they seem. We have all learned that hard lesson many times over."

Faced with yet another conundrum, Sebaste found himself making a violent inner effort to shut off the inexhaustible spring of his memories. A new player in the game; how many times had that been seared into the collective memories? Sebaste saw the pattern repeated far back into the past and physically staggered at the prospect.

He flung out a hand to steady himself against the pillar. Torkild ducked in a little closer, as if even here his reflex was to serve one who needed him.

"Are you all right?" asked Torkild.

"Yes," replied Sebaste taking a deep breath. "There's just so much...so many memories."

"Ah, I see," said Torkild. "Be careful who you show this sort of weakness to. I know you are but recently an heir to the memories, and there are many in Hold and Camp who would lunge in at the slightest sign of weakness."

Sebaste straightened himself. His hand scraped across a rough section of the pillar and the pain snapped him out of the vortex of memories which threatened to pull him down. "You are not one of those?" questioned Sebaste.

"I know weakness," he said simply. "When to exploit it, and when to protect the one who shows it."

"Thank you, I think," said Sebaste.

"You will not come to the Camp, then." The servant of the King/Lord made it clear it was a statement and not a question.

"Not now. Perhaps never. I can't say. As you graciously pointed out, I have but recently inherited my position and I need to know where and how best to use it."

"I understand. I did this for him," said Torkild in a subdued voice. "He is my...friend, for lack of a better word. He would never believe it, of course, but there it is. I don't want to see him suffer any more than he has to. I thought perhaps you could help me. But, I understand."

All the time they had spoken, the opposing factions had clashed down along the gallery. At one point the silence from that direction had startled Sebaste. He assumed they had left to play elsewhere. But even as Torkild murmured his small confession, the boys suddenly burst from cover. They tore past the two men and did not even bother to look at them.

Torkild shrank back from the wild shouts as if the noise hurt him. Sebaste turned to watch them scatter among the pillars. He was turning back to Torkild, having decided to end their interview and get back to Steelstain Alley as soon as he could, when an image among the ruins arrested him.

To avoid capture by the enemy, one of the boys had taken refuge upon a window sill beneath a broken archway. The clouds which had covered the sun most of the afternoon suddenly tore apart and a shaft of pure gold struck the gallery just where the boy crouched. His thin form was lit up.

Sebaste waited. He was instinctively aware that the image was a memory hook which should lead from one sensation to another to establish the memory sequence. But, the image was all. The memory sequence was not broken but suspended.

"What...?" began Torkild, who was perplexed by the rigidity of the Seer.

That word in a questioning tone caused a definitive click within Sebaste's mind. In that instant, he realized the visual cue pointed to the complete memory sequence, but did not lead directly to it. The sequence consisted of only one sense, that of hearing.

Two voices speaking; that was the memory. And with a rush of understanding, Sebaste knew the two voices speaking created the key to the schism, the seminal event which sent the King/Lord out of the Hold to lay siege to it.

"Yes," hissed Sebaste through clenched teeth.

"Yes, what?" asked Torkild.

But Sebaste could not answer him. He was immersed in a torrent of memories which left him aware of what was happening around his physical body but unconcerned with anything as gross and temporal as bodies or walls or air.

"What have you been doing?"

"Nothing."

The question was uttered by the King/Lord long ago. The reply came from the Queen/Lady and the schism was begun. Torkild's aborted question had set it all in motion and now it poured through Sebaste like water directly from the River Ice. Like the water it numbed and cleansed and rejuvenated and shocked.

The remembered words went back and forth, probing and feinting like blood blades. The King/Lord asked if the Queen/Lady had a lover, an illegal consort. She admitted it and in her pride, and to be as hurtful as possible, said that she no longer loved the King/Lord. He demanded she throw off the lover and adhere strictly to the Rituals. She refused and began to taunt him with her extra-Ritual infidelity. The King/Lord continued to demand she return to him and the Rituals. She continued to refuse and finally lashed out by saying he loved his kingdom more than he did her and that the Rituals meant more to him than she did. The King/Lord could only say 'No,' over and over again. The Queen/Lady said that once they had been free together at the heart of the Rituals, but the heart had died. The King/Lord maintained his litany of 'No.' At the last, she told him to get out. He went and took more than half of the heart of the kingdom with him.

As the words died away, back into the structures of stored memory once again, Sebaste recognized the telltale signs that his own immediate predecessor had discovered this very memory for himself and in much the same way. His teacher had kept the memory to himself. He had not revealed its hiding place even at the last. Sebaste knew it was such a powerful memory that each Sebaste in turn had to come to grips with it and decide for himself what to do with it. It had remained hidden for generations, and even as the last dregs of the memory slipped away, Sebaste knew he too must maintain the secrecy.

"Are you all right?" Torkild questioned Sebaste even as he scanned his face for any signs of what had gone on inside that memory crammed head. He hoped to glean some information he could use to apply even the lightest of pressures to this obviously difficult Seer.

"I am...all right," replied Sebaste as he reentered the immediate world about him. The heavy dampness of the air weighed down upon him and his head ached as much from that as from the flood of memories which was just then receding.

"You had a rough recall, if appearances are any indication," ventured Torkild, still watching for any opening which might present itself.

"Yes, I guess you could say that," said Sebaste as he sucked in the damp air and shook his head to clear it.

"Just to clarify things; you refuse to come to the Camp and take up your traditional position as Seer to the King/Lord?"

"I refuse the honor. You certainly understand that at the time Sebaste was dismissed from direct service to the King/Lord, the traditions were altered. I am a free agent now and must remain so."

Torkild twisted toward him as if to emphasize what he said next. "A free agent. That means you will not offer your services to the Queen/Lady?"

Sebaste smiled. "Is that what you fear? That somehow the Queen/Lady will gain an unfair advantage in the ongoing war between the monarchs? I can see you do love your King/Lord. But I can also see you cannot help being the creature he has made you in to. Watch for the signs of weakness, watch for the flaws in the defenses, and press the attack."

Torkild smiled himself and nodded once.

"You may tell your monarch that Sebaste will not work for King/Lord or Queen/Lady again. Even in the short time I have possessed them, I have come to realize the importance of the memories which I hold in trust outstrip the petty concerns of even a century of rulers."

"Well, then, our meeting is at an end," said Torkild. "It has been illuminating. I must return to the Camp to attend to the needs of the King/Lord and before some wandering Ice Guard finds me. It would not do to have the personal servant of the King/Lord detained within the Hold."

Torkild swept Sebaste a lopsided bow and shuffled quickly away toward the causeway. His limping figure ascended the steps and slipped into the thinning crowds before the edifice of Hold Gate.

Sebaste watched him go and then turned toward the River Ice. The boy, who still crouched on the sill, suddenly realized he was being watched. He stood up, touched the top of the broken arch above him, darted a rebellious smile at Sebaste, and was gone. The noise of disturbed tiles marked his departure.

The clatter was then swallowed up as the snow, which had threatened for so long, began falling. Heavy clumps of whiteness settled on Sebaste's shoulders and brushed across his cheeks. He shook his head once to clean the snow off his hair before he slipped up the hood of his singlesuit. His mind relieved of memories for the moment, he made his way up through the smothering snow, back to his rooms on Steelstain Alley where he knew a brightly burning fire awaited him.

## XV

FUNCTIONING chimneys seemed to be a measurement of wealth in the Hold. In his descent from Upper to Low Hold, Trys was struck by the steadily increasing amount of coal smoke which hung in the air and the correspondingly thickening layers of greasy soot which covered most surfaces. He had left the upper reaches where the smoke was discreetly vented and had arrived in regions where it was not uncommon to see dark smoke billowing out of a crooked doorway.

And doorways were not the only crooked things in Low Hold. The streets crawled about in sinuous ways and more than once he had been stopped by a cul-de-sac and been forced to retrace his steps to find another way to continue his descent. The volcanic activity of the mountain did account for some of the twisting of streets.

In Upper Hold the slots cut into the rock which allowed sections of the city to slide downward with relatively little damage being done to them during an earthquake were well maintained. The slots in Low Hold were clogged with garbage as well as the residue from the upper reaches which had descended over the centuries. In many respects, Low Hold was the dumping ground for what was no longer needed nor wanted in Upper Hold.

What disturbed and saddened Trys the most was the fact that the abundance of material refuse was matched by the amount of human refuse which he saw on every hand. While smoke issuing from doorways was an indication that the inhabitants could not afford a proper chimney, the pinched faces of the people was a grimmer sign of the poverty which covered Low Hold like its pall of smoke. In the North, people were not allowed to suffer simply because they could not afford the necessities of life. Clan members shared with one another to uphold the dignity and the vitality of the clan as a whole. There were no signs of clans here. Everyone was simply an indistinguishable part of the blackened world of Low Hold.

Trys followed yet another broken backed street to a corner which appeared to be clogged with stones and garbage. He thought he would have to turn around and retrace his steps to find a street which did not dead end, when a breeze sluiced away the pall of smoke which hung before him. The corner was only partly clogged. A well-worn path led over the major obstacles and out to whatever lay on the other side.

He climbed the midden heap and paused at the top. There before him, framed by the jagged ends of the houses on either side of the street, lay a sight which further shook his perspective on Low Hold. It was Hold Gate itself. An immense square opened up just beyond the street in which he stood and while it dipped down here and rose up there, obvious results of centuries of volcanic activity, its proportions were so large that it appeared to be simply a tremendous open field.

The gigantic scale of the square was matched by the monolithic structure of Hold Gate proper which seemed to rise up and up and up. Where the side turned to the Waste was embellished to overflowing with carvings, the side facing the Hold was less cluttered but still well covered. Its walls rose straight up, broken by narrow windows and a series of defining ledges among the carvings which helped to slow the upward thrust of the man-made mountain. It was astounding in its scale.

Trys half slid, half walked down off the heap and into the square where he was immediately caught up in the currents of humanity which swirled here and there throughout the vast space. Life flourished in the square before Hold Gate in all of its vitality and all of its squalor. Items of every conceivable type were bought and sold, food was consumed or thrown away, voices were raised and whispers were heard, people shuffled along with no goal and they ran with desperate urgency to appointments on which their lives depended.

Trys let the currents carry him as they would, fascinated by the sheer numbers and diversity of the people he saw there. The Northern clans were blandly homogenous compared to the riot of ethnic groups which swarmed about the young Interpreter. He had not known that Winterhold held such diverse populations and he was stunned by being plunged into the midst of it all.

Eventually, the currents deposited him at the base of Hold Gate and off to its left hand side. There he found himself standing, somewhat unsteadily, in front of what appeared to be an apothecary shop. The shop was tucked into a corner beneath one of the massive arches which formed part of a gigantic porch running along the entire facade of Hold Gate. The groined ceiling, hundreds of feet above the floor of the porch, caught and tossed back the myriad sounds which drifted in from the square just outside. The shop, which was really not much more than a collection of roughly made walls designed to enclose its contents, seemed to huddle beneath the arch to avoid as much of the noise and bustle as possible.

Trys had come to Hold Gate to watch the performance of his two acquaintances, Englerth and Bledsahl. They had told him to meet them on the left hand side of Hold Gate. That was where he was, but he saw no sign of the two unlikely actors. Since he had no idea where they were nor where the performance might be put on, he decided to step inside the apothecary shop to ask if anyone could help him.

It was quiet in the apothecary shop. The noise from the square did not penetrate the flimsy walls. Trys felt as if he was wrapped in a blanket. But this was an overwhelmingly aromatic blanket. The raw materials for the making of unguents and elixirs were piled on nearly every open foot of space, leaving only a narrow and winding path which ran toward the back of the shop.

Trys took a few steps along this path when a combination of scents struck him as particularly heady. The bitter and sour surged up his nostrils and tangled in his brain. He swayed and reached out to steady himself. A slim hand caught his arm and guided him to a bench tucked back in a nook between bales of herbs.

"Are you always this lightheaded? Or do I just catch you at bad times?" said a woman's voice close to his ear.

Trys began to take a deep breath, thought better of it when he realized the air was heavy with a riot of smells, and held it for a moment while he focussed upon the person who had gotten him to the bench.

He let out his breath in a rush when he realized she was the woman from the ruined gallery near the entrance to Hold Gate. She appeared to be wearing the same singlesuit. It fit her limber body snugly. Her red hair was cut short and close to her head which was tilted at a questioning angle just then.

"You," Trys said rather lamely.

"Yes, and you. I'm glad we've got that straight," she quipped. She raised her head then and smiled. It was meant to be mischievous but came across as pleased toward the end.

Trys was startled by the sudden appearance of the mysterious young woman. She had popped into his thoughts at the oddest moments since he had first seen her upon his arrival at the Hold. Her expression and her scent had tantalized his memory. He now realized where the scent came from, but he had yet to figure out the expression. He then smiled to himself as he realized that his visit to Low Hold had been in part prompted by a vague hope of seeing her again.

She noticed the bemused smile and raised her chin. "Now, that's a strange little smile."

Trys coughed, ostensibly to clear his throat of the aromatic fumes which filled the air, but it came out as a transparent attempt to cover his embarrassment. "I just...thought of something. That's all."

"Something pleasant, I warrant."

"Well, yes, pleasant."

"I don't make a practice of asking young rakes what they find so pleasant about this grungy shop, but I will make an exception this time. What is it, my most noble Lord?"

Confronted by the honest look on her face and the challenge in her eyes, Trys found himself saying what he had not planned on saying. "I came to Low Hold to meet some friends of mine, but discovering you seems much more pleasant."

"That shows you how much you know," she said in a firm voice. "I'm not such a pleasant person to know. Ask any of the vagabonds about the square. They'll tell you I have little time for and even less patience with flatterers."

"Oh, I didn't mean to..." stumbled Trys.

"To flatter. I know. You young rakes are all the same. Deigning to descend from the High Hold for a few hours of dalliance among the scum of Low Hold. Well, ask anyone around here and you'll find out I'm what they call a revolutionary." She paused as if expecting her declaration to have a devastating effect.

"That's very nice, I suppose," said Trys, cautious about how he progressed now.

"Nice? No, it's not nice. If you were a spy of Lord Grendyl, I could be hauled away to the dungeons of the Hold in an instant. I only mention it because I can see you are most definitely not a spy."

"How can you be so certain?" said Trys, his pride slightly wounded by her assessment.

"I've seen them all. The cringers and the braggarts, the cajolers and the threateners, and no one has been able to catch me up in any revolutionary act. I'm too clever for that by far. And too attractive." She smiled her mischievous smile again and waited for a reaction.

"I can see that," agreed Trys.

"No, you look like a young Lord with too much time on his hands. One who might be ripe for recruitment. Our leader is on the other side of the Hold at the moment, fomenting violence among the workers on the docks. But if you listened to him, I'm sure he could help you see the gross inequities which ravage the people of the Low Hold. I'm just one of his lieutenants."

"Don't underestimate your powers of persuasion. I'm more than half convinced already," replied Trys.

"I'll bet," she snapped back.

"No, really," insisted Trys.

She grinned wryly and picked up a handful of dried leaves from the bag next to her and crushed them between her fingers. The smell stung Trys's nose and made his eyes water. She remained dry eyed and unmoved.

"You mentioned some friends. What kind of friends could someone like you have in Low Hold?"

"Actors."

"That makes some sense. Actors are classless. Low Hold is about the only place that will have them," she observed.

"I was supposed to meet them here. A tall man and a short man whose names are..."

"Bledsahl and Englerth," she finished for him.

"You know them?"

"All of Low Hold know that pair. They've been around for many years and are likely to be around for many more. It's not that their acting is so good, but rather that they perform their lives so well. Survivors from a different time." She studied him for a moment and then asked, "All right, I know your business here. Now, how about your name?"

"Trys pyr..."

"Ah, stop there. No patronymics or matronymics here. This is Low Hold. Try to remember that. The rules are different."

"I'll try to remember. And your name?" he ventured.

She smiled another devastating smile with less mischief and more pleasure in it before she answered. "Roxyna."

"A strong and appealing name," said Trys, believing that he would only get snapped at for his straightforward flattery, but saying it all the same.

But she surprised him. "Thank you," replied Roxyna. The softened tone of her voice and the slight wrinkle of her forehead was evidence she appreciated the compliment but was not too certain how to react to it.

"It's almost time for the performance to begin in the square. Knowing those two, they probably got into a squabble about some difference of philosophy or where the best ale is to be had. I shouldn't imagine that either one will be along to collect you now. Bledsahl will be doing the prologue, as usual, and Englerth will come on right after him."

She glanced around at the empty shop and then turned back to him. "Since business is just a little slow at the moment, I'll take you over to the performance."

"You'd do that for me?" asked Trys standing up.

"I'd do it for almost any poor soul from Upper Hold who wandered down here," she said in a tone of voice which put rather too much emphasis on the fact he was not someone special.

"Of course. Thank you."

"Well, let's go," said Roxyna, who turned and strode out of the shop.

Trys followed and paused just outside the door. "Don't you

need to lock up the shop, or anything?"

Roxyna stopped and spun about. She put her fists on her hips and looked defiantly at the passers-by. "Everyone in Low Hold knows better than to steal from this shop. They would have me to deal with."

"I see," said Trys, suppressing a slight smile. "In that case, lead on."

Roxyna nodded once and spun about again. She walked purposefully along the porch which extended along the base of Hold Gate, headed for the center of the monolithic facade.

Trys quickened his pace to catch up with her. He walked on her right and kept one step back. In that position he could study her face, an activity he discovered filled him with a mingled sense of excitement and pleasure. The girls he had known among the clans of the North were nothing like her. While they had been independent and certainly capable of surviving amid the desolation of the Waste, they had lacked the spark which Roxyna possessed.

The crispness of her stride and the self-possessed expression on her lovely face seemed to declare to all who saw her that here was a unique personality. He noticed a reaction to her in the sly, lewd looks of the grimy, classless men who slouched along the pavement as well as the ones obviously possessed of wealth and status. That initial leer faded away as she stared them down and they all looked slightly puzzled as she left them behind.

But as enjoyable as Trys found his examination of his companion, he suddenly found his attention being drawn to what lay beyond and above the piquant face. The porch, into a corner of which the apothecary shop was tucked, ran on for hundreds of yards. They reached the end and stepped out from under its protective roof. Hold Gate loomed over the square immediately before it, towered over the buildings of Low Hold which crouched around its foot, and even seemed to challenge the dizzying heights of the Hold proper.

The facade of Hold Gate leaped upward in all of its glory and decrepitude. Like the facade of the Gate turned to the Waste, this side of the mass of stone was amply covered with carvings from base to crown. But where the images out there were on a colossal scale, the ones on the inside of the Gate were on a more human scale. Warriors and merchants, Lords and Ladies, upper, middle, low and even the classless were represented in all aspects of life upon Winterhold. And behind them all was the ubiquitous climate. Drifts of snow, storms of snow, wastes of snow formed the background for the myriad figures. The rendering of the icy world made Trys long for the clean open spaces of the North. But he was jostled by a bent and grimy beggar and brought rudely back to the world of Low Hold.

He was about to help the man, who appeared to have fallen down, when Roxyna's booted foot sent the man sprawling. "He nearly got your pouch," she said drily.

Trys looked at his side. His pouch, which contained a few coins and a small prayer horn, hung from only one of its two thongs.

"How did he do that so fast?" asked Trys as the man leaped up and ran energetically away to be lost in the crowd.

"Practice. The thieves of Hold Gate are the best," said Roxyna. "This way. The stage is over here."

She nodded to their left where people milled about an alcove in the Gate. However, being on a scale with the rest of the Hold Gate, the alcove was the size of the main cave of the Caynruhl where all of the clan members could gather and not be crowded.

"There's a low wall over here. It's not too close to the stage but we'll have a good view." With that she grabbed his hand and pulled him firmly through the thickening crowd.

Trys held her hand but was careful not to squeeze it, being uncertain as to how such a familiarity would be received. Her hand was warm to his touch. Her grasp was strong and he could feel the ridges of the callouses on her hand. There was no doubt she was a worker, but one who lived for more than her work.

Roxyna reached the wall and pulled Trys to her to disentangle him from the shifting throng. She gave his hand a quick squeeze and, before he could return the pressure, she dropped his hand and hopped up and sat on the wall. Self-conscious now, Trys made a show of trying to figure out the best way to climb up the crumbling wall.

Roxyna leaned over and smiled. "Just get up here. Do you need my hand again?"

"No, no, I can manage," spluttered Trys as he lurched forward and up and scraped his shins on the rough blocks. "Thank you, anyway," said Trys as he sat next to her on the wall. He offered a hesitant smile of his own, but she was not looking at him. She was watching the stage where the performance was already underway.

The stage occupied the space at the very front of the alcove in Hold Gate. Thus, the huge vault of the alcove's arch acted as a proscenium for the stage. Torches flared at different spots on the stage to give the actors needed light in the deep shadows of the alcove but also to illuminate the actors so they could be seen by the audience.

The penetrating tones of the actor delivering the prologue rolled out across the restless audience and soothed it. People still moved about and conversed, but they did so with more care and less noise.

At first, Trys could not see the actor who was speaking, but then he realized that a cluster of torches off to one side was designed to spotlight the speaker. In the moment he saw the actor, he also recognized the voice. It was his acquaintance from the inn in the Hold, Bledsahl. His black singlesuit was a dark shadow before the torches.

The story he told was of a young and foolish princess who, isolated in the palace, wanted to experience the reality of the marketplace. To accomplish this whim, she changed clothes with her serving girl.

Bledsahl had just reached this point in the action, when Trys became aware of a disturbance in the crowd below the wall. It rippled and shifted and complained as a short man plowed his way through it and up to the wall where Trys and Roxyna sat.

Trys looked down. There below him, his round face red with his exertions, stood Englerth.

"I do apologize most heartily, my dear friend Trys. Oh, hello, Roxyna, I see my new friend here has made your acquaintance. We were unavoidably detained. Or rather, I should say I was, since Bledsahl would shudder at the thought of partaking in the wonderful debauch of which I was a part just a short time ago. It's still going on, up there in Hold Gate. It was quite a group. Let me see, there was me, of course, and Myrsa, a special friend from the old days, you know the ones I mean, the ones we chatted about in the inn in the Hold. Those days when a certain young Consort nearly upset everything and did end up dying for his boundless love. Those days..."

A distinct cough from the stage stopped Englerth cold. He smiled sheepishly and shrugged his shoulders. "Got to be going. I'm supposed to be on stage right now."

With that, he turned and plunged through the crowd toward the stage. In a surprisingly short time, Trys could see him grab the edge of the stage and pull himself up and onto it. Bledsahl tapped his foot impatiently and fixed him with a withering look. Trys could see that Englerth said something to Bledsahl which made him stiffen. Englerth then turned to the audience and spread his hands wide in a gesture of welcome. Without a trace of embarrassment, he launched into his first speech and the crowd cheered him, drowning out his words.

"They like him," commented Trys.

"Everyone likes Englerth, except perhaps Bledsahl, and I have my doubts about him, too," said Roxyna.

Trys enjoyed the play. The gestures were overdone and the lines delivered in an overwrought manner, but that lent it a certain charm. He glanced over at Roxyna. She was smiling at the broadly done humor and he decided then and there she was really quite beautiful.

But two events occurred, the second following hard upon the heels of the first, to stop the play. First, it began to snow. Huge flakes descended in a smothering blanket. Most people simply pulled up the hoods of their singlesuits and ignored it.

The second event could not be ignored. It announced its arrival with the strident clash of metal on metal. The sound rolled down a street which opened on the square not far from the stage and grew in intensity until the actors were hard put to shout above the noise.

All eyes turned to the street. A tide of ill dressed and poorly armed men and women flowed into the huge square in front of Hold Gate. The ones in front were simply running and shouting and waving their assortment of weapons over their heads.

Behind them was a contingent which moved more slowly and did less shouting. They were too busy fighting to shout. They were led by a tall, thin man dressed in a singlesuit unique within the mob for its cleanliness. He urged them to give way slowly but to contest each foot. Despite their ragged appearance, the mob seemed to be well trained and certainly dedicated to the man who led them, for they were being pressed back by a well armed and disciplined phalanx of Ice Guards.

Roxyna leaped to her feet on the wall and the moment she saw the tall man in charge of the rabble, she cried out, "Lyrdahl!" She turned to Trys who stood up next to her. "That's Lyrdahl, the leader of the revolution. And that man in the center rank of the Ice Guards, is Lord Grendyl himself."

She pointed out a burly man with silver hair and beard who kept his head down and his blood blade slashing in a short but deadly arc. He mowed down one opponent and moved on inexorably to the next. He seemed intent upon reaching Lyrdahl who danced back and forth several rows away from the determined First Lord. Lyrdahl urged on the men and women who fought and died just in front of him, but Trys could see the sheer determination of Lord Grendyl, as much as his cutting blade, created a ripple of panic in the ill clothed ranks of the revolutionaries.

They faltered and then flowed away from the crushing advance of the Ice Guards. Lyrdahl shouted at them to stop and grabbed those within his reach to try to get them to stand up to the professional troops behind them. His words were ignored and his hands shrugged off.

As soon as he saw resistance ebbing, Lord Grendyl halted his troop and surveyed the enormous square now teeming with groups of panicky people moving this way and that in attempts to get away from the unsheathed blood blades of the Ice Guards. The revolutionaries mingled with the crowd in the square and it became difficult to discern who was an enemy and who was simply a bystander.

Roxyna swore a low oath and then began to shout at the top of her lungs. "Kill the Ice Guards! Destroy the classes! Tear down the Hold!"

Amidst the swirl of the crowd, Lyrdahl looked up at her and smiled. He then took up the chant. As if by magic, others joined in until the entire square rang with the provocative phrases. It was obvious that not only the revolutionaries who had fought the Ice Guards were chanting as hard as they could. The huge mass of people tottered on the edge of riot.

Lord Grendyl raised his face to the falling snow. The flakes whitened his beard and nose and eyes. He wiped his eyes to clear the wetness from them and looked at the surging square once again. He then raised his reddened sword and swung it toward the wall where Roxyna and Trys still stood.

Silently, the phalanx of Ice Guards advanced, a solid mass of warriors glittering with brandished blades. People closest to the oncoming warriors paused in their shouting. The Guards kept going. People turned and tried to move out of their way. The Guards kept marching. People began to shove at each other to try to get away. The Guards reached the edge of the crowd and, still without a sound, they raised their swords and began slashing.

Screams overwhelmed the chant as the square convulsed like one gigantic body cut to the quick. Two areas floated above the chaos which erupted, the wall where Trys and Roxyna perched and the stage where Englerth and Bledsahl stood. Even as panic gripped the square, Trys glanced over at the stage.

He noticed Englerth and Bledsahl had tried to carry on with the play, for they still occupied the same positions and still struck the same poses they had before being upstaged by the carnage below. At first, Bledsahl looked disgusted with the turmoil and then, when the full realization of what was occurring down there hit him, his long, thin face grew pained. He made a sad, dismissive gesture and left the stage.

Englerth danced about at the edge of the stage. As if to see which suited him best, he first chanted the revolutionary slogan and then switched over to a cheer for the Ice Guards. The sudden appearance of a rusty brum pike quivering in the stage floor inches from his feet, made him dance faster toward the back of the stage where he quickly disappeared.

Trys and Roxyna were then the only ones left standing above the chaos. Trys grabbed Roxyna's arm. She was still chanting.

"Let's get out of here!" he yelled at her above the din of the struggling crowd.

"Why?" She shouted back and grinned. He could tell she was enjoying herself.

"Because of them!" Trys pointed to the rapidly approaching troop of Ice Guards led by the determined Lord Grendyl. Trys had to believe their exposed position and Roxyna's continued defiance made an excellent objective for the murderous intent of the First Lord.

"Well, you may be right! Jump!" With that she grabbed his arm and leaped into the milling mass next to the wall. Trys half fell, half jumped after her and landed heavily on his knees. He stood up immediately and followed the swaying back of the girl as she darted through the throng.

He had just begun to think that perhaps their escape was assured when Roxyna stopped abruptly and he bumped into her.

"What is it?" he asked.

"It seems we're caught," replied Roxyna calmly.

The crowd immediately about them dissolved, leaving the two of them face to face with the scowling Lord Grendyl and half a dozen of his men. The warriors edged around them and Trys and Roxyna found their backs pressed to the wall.

"You are the one who began the chant," stated Grendyl. "You are a rebel."

"I am a member of the revolution which will topple you and your class. The revolution will right the injustices rampant in Low Hold. It will crush the oppressors..."

Trys put his hand on her shoulder. "Roxyna, settle down. Talking that way won't help..."

"Won't help who?" she spit out as she turned on him. "Won't help me? No, it won't. But I'm sick to death of helping just me. That's why I joined the revolution in the first place. Others need help. Others need freedom from the bullying of beasts like the fine Lord Grendyl who you see before you. He is one of the prime murderers from the High Hold. He and his kind have trodden us underfoot for too long!" Her voice rose as she warmed to her topic.

"Silence, you rebellious bitch," growled Grendyl. He raised his blood blade which pulsed with heat from the blood which coated it from tip to hilt. It was clear from his face he intended to cut her down and silence her forever.

It was the look which decided Trys. Even as the blade reached the top of its swing and began to descend, Trys stepped forward. He swung his left arm up and out to catch the side of the blade on his forearm and deflect the blow. He then stepped in and struck Lord Grendyl a hard blow to his stomach.

The First Lord stumbled back and crashed into his men who

had surged forward as Trys had attacked. He flailed to keep his balance and his men ducked to avoid the slashing sword still in his hand.

Without a pause, Trys turned to Roxyna and grabbed her under her arms. He heaved her up toward the top of the wall. She understood instantly and grabbed for purchase on the crumbling blocks. With a scramble, she was up and over the wall and gone.

Trys turned to face the Ice Guards. He knew he had no chance to climb the wall before they were upon him and he decided to hold them back from pursuit of Roxyna as long as he could.

Grendyl stood up and stabbed the point of his blood blade at Trys. "Take him," he gasped.

In an instant, Trys's arms were pinioned and he was slammed back hard against the wall.

Grendyl took a deep but ragged breath and stalked over to Trys. He stared intently at the young Interpreter's face.

"I know you. You are the new protege of Dwilkon. You were brought from the North by Cyln." He said it as if he did not quite understand how Trys could have two such unlikely benefactors. "You are a rebel," he then said with satisfaction, since the label wiped away all other considerations for him.

"I am not a rebel," protested Trys. "I was just visiting Low Hold when I met up with..."

"Trouble," interrupted Grendyl. "You are a prisoner who will be taken up to the Hold and interrogated."

An officer of the Ice Guard suddenly appeared out of the snow which was falling thicker by the minute. He marched up to Lord Grendyl and saluted.

Grendyl turned to him, "Report."

"The fighting is over. Most of the rebels have retreated into Hold Gate."

Lord Grendyl nodded. "Reassemble the troop and gather up the prisoners. It's not worth following the scum into their hole. They have been taught a good enough lesson for today."

He fixed Trys with one last burning look. "Let's get back up to the Hold. We have some interrogations to perform." With that he turned and strode off into the snow where he was lost to Trys's sight in a moment.

The Ice Guards yanked him forward roughly. They half led, half carried him around the end of the wall and shoved him toward a small group of men and women who were surrounded by Ice Guards with drawn swords. Trys searched the faces but he saw neither Roxyna nor Lyrdahl, the tall leader of the revolution. He felt a sense of relief.

Lord Grendyl barked an order and they set out across the

square and up toward the Hold. Trys looked back once. The snow blanketed the square, leaving white mounds to mark the bodies of the fallen. He looked up. Hold Gate was nothing more than a dark bulk rising up through the swirling snow.

## XVI

HIGH INTERPRETER Dwilkon left the corridors of the Hold with which he was familiar and glided into a region set deep in the rock of the mountain. Gone were the expansive halls, gone were the meticulously spaced torches to light the way, and gone were the smooth floors over which he usually glided so easily. He stumbled in a wide pool of shadow and only recovered his balance by thrusting out a thin hand to catch himself. The walls too were rough. He drew his hand back and ruefully examined the scrape on its heel.

He hoped that was all he would rue this day. The summons from Lord Grendyl had mentioned a matter of vast importance concerning his new Interpreter, Trys. And, given the current state of his investigations into his novice's past, he decided it was worth submitting to the overbearing Lord's demands this once. He had gained knowledge which could provide him with great power, but he needed to confirm the facts and also be sure that no one else had beat him to the discovery.

Dwilkon had entered the old holdings within the Hold. The corridors and chambers were some of the first carved out of the rock when the clans had climbed the mountain in search of warmth and life. Desperate for warmth, they had burrowed deep to tap into the heat buried within the stone. These regions belonged to First Lords and Ladies who were direct descendants of those first clan members who left the Waste behind.

Lord Grendyl's family was the first among the first and, as such, his holdings were extensive if obscure. Dwilkon began to understand just how obscure as he ventured deeper into the inner Hold. The corridor dipped and turned, rose and fell as it followed the path of least resistance through the solid rock. Dwilkon reminded himself they had only had primitive tools to cut the stone at that time, even as he bumped his head on a low part of the ceiling obscured in darkness.

He quickened his pace toward the next torch, keeping his head down slightly. It was this posture which prevented him from seeing the man who stepped suddenly into his path from a shallow alcove in the side of the corridor.

He jerked up his head and stopped. A low voice with a definite trace of amusement in it, greeted him.

"High Interpreter Dwilkon, I'm so glad you decided to come." Lord Grendyl himself stood beneath the guttering torch.

"I don't believe I have ever had the honor of visiting the old holdings before. It has been interesting so far," said Dwilkon rubbing his sore hand unobtrusively on his robe.

"I hope it will be more interesting before we're through. Follow me to a chamber where we can talk," replied Grendyl. He then turned and marched off down a much narrower corridor branching off from the main one.

Dwilkon now found he had to keep his elbows in or else they rubbed against the walls. He was silently cursing the reactionary First Lords and Ladies who would continue to live in such primitive conditions, when Grendyl slid out of sight from in front of him.

The High Interpreter paused and poked his head forward and to the left. There was his host, fists planted on hips and a grin on his face, standing in an oddly shaped chamber. He sidled through the narrow slit which was the door and approached Grendyl.

A draft of frigid air tugged at the hem of his long robe. He glanced around. Four torches fitfully illuminated the chamber. The moving air caused them to twist and flare, but even then their light did not reach into all of the corners. Dwilkon counted eleven before he gave up.

Placed as the torches were at shoulder height, they also served to accentuate the vast darkness which occupied one narrowed end of the chamber. Dwilkon looked toward the darkness. A blast of warm air surged across his face. He narrowed his eyes against the unexpected warmth and also to tried to penetrate the darkness. He could make out a few outcroppings of rock and the glint of a vein of some reflective mineral which ran out of the light and into the darkness in a jagged line, but that was all.

"This is an ancient chamber," observed Grendyl. "When it was being cut, the builders broke through the rock to discover this natural gallery." He waved his hand in the direction of the dense darkness. "It is said, there is no end to it; that it runs on forever into the heart of the mountain."

"Is it so ancient it lacks furniture?" asked Dwilkon, trying to regain any advantage he could.

Grendyl smiled. "No, of course not. Please take a chair." And with that he slid two chairs of extremely modern design out from the shadows which filled one of the many corners of the room.

Dwilkon sat down carefully but gratefully. Grendyl threw himself onto his chair. He placed a hand on either knee after adjusting the blood blade in the scabbard on his back so it would not hit the chair. He thrust his head forward and looked hard at the High Interpreter who was doing his best to look both composed and guarded at the same time.

"I called you here," announced Lord Grendyl.

"Yes, you did. And I came."

"Yes, you did," echoed Grendyl. "I must admit I'm a little surprised by that."

Dwilkon narrowed his eyes and said nothing.

"You know I have little use for Interpreters. Not as little as our Queen/Lady, but not much. But the situation being what it is..."

"What situation is that?" interrupted Dwilkon, perhaps a bit too eager for information which might serve his own pressing needs.

Grendyl leaned back slightly. "Why, the rebellion, of course. What did you think I meant?"

"Just that. The rebellion. The situation of the moment," purred Dwilkon in his best soothing voice.

"I have Trys," said the First Lord flatly. "He's under heavy guard not far from here."

"I see. Why is he being detained?"

"He has joined the rebel scum. I caught in him in the square in front of Hold Gate, associating with known rebel leaders and fomenting a riot. He even went so far as to strike me so that one of his gang could make her escape."

Dwilkon did not smile but he wanted to. "I am very sorry to hear that. However, he is a novice Interpreter and, as such, under my protection. I demand you hand him over to me or the Queen/Lady shall hear of this."

"What difference would that make?" asked Grendyl

"The Queen/Lady does not approve of your heavy handed tactics in the suppression of the revolution. You crush the innocent along with the guilty too often. She may be looking for an excuse to exile you to the Waste. Intrusion upon the jurisdiction of the Interpreters might be just the excuse she needs."

Grendyl laughed outright. "She despises the Interpreters. She would probably see it as getting rid of one more. No, you'll have to come up with something better than that."

"Or else?" asked Dwilkon.

Grendyl growled. "How is it you Interpreters always know there's something more behind a demand? Your drug twisted minds, I warrant."

Dwilkon nodded as if to say that was only the First Lord's opinion.

"I want more cooperation from you, High Interpreter. I want your help in smashing the rebellion. You know how much I hate it, even more than I hate you. I suspect you are not completely opposed to the rebels and their cause. I'm sure you have your own devious reasons for that. Well, I don't care about them. All I care about is the eradication of the rebellion."

Dwilkon smiled thinly. "Direct, as always, my Lord Grendyl."

And Lord Grendyl was also correct in his assessment of the Interpreters and their attitude toward the revolution. During the first stirrings of the nascent revolution, Dwilkon had looked upon it as an inconvenience, something which disrupted the normal order of things. But as it continued and disrupted more and took more and more time to suppress, Dwilkon had begun to think differently about it.

It bothered Lord Grendyl, that in itself was worth much to him, but it also kept him extremely busy. And if he was busy with the revolution, he did not have time to monitor the precise movements within the ranks of the Interpreters. Dwilkon had already used the lack of attention to make small shifts of power; everything from the installation of an especially observant Interpreter to tend to the religious needs of the Ice Guards to persuading certain key servants, who were devoted to their religion above all else, of certain First Lords and Ladies that a casual report now and then was in the best interests of the Rituals.

Dwilkon's thinking had now progressed so far as to toy with the heretical idea of starting a ground swell among the common people, the lower classes and even the classless, which might be used to sweep away the old divided monarchy, and all of its encrustations, and leave behind a powerful and concentrated coterie of Interpreters who could found a strong religious state upon the ashes of the old regime. Revolutionary fervor, while blind and ugly, did have its potential uses. The High Interpreter was feeling his way cautiously toward a position where he could grasp all of the reins of power in his own thin hands.

His recent unconfirmed discovery was part of his reason for even conceiving of such all encompassing ideas. It could cause a radical shift of power within the Hold and, perhaps, just perhaps, even have repercussions within the Camp. Even as he sat uncomfortably before the gruff First Lord, he held on tightly to all of the diverse threads of his plots and reassured himself he did indeed possess power, not of the sword but of the word.

That was why he decided to speak a word which might bring some pain to the Lord who faced him so belligerently within the ancient chamber. "I know, Lord Grendyl, it is the death of your son at the hands of the revolutionaries which hurts you. His cowardly murder, ambushed as he was in a narrow alley in Low Hold, not even given a chance to draw his blood blade and die like a warrior, must be a constant source of pain to you."

However, the High Interpreter had not reckoned with the reaction which his words would have. His face a mask of contorted shadows, Grendyl stood and drew his blood blade from its back sheath in one fluid movement. The sword hung in the air over the narrow skull of Dwilkon.

His eyes locked upon the burning eyes of the old First Lord, Dwilkon surreptitiously loosened a poisoned dart from its sheath strapped to his arm within the bulky sleeve of his robe. He judged he would have just enough time to impale the throat of the warrior before the edge of the blood blade sliced through his skull. It was not a judgement he reveled in, but he had lived long enough within the violent world of the Hold's plots and counterplots to accept his end when it came.

It was not to come that day. Grendyl swung his blade to one side and lowered it carefully until its point touched the floor of the chamber with a light ping. As the rush of anger left him, he seemed to be aware his adversary would have a defense of some sort and he did not want to leave any excuse for its use.

"Cruel, as always, High Interpreter Dwilkon." Grendyl took two short steps backward and sat down heavily on the chair. It creaked but held. His blood blade remained naked in his hand. The point scraped along the floor as he dragged it closer to him.

"You know how to touch a man in his most vulnerable place, High Interpreter. I despise you for that, and admire you at the same time. But I have my own form of strength and I am using my greatest weakness to fortify it. Yes, I loved my son. I still grieve for his death. And to help me, I have focussed all of my energy and strength on the destruction of the rebellion. Now, I am demanding cooperation from you. I hold one of your Interpreters. He appears to be a rebel. I will make as much of that as I can and force you to help me."

Grendyl raised the point of his blade off the floor to emphasize his last statement. Dwilkon watched the deadly tip of metal rise, waver about, and then settle again before he answered.

"I believe Trys might be much more important than merely an Interpreter turned revolutionary," he said in carefully measured tones. He paused.

The First Lord shifted forward. "What do you mean?" Doubt was evident in his voice, but his curiosity was piqued.

"Perhaps one son may make up for the loss of another son," replied Dwilkon. He kept his face blank and watched the reaction his words had upon Grendyl.

They seemed to confuse him. "What Interpreter mumbo-jumbo are you spouting now? Say it clear and straight."

"Yes, I suppose it is time for such talk. Very well, then. I am in the process of searching for absolute proof that Trys is the child of the Queen/Lady Alisande, the child who everyone believed was stillborn."

Grendyl frowned and then burst out laughing. But his laughter stopped suddenly after a moment of thought. He stood up and shoved back the chair. He began to pace about the chamber, his sword held lightly in his hand, as if it were nothing more than a stick.

"The son of Alisande and the Consort Gerred. That would make him..."

"A legitimate heir to the half throne of Nordseth," Dwilkon finished his sentence for him.

"Why just Nordseth's half? Even though he has been dying for decades, he is still very much alive and very much in control. You are an Interpreter. Is there anything in the Chronicles of Blood which demand a Queen/Lady to sit upon one half throne and a King/Lord upon the other?"

"My dear Lord Grendyl, you do have a devious turn of mind yourself. I am delving deep into the Chronicles to research that precise point."

Grendyl stopped pacing and stabbed his blade at Dwilkon, but merely to emphasize his point. "I want to destroy the rebellion. That is my one overarching goal. Alisande has shown she is unwilling to let me do what is necessary to obliterate the rebellion. I do not like devious means, but I am willing to use any means to achieve that goal."

"Of course. I understand," murmured Dwilkon.

"It pains me to even talk of betraying my Queen/Lady, but something must be done or there will be no half throne left within the Hold. The rebel scum will rule in their own perverse way," continued Grendyl.

Dwilkon let him talk. He wanted the First Lord to convince himself that this new development might be useful to him, for he did not want him as an enemy. A neutral Grendyl, or better yet, one who was a grudging ally, would help along Dwilkon's schemes immeasurably.

"It is not truly betrayal. My first duty is to the Hold and to the Rituals. Alisande is merely a person who rules for a time and then dies. Ancient principles are at stake here. They rule us. The Queen/Lady, or King/Lord, are merely representatives."

Dwilkon could tell his mind was made up. "You are absolutely correct, my Lord Grendyl. We are merely instruments of much larger forces, and we must obey them," he purred convincingly.

Grendyl raised his blood blade before him and slashed the air to left and right. "What is the next step?"

"Ah, first, I must determine beyond a reasonable doubt that Trys is indeed Alisande's son. My informants are busy at work on that right now. We must make sure Trys remains within your grasp. We cannot afford to lose him now."

Grendyl tipped his blade over his shoulder and slammed it hard into his back scabbard. "That might not be too easy."

Dwilkon jerked his head up. "What do you mean?"

"The Queen/Lady has decided to interrogate him herself. I received the order just before you arrived. Depending on what she finds out, she might decide to let him go or take him under her custody."

Dwilkon saw their chances wither before him. "Curse her interference. She could spoil everything."

"Everything may be spoiled if he is indeed a true rebel. If he was just caught up in the excitement of the moment and has no particular feelings for the scum, then she might see that and release him. If he is a rebel and she perceives him as a threat to her vision of what the Hold ought to be, then she might detain him within the royal prison. I'm afraid it all depends on her."

"Upon her and Cyln," pointed out Dwilkon. "She relies very heavily upon her bodyguard. And Cyln has been ordered to the other side of the Hold to look into the escalating revolutionary violence among the docks. I think we may be in luck. With Cyln not at her side, she is more likely to be lenient than otherwise. We must trust he will be released so we can shadow his every move."

"Agreed," said Grendyl. "Between the two of us there is no corner of the Hold into which he can crawl where we can't follow." He paused then and looked hard at Dwilkon who still sat in his chair. "I have made an unholy pact here, High Interpreter. I have done it for a greater purpose. I will honor my end of the agreement, see to it you honor yours."

Dwilkon smiled thinly and nodded. "The 'or else' is not even needed. I believe we understand each other completely. It will be a pleasure to work with you instead of against you, my Lord Grendyl. I have always admired your power and your methods of using it."

"Well, I can't say the same for you," growled Grendyl. "But I'll put aside my personal distaste for now. Just remember, this will not last forever."

"Indeed, what does?" said Dwilkon as he stood in one fluid motion. "Now, if you will direct me back to the more civilized portions of the Hold, I will get to work."

Grendyl chuckled and waved the High Interpreter toward the door of the multiple cornered room. Dwilkon swept out. Grendyl took a deep breath and gazed off into the thick, warm darkness that was said to go on forever. He shook his head once, squared his shoulders, and followed him out.

## XVII

SHOUTS OF anger mingled with the clash of metal and rolled across the water cut grid of the royal Hold Docks. The sound tried to fill the huge basin which contained the complex system of main and branch canals, but it dwindled and died out among the squat structures of the warehouses.

From where she stood at the second story window of a warehouse perched on the edge of the main canal, Cyln could see, and more importantly on that day, hear what was going on within the wide basin. Laid out before her was the system of cunningly cut canals which allowed boats from the River Ice to sail right up to the warehouses where their cargoes were either unloaded or picked up.

The royal Docks occupied the floor of the natural basin at the base of the mountain on the side opposite to that of Hold Gate. Goods and supplies from both North and south flowed through the docks, keeping the Hold well stocked and affluent. It was the key to its wealth and well being.

But the noises which echoed through the basin on that day told of a threat to that well being. The revolution had come to the Hold Docks; that was why Cyln was there. Not as an overt representative of the Queen/Lady, but rather as a secret agent. An enemy who gained control of the Docks would have a stranglehold upon the Hold's life line of supplies. She had come to assess the situation and do what she could to prevent just such an event from taking place. To that end, she was posing as a Northern trader in brum furs.

Cyln strained to hear the progress of the crowd of revolutionaries as it wound its way among the canals of the Docks, crossing the bridges of roughly hewn stone and pouring along the main thoroughfares of the basin. The sounds subsided for a moment and that was when Cyln realized the merchant in the room behind her, the one she was supposed to be selling her brum furs to, had been talking to her for some time.

"I say, these are very fine brum furs. Thick and rich. I particularly like the blue tips on the head fur. That means you must have acquired these from the upper reaches of the Northern Range. From the Brumkysh clan perhaps, or the Brumruhl. Only they hunt such brutes and in such quantity. They are spectacular hunters, don't you think?"

"Ah, yes, right," answered Cyln, trying to suppress the petulance in her voice. Her anger came from the fact she was trying to hear where the mob was headed for next and from the fact her clan pride was touched by the babbling of the merchant. The Brumruhl as spectacular hunters? Absurd.

"Well, I, Lon myr Pyta pyr Ghyn, have seen thousands, perhaps millions of furs in my day, which has been a long one after all, and these are easily among the best. Now all we have to do is arrive at a price which will delight both of us."

A harder edge could be heard in his voice as he said this and if Cyln had looked around, she would have seen him sizing her up yet again. He knew she was no Northern trader in brum furs, based upon the way she presented the furs to him to paw over and the way she held herself erect, as if every second she were aware of the clean line of her blood blade which lay along her back.

When she did not answer immediately, he went on. "Now you can ask anyone on the Docks about old Lon. And anyone will tell you he gives a good price, more than fair usually, and everyone walks away from one of my deals with a sense of accomplishment. I've finished examining the wares and I'm thinking of a price just now which should send both of us home happier than when we left it. At least I know I will, since I left it in a bad mood this morning. A shipment of bryl meat for which I gave a very fair price the day before turned out to be rotten. The owner of the boat which transported it out of the North didn't pack the ice around it properly. He left big gaps down under where the meat just didn't stay cold enough. I should have known, he was young, but one wants to give the young their chance too. Headstrong and stupid, I'm afraid. Him, not me. Possibly even involved with this revolution, as well. I mean, it seems pretty ridiculous to me, but it does have its points. Points which even an old merchant like me can see and appreciate."

Cyln turned to the merchant at that and asked a question with a very un-trader-like edge to her voice. "What do you know about the revolution?"

Lon spread his hands wide in a noncommittal gesture and answered with a question. "There is no time for such things as revolutions in the Waste, is there?"

Cyln turned from the window to face the merchant. He was of average height but slightly stout, which made him seem shorter to Cyln than he really was. The brightness of his eyes also contributed to the slight air of deception which seemed to hang about him, as if he were trying very hard to project a sense he was alert but not too smart. Cyln was excellent at sizing up an opponent when he came at her with a drawn blood blade in hand. But this merchant confounded her abilities to find his strengths and weaknesses.

"In the Waste, the struggle for survival dictates what is and what is not important."

"Succinctly put," said Lon. "I have traveled far and wide, North and south, and I must say that towns do strange things to people and cities even stranger things."

"This rebellion seems like utter stupidity to me," said Cyln. "Why are those people wasting their time and even putting their lives in jeopardy?"

Lon's eyes brightened even more for a moment and he moved to stand next to her at the window. The noise of conflict drifted over the main canal as the mob surged through the streets. Cyln caught a glimpse of the throng as it flowed across a distant intersection visible from the warehouse window.

Lon glanced behind him and even took a quick look out of the window before he spoke again. "It is a revolution, not a rebellion. There is a difference. Would you like something other than money for your furs?"

Cyln raised her head and glared down at him.

He smiled a dark little smile and shook his head. "Nothing illegal, just information. You seem to be interested in what is going on out there. I might have something to tell you about what is happening, and why it is happening."

"Fine, as long as it costs me nothing," said Cyln, trying hard to act the part of the trader driving a tough bargain.

"It will cost you nothing in the coin of the realm. There are other costs, much less tangible."

"I'm willing to pay, whatever the cost."

"Good. Good. The price might be a change in your attitude toward the 'utter stupidity' out there," said Lon. "Some people find that too high a price." He moved up to the window and placed both his hands on the sill. He listened for a moment to the turmoil sweeping through the streets.

"That noise is the revolution. It is the sound of people awakening to the inequalities which have been perpetuated for centuries. Only now are people beginning to realize it may not have to go on forever. It's the sound of anger. Not anger with outright oppression, although there is enough of that to go around, but rather anger born of disgust with a system which has ground slowly but surely over generations since the Hold has been occupied. There were no classless before the Hold. In the Waste everyone has a place and a use, however small it may be. In the Hold everyone has certain material advantages, adequate levels of heat, for instance, at least relative to the middle of the Waste, but not everyone has the same dignities afforded them. Certain classes of people were dropped out of the system because they were not needed. Their skills were unnecessary and soon they lost even those, until the classless of today are truly without status and without use in the society of the Hold. The Hold gives and the Hold takes away. The people out there are merely trying to regain some of their dignity, some of their usefulness, some reason for their existence. You would fight for that, wouldn't you?"

He turned to Cyln with his eyes glowing. She looked him straight in the eyes and knew, while he seemed an unlikely revolutionary, he was a true one.

"Yes, I would. I feel like I hover about on the edge of uselessness myself sometimes." She smiled ruefully to herself as she thought of her constantly confounding position as bodyguard to the Queen/Lady. But then she asked a question to try to catch the merchant off guard. "But why are you willing to fight for that? You are not classless."

"My mother was only one class above the classless. She married into my father's class, but it was never the same. The imprint of banishment was there. Before she died she told me how it had been. I decided it was worth struggling in my own small way to end that type of existence. And besides," here he smiled and folded his hands together, "it's good business. The more people with a recognized social status, the more people with recognizable money to spend."

It was evident now to Cyln that the revolution was not merely a rabble of zealots eager for instant change. It impressed her more than she had anticipated. Life in the Waste was necessarily a blend of the communal and the dictatorial. All had to pull to together to survive under the direction of a solid leader who could make and enforce decisions rapidly for the good of the entire clan. If the revolution had formed itself into such an entity, it was a force to be reckoned with.

Cries from the streets reached them at the second story window. Cyln could not make out the individual words but recognized the tones of frustration and anger. "I want to go down and see the revolution close up," she said.

He nodded slowly as if gauging the results of such an action. "Yes, you should see it close up. I trust you can use that blade at your back?"

Cyln grinned and flexed fingers which were eager for the feel of the hilt. "This blade has saved my life many times in the Waste."

"Let's hope it serves you as well in the no less wild Hold."

"Yes, let's hope," muttered Cyln.

They left the warehouse, with Lon leading the way, and turned down the main street which ran along the main canal upon which the warehouse sat. The noise from the crowd grew as they neared the intersection of another large street. The street which crossed the one they were on went over a wide bridge which spanned the main canal.

With her practiced warrior's eye, Cyln noted the bridge was one of the newer ones and as such possessed certain embellishments. Along with the fancy scrollwork carved into the stone along its sides, it also had nooks every dozen yards. These created small balconies from which one could step out of the main flow of traffic on the bridge and view the waters of the canal below.

A shout and then a steady chant announced the approach of the crowd as it turned a corner and flowed into the street along the main canal. The ill clad and ill armed men and women reached the end of the bridge where Cyln and Lon stood and stopped. They filled up the intersection and milled about. To avoid being shoved and to gain some protection should the crowd turn nasty, Cyln tugged on the sleeve of Lon's singlesuit and drew him into the first nook on the bridge. She reasoned that there at least an enemy could only come at her from one direction.

Lon seemed preoccupied and kept scanning the crowd. Cyln was about to ask him if he was looking for someone in particular, when a man emerged from the mob and climbed onto the top of a low column which marked the end of the bridge. He raised his hands for silence and got a relatively good imitation of it for a crowd so large.

Lon leaned over to Cyln. "Now you will hear some of what the revolution is about."

Cyln nodded and watched the man wave his arms about. His singlesuit was old and a couple of sizes too large for him, so the ragged sleeves slid back to reveal his thin arms.

"The weight of the Hold lies upon our backs!" A cheer went up. "They take from us and give us nothing in return!" Another cheer a little louder. "We are useful! We are important! We are people!" He screamed the last and a cheer surged into a shout of defiance from the mob.

"We are winning the war, my friends!" shouted the man as the cheer trailed off. "The Hold Docks are nearly ours; nearly yours! Hold Gate is a bastion of the revolution and the square before it the first true territory of the classless! We have taken it back as we shall take the rest of the Hold! The upper classes will not stop us! They cannot stop us! The Interpreters pretend to be our friends! Beware of friends in high places, I say! We must stay together and forge ahead! Our strength is in numbers and in being right! Nothing can stop us! Nothing!" The man's voice cracked on the last word.

The mob screamed back and began to mill about as if eager to put their newly discovered power to the test. A movement from the other side of the bridge caught Cyln's eye. She turned to look. A troop of Ice Guards in tight formation marched toward the end of the bridge on the other side of the main canal.

Cyln saw the captain of the troop signal for his men to prepare their weapons and move forward at a double quick march. She glanced back at the speaker on the end of the bridge. From his elevated position, he too could see the oncoming Ice Guards.

"We are about to be attacked! The arrogant and brutal Ice Guards approach even now! What are we going to do?"

A loud mutter arose from the mob but no clear words emerged until three men who stood at the base of the column on which the speaker stood shouted out, "Resist!"

Instantly, the mob took up the cry. "Resist!" boomed forth and echoed across the waters of the canal.

The man bent down and spoke to the three men at his feet. They nodded and fanned out into the crowd, issuing instructions as they moved.

The Ice Guards swept past Cyln and Lon where they stood within the nook upon the bridge. Cyln did not know the captain, but he was young and appeared to be eager for battle. As an experienced warrior, she did not like that combination.

With the captain in the lead, the first warriors crossed the bridge and charged into the intersection. The mob dissolved in front of them like snow upon the hot side of the mountain of the Hold. They continued their charge, maintaining their formation with textbook precision, until the entire troop was off the bridge.

The captain then halted his troop. It was either that or continue the charge right into the canal on the other side of the main street across from the bridge. He looked around, puzzled at the lack of resistance from the mob and their continued presence.

Cyln turned to Lon. "Dissolve and fight, that's the pattern, isn't it?"

Lon nodded. "It has proven to be a very effective method of street fighting. Also, note there is no single leader of this throng, but rather squads of leaders which vary from day to day so no one man or woman can be captured and accused of traitorous acts."

The chant of "Resist," suddenly stopped. A deep silence filled the intersection even though it was crammed with hundreds of men and women. Cyln saw the young captain size up the situation. He turned to face his men and rapped out in a clear, firm voice. "Ice Guards, form square!"

In obedience, the warriors shuffled about until they formed two concentric squares. The men in the outer square left some space between each other to allow the ones in the inner square to be able to reach forward and past them to give them support as needed. Cyln silently applauded the maneuver, even though she knew they would be hard pressed to hold back the overwhelming numbers which surrounded them.

The mob seemed fascinated by the maneuver. It paused and allowed the warriors to dress their ranks, as if acknowledging it was only honorable that the foe should be prepared for the attack.

The captain then raised his sword in a salute to the mob, as if to let them know they were ready. Cyln found it absurd, yet heroic.

His salute was the signal for the onslaught. With one savage scream wrenched from hundreds of throats, the mob launched itself upon the Ice Guards.

The blood blades of the troop slashed forward to meet the attack. The front rank of the mob fell like broken sticks. But others behind them pushed them down and kept on coming.

In the close quarters, the blood blades of the Guards were not very effective. Each warrior needed room to swing it to use it properly, and room was one thing they did not possess. The knives and broken off brum pikes of the mob were better suited for the short stabs which took out Ice Guard after Ice Guard.

The square held at first but then contracted to close up the empty spaces left behind by the falling of warrior after warrior. Soon there was only one rank and they were nearly shoulder to shoulder. The young captain seemed to be everywhere, closing up a gaping hole here and cutting down a revolutionary who somehow got past the flailing blades there.

Cyln watched, her hand itching to draw her own blade and help out the beleaguered Ice Guards. Generally, she had little use for the warriors she perceived as sloppy and unskilled, but what she saw that day gave her new respect for some of them at least.

It was because she was watching the battle in the intersection so closely that she missed the first signal from Lon to a group of seven men who kept to the back of the mob and near to the end of the bridge. While they were as raggedly dressed as the rest of the people in the mob, they did carry well maintained blood blades and daggers.

When they all turned in her direction, Cyln darted a quick glance at Lon who was just completing a nod to them. Realizing he had been discovered, the merchant stepped to one side and out of the confining walls of the nook.

"What is this, merchant?" snarled Cyln

"It's the revolution," replied Lon. "She's the one! She's the Queen/Lady's own!" he shouted to the seven advancing men.

"Damn you," she hissed even as she drew her blood blade and took two steps backward to place herself just within the nook on the bridge. A quick look told her it was narrow enough to force her opponents to come at her only two at a time. She knew she could handle those odds.

She brought her sword up before her and slashed left and then right. The familiar balance of the blade reassured her. She had not fought for some time. She gave a little grin which made the first two approaching her frown and hesitate for a moment.

"I'm ready anytime you are," said Cyln.

The two nodded, thoroughly confused by this too willing adversary. They glanced at each other and then both lunged forward, trying to time their thrusts precisely. The man on Cyln's left was a bit quicker though, and she flashed her blade left to deflect his blade and then high and to the right to parry the other incoming sword.

The man on her left tried to slide in low to skewer her. But she neatly finished the parry on the right and swung her sword about in time to stop the thrust. A lightening fast backhanded stroke followed and the man sank back against the wall of the bridge, his throat pumping blood.

The man on her right hesitated at the sight. That was a mistake. Cyln coolly beat aside his blade with two hard slashes and thrust him cleanly through the heart. He stumbled back out on to the open bridge before he went down.

His blood formed a pool on the bridge which the others could not entirely avoid. Two more went in, cautious of the blood underfoot and the killing blade in the hands of their adversary. Cyln kept her head down to watch the nuances of movement of the two now opposing her. She let them come. She fended off their searching blades with a skirl of metal on metal and then drove them each back a step with rapid, probing thrusts.

They attacked again, and again retreated before her savage repulse. But this time, the one on her right clutched a long gash on his sword arm even as the hilt of his sword dropped from the nerveless hand.

Cyln looked up and grinned, as the heat from her blood blade warmed her face. It felt good to practice her trade once again. She then settled into a battle rhythm which tested the capabilities and weaknesses of her foes since she knew that none of them would make any unnecessary mistakes now that they had seen a display of her skills. She made long clean strokes to save her energy and let the walls of the nook protect her flanks as much as they could.

Meanwhile, the troop of Ice Guards remained bogged down in the morass of revolutionaries in the intersection. The mob kept pressing them but did not try to overwhelm them, seemingly held back by the dogged determination of the Guards whose swords rose and fell in a deadly, repetitive pattern.

And then, just as suddenly as it began, it was over. The mob dissolved like snow before an overheated blood blade. Even as they retreated, the Ice Guards left in the decimated ranks continued to swing their blades, not quite believing their clamoring foes were actually going for good.

The young captain, a cut down one side of his face which created a half mask of drying blood, shook his head as if to clear it. He told his men to stand at ease. Some fell down, others leaned wearily on the hilts of their swords. He looked about at the heaps of dead before him. They were mostly bodies of revolutionaries but there were many of his own troops mingled with the carnage. He then gave orders to reassemble the remnants of the troop and prepare to march back to quarters.

The mob flowed down the main street or across the bridge. Cyln saw them going from where she still slashed and cut and parried. The rapid departure also made her attackers hesitate. With the mass of angry people at their backs, they had felt stronger, assured of help if it was needed. As the crowd dissolved, so too did their determination to overcome the wild warrior who had killed so many of them. They paused.

Cyln did not. Yelling, she charged the remaining attackers. The heat of her blade flashed past her face once, twice, three times and another opponent crumpled to the pavement of the bridge, his chest open and bleeding. The three remaining danced backward and held their blades out stiffly before them to fend off the mad attack.

As Cyln left the protection of the nook, she saw Lon standing to her right, higher up along the bridge. She changed her direction in a split second and lunged toward him. He turned to run, but she caught the hood of his singlesuit and yanked him back.

Her blade flashed to his throat. He winced from the heat which beat into his face. "Call off your men or you die," she rasped out.

He straightened up then and looked at her with a mixture of defiance and resignation on his face. "You will not kill me," he said quietly.

She nearly laughed hysterically at that. She was not one for gratuitous revenge but his betrayal of her angered her beyond measure. "Oh, don't be so sure of that, traitor."

"No, you won't because they will." He then nodded toward the three men.

Cyln spun about to get her sword in front of her even as the three lunged as one. But she had nothing to parry. The points of the three blades found their target in Lon's chest at the same instant.

He was rammed back hard into her. She stumbled back against the low wall of the bridge. With a heave she straightened up the slumping merchant and raised her blade. They were gone. The last one reached the crest of the bridge and disappeared. She glanced in the other direction. In the intersection below, the Ice Guards picked over the heaps for their dead. Otherwise, the entire area was empty and silent.

She jerked the merchant back against the wall and lowered her blade, although she kept glancing around to make sure there were not any last minute assassins lurking anywhere close by. Lon slid down the wall until he sat with his legs straight out before him and his arms limp at his sides.

In a voice surprisingly clear and strong, he spoke. "You see, this is the revolution. I was informed you were Cyln, bodyguard to the Queen/Lady Alisande, and told to have you killed. I don't look much like a revolutionary, do I?" He did not wait for an answer. "But I guess, I am. Or rather, was. I surprised myself, quite frankly. I didn't think I had it in me. Profits of money were once all I craved. Now, just now, I realize there are other profits to be made. And I have made them."

He stared straight at her and smiled. Blood gurgled from the smile and he slumped over dead.

Cyln stood up and straightened her back. She looked down at the crumpled figure before her and at her blade which radiated heat like a furnace. She carefully wiped off the blood and slid the blade into her back sheath. There was much more to the revolution than she had imagined. She would have to think long and hard about the ideas which drove men like Lon to become something they did not seem to be.

She then turned and walked toward the Ice Guards. She would see if she could help them regroup and get back to the Hold. They had both taken a beating at the hands of the revolution that day, and both needed all the help they could get.

## XVIII

THE MOUNTAIN talked to the Queen/Lady. It muttered and moaned, coaxed and cried. But Alisande could never quite make out what it said. It only talked to her in one place; within the Chamber of Judgement. The Chamber was a special place set aside for the hearing of grievances and the dispensing of judgments which, in the best tradition of the ancient Waste ways, were tempered by mercy.

The Chamber was made from a knife-like fissure which ran from very near the top of the mountain to about halfway down the upper slope. During the centuries in which the volcano had erupted and shuddered its sides downward, the fissure had remained intact, as if this ancient wound in the side of the mountain was inviolate from further destruction.

At its top, it was open to the wind which blew constantly across the mountain. The sound varied depending upon the strength of the wind, but it most often sounded like the cry of a lost soul filtering down to the occupants of the chamber. In ancient times, it had been used to impress the superstitious and to give the monarch a greater sense of power within the room.

Alisande had never used the chamber to cow anyone. She used it to dispense justice as she saw fit. For that reason, she heard the cry as the plea of the thousands who asked for mercy and were granted it.

On a day of intermittent wind and sporadic sun, she sat alone in the chamber waiting for the arrival of the young Interpreter. The starts and stops of the wind far above created a veritable symphony of sounds, accompanied by flashes of sunlight which managed to follow the wind down into the fissure now and then. It pleaded one moment and crooned softly and secretly the next. It was a day on which Alisande truly felt the mountain was trying to say something to her. But, as always, she could not quite make out what.

As was her practice, she sat alone on the low throne in the Chamber. She preferred to face the person brought before her without the distractions which retainers were bound to create. It was one of the few times she could be truly alone within the Hold and she relished the comparative solitude.

The low throne, carved out of an outcropping at one end of the fissure itself, was strangely comfortable. It fit each curve of her body as if it had been carved with only her in mind, even though it had been hacked out of the stone centuries ago by some unknown stonecarver. She snuggled back in its expansive embrace and considered the interview about to begin.

The young novice Interpreter Trys, the one Cyln had brought down from the North, was to be brought before her. He was accused of being a rebel by Lord Grendyl. Normally, such an accusation would not have been brought before her. Lord Grendyl was swift and unrelenting in his dealings with the rebels.

But Trys was a special case. For one thing, he had been brought to the Hold by Cyln. Just then, Cyln was on the other side of the Hold dealing with the revolutionary activities at the Hold Docks. Alisande felt she owed it to Cyln to stall any decision about his fate until she could return and advise her concerning the matter.

Alisande also felt the young Interpreter was somehow special, both to Grendyl and High Interpreter Dwilkon. Grendyl had mentioned his treasonous acts, but had done so in a gruff and offhanded way as if he did not want to execute Trys out of hand. And, as expected, Dwilkon had protested the detention of someone he declared to be under his jurisdiction. He had demanded his release, but in a curiously strident manner which made Alisande question his motives. Why did she get the sense the two bitter enemies were somehow in agreement in wanting the novice Interpreter to go free?

Through long hard experience, she had learned to trust her intuition. It told her now to talk to the Interpreter but to keep him imprisoned until Cyln could return, perhaps for his own good as much as for hers.

Far above on the top of the mountain, the wind paused. It was silent in the fissure. Alisande could clearly hear the clattering approach of the Ice Guards with their prisoner. They stopped just outside of the chamber. She sat up straight in the low throne and composed her features to resemble one of the masks which she wore during Rituals. This one was a stern face; the face of a monarch dispensing justice.

A spear shaft tapped three times on the stone floor just outside the door of the chamber. Alisande took a deep breath and spoke. "Enter!"

The door scraped open and one person entered. She could tell by his footsteps that he paused at first but then proceeded resolutely along the narrow length of the fissure room. He could not see the throne from the door since the fissure bent twice before opening up at her end. He is brave, she thought, it takes bravery to walk so resolutely toward your fate.

Just as he turned the last bend, the wind picked up again on the mountain. It gusted down the knife cut of the fissure with enough force to stir the stiff brocade of the Queen/Lady's complicated gown. It boomed in the chamber as it hit bottom and swirled upward.

Trys looked about him even as he strode forward. Alisande could see he was more curious than frightened. She liked that.

While the light of the sun did sometimes reach the bottom of the fissure, the low throne was set under an overhang of rock so it was always in shadow. However, the floor immediately in front of it was directly beneath the widest point of the cut in the rock. Like the wind, the bright light flashing mysteriously from above often proved intimidating to the men and women who stood before the throne.

Trys stepped confidently into the pool of brightening light and stopped. It blinded him for a second, coming as he did from the torch lit corridors of the Hold. Not sure what lay beyond the circle of intense light, he decided it would be best to wait until his eyes adjusted to the brightness or he received other instructions.

He shaded his eyes with one hand and squinted. He could then make out the low throne before him and the figure sitting in it. He bowed deeply and remained that way until the Queen/Lady spoke.

"You may stand up straight. I prefer to see your face."

"As you wish, my Queen/Lady," Trys murmured as he straightened up and even raised his face slightly so the full force of the light from above illuminated it.

A cloud scudded across the sun and a shadow darkened the bottom of the fissure for a moment. In that moment, Trys could clearly see the stiffly held figure of the Queen/Lady upon her throne. She contemplated him with interest, but not anger. He realized he had no reason to fear her. In fact, she looked upon him just then with an expression approaching sadness. But the cloud passed and the light returned and she was no more than a darker shadow among shadows.

"Interpreter Trys, certain charges have been brought against you," said the Queen/Lady in a matter of fact way. There was the rustle of bryl hide parchment in the shadows. "I will read them out to you so you understand your precise position."

She paused. Trys was not certain whether she wanted him to respond or whether she was just finding her place on the parchment, so he nodded and then said, "I understand."

"You were detained at the sight of a riot during the course of which five Ice Guards were killed and fourteen injured. You were discovered consorting with a known revolutionary. You offered physical harm to First Lord Grendyl pyr Tal myr Joryth as he was carrying out his duties to his Queen/Lady." The parchment rustled as it settled into her lap. "In and of themselves, each charge is relatively minor. Together they point toward what appears to be a calculated plan of treason. How do you answer these charges?"

Thin cloud cover rolled across the face of the sun far above the mountain. The sunlight in the fissure dimmed but did not go out entirely. It allowed Trys to see the Queen/Lady where she sat upon her throne. It appeared to him she leaned forward with some expectation and interest.

"Most gracious Queen/Lady Alisande, I answer the charges in this way. I did not plan to be at the center of the riot. Riots happen and I was caught up in it like many others. From my observations, I must say it appeared to me the Ice Guards were as much at fault for the violence which ensued as any so-called 'revolutionaries.' They were the ones who charged into the square with drawn weapons and in attack formation. I had no idea the woman I was with was a 'known revolutionary.' While she did hold very firm opinions on certain social issues, I was not aware that holding such opinions was a crime. But then, I have just come from the North where such things are not a crime. I do freely admit I did strike Lord Grendyl, but only after he had threatened my companion with his blood blade. She was unarmed and not threatening anyone, unless her tongue could be classified as a dangerous weapon. I must admit she was very free with it and it did possess a definite edge." He stopped.

Alisande smiled at his answers and the manner in which they were delivered. He was brave and held onto his convictions, which was very different from most of the people who were willing to crawl before her in this chamber hoping to preserve their life and liberty.

"Just as a matter of clarification. Where did you hit Lord Grendyl?"

"In the stomach, my Queen/Lady."

"Hard?"

"Hard enough to knock him off balance and to give my companion time to leave the scene of the riot."

"Ah, so you also aided and abetted the escape of a known revolutionary," observed the Queen/Lady.

"If you wish to call her that, then, yes, I did. I see it as performing an honorable action. In the North, armed men do not attack unarmed women," retorted Trys with some heat in his voice.

"This is not the North," said Alisande with some resignation in her voice. "The laws of the Hold apply here and the security of the Hold is at stake. I find I must detain you for the time being. I need to consider what punishment, if any, will be meted out."

"I understand," replied Trys.

"Thank you. Usually, the people who appear before me in this chamber are not so flexible."

"I believe that." He stared hard at her then and clenched his fists at his sides.

"Do you wish to say something more?"

"Yes, I do. I just want to say I understand much better now why the classless have created the revolution. You were not in the square. You did not see the oppression of the Ice Guards. You did not see the oppression of everyday existence for so many people in Low Hold. I know laws must exist. I am an Interpreter. But as an Interpreter, I do my best to take each Ritual and to interpret it with as much mercy as I can. I have seen precious little mercy here in the Hold. Why do you not dispense more mercy and less justice?"

Alisande watched the anger and frustration move across his young face in the sunlight. Another cloud dimmed her view for a moment but could not dim the intensity of the feelings emanating from the young man who stood before her.

"I ask myself that everyday. And everyday, I discover I am just as much a victim as you are," said the Queen/Lady quietly. "I may have the title of Queen/Lady of the Hold, ruler of the half kingdom, but I am held in the iron grip of the Rituals. You, at least, may bend them to a certain extent. I must live with them and by them."

Trys bowed his head. "I'm sorry, my Queen/Lady. My anger got the best of me."

"Yes, I know," she said. "And it is admirable that strong emotions can still be expressed somewhere in the Hold. Tell me, do you believe the revolution is right?"

Trys raised his head and tried to see the Queen/Lady's face. He knew he had to be careful about answering questions like that. But in the backwash of the sunlight, he could see her leaning forward and he could tell she wanted an honest answer. So, even if it was risky, he decided to give her one.

"The revolution is necessary, but not necessarily right. The oppression of Hold and Ritual is crushing the people at the bottom, the people of Low Hold. They have nothing left to lose. I realize now that that is the time when people will stand up and fight to survive. Survival in the Waste is a daily struggle. Survival in Low Hold is quickly approaching that."

"I see," said the Queen/Lady.

In that moment, the light full upon his upraised features, she thought she caught a glimpse of herself as she used to be, strong and defiant. It passed in an instant but left behind it a disturbing sense of connectedness to the young Interpreter. She wanted to ascribe it merely to her appreciation of his fervent stand against the mindlessness of the established order, something to which she had once been more committed herself. But it was more visceral, and it brought back a wave of old memories which still pained her. In that moment, she hated what she had become and mourned the passing of younger and more fervent passions.

The light went out then in the Chamber of Judgement and the moan of the wind returned. Alisande raised her head and listened. A storm had moved in from the Waste. She could tell by the sustained scream of the wind and the few flakes of snow which managed to find their way down the fissure to fall and melt on the bare head of the young Interpreter.

With the departure of the soft light from above and the return of the cruel wind, Alisande found herself snapping back into her official mode. She pushed away the memories and raised the mask once more.

"I see."

When she said it this time, it was dismissive and Trys wondered if he had ever seen a sign of sympathy from the figure upon the throne. He felt he had made a big mistake in expressing himself so openly, but it could not be helped now. He sighed and straightened up to face what was to come.

In her best official voice, she said, "You will be placed in a detention cell until such time as I decide what is to be done with you. Do you understand?"

"Yes."

"Very well. You are dismissed. The Ice Guards at the entrance to the Chamber will escort you to your cell."

Trys turned without another word and left the Chamber. Alisande sat still upon the low throne and listened to the barrage of wind and snow which battered at the mountain. The mountain cried out to her, but she still could not make out what it said.

## XIX

TRYS'S PRISON cell was palatial. Brum fur covered both the floor and the walls up to a height of five feet. Ornate cressets fixed to the wall just above the fur provided a soft and consistent light. The cell was kept at a very comfortable temperature by a small but efficient fireplace. A sleeping couch of antique and sumptuous design, several well padded chairs, and a finely wrought tapestry which covered fully half of the curved wall in the cylindrical room, created a charm which might have lulled Trys into a sense of false security if he had not been so recently introduced into the room.

As it was, he was more puzzled than worried about his fate. The Queen/Lady had seemed to imply he might remain a prisoner for a while or that he might go free at any moment. He settled back in one of the chairs and thought about his exact position, both within the physical confines of the Hold and within the society into which he had stepped from the relative simplicity of the Waste.

He was imprisoned, even if his prison was ornate and comfortable. The cell itself consisted of a chamber within a chamber within a chamber. This concentric arrangement allowed for a certain freedom of movement but little chance of escape. The door of the inner room was in a direct line with the door of the middle and the outer room. Therefore, a single guard, by throwing open all of the doors could see the heart of the cell. Trys was given free access to the two inner rooms while two guards patrolled the outer one. One guard was always posted by the door, which was secured but not heavily laden with locks. The other guard slowly but continually walked the circle of the outer room.

The walls of the outer room arched inward at the top to create a high dome above the other two rooms. The walls of the middle and inner room were not solid all the way up to this overarching ceiling. Rather, the architect had joined the two inner walls to the outer by a set of fantastically carved stone supports. In fact, there was no complete ceiling for either the inner or the middle room. They were both open to allow an unobstructed view of the delicate stonework of a huge sun design which occupied most of the center of the outer room's ceiling.

Trys thought the irony of the design was rather heavy handed. But then the prison itself was an example of irony on a classic scale. He had been told by the guards why such an oddity even existed. The prison cell had been expressly designed for a notable and notorious First Lord when the Hold was first established.

The Lord had been blatantly guilty of treasonous acts. He had tried to overthrow the monarchy at a time when the transition from Waste to Hold had placed huge strains upon the institution and its final incarnation was in doubt. His intimate connections with the ruling clan, and several friends in high places, precluded severe punishment. Therefore, he was allowed to design his own prison.

He did so with a flair, managing to create an efficient prison, which only required two guards, at the same time that he created a sumptuous environment for himself. He even selected the furnishings and had the tapestry commissioned. It portrayed him as a gallant warrior climbing toward the top of the mountain. All about the figure were symbols of his career and ambition; everything from his first victory in battle at the base of the mountain to his strangely twisted view of his end where a figure which closely resembled the King/Lord of the time appeared to be lowering a crown onto his head.

Trys knew no one would lower anything resembling a crown onto his head. In fact, at moments when he soberly considered his situation, he fervently hoped he would be allowed to keep his head. His brief encounter with the revolutionaries had only served to complicate his feelings about the Hold and his role as an Interpreter.

He had been uncertain about coming to the Hold in the first place. His distaste for the Hold ways had only been confirmed once he had arrived. And now he felt the aims of the revolution were not all that outrageous. As if in a dream, he seemed to be tugged further and further away from the things he had once believed in. The cold clearness of the Waste appeared very desirable to him just then.

A chunk of coal in the fireplace burned through and fell apart. A puff of hot air blew into his face and a handful of glowing embers scattered across the brum fur directly in front of him. He wiped the sweat from his face and got up to scrape the embers back inside the firebox with his booted foot.

"In the Waste, that much heat would keep an entire clan warm for a day."

Trys spun about at the sound of the familiar voice. Cyln stood framed in the three open doors of the cell. Over her shoulder, Trys saw the guard close the door of the middle room and he heard the outer door close a moment later. Cyln stepped into the cell and closed the inner door after her.

"Cyln, thank the gods, you're back," exclaimed Trys.

"The gods have less to do with it than you think. Thank the revolution, in this case."

"Yes," agreed Trys. "The revolution does seem to have an effect, for both good and bad, on most events in the Hold."

She moved across the room and clasped him by the shoulders, but held him at arm's length. He knew for Cyln it was a mark of extreme emotion.

"I was delayed by the revolution, but it seems you've been imprisoned because of it. What's the story behind that?" she asked gruffly.

Trys motioned her to a chair and sat down himself. He then told her the whole story from beginning to end. He noticed she looked at him sharply when he mentioned his encounter with Bledsahl and Englerth, that she gave a slight grin when he talked of Roxyna in what he thought was a highly objective manner, and that she laughed out loud when he described how he had sent Grendyl reeling back into his own men in order to save Roxyna. By the time he reached the end and told of his talk with the Queen/Lady, she was somber and listening attentively.

When he was through, he sat back. "And here I am, a prisoner due to a chance encounter with the revolution."

Cyln stood suddenly and paced back in forth in front of the fire. "It might not be only due to the revolution. What do you think of the revolution?" she asked as she stopped and turned to him.

"I saw the squalor of Low Hold. I saw the oppressive tactics of Grendyl. I saw the determination of Roxyna and the others to break an old pattern. I'm not a revolutionary, but neither am I a true Hold Interpreter. I feel like I've wandered into the middle of something I don't really understand but which I'm supposed to be a part of."

That started Cyln pacing again. "Yes, yes, you're right. Right about most of what you say. Some of it is simply beyond us to understand right now. But I too have seen the revolution close up. It is dangerous but it does hold small yet true seeds of change. I have doubts myself."

Trys frowned. He had never seen or even thought of Cyln as having doubts about anything before. It disturbed him somehow, as if the solid rock beneath his feet had suddenly started to shift.

Cyln stopped again. She stared hard at the fire for a moment and her right hand drifted to her shoulder. Trys had seen the unconscious movement before. She was checking to make sure her blood blade was secure in its back scabbard. Her fingers fumbled about the empty top of the scabbard for a second until she realized the guard in the outer room had taken her blade from her before she entered the cell.

That movement as well as the pained expression on her square face beneath the straight line of her closely cropped hair, told Trys she was struggling in ways he had never seen before. She was fighting an inward battle, and the sweat stood out upon her brow as if she were swinging her blood blade in deadly earnest.

She glanced over at him. "I wish I could explain more. I wish I could explain..." She broke off.

"Explain what?" asked Trys.

"My first duty is to my Queen/Lady," stated Cyln. She said it as if it were an article of faith designed to remove her doubts. It seemed to work. "I must protect her. And I must protect you."

"I'm all for that. But how much danger can there be for me here in this cell?"

"The sharpest blade is easily concealed beneath the softest brum fur. That is a fact here in the Hold." She glanced around the room and up at the high vault of the ceiling before she knelt by Trys's chair and spoke in a low voice. "Even though I've only been back a short time, I did check with my informants. Your life is in jeopardy. For reasons unclear to me, Grendyl and Dwilkon have come to some sort of agreement regarding your fate. They did not expect the Queen/Lady to put you into a cell, and now it appears they feel only your death will suit their purposes. I can't fathom the reasons. I just know the facts."

"How is it to be done?" asked Trys, trying to keep his voice low and attempting to master the quaver which threatened to creep into it.

"They have bought off the Ice Guards who will take the next watch. From what I know of plots like this, they will make it look like you attempted to escape. The watch is due to change very soon. We don't have much time."

"What do I have to do?" Trys found himself gathering courage now that he knew what lay immediately before him.

"You must get out of the Hold and down to a place called Steelstain Alley. There you will find Sebaste, a former Seer to the King/Lord. He will be able to tell you certain...things." Again Cyln paused with the same sort of hesitation which Trys had heard before when she had said she wished she could explain things. "Ask him for a blood blade which he has in his keeping. Tell him the sword is yours by right."

"By what right?" asked Trys.

Cyln banged the arm of the chair in frustration and smothered a curse. "I can't explain more right now. There's simply not enough time," said Cyln as if trying to convince herself as much as she was Trys.

"I'll do it. Don't worry."

She gripped his arm then and squeezed it. Awkwardly, Trys patted the back of her strong hand. He was not sure who was comforting whom.

"Do you still have the medallion?" Cyln asked it suddenly, as if she had just thought of it.

"Yes. I keep it laced into the pocket on my left thigh."

"The Queen/Lady has not seen it?"

"No, it's been in my pocket."

"That's all right then. The time will come for you to wear it. The time will come."

Trys was about to ask her why the medallion was so important when she suddenly sprang to her feet. "The ones sent from Dwilkon and Grendyl will not make a move until I leave, so we must act now. You must remember they will be vigilant since they plan to murder you."

"Yes," was all Trys could force out.

Cyln began to unwind a thin leather strap from about her waist. It was very long, nearly thirty feet or so, Trys judged. After she had the end in her hands, she measured back about six feet and stepped to the fireplace. Without hesitation, she held a portion of the strap taut between her hand and over the flames. She winced as the flames licked upward and ate through the strap. A jerk and the strap broke. She stood up and stepped back, blowing on the heels of her hands which had gotten slightly singed in the process.

The Queen/Lady's bodyguard then dropped the shorter section at her feet and made a loop in one end of the long section of the thong. After a quick circuit of the room close to the curved wall, she stopped approximately three feet to the left of the doorway. She peered up into the dimness above the burning cressets.

She cast the loop up three times unsuccessfully, but on the fourth try snagged it on an outcropping on one of the ceiling supports. A quick tug secured it about the stone. She then hopped up and hung from the thong for a moment. It creaked but held her weight. Satisfied, she jumped down and motioned to Trys to join her.

"I know this cell. I know how it is constructed," she said in a low, serious tone. "The ceilings of the two inner rooms do not connect solidly to the ceiling of the outer room. There is a narrow gap among the supports up there. You can move all the way to the wall of the outer room and drop down close to the door. You must listen very carefully for the guard who is making the circuit of the cell and be sure he is on the far side of the wall before you drop down on the guard at the door. It should be relatively easy to overcome the guard at the door. He will certainly not be expecting anyone to drop on him from above. Once you have taken care of that guard, take his weapons. The remaining guard walks to the left, away from the door if you're facing out. Follow him around that way and come up behind him. Kill him. Understand?"

Trys nodded and rubbed his sweaty palms on the thighs of his singlesuit. He felt it must be the high banked fire which made him so hot.

"One last thing," said Cyln. "You must tightly bind and gag me so I cannot be implicated in your escape. I will have a hard enough time explaining how the Queen/Lady's bodyguard was overcome by a mere youth." She grinned at Trys. He tried to grin back.

After he had tugged the last knot tight and Cyln had grunted at him through her gag, Trys went to the leather thong and looked up. It hung about three feet away from the wall. He reached up and gripped it tightly. One last look back over his shoulder to where Cyln gave him an encouraging nod and he began to climb. He pulled himself up hand over hand while he walked up the wall. He had to swing out slightly to avoid a cresset and soon he was in the dimness near the ceiling.

The ceiling supports were much as Cyln had described them. Their design allowed for strength with openings between them which someone of Trys's size could probably get through. He transferred one hand from the thong to the rock of the downward sloping ceiling and peered in. The light from inside the cell did not reach into its recesses while the torches which burned in the outer room created only a faint glow from far below.

Brushing off the thick layer of dust which covered the edge of the rock with one hand, Trys then let go of the thong and grabbed the edge with both hands. He pulled himself over the lip and slid head first into the opening between two supports. He discovered he had plenty of room for his elbows and clearance for his head and back as well.

The dust which coated the stone actually helped him to slide along the relatively smooth surface but it swirled about his face and clogged his nose and eyes. He narrowed his eyes and kept sliding downward. The going was easy until he passed the wall of the middle room. A bump in the slope told him he had reached that point.

The glow from the torches in the outside room was stronger here but still only provided enough light for him to make out vague shapes. It appeared the channel narrowed quite dramatically just ahead of him. He paused. There was no way to go back even if he wanted to. He could only go on.

Nearly standing on his head in the dark, dust choked space, he took as deep a breath as he dared without suffocating, and slid forward. The slope suddenly steepened. He slid forward in a rush and wedged himself into the narrowing chute of rock. He pushed forward with his feet. Nothing. He pushed backward with his hands. No movement. He was stuck.

A surge of panic swept through him. He twisted his body in a vain attempt to move. He clawed the stone with his hands which were stretched out in front of him and dug at the stone with his toes at the same time. No movement. He clamped his teeth down tightly to suppress an hysterical scream from erupting.

With a growing consciousness of the weight of the entire Hold pressing down on him, he went a little crazy. He shoved and wriggled and kicked and squirmed until he felt two things happen. One was a burning along his back and chest where singlesuit and skin were torn away by the rock. The other was a downward slide. He was through.

With the blood on his back and chest helping to lubricate his passage, he slid past the bottleneck and had to brace himself awkwardly with his hands to prevent himself from falling down through the widening channel. He moved down until he reached a rock buttress which connected the middle and outer walls. There he braced himself with his hands and tried to figure out just where he was and what lay below him.

A torch burned on either side of the doorway on the wall of the outer room. Trys hung about twelve feet above and five feet to the left of the one on the left hand side of the doorway. Both guards stood beneath the torch. They kept glancing toward the corridor which led back into the main part of the Hold and also toward the door into the cell.

"How much longer do we wait?" asked the one facing the door into the cell.

"The other guards said she went in a few minutes before we arrived. We wait until she comes out and leaves. We have to. She can't be here when we do it, you know that," growled the one with his back to the door.

"I also know I can't wait too much longer. Isn't there a limit on how long visitors can stay?"

"She's the Queen/Lady's bodyguard. You don't mess with her," said the one close to the door.

"Right," sighed the one in the hall. "Well, I guess I'd better do my round. Make it look like we're doing our duty."

"We are doing our duty," snapped the other one.

"You know what I mean, our guard duty. Not the other thing. That's bonus work as far as I'm concerned."

"Oh, yeah," acknowledged the one by the door. "I thought you meant...Well, you know."

"Yeah, I know." He settled his scabbard belt more comfortably across his shoulder and slouched away to the left around the curve of the outer wall.

Trys studied his gait. He was walking slowly. How long would it take for someone walking that slowly to get to the opposite side of the outer room? His arms began to ache with the strain of supporting nearly his entire weight, but Trys held still and tried to count the number of steps the man had probably taken.

A drop of blood from his chest splattered on the stone of the buttress near his hand. His arm quivered from the strain. He had to do it now.

Just as he made his decision, the guard near the door pushed himself off from the wall and took three steps to the left, which placed him almost directly beneath Trys.

Trys gripped the buttress with sweaty hands and let his body slide down and out of the narrow chute of stonework. His boot scraped against the rock as it slid out. The guard looked around him.

That moment gave Trys the time he needed. With a grunt of pain and determination, he slid out of the chute and twisted his falling body. He managed to miss the buttress even as he clung desperately on to the stone with his wet hands.

The guard looked up. Trys swung down fast. His grip slipped but held long enough for him to swing around the buttress in a arc which ended when his booted feet smashed into the upturned face of the guard.

The man fell back and Trys followed him as his hands lost their grip. The guard was only stunned by the kick as he stumbled backward. It was Trys's landing heavily on him which finished him off. Trys heard a sickening crunch as he crashed into the man and they both went down in a pile.

Trys pushed himself off the man and tried to get to his feet. His knees buckled and he slumped against the wall beneath the torch. Trys readied himself to jump on the man if he should fight back. But he lay unmoving. A streak of blood covered the side of his face which was turned at an unnatural angle to the rest of his body. At first, Trys thought he had cut him until he realized the blood had come from his own lacerated chest.

Trys sank to his knees beside the dead man and worked at the buckle which fastened his back scabbard across his chest. His fingers refused to work the simple device until he sat back and took a deep breath. The other guard still walked his round. He had to get the blood blade off this man and kill the other one or else all of his efforts would be in vain.

The buckle yielded to his fingers. He rolled the man over and dragged the sheathed sword out from underneath him. It was but the work of moment to fasten the scabbard about his own shoulder and pluck the dagger out of the dead man's belt.

He balanced the hilt in his right hand. What was the best way to kill the other guard? He had never been any good at throwing blades, but he would have to try now.

The guard must be well past the half way point of the circuit. Trys ran as quietly but as quickly as he could to the left away from the door to come up behind the guard.

When he had circled nearly the entire outer room, he heard the shuffling of boots just ahead of him. He slowed down and crept forward. The guard was close to the door. A few more steps and he would be able to see the body in front of it.

Trys sprinted forward even as the guard, who had not been paying much attention to where he was going, suddenly looked up and stiffened. He saw the body.

Even as he ran, Trys drew back his arm and threw the dagger. It flew end over end and crashed harmlessly against the curved wall next to the guard. The man jumped and spun around, drawing his blood blade at the same time.

Still running full tilt, Trys drew his own and swung the heavy blade in front of him. The guard was too surprised to move. His companion lay dead behind him and bearing down on him was the man who was supposed to be safely locked behind two doors, looking like a dead man himself, his chest covered with blood.

The guard's blade came up automatically and he set himself in a defensive posture. But Trys's momentum and desperation swept his defense away. Trys smashed the blade to one side and struck the man full in the chest with his shoulder. The man stepped back and tripped over the dead body just behind him. They both went down hard.

With a sudden jerk, Trys managed to raise himself on his left hand and slash the pommel of the hilt across the man's face. He grunted but struggled to fight back. He dropped his sword, useless in such close quarters, and snatched a dagger from his belt.

Trys saw the flash of the blade and, still balanced on his left arm, he swung the point of his sword around and shoved it hard into the man's exposed throat beneath him. Without waiting to see if the thrust had done the job, Trys let go of the hilt and rolled off to the right. That roll saved his life since the rising dagger merely slit open the side of his singlesuit and carved a shallow slash along his ribs.

Trys rolled until he hit the wall. He then lurched up and set his back to the wall, waiting for an attack. None came. The only thing which came was a gurgle from the severed throat of the dying guard. The hilt of Trys's blade wavered over the man even as the dagger slipped from his lifeless fingers to clatter on the floor.

It was over. Trys was free of his cell, but not out of the Hold. He winced at the new pain which laced up his wounded side. He touched the cut. Even though his hand came away red with blood, he could feel the cut was not deep. He wiped his hand on his singlesuit.

"I can't walk through the Hold like this," he said. His voice sounded strange in the silence of the curved room.

With that he began to unlace his singlesuit and stripped it off. Using his old singlesuit as a towel, he wiped off as much of the already drying blood on his chest and back as he could. He then moved to the first guard and went methodically about getting him out of his Ice Guard uniform.

After tying the last lace, settling the belt of the back scabbard on his shoulder, and touching the medallion now laced into the left thigh pocket of his borrowed singlesuit, he looked down at himself. No blood was evident. He felt his face. There was no stickiness there and he hoped that meant no blood.

He thought about dragging the bodies inside the middle room, but decided against it. He was not sure he had the strength just then and the cell was distant enough from the well traveled halls of the Hold to ensure that no one, other than the change of guards, would venture into this area for some time. No, he had to get out and do it now.

He tugged at the front of his singlesuit where the still flowing blood made it stick to his chest. Miles of halls lay before him. But he had to get out, out of the Hold and down to a place called Steelstain Alley. He turned and practiced walking at a reasonable pace, the pace of an Ice Guard on important but not urgent business, a pace which would eventually take him far away from the Hold.

## XX

TRYS STUMBLED into the broken defile of Steelstain Alley more by accident than by design. He had passed through the halls of the Hold on his way downward, like someone lost in a waking dream. His disguise, flimsy though it was, served him in good stead. No one questioned an Ice Guard on business in the Hold.

In Low Hold, the dream had continued but was somewhat altered as he trudged up and down and around the twisting, squalid streets. Dressed as an Ice Guard, people gave him only contemptuous looks and shrank furtively away. There was no one to ask directions of, even if he had dared.

Since the streets of the Hold shifted periodically due to the volcanic activity of the mountain, signs were of limited value. A sign which clearly labeled a complete street today, might be left to languish upon a single house within a few months if the mountainside shifted and the bulk of the street moved on its torturous way downward.

So, Trys wandered here and there and, it seemed to him, everywhere, until he nearly fell when he crossed a frozen stream of dirty water which acted as a rudimentary sewage system when the mountain warmed enough to permit it to run downhill and carry along the garbage it now held in suspension. As he straightened from his awkward slide, he glanced up at the corner of the building he was then using as a means of support. There above him was a street sign. The word "Steelstain" was clearly emblazoned across the piece of cracked stone, although only the "A" had managed to cling to the splintered sign just behind the first and most important word.

Now that he had found the Alley, Trys wondered how he could find Sebaste's chambers. Cyln had neglected to tell him exactly which building it was. He peered down the steep slope of the Alley. The houses tumbled in a haphazard fashion down either side, swaying toward each other at one level and away from each other at another. At points, the Alley was little more than a tunnel created by the tilting walls.

As he stood there, halted by uncertainty but urged forward by necessity, a figure engulfed in a Waste cloak turned one of the sharp corners down along the Alley and labored up the incline toward him. The person kept stepping on the hem of the cloak, which dragged along the uneven ground, and lurching forward. When the person had stumbled to within a few feet of him, Trys called out.

"Excuse me. I need to find the chambers of Sebaste. Could you direct me to them?"

The person stopped and shoved back the oversize hood with hands which fought their way free of the folds of the cloak. An old woman peered up at him. "You want the new one?"

"I guess so."

"Well, the old one's dead, so you'd have to see the new one, wouldn't you?" The woman cackled to herself at the thought. "But then, they're all the same aren't they?" She had to cackle again, as if she found herself terribly amusing.

"Yes, of course." Trys was having trouble following the conversation and was getting a bit impatient.

"Let's see. Right now, it would be the fifth house down on your left. Yes, that's where it ended up after the last quake."

"Thank you," said Trys, who was already moving down the incline of the Alley.

"Knock hard. He's usually in a trance or something. At least, the old one was, so I suppose the new one does the same thing, since they really are the same." Her laugh was muffled as she pulled the hood of the cloak over her head and continued on her way.

Trys hurried down along the Alley. A level area just in front of the fifth house had caused the icy sewage stream to spread out and form a sewage pond. Trys skated across a corner of it and slid into the door. He looked up. The second story overhung the street so he could not tell if there was a light in the window. He decided to take the advice of the eccentric woman and began to bang on the door. Not knowing how extensive the search for him might be, he felt the desperate need to get off the street as soon as possible.

He had banged once and was swinging his hand forward for a second blow when the door swung open. He nearly tumbled into the arms of the man who stood there as he tried to stop his forward momentum.

"You're quick," said Trys, somewhat lamely.

The man, whose face was thin and straight with seriousness, smiled unexpectedly at the observation. "I've been told that before."

"And you're Sebaste?" asked Trys, even more lamely.

"Yes, I am. You need help. Come in."

"I do need...help. How did you know? You're a Seer, but I thought they looked into the past."

"A Seer needs to notice things. The blood on your chest has soaked through your singlesuit. Get inside and I can dazzle you more, if that's what you want." Sebaste grinned and stepped to one side to let Trys enter the doorway. As he did so, he felt a rush of weakness suddenly wash over him. He stumbled to the stairs where he nearly fell over.

Sebaste poked his head out of the door for a second. He scanned the empty street before he slammed the door closed and slid a heavy bolt into place. He then hurried to Trys's side and helped him to climb the winding and rickety stairs to the second floor.

The door into the chamber was open. The two entered the room where Sebaste guided Trys through a maze of artifacts which covered most of the floor to a chair next to the hearth. He then ran back to the door, closed it with a lift and shove of his shoulder, and turned to Trys.

"I'll get you something for the wounds and for your stomach." With that he disappeared among the piles of things toward the back of the low ceilinged room. Trys heard a door open and close and assumed he had entered another room in search of medical aid and sustenance, both of which Trys suddenly realized he was in dire need of.

He sank back in the chair only to lurch forward when his sore back touched the cushions. More flesh had been scraped off than he had at first supposed. He began to unlace the front of his borrowed singlesuit. It was sodden with blood and the laces were difficult to untie.

"Let me help you."

Trys glanced up. There was Sebaste, just setting down a tray piled high with bandages, jars of ointments, a platter of cold meat and dark bread, and a thin necked bottle of snow wine. A singlesuit of dark leather was draped over his shoulder.

"Yes, I guess I need help. A lot of help. I..."

"Don't talk right now. Let me get you cleaned up and fed first," ordered Sebaste. "I've also brought another singlesuit which should fit you," he added.

With that he went to work. In a matter of minutes, Trys was stripped of the blood soaked singlesuit and his wounds cleaned and bandaged. Then, dressed in the clean singlesuit with its laces pulled snug but not too tight and the medallion transferred to the new pocket, its familiar weight a comfort against his thigh, he set to work himself and devoured all of the food on the platter and half of the bottle of snow wine.

Glowing inside and out, the warmth of the wine nicely complementing the warmth from the newly stoked fire, Trys closed his eyes and sank back in the chair once more. This time there was only a dull ache from his thoroughly bandaged back.

Trys opened his eyes to find Sebaste studying his face. He wanted to prolong the moment of comfort and the feeling of security. It had been a long trip out of the Hold, and there was a long trip ahead of him, the end of which he could not even imagine. He remained silent.

Sebaste spoke. "Once upon a time, someone came to me, to us actually, much like you have. I was there in two senses. I have my own personal memories of it, and I now possess Sebaste's memories of it. It gives it a curious doubling effect, like seeing the same event from two different angles. The one who came before was also on his way out of the Hold. He was headed south, although eventually he did come back, headed in the opposite direction. Where are you headed?"

Trys gathered his strength and sat up straighter in the chair. "I don't know. I just escaped from a prison in the Hold, and I don't have any place to go to. Cyln did not tell me where I should go, other than here."

At the name of his friend and rescuer, Sebaste took a deep and steady breath and nearly closed his eyes, as if he was making a physical effort to not slip away from the immediate physical surroundings. He stood up suddenly, and stalked to the fire and back.

"Your name?"

"Trys myr Lyn pyr Drun."

"That's not all of it," muttered Sebaste to himself. "There is more here, much more." And then to Trys, "You are the young Interpreter from the North. Someone who the King/Lord Nordseth has decided requires watching. You are more than you seem, and much more than you know."

"Maybe it's the wine, or maybe the tiredness, but you're not making any sense to me. I am Trys myr Lyn pyr Drun of the Caynruhl clan. I came to the Hold at Cyln's request. I came to be an Interpreter, although I don't think I'm going to make it. Not after what's happened. I'm confused, to say the least. And the only other thing I can tell you, is that Cyln told me to ask you for a blood blade you are holding which is mine by right. Does it make any sense to you? Because if it does, please explain it to me."

Suddenly and completely, Sebaste came to rest. Trys saw his eyes close and his muscles relax, and marvelled that someone so at rest could still stand up. Indeed, Sebaste did sway, but he did not fall down.

He was plunged deep into memory recall; quicker and deeper than he had gone before. All he had learned from the former Sebaste, all he had learned on his own, snapped into place within his finely tuned mind.

As he swayed, he discovered the myriad connections among facts which flowed together like disparate pieces of colored stone to suddenly form a complete mosaic. He knew then the ability to judge what the pattern represented was as important as the ability to recall the pattern. Facts required interpretation, otherwise they remained simply dead, unconnected colored bits of stone. In that sense, he was more of an interpreter than the Interpreters.

He saw how the secret which only Cyln could have known, the existence of a living heir of Alisande and Gerred, was hidden in between the facts which Sebaste had within his collective mind all of the time. No Sebaste had been anywhere near the birth in the far North those many years ago. But the request from Cyln, sent through the very subject of the secret, aligned all of the facts and allowed the true pattern to finally be revealed.

A beatific smile formed on the face of the Seer. Trys watched it and marvelled again. He did not know what had just happened, but he did know it had transformed the man before him.

With the smile still wreathing his face, Sebaste turned and prompted his still relaxed body into motion. He wove his way through the piles which cluttered the room to a far corner where he bent over an ancient trunk.

Trys heard the top bang against the wall as it was opened. He watched as the Seer returned to the hearth carrying a long object bound in soft bryl hide. He laid it reverently upon the stones of the hearth. With movements which seemed to be part of a natural and spontaneous Ritual, he untied the thongs which bound the object and drew back the hide.

A blood blade of simple and ancient design was revealed. The light from the fire puddled and ran along its length. In that moment, Trys felt as if its inherent heat, so long locked away, leaped about joyously.

"This blade was given to your birth father by the former Sebaste. He returned it to Sebaste just before he climbed to the garden of the Queen/Lady. There he fought Lord Kysel and his men, and died in your birth mother's arms."

Trys looked at Sebaste. The smile had softened but the impulse which had created it was still there. Trys tried to understand the words just spoken to him by the blissful Seer.

"My father never had such a fine blade." He spoke slowly and deliberately as he tried to match what he knew to what he thought he had heard.

"This blood blade belonged to your birth father, not your adoptive father."

"My father is...my father. I don't know anyone else who might or might not be..."

"You have had two fathers. One helped you to grow up. He was very important to you. The other left you a legacy which is both dubious and glorious. You will have to decide for yourself how to accept it, and what to do with it."

"My father is Drun pyr Khun myr Jynth," said Trys in a shaky voice.

"And your other father was Gerred pyr Nordseth myr Phylla," replied the Seer.

"That means my mother was...is not my mother?"

"Your mother is still your mother. But now you must know your birth mother is Alisande myr Rystarte pyr Grendyl."

"The Queen/Lady?" Trys sank back into the chair. His wounds stung him, but the pain seemed to be happening to someone else.

"I, too, am just finding out who I am," said Sebaste in a determined way. "Only a short time ago I had a different name and a single history. Now I have vast structures of memories crowded into my mind. Yes, I can wander amongst them and examine every nook and cranny, but I often lose sight of who I was before. That person is there somewhere, but dwarfed by the edifice which has become my responsibility. I would advise you to absorb it a bit at a time. Don't question too much, and don't judge anyone's motives just yet. It is so hard to tell whether some have done right and others have done wrong. Such distinctions can easily become muddled in the light of a single new fact."

Trys nodded. With the muddy swirl of his past now revealed to him, he found himself staring hard at the clear stream of the future. He stood up then and moved stiffly to the hearth where the sword lay in the firelight. He ran his fingers along its shimmering length. What did the object mean to him now? It was something from his past and the past of others whom he had never known. He needed to take it up. He needed to use it in his present to try to forge his future.

He gripped the hilt hard and lifted the well balanced blade. He slashed the blade in a figure eight. The warm air of the room sighed as its keen edge rose and fell and rose again.

"I am a fugitive from the Hold, no matter who my birth mother is." It cost Trys some pain to say it. "I am perceived as a revolutionary. Perhaps, I am one." Trys spoke to himself as much as he did to Sebaste, trying to sort out his suddenly complicated situation. "As you said, in the light of the new facts certain things seem clear. My status is, shall we say, dubious. I can't know how I would be received by my new found mother. She might have to lock me up forever if I go back to her. The revolutionaries might receive me with open arms. But one of those arms might have a dagger clutched in the hand. And then there is my...grandfather."

Trys paused. He glanced over at Sebaste who stood at one side of the hearth with a quizzical expression on his face.

When the silence lengthened beyond a minute, Sebaste shook

himself and turned to Trys. "Memory recall," he said by way of explanation. "It comes on unbidden at times. And, I'm sorry to say it does not always provide any clear precedents for situations underway. Your grandfather, the King/Lord Nordseth pyr Nystrin myr Olda, is an unknown factor here. His reign has grown bloodier of late, but it is nearly impossible to predict what he might do if you went to him and revealed yourself, if he doesn't already know what you have just discovered."

"He might find a use for me," said Trys somewhat hopefully.

"True, but you might not like what it entails, either for yourself or for others. I just don't know. In this case, I'm not a very good Seer."

"No. You have given me my past. That is more than enough. I'm the one who has to figure out how it fits with my future."

Sebaste nodded, and then snapped his head up at the loud pounding which erupted at the street door. Trys spun to face the chamber door, his blade held straight out before him.

Muffled shouts and the clatter of numerous weapons could be heard down in the Alley. Sebaste raised his hand to Trys to indicate he should stay where he was, while he slid across the chamber and into a corner from which he could look out of a window without being seen. He craned his neck to get a good view of the narrow defile outside the house, and then drifted back to Trys where he stood near the hearth.

"Lord Grendyl's men. At least a dozen, maybe more. They will respect the sanctity of the chamber of the Seer for a short time. That should give us enough time to get you out of here and on your way."

"To where?" asked Trys. An edge of panic crept into his voice. He was being hounded from one end of the Hold to the other, and he had no idea where to go next.

"The Camp. If Nordseth doesn't know of your existence, he soon will. He will decide quite quickly how you fit in with his plans. That means either he will want you alive or quite dead. Based on some rapid memory recall, I would say Nordseth will not eliminate you right now. You are an unknown factor, something he has played with in the past to his benefit. You represent a source of power, and he will want to secure that source before others do. It's a chance, but I think it's your best one."

"That's it then. The Camp." Trys wished he could say it with more conviction.

"But first, out of here."

"How?"

"As you noticed on your way in, there is not one straight line in the entire length of Steelstain Alley. An energetic man can slip past a large numbers of searchers who might be just around the corner from him. When I was younger and an apprentice here, I used to practice finding alternative ways to get to and from the Seer's chamber. Believe me, there are many. Just remember to hug the walls and take advantage of the shadows." Sebaste grinned as he gave this advice and recalled his youthful exploits along the Alley.

The grin was wiped off his face as a spear smashed through the window and buried itself in the plaster of the ceiling. "They're getting serious." This statement was corroborated by the sound of axes smashing heavily into the panels of the street door.

"Grab the scabbard for your blade and follow me," said Sebaste.

Trys did just that, sliding the blade into the scabbard and tying the thong which held the blade in securely, as he followed Sebaste among the piles in the chamber.

Sebaste led the way into a back chamber, the door of which was hidden by a formidable pile of brum pike shafts wrapped up in moldering bryl hides. It was obvious the pile had not been touched for many years.

Inside the other room, Trys was surprised to find just as much material but in much better order. Items seemed to be stacked with an overall scheme of organization, although just what that organization was escaped Trys upon his cursory inspection.

Sebaste went as straight as he could to the center of the room and stopped. He closed his eyes, and then opened them to turn to Trys.

"I'm trying to recall exactly where the secret passage out of this room is located. I know its here, but Sebaste, like all of us, I'm afraid, tended to be a bit fuzzy on specific details of specific rooms. I was never allowed in here when I was his apprentice or else I would have found it right away," he added in defense of his former self.

He closed his eyes and spun slowly around in a complete circle. As he came around toward Trys, he opened one eye, shrugged, and then closed his eye as he returned to his circling. He had made three complete circuits when he suddenly stopped, nodded, and headed for a corner of the slightly skewed room.

After pawing about among several piles of primitive works of art executed in herb based paints on thin slabs of stone, muttering all the time he would have to come back at some point and make sure they were back in their proper order, he pulled two of the largest aside to reveal a gash in the wall. The hole appeared to be very narrow and shallow as well.

"This is it," announced Sebaste.

"You're sure?" asked Trys. "It looks rather small."

Sebaste looked at the hole. "Well, it is, but it's all I've got."

Trys nodded. "It looks like squeezing through narrow openings has become my specialty."

Sebaste gripped him by the arm and squeezed. "Just keep going down. There's bound to be an opening at the bottom, somewhere."

"Great."

"Remember, once out in the streets, keep close to the walls and in the shadows."

"Thank you for all of your help."

"I hope it proves to be a help in the long run. The gods be with you," murmured Sebaste. "Now, get going."

The sound of splintering wood from the direction of the street door emphasized the sudden need for action. Trys turned, shoved his scabbarded blade into the gash first, and followed it.

The space was cramped but there was a strong current of cold air flowing up through the shaft. Trys discovered if he pushed hard with hands and feet that some of the ancient plaster crumbled away to give him a bit more room to maneuver.

As his feet came to rest on a stone support within the wall, he craned his neck to look back into the room. Sebaste was gone and the room darkened as the door closed behind him. Trys was on his own.

In a series of wriggles, which took him past the tight spots, and falls, which resulted from entering slightly wider spaces, Trys made his way down inside the wall of the house on Steelstain Alley. He scraped knees and elbows, shoulders and heels, and was saved from serious injury by Sebaste's expert application of the bandages to his already sensitive areas.

He discovered that, while the builders of the house were conscientious and made each support wide and sturdy, they were not consistent when it came to the distances between the stone supports. After squeezing between the wall and the support, he would have to feel around with his feet in the pitch blackness for the next support, only to be forced to let go and drop about two feet, landing heavily on the stone ledge of the next support. Other times, he would find the next lower support just a couple of feet below the one he was on, which meant he had to push himself into the tight space between the supports and remain crouched there until he could feel his way downward to the next level.

After what seemed like hours of downward crawling and falling, he reached bottom. The only reason he knew it was bottom was that the plaster gave way to solid stone which fitted flush to the other stones. He could go no lower.

He stood in the absolute darkness and wondered how he could

get out of the pit he was in. By way of experiment, he tapped the wall in front of him with the hilt of his blood blade. The plaster absorbed the blow with a dull thud and a chunk fell onto his feet. It sounded like the wall was not very thick.

He strained his ears to pick up any noises from beyond the layer of plaster which separated him from he knew not what. He heard nothing. Deciding that caution would only keep him entombed within the wall, he drew back the hilt of his sword as far as the narrow confines would allow him and swung it forward as hard as he could.

The wall gave way and Trys tumbled through head first. He landed heavily on his blade with his legs buried in the crumbling plaster of the demolished wall. He pushed himself up onto his elbows and as he did so he saw something which made him freeze.

Directly in front of him were the Waste boots of a fully armed warrior. Still protruding awkwardly out of the wall, Trys looked up into the surprised face of a warrior with the device of the Lord Grendyl worked onto the breast of his singlesuit.

The man poked his drawn blood blade at him and uttered an order. "Give up."

"Of course," replied Trys, "I can see I have little choice."

"Right," agreed the warrior, who then studied Trys's nearly upside down posture. "Get up."

"Gladly, but I seem to be stuck." Trys wiggled to show the man that his legs appeared to be firmly held by the broken wall. "Help me up."

The warrior stepped forward automatically to help. As he bent over to grab Trys under his arm, Trys flipped himself to the left and brought the hilt of his previously hidden blade up sharply. It caught the man on the point of his chin. He crumpled into an unconscious heap.

Trys kicked his way free of the constraining plaster and stood up. He found himself in a deeply recessed doorway. He checked the warrior to make sure he was completely unconscious, and then moved to the end of the recess. He peeked around the corner. The street was empty.

He stepped out. In the instant he reached the center of the narrow street, he realized the twisted angles of the buildings had hidden three of his pursuers. They stood only a few feet away.

Trys turned and walked slowly and deliberately away from them, hoping they would take him for just another denizen of Low Hold. Just as he turned a corner, he heard one of the men shout.

"He's got plaster dust all over him! It's him!"

Trys broke into a run, dodging around the twists of the convoluted street. He turned corner after corner, and did not hear any sounds of close pursuit.

Thinking that perhaps he had eluded the men out of sheer luck, he rounded yet another corner and ran full into one of Grendyl's men. In a flash, the man drew his blade. Trys struggled to undo the thong which held his blade securely in its scabbard, but it resisted his violent and hectic efforts.

Swinging his sheathed sword wildly at the head of the warrior, Trys drove him back a step. But the man recovered quickly and lunged forward. Trys threw his body against the wall of the nearby house and managed to smash the thrusting blade upward. The impetus of the warrior buried the point deeply in the plaster of the wall behind Trys.

Having had success with using the hilt of his blade before, Trys gripped the length of his sheathed blade in both hands and brought it around sharply. It hit the side of the man's head with a crack. The force of the blow slammed his head into the wall on the other side of the narrow alley and he went down. His nerveless hand slipped from the hilt of his buried blade, which bounced up and down above the unconscious warrior.

Trys did not stop to check to see how effective his unorthodox method of dispatching warriors had proven this time. Instead, he set off at a dead run, heading always downward and ignoring, as best he could, the sounds of pursuit which came closer and then receded.

He ran until he reached the edge of the crowds which milled about on the causeway beneath the monolith of Hold Gate. There he slowed to a walk and slipped into the swirl of humanity, and eventually slipped out of the Hold entirely.

## XXI

THE DESOLATION within the Royal Tent of King/Lord Nordseth pyr Nystrin myr Olda reminded Trys of certain tracts of the far Northern Waste where life clung tenaciously to the landscape only in small patches. While such tracts lacked vitality, they did retain a profound sense of determination to hold onto the minute scraps of life scattered across their austere surfaces.

Taken into custody immediately upon stepping off the causeway and entering the official domain of the King/Lord, Trys had been marched directly to the Royal Tent by the perplexed Blood Guards. They had not understood his insistence upon being presented to the King/Lord. With the general mood in the Camp being one of suppressed anxiety about what the arbitrary and bloody minded monarch might order to be done next, a stranger arriving from the Hold and asking to be taken to the source of that anxiety seemed like a death wish to them.

The high blaze of the sun nearing noon in a cloudless sky was blotted out as Trys and his escort of four Guards stepped through the flap which marked the western entrance to the Tent. They stepped into deep shadows and flickering lights where here and there a torch burned to facilitate the work underway within the Tent. And the work was of a curious nature indeed.

As the health of King/Lord Nordseth deteriorated into a series of fitful bursts of energy and depressions of the spirit, so too did his inclination for light and shadow. At times, every torch within the great dome of the Tent was set ablaze to create a minor constellation to rival those outside of the bryl hide. But more often than not, all torches, except those absolutely necessary for ongoing work within the Tent, were snuffed out, to create a vast lightless realm beneath the overarching dome.

Trys and his somewhat reluctant escort, reluctant to approach too closely to the throne where there sat such a capricious monarch, moved from station to station within the imposed twilight of the Tent. As they did so, they were challenged with varying degrees of thoroughness and interest by the Blood Guards at each post. Most did not seem to care who they passed on, while others were curious in a bloody minded sort of way who had asked to see the King/Lord on one of his admittedly bad days.

As they moved on their slow way inward toward the center of the vast Tent, Trys realized they were not moving in a straight line, but rather were following the tightening coils of a huge spiral. The spiral encompassed much of the floor of the Tent and it allowed Trys to see the work which was going on.

The floor of the Tent was cluttered with objects which had once, perhaps in as short a time as a few days or a few hours ago, been arranged to form rooms, or at least living areas, upon the darkened plain. Trunks and tables, chairs and hangings, which consisted of ornate tapestries draped over frames, were all being taken down and then away. The moribund rooms were falling into nonexistence.

When asked about this curious project, the Blood Guards simply shrugged and said it was the will of the King/Lord. It appeared his paranoia had surged of late and he had ordered that the spreading floor be cleared of all extraneous objects so he could see from far off who was approaching him. The clearance of the living areas also effectively kept everyone, servants included, away from the throne. His paranoia had expanded to include just about everyone.

Soft light and air from the baffle flaps in the dome high above, as well as four tall braziers set at the four corners, marked the throne and its dias. About a hundred yards from this island of subdued light in the ocean of darkness, Trys came upon a piece of furniture which had not been cleared away and which marked the last remnant of a room. It was a much scarred four legged stool missing a leg. It was balanced on its three legs, but looked as if a light breeze could knock it over.

As he passed this mute reminder of the dismantling process underway, Trys could clearly see the throne in its spotlight. He was able to discern a figure huddled back within the massive arms of the throne. He could not see the face of the one who crouched there, but he did notice the stooped presence of a second person standing on the first riser of the dias and to the left of the throne itself.

The Blood Guards slowed and then halted about fifty feet in front of the throne, as if they were not sure how close they were allowed to approach. They looked at each other and then jumped when they heard a voice from the throne.

"Torkild, tell them to come closer. I can barely see them and certainly can't hear what they have to say."

The curiously stooped man on the first riser of the dias nodded his head down and to the left and motioned for the group to move closer. It was then that Trys noticed his scarred face and twisted body. The left side of his face was frozen in a gruesome smile which conveyed no mirth. His left arm and leg were likewise fixed in a twisted attitude.

As they shuffled to within ten feet of the dias, the Guards

moving forward hesitantly to obey the order which they seemed to fear, Trys could clearly see the man upon the throne. He slouched back in the throne, like a pile of finely wrought material with a head floating above it. His eyes were fever bright and eclipsed the rest of his painfully thin face, not to mention his skeletal body which was thoroughly enveloped in the flowing robe. Trys knew he was in the presence of King/Lord Nordseth.

Torkild stepped down from the riser with a turning motion of his injured leg. He moved quickly to Trys and looked him hard in the face. Trys stared back at the half frozen, half mobile features. Torkild must have approved of what he saw, for he arched his right eyebrow and crinkled the right side of his mouth in a rueful smile.

He then turned to the Blood Guards. "You may step back. You know to where."

They did not need to be told twice. As one, the four turned and marched briskly back into the shadows which held sway about a hundred feet from the throne.

The servant of the King/Lord then swept his right arm toward the throne to invite Trys to step even closer to the place which the Guards could not wait to get away from. Trys had no idea what he was in for, but he no longer had a choice. He had to keep moving forward.

Together they moved to the dias. Trys stopped just in front of the first step, while Torkild hunched himself up and onto the step and took up his previous position.

With a sudden movement, the King/Lord leaned forward. He thrust his head out and cupped his hands about a decahedron of blood metal partially wrapped in a dark red cloth. As had his servant, he too closely studied the face of the young man before him. However, he did not end his inspection with a smile, even a rueful one.

"Trys myr Lyn pyr Drun." Nordseth spoke his name and then paused, as if to test it and Trys's reaction to his knowledge of it. Trys frowned slightly, but stood straight and continued to face the sickly King/Lord. "I know your name. I know other things about you. Perhaps, even more than you yourself know."

"That doesn't surprise me. I've only recently discovered there are many things I don't know about myself."

Nordseth's great eyes burned brighter for a moment and the beginning of a smile curved his thin, bloodless lips. "Spirit. He has spirit. But then he would," said the King/Lord more to himself than to Trys.

The smiled ended. "As you can see, I know many things. Now, I want to know why are you involved with the revolution?"

"I'm not involved. I just got caught up in it," protested Trys.

"Lord Grendyl saw fit to arrest you in the square in front of Hold Gate, and the Queen/Lady Alisande detained you in a prison cell within the Hold, from which you obviously were able to escape. That is involvement."

Trys sighed. The revolution simply would not leave him alone. "I came south to the Hold to be an Interpreter. I have discovered it is more difficult than I thought possible. Since I've been in the Hold, I've seen inequities and, while I don't believe in the violent and radical methods of the revolution, I do believe that certain portions of the system do require reform. The lower classes and the classless deserve better treatment. In the Waste, everyone has a duty to perform. In the Hold and Camp, you seem to have lost sight of that."

"I have lost sight of nothing," hissed Nordseth. "I see all of it every moment of every day, and I am sick of it. The classless deserve their exile from the system. They have earned it."

"But their contributions to society are lost."

"You honestly believe the revolutionaries want to contribute to society? They want to tear it down and build it up to suit their own ideas. They want the power I wield now. They want to be just like the ones they despise. That is the revolution."

The King/Lord had risen nearly to his feet as he held forth upon the revolution, but a spasm passed through his frame and he collapsed back into the massive arms of the throne. Trys glanced over at Torkild, looking for some explanation of the sudden deflation of the overwrought monarch. All he saw was a pained expression flit across the undamaged side of his face.

And then the King/Lord began to cough. It was a wrenching cough which gathered deep down in his body and tore its way outward. It was a cough which shook his thin limbs but did not seem to affect his eyes, which stared out in an expression more of boredom than of pain. It was a cough he had come to terms with in order to live, even though he knew eventually it would be his death.

As soon as it began, the King/Lord raised the cloth wrapped decahedron of blood metal to cover his mouth. It remained there steadfastly during the violent fit. The coughing slowed and stopped.

The hands of the King/Lord quivered as they slowly lowered their burden to his chest. Trys could clearly see the cloth was darkened with blood and sense the glow of intense warmth from the activated blood metal of the decahedron. Nordseth appeared to relish the heat which he cupped in his thin fingered hands.

"As you can see, I am not well," said Nordseth in a completely matter of fact tone of voice. "But I am not so sick I do not know my duty as King/Lord. The status quo must be maintained. I am the caretaker of half of this society and, as such, it is my duty to see that the things which function, continue to do so."

Trys was sorry for the sick monarch. He imagined the terrible burdens which must weigh down upon the frail body before him. And then, feeling the King/Lord was being quite reasonable in the aftermath of his coughing fit and burning with the ardor of youth to point out what he saw as the fallacies of the King/Lord's argument, Trys spoke up.

"Things do change. One does not have to shove them along, but one should not impede their progress. If it is revolutionary to try to see change, acknowledge it, and help it along with the least amount of disorder for all concerned, then I am a revolutionary."

With a convulsive movement, Nordseth sat bolt upright on the throne. His knuckles whitened about the decahedron. He began talking in a low snarl which built to a scream.

"You are a hypocrite. You are a revolutionary, and yet you deny it. Be a revolutionary. Be one completely. Even though I despise Lyrdahl for his radical beliefs, I admire him for the extremity of his position. You are nothing more than an opportunist, and a lukewarm one at that. Burn with the need for change if you will achieve any at all! Storm the moldering fortress of the status quo and tear it down until not one stone remains upon another!"

A darkness passed across the tense face of the King/Lord. Trys noticed Torkild shifted his position to be ready to leap to his monarch's aid, even going so far as to allow a portion of his distorted left side to be revealed. But he did not begin to cough. Instead he went on speaking, the scream held in check but the violent energy still propelling his words.

"Exterminate the rot. No, better, exterminate the cause of the rot." Nordseth paused and Trys could tell he was casting about in his fever wrapped mind for the thread of what he wanted to say. Finally, he found it. "Yes, exterminate the cause. And the cause is the rebellious throngs holed up in Hold Gate. A den of vile habits and unclean thoughts, a breeding ground for rebellion and disease of all kinds. Send them back to the Waste. All of the classless. All of the lower classes. All of them. Back to where the wind will scour them clean. Back to where the cold will freeze out any thoughts of their being something they never were and never will be."

Nordseth stood with a lurch which surprised both Trys and Torkild, who moved up one riser closer to his monarch, even as he awkwardly shifted away his left side. Nordseth swayed and then steadied himself by grasping an arm of the throne with one hand. His other still clutched the warm decahedron to his chest.

"Come forward," hissed the King/Lord. "Up on the second step."

Trys gave Torkild a quick glance to check the propriety of the move. Torkild nodded slightly. He was not certain where this was all leading, but he knew better than to try to circumvent his King/Lord when he was in a mood like the present one.

Trys walked forward and stepped up and onto the second riser. He stood still as Nordseth leaned forward and studied his face intently. The King/Lord then frowned and looked down at the decahedron, as if he just realized he still had it in his hand and wondered where it might have come from.

"You are..." The words trailed off below a whisper.

Trys shook his head. "I'm sorry, but I couldn't hear what you said."

Again the subdued whisper which vanished, "You are my..."

All Trys could do was to shake his head to indicate he still had not heard what the King/Lord had said.

With a visible effort, Nordseth gathered himself and shouted out, "You are my grandson! The illegitimate offspring of a disowned Consort and a slut of a Queen/Lady!"

Trys stumbled back from the violence of the assault and nearly fell off the dias. He suddenly found Torkild's hand on his back, steadying him.

But the King/Lord was not through with the violence. "Blood Guards! To me! Now!"

The four who had escorted Trys to the throne came running and were joined by four others who appeared out of the shadows all about the dias. They came with blades drawn and looked about wildly for assassins to subdue. When they saw none, they stopped and waited in some confusion for the next order. It was not long in coming.

Nordseth pointed a long finger at Trys and said, "Execute him. Immediately."

Torkild removed his hand from Trys's back and took a step away from the object of the King/Lord's fury, but stared hard at his monarch with both his good and his bad eye. Trys focussed on the chief servant in the moment after the sentence of death was pronounced. He felt sure Torkild was trying to gauge just how serious Nordseth was about the command, and whether or not he would actually have it carried out. He also seemed to be trying to catch the eye of the monarch, as if that might mitigate his bloody mood.

The Blood Guards had no doubts. Their King/Lord had spoken. They advanced with drawn swords and stern looks upon their faces. Obviously, they did not relish the idea of slaughtering an unarmed man, but they knew only too well that disobedience would result in their own deaths. As one, they aimed the points of their blades at the heart of the victim.

Trys stepped down off the dias to meet his fate. He found he was strangely calm. He had gambled his grandfather would help him, and he had lost.

While he had no prayer horn, he could pray, and picture the infinite spiral of the horn in his mind as he did so. His fingers moved as if they were following the carved lines. His lips moved as he whispered the prayer of death. He had spoken it for only a handful of souls back in the North, but its simplicity and serenity were as familiar to him as his own voice.

"Mother Ice, take my body into your loving embrace. Father Sun, let my soul wing to you in all of your burning splendor. Let me go quietly to where everyone goes. Let me go courageously to the ice bound realm of peace. Let me go..."

Trys's murmured prayer was interrupted by a stifled cry from behind and above him. Trys saw the advance of the blades falter, and then stop.

He turned to face the King/Lord. Nordseth still stood by his throne, one hand clasping the decahedron and the other the arm of the throne. Even as Trys watched, the expression of pure fury melted away to be replaced by a look of wonder and bafflement.

"What are you doing?" The question was one of true curiosity.

"I am reciting my death prayer."

The baffled expression dissolved, to be replaced in rapid succession by ones of disgust, fear, and finally resignation. One melted into the other, and each one seemed to sap Nordseth of some of his manic strength of will.

"You would have to do that, wouldn't you? You would have to face death calmly and make peace with the gods that way, wouldn't you?"

Trys could tell the King/Lord did not really expect him to answer.

Nordseth collapsed slowly back onto the throne. The decahedron of blood metal clanked dully against the ice marble of one arm as he sank back. The blades of the Blood Guards wavered. He noticed them and waved them back with one thin hand.

They dropped the points of their swords but kept them at the ready, in case the arbitrary King/Lord might change his mind yet again.

When Nordseth recognized the fact they still had blades drawn, he scowled and spoke. "Sheath those blades. Take him away. Take him away and put him...somewhere. Torkild will tell you where, and what to do with him. Take him away. Now!" A bit of the old fire flared up on the last order and the Guards hurried to put their swords away and surround Trys as quickly as they could.

Trys felt sorry for the man on the throne. And even as he did, he realized it was his grandfather for whom he felt that emotion. The man before him was the father of his father. The man before him had nearly had him put to death on the spot. But he had no fear now of the man who had paused and rescinded the order; merely sadness, and a certain fascination with all of the contradictory emotions which were crowding in upon him at the end of the somewhat ludicrous and yet nearly deadly scene which was just ending.

The Blood Guards moved to surround Trys. They tried to act threatening, and yet kept their distance, not at all certain how tough they were supposed to be with this particular prisoner who the King/Lord seemed so uncertain about. Previous to this, an edict of death was swiftly and summarily carried out. Now, they just did not know.

Torkild helped to resolve some of their doubts as he lurched down from his place near the King/Lord and curtly ordered the prisoner taken to one of the smaller tents at a short remove from the royal one. They obeyed his order eagerly, glad to have a firm command they could understand and carry out. They all marched away from the dias, with only Torkild not keeping perfect time with their swinging step.

When they had all disappeared from sight amongst the shadows in the Tent, Nordseth raised his head to listen to their steady tread, accented by Torkild's awkward gait. The sound could be heard all the way to the flap in the outer skin of the Tent. Nordseth listened until the flap fell. And then, his eyes, bright with fever, grew even brighter for a moment before they were dulled by the tears which welled out of them. They dropped one at a time onto the decahedron where they hissed and evaporated.

## XXII

NEAR THE middle of a midwinter's night, the moon's light was by turns dazzling in its brilliance and shrouded behind high, wind driven clouds. Over and over again, the light chased the dark away, and was in turn smothered by the darkness. During a period when the wind scattered the clouds yet again, the silvered light of the moon swept down the grim bulk of the Hold and flashed across the sprawl of the Camp.

On a mount which lay close to the Royal Tent, challenging its preeminent position but being overtopped by the bloated dome of bryl hide, lay a small group of subsidiary tents which housed the prisoners of the King/Lord. In the harsh, metallic light, they looked pitiable, as if they crouched together to share the meager bits of warmth each contained.

Here and there a brazier burned to illuminate the small tents from the inside and give an indication that some small flicker of life still existed upon the exposed ground. A modest number of Blood Guards patrolled the upper perimeter of the mount on the frigid night. Most had been driven into their own tent, which lay at the foot of the mount and which blazed with light and rang with song and laughter.

It was toward this mount that two figures hurried, until they reached a large drift of snow which had crept into the Camp over the past few days and which lay about a hundred yards from the tent of the Blood Guards. Since it offered some protection from the cutting wind, they paused in its lee.

The tall figure bent down to try to get his head below the curled edge of the wind shaped snow, while the short one stood on his tiptoes to try to get a glimpse of the mount which lay before and above them.

"There it is," said Englerth, craning his neck above the drift and spitting out the snow which blew into his mouth.

"And here we are," grumbled Bledsahl, hunching over to keep the wind driven snow from crusting over the hood of his black Waste cloak.

"He's got to be up there. Roxyna said he was the King/Lord's prisoner, and that's the King/Lord's prison."

"To which we may be introduced all too soon. He may be up there, but how do you propose we get him down from there and out of the Camp? After all, we are actors, not magicians."

Englerth sputtered as a gust threw a handful of granular snow in his face, and then moved into the protection of the drift by the simple expedient of getting down off his toes.

"Well, let me think about that," answered Englerth.

"You mean you didn't have a plan to begin with? But you told Roxyna..."

"I told her what she needed to hear. You can see she loves Trys. She needed reassurance."

"As do I."

"Oh, Bledsahl, don't complain so. Just give me a minute to think."

"A century might not be enough to get us out of this spot," observed the tall actor.

Bledsahl and Englerth were in the Camp performing with a minor and rather ragged acting company which normally Bledsahl would have simply turned his nose up at, but which they had joined temporarily, with the emphasis on the temporary at Bledsahl's insistence, due to the sincerely desperate urgings of Roxyna.

The network of revolutionary spies in the Camp had informed those in Hold Gate that Trys was a prisoner of the King/Lord, that he had escaped immediate execution, but that the King/Lord's thinking was once again swinging around to an elimination of the newly discovered potential heir to the half throne.

The recently revealed truth about Trys's birth had blanketed Hold and Camp like a particularly insidious snowstorm. Many made nothing of it, waiting for the Interpreters to put their seal of either approval or disapproval upon the potential heir, while others, Lyrdahl included, saw the unexpected arrival upon the political scene as the final boost which the revolution needed to put it over the top and to help it gain widespread support. To that end, he had used Roxyna, who was anxious for Trys's life in any case, to implore Bledsahl and Englerth to try to help Trys to escape from the Camp and get into Hold Gate, where the ragamuffin troops of the revolution were massing for what promised to be a final confrontation for good or bad.

For a while, it seemed Nordseth had forgotten Trys's presence in the Camp. He had shivered in his tent upon the prison mount for a week. But, as was the King/Lord's wont, just two days ago, an order of general execution had gone out for all of the prisoners on the mount.

The excuse, used often enough before to seem routine, had been that the tents were getting rather overcrowded and that they needed to be cleared out for a new batch of prisoners, the supply of which seemed unending under Nordseth's current paranoid reign. It was this which had prompted Roxyna, after not so subtle hints from

Lyrdahl, to seek out the two actors and beg them to make an attempt to save Trys's life, which might or might not be in peril.

They had hesitated at first. But when Englerth had pointed out that Trys's birth father had been none other than their friend Gerred, neither one had been able to come up with any overriding objection to the attempt. Although, Bledsahl had made it clear to Roxyna they would try, but not necessarily succeed in the attempt. She had taken what she could get.

And so, they found themselves prowling about the Camp in the middle of a bitterly cold night, trying to formulate a brilliant plan of escape on the spur of the moment.

"I know," chirped up Englerth. "Let's storm the mount and overcome the guards."

"Our reduced numbers and disadvantage in arms mitigate against that particular plan," observed Bledsahl drily.

"Well, yes, there is that. Do you have any ideas?"

"As a matter of fact, yes. I propose we do what we do best. Act. And in this case, you may have the lead. You will be a First Lord just in from some obscure Northern clan eager to see the dangerous prisoners and I will be your silent, albeit deadly looking, retainer."

"Yes, that might work."

"Merely be insufferable and arrogant. You should be able to carry it off with a modicum of acting," said Bledsahl.

"Exactly. I was made to play the part. At this late hour the Blood Guards are unlikely to hunt up someone higher in authority to verify my identity, and once in we'll be able to help Trys to escape. How exactly should we do that, once in, I mean?"

"We will get in by cunning and talent; we shall get out the same way."

"In other words, you don't know."

Bledsahl gave him a withering stare but said nothing.

"Fine," said Englerth. "I love improvisation. We'll think of something when the time comes."

"Let's get going. Daylight will be here soon and we need to finish this little play before then. Remember, Roxyna waits on the causeway."

"Right. Let's go."

With that he drew himself up to his most impressive height, which was done impressively but turned out to not be very high, and threw open the front of his cloak, borrowed from the costumes of their current acting company. It was a deep purple in color and cut to flatter his short, stocky figure.

Bledsahl shook his head and muttered something about how he hoped even if they were caught they would be lenient with two madmen. He then drew his own black cloak about him and hunched himself over slightly, trying to exude the essence of a humble retainer while maintaining his own innate dignity, no small feat he soon discovered.

They approached the prison mount by a roundabout means to avoid having to pass too closely to the tent of the Blood Guards pitched at the base of the mount. As they struggled up the slippery slope of the mount, the clouds obscured the moon and they were forced to inch forward along the unfamiliar path. Englerth kept sliding backward into Bledsahl who would then shove him forward, even as he slid backward himself on the uncertain footing of the icy walkway. In this manner, they laboriously climbed to the top of the mount.

Once at the top, they paused to get their bearings. The moon burst from behind its cloud cover and washed the entire top of the rise in its garish silver light. The tents were huddled together in the center of the plateau with only a flickering light to be seen here and there within them. The unevenness of the light and the meanness of the tents contrasted sharply with the huge, resplendent dome of the Royal Tent, blazing brightly in spots even at the late hour and clearly visible just beyond the edge of the mount.

The bright light also revealed two Blood Guards making their rounds along the perimeter and even then approaching Englerth and Bledsahl where they stood at the top of the path. Bledsahl could clearly see their suspicious looks and he nudged Englerth, who managed to throw out his chest a few more inches to make himself even more prepossessing than he had been a moment before.

Both Guards lowered the points of their brum pikes and advanced to within comfortable striking range of the intruders. As they got closer, Bledsahl could also see they looked tired, as if they were near the end of their watch and eager to get it over with and into the tent at the bottom of the mount. Bledsahl whispered his observation to Englerth, who nodded and stepped forward bravely.

He stepped so close to the Guards they were forced to raise the points of their pikes to prevent him from impaling himself upon them. Bledsahl silently applauded the maneuver, for instead of ordering him back, they raised their pikes and leaned upon them, scowling but obviously tired.

"What do you want?" asked the one on the left. "No one is allowed up here without the permission of the Captain of the Blood Guards." He spoke his lines as if he had repeated them a thousand times and they had lost all real meaning for him.

Englerth picked up on the poor delivery of the lines and launched into his own brilliant interpretation of an overbearing First Lord out for a midnight stroll.

"I am First Lord Brack pyr Brack myr Gysh. You will take me to the tent of the prisoner called Trys. Now."

They both blinked their tired eyes, but did not move. They had seen their share of Lords and Ladies who demanded this and that, and they knew their official duties did not include giving in to every one of them.

"Not without permission of the Captain of the Blood Guards," repeated the guard.

"The Captain and I have an understanding, you may be sure of it. He is...courting my sister. He is virtually a member of the household," said Englerth, scrambling hard to find a reason to justify his presence.

Bledsahl groaned inwardly. Such an outrageous reason was bound to get them caught and thrown into one of the drafty tents themselves.

But miraculously, both guard perked up at the mention of Englerth's fictitious sister. They straightened up and glanced at each other. They then leaned toward one another.

"Do you think that's it?" said the one on the left.

"Could be," replied the one on the right. "He's been swaggering a lot. It would be just like him to have something like that under his hood and not tell anyone about it."

"Yeah, he's been acting like he wouldn't have to put up with us for much longer. A good marriage might just do it."

"So, what do we do with these two?"

Both guards turned to examine the pair in the garish light which streamed down from the wild sky.

"Let them see him. We'll be right outside, and if what he says is true, then maybe he'll put in a good word for us," said the one on the left.

Englerth drew himself up and fairly quivered with excitement at his unexpected success. "My good fellows, you may be assured I will describe your admirable talents in great detail to the dear Captain upon the first opportunity. Men like you should be officers. I will emphasize that particularly."

That did it. Their greed, and the fact they had trudged the same midnight round of duty on the mount for two weeks in a row, overcame their reservations. They shouldered their pikes and indicated that Englerth and Bledsahl should follow them.

They led them through the tents which were arranged in a roughly circular pattern upon the top of the mount to one at the very center. It occupied a relatively open area. The closest tent was about eight yards away. A single light illuminated it from the inside, although the light did burn brighter than any of the other lights in any of the other tents around it.

"This is it," said the guard on the left, as he dragged open the flap and grinned up at the ersatz Lord Brack.

"Well done, well done, indeed. I will remember this. Stand back now and we shall be out in a short while."

The guard suddenly frowned. "But wait a minute."

Bledsahl felt his stomach drop and Englerth tensed.

"What is it now?" asked Englerth, careful to put enough authority in his voice to command respect but not be pushy.

"You don't know our names."

"I don't know your names," repeated Englerth, relieved that that was the cause of his sudden hesitation. "Well, tell me. I shall commit them to memory and be sure to link them with all sorts of glorious phrases when I next see the Captain."

The man grinned. "I'm Gursec pyr..."

Englerth interrupted. "I don't need your patronymic and matronymic. I will wreath your own given name alone with glowing praises."

"Oh, right. Then, I'm Gursec and he's Tomsur, Blood Guards to the most magnificent King/Lord Nordseth pyr..."

"You're getting carried away again," warned Englerth. "Now kindly step back and let us enter."

Gursec grinned again, but sheepishly this time and bobbed his head in acknowledgement he had gone a bit far. They both picked up their pikes and retreated to the required distance, smiling as they looked back over their shoulders.

"Excellent improvisation," muttered Bledsahl under his breath.

"Why, thank you, I did enjoy it," whispered back Englerth.

"Let's get inside quick, before they think of something else they think you should know about them to better sing their praises," said Bledsahl.

Englerth and Bledsahl ducked through the opening and into the close yet chilly atmosphere of the tent. Like all tents, it consisted of bryl hides stretched tightly over bryl bones which formed the dome and a floor, also of bryl hides, which was sewn to the walls. This arrangement formed a pocket which could be warmed by a small fire and ventilated by baffle flaps near the top of the dome. This particular tent was not overly warm, even though a small brazier, standing on three wobbly legs near the center of the tent, did contain a modest but smoky fire.

Both Englerth and Bledsahl could tell from the steady draft from overhead that the baffle flaps were either wide open or nonexistent, thus allowing the cold to overwhelm the meager warmth from the brazier. But, while the flaps let in the cold, they did not seem to be allowing the smoke from the ill tended fire to escape. As a result, the tent had the worst of both elements, too little warmth and too much smoke, which made it difficult to see clearly.

Other than the brazier, the only other furnishing of the tent was a small pile of hides, most of which had lost their fur at some point in the distant past. Crouched upon these paper thin hides were two men. A long bundle of well cured bryl hides which appeared to contain something within it, did lie next to one of the men, but it did not appear to be a part of the furnishings of the tent.

Bledsahl gave Englerth a quick warning glance. Englerth noted it and nodded ever so slightly. They had not expected to find anyone other than Trys in the tent and would have to act accordingly.

Englerth decided to continue with the act which had carried him this far. "Trys? I come to see the prisoner, Trys. Which one are you? Speak up now."

The taller of the two men rose and straightened himself up, or at least as straight at the low dome of the tent would allow. "I am Trys. Who asks?"

"And your companion. Who is he?" asked Englerth, throwing out his chest as he decided to keep the act going until he could determine with whom they had to deal.

"And I say, who asks? It's bad enough I'm kept imprisoned here without offensive little Lords pushing their way in to gawk."

The other man turned the right side of his face toward them and stared hard with his right eye. He then raised his right hand and touched the sleeve of Trys's singlesuit as if to calm him.

"I'm Torkild, servant of the King/Lord Nordseth."

Englerth gulped and deflated. Bledsahl stirred at his elbow and spoke quietly to him, "Now we're in for it."

Englerth half turned to him, his assumed attitude dropping off him like an old rag which would no longer hold together, and began to berate him. "It was your idea. This was your idea, remember?"

"It might have been my idea, but you were the one who overacted your way up to this point. Subtlety is not your strong point."

"It got us this far, didn't it?"

"Yes, and where is this? Caught by the King/Lord's own personal servant."

"Englerth! Bledsahl!"

The sound of their names made them stop. They turned to Trys with some fear, thinking he had just revealed their true identities before the right hand man of the King/Lord, and not being able to see any benefit for themselves from the revelation.

"It is you. I could tell once you began to fight. What are you doing here?" asked Trys who moved around the brazier so he could see his old acquaintances better.

"I believe," said Torkild from the other side of the brazier, "that like me, they are here to help you escape. But unlike me, I believe they might have a fair chance to accomplish that feat."

"Escape? But, why should you endanger yourselves to help me?"

Bledsahl raised his eyebrows and Englerth sniffed at the intimation they had no real reason for being there. Englerth spoke up. "Your birth father was a very close friend of ours. We are doing this for him as much as for you."

Trys reached out and touched Englerth on the shoulder. "He must have been lucky to have such friends as you two. I wish I could have known him."

"Someday, when leisure allows," said Bledsahl, "we shall tell you all about him. He was someone special."

"Leisure barely allows this," interrupted Torkild. "I'm sorry to break up this little reunion, but necessity demands that we act now."

Trys turned to Torkild. "I do need to know one thing, Torkild. I can see why Englerth and Bledsahl here would try to help me escape. But why are you aiding me?"

"A fair question," he replied as he ducked his head in acknowledgement that he had to reveal his reasons for joining in what appeared to be an act of treason to his King/Lord. "The King/Lord's health is failing. He will not die tomorrow or the next day, or even the next, but his days are numbered. When he does die, there will be chaos for a time as one faction fights another for the power which lies unclaimed. All of my years of watching the machinations of power close up have led me to one assumption; you could well be the next King/Lord."

Trys nearly laughed out loud at what he perceived as an absolutely preposterous statement.

Torkild held up his right hand. "Do not predict the future merely from what exists in the present. Ask Sebaste about that old maxim. You do possess the proper bloodlines to assume the throne, and you are outside of the current political system which grips the half kingdom in its death-like embrace. That might be a true advantage when the time comes. I help you now so that perhaps you can help me later. When you do come into your share of the power, I hope you will remember me."

"I will certainly do that. But I don't believe I will ever hold any of the power of which you speak. In fact, I'm not sure I will even live to see the sun sink beneath the horizon."

"Don't worry," said Englerth in his best heroic voice, "we'll see to that."

"So, you have a plan to get me out of here?" asked Trys eagerly.

"Well, not exactly," said Englerth in a suddenly less than

heroic tone of voice.

"I came up with the plan to get us in here," said Bledsahl, "but we figured that once here something in the form of an inspiration would strike us. Any bolts of inspiration, dear Englerth?"

"Well, no. But if you would give me a chance to think, I might come up with something."

"The only thing you'll come up with is a headache from trying to use that severely underutilized portion of your head called a brain."

"I have plenty of schemes for helping Trys escape," countered Englerth, beginning to warm to the conflict. "I just have to sort through them to find the best one."

"May I suggest something?" said Torkild quietly but firmly.

The actors stopped their squabbling and turned, with thinly veiled relief that someone had a practical scheme to get them out of the mess they had put Trys and themselves in, toward the servant of the King/Lord.

"If, on the way in, Englerth played the part of the First Lord and Bledsahl that of his aide, I would suppose that Englerth did almost all of the talking, while Bledsahl remained silent?"

"It is ever so," intoned Bledsahl solemnly.

"That's just because I'm better at it," quipped Englerth.

"In your case, practice, long, insufferable practice, does not make perfect," retorted Bledsahl.

"You're simply jealous. Why..." Englerth stopped as Torkild made an impatient gesture and scrambled to his feet.

"My proposal, if you will be so good as to be quiet long enough to hear it, is that Trys wear Bledsahl's Waste cloak, and that he and Englerth simply walk out of here."

No one said anything for a moment. Both Trys and Englerth then looked at Bledsahl who drew himself up, raised his eyebrows, and at first tugged his cloak tighter about him but then loosened it slightly.

"It's a good idea, Torkild," said Trys, "but I couldn't ask Bledsahl to jeopardize his life to try to free me."

Bledsahl nodded, but then frowned and shook his head. "I certainly wish to aid the son of an old friend, but I must admit I'm not keen on offering up my life in such a manner."

"It would be the best role you've ever played," said Englerth quietly.

"And it could be the last one," observed Bledsahl.

Torkild limped around the brazier to join the group. "Consider this, then. Once the alarm is raised, and I plan on raising it myself to throw suspicion off of me, I will probably be able to help you to slip away undetected. Since the Blood Guards will be looking for a man in a black Waste cloak, I will be quite specific on that point, you should find it relatively easy to slip away in the confusion."

It was now Englerth's turn to look skeptical. "If you raise the alarm and tell the guards just who to look for, what are our chances of getting away?"

"I will give you as much time as I can. I will send them off toward the other end of the mount to begin with. They will be so scared that such an important prisoner has escaped they will listen to me as if I were Father Ice himself telling them where to look," said Torkild.

"It's simple and bold. It will work," declared Trys.

Both Englerth and Bledsahl agreed, although with less certainty. Bledsahl took off his black Waste cloak and Trys put it on. He pulled the hood up and thrust his hands deep into the wide sleeves. He was almost the same height as the tall actor and in the relative darkness could easily be mistaken for him.

"We're ready," announced Trys.

"One more thing," said Torkild. He shuffled hurriedly back around the brazier and picked up the long bundle which had lain near him on the tent floor. "Your blood blade." He handed the bundle to Trys. "I thought you might need it."

Trys gripped the bundle and felt the familiar shape within. "Thank you, Torkild. I will never forget this."

"See that you don't. You're my insurance." The right side of his twisted face grinned and then he ducked his head. "Get going now. Bledsahl, come and warm yourself at the brazier. We'll venture forth in a little while."

"Not too little, I hope," said Englerth.

"I will give you as much time as I can without throwing too much suspicion on myself."

"A true survivor," muttered Englerth under his breath. "Take care, Bledsahl," he then said out loud. "I'll see you soon. I hope."

Bledsahl smiled grimly and nodded. "Gods' luck to you two."

With that, Englerth and Trys moved to the flap where Trys poked his head out. No clouds covered the moon and the silver light flooded the top of the mount. The two guards leaned on their brum pikes several yards away.

Trys pulled his head back in. "Two guards are out there."

"Oh, don't worry about them," said Englerth airily. "They won't bother us."

"I certainly hope not."

Trys, followed by Englerth, slipped out of the tent. Both stood there and Trys made sure his cloak covered him entirely. He also tried to stand just a little taller to better match the former owner's height.

"That's it. The costume is as good as it's going to get. Let's get moving," said Englerth in a low voice.

Englerth waved to the two Blood Guards who still stood at their post. They nodded and grinned, thinking of the good things which would be said about them. The short actor then began to swagger as quickly as he could toward the edge of the mount, while Trys glided along just behind him, trying to act as much like a subservient retainer as he could. Both found they wanted to break into a run, but they curbed the impulse and walked slowly but tensely.

They reached the path which led down off of the prison mount and were just beginning to quicken their pace on the steep slope, when they heard a shout go up from the center of the tents. In an instant, more shouts were heard and then the clatter of armed Blood Guards as they charged through the prison tents.

"That's not much time," complained Englerth.

"Those guards probably decided to check on the prisoner. It doesn't matter. Run," said Trys. "Just run."

They ran. They ran down the path and out onto the Waste plain which lay near the River Ice. And as they did so, the tent which held the company of Blood Guards and which lay near the base of the mount, flared with light and then spilled forth most of the company. Most charged up the path to the mount, but a good sized contingent veered off and took the same path which Trys and Englerth were on.

The two ducked behind the large drift where Englerth and Bledsahl had paused on their way toward the mount. They were hidden in the deep shadows which crouched there. But both looked toward the coming guards and then ahead to where the causeway over the River Ice seemed so distant.

"You've got to make it to the causeway. Roxyna is waiting there for you. If only the moonlight would disappear for a while," said Englerth.

As if at his request, clouds scudded over the face of the moon and they were plunged into near total darkness. Englerth fumbled for Trys and shoved him along the path toward the causeway.

They left the protection of the drift and were making good time toward their destination when they heard the clank of pursuing Blood Guards behind them. And then, as if to mock the granting of the previous request, the clouds were blown from the face of the moon and it glared down in all of its whitened glory. The two men were caught in the midst of the open landscape. The Blood Guards saw them and quickened their pursuit.

As they ran, Englerth gasped out, "Make for the causeway. Roxyna is there. She's waiting to get you into Hold Gate. Hurry."

"What are you going to do?"

"Decoy," puffed Englerth, and with that the short actor darted off to one side and disappeared in a section of low snow dunes which bordered the path. In a moment, an unearthly caterwauling erupted from the dunes which nearly stopped Trys in his tracks until he realized it was Englerth acting the part of the decoy.

It almost worked. When Trys spared a glance back over his shoulder, he could see the Blood Guards falter in their pursuit and then split up, a large portion of them charging out toward the dunes where sounds resembling a wounded brum rumbled and roared.

Trys kept on running. His side was stitched with pain and his feet grew heavier with each step. Suddenly, he felt the stone of the causeway beneath his feet and not the frozen earth of the path. He had made it that far.

A shout of anger went up from behind him as the Blood Guards realized he was almost out of their grasp. A shout of victory rang out from in front of him as he glanced toward Hold Gate. There, spanning the entire width of the causeway, was a group of warriors whose singlesuits marked them as Lord Grendyl's men. Enemies before and behind, Trys continued to run until he reached the center of the long span. There he stopped and bent over, laboring to suck in enough of the frigid air to ease his aching lungs.

He looked both ways. Warriors approached from both sides at a slow but steady pace. No one seemed to be in a rush now that his capture by one group or the other seemed inevitable. In fact, Trys could tell they were sizing up each other, trying to determine who would win the battle for the lone figure at the center of the causeway.

He undid his borrowed Waste cloak and let it slide to the surface of the causeway. Even as he did so, he chuckled to himself and hoped it was not Bledsahl's best cloak. It looked like Bledsahl would never get it back.

He began to unwrap the blood blade from the bryl hide, but was having trouble untying one of the knots, when he sensed someone walk up behind him. Even as he tensed, he was puzzled. None of the warriors could have reached him yet. He gripped the still wrapped sword and prepared to whip it around to cudgel whoever approached him.

He spun, and then stopped. There, a few feet away and smiling, was Roxyna. In that split second of recognition, he thought he had never seen her looking so beautiful. The pure white light from the full moon flooded down and illuminated every lovely line of her face and curve of her body.

And, like some angel of the snow, she beckoned to him. "Trys, this way. Hurry."

He followed her as she turned and sprinted for the edge of the causeway, even as he wondered at the choice of her direction. As suddenly as she had appeared, she disappeared over the edge.

Trys slid to a halt, but was then urged on by her voice.

"Jump. It's just a small jump down."

He jumped off the edge of the causeway into what looked like open space. But instead of plummeting into the icy waters of the River Ice far below, he landed heavily on a small platform just a few feet below the level of the causeway. Roxyna grabbed and steadied him.

She gave him a brief hug and brushed her lips across his cheek. He fumbled for her but she had already slipped away, although she did retain his hand and drew him after her.

"This way. Hurry. We'll be safe in a moment."

He ducked down and into what proved to be a low corridor which ran toward the center of the causeway. He soon found the corridor intersected another larger one which ran both toward and away from Hold Gate itself. They turned and hurried along the corridor which led to Hold Gate.

Overhead, he could distinctly hear the clash of the Blood Guards engaging Lord Grendyl's men as the two groups swirled in confusion and anger at the disappearance of their prey. He marveled at the resourcefulness of his companion, and at the delicate yet tough fingers which firmly held his own. He squeezed her hand. In the darkness of the narrow corridor, heading toward he knew not what fate, she squeezed back, and he felt that somehow all would be right.

## XXIII

TRYS AND Roxyna reached the Hall of the Revolution deep within Hold Gate just as the sun rose. A bright ray of sunshine made its way through a series of serendipitously arranged cracks in the fabric of Hold Gate itself to fall upon an ancient wall. The wall glowed soft and yellow and the faint images of a mural, once vibrant with color but now muted with age and dust, could be seen but not understood. The image might have been that of the Hold or of the mountain itself. All that remained was a sense of a rising and then falling line amongst the cracks and the dirt.

The wall was the first thing Trys saw as he stepped into the Hall of the Revolution. The rest of the huge yet surreal room fell into place about it as he and Roxyna walked across its floor of randomly alternating black and white and red slate tiles. It drew his eyes and seemed to offer a sense of stability and comfort which was sorely lacking from the rest of the monolithic structure.

In many ways, the Hall was a reflection of the rest of Hold Gate which they had seen as they climbed upward through its ancient, idiosyncratic corridors and stairways. Hold Gate was a paradox; an inhabited ruin which nurtured life in its odd corners even as it threatened to come toppling down to crush that very life.

Trys and Roxyna had begun their tour of the Gate when they scooted from the causeway into the lowest corridors, like animals going to cover. There, amidst a warren of tunnels, they had been greeted by the tenacious defenders of the outer reaches of Hold Gate. The revolutionary warriors, both men and women, had struck and slipped away, only to reappear and strike again at the imposing phalanx of Blood Guards who had pursued them onto the causeway.

The Blood Guards, covered in blood from numerous but superficial wounds caused by swords made from strips of rough metal and spears with chipped obsidian points, had finally fallen back, more baffled than defeated by the quick rat-like attacks, and had formed an imposing wall of armor and flesh across the entire width of the causeway as if to say, you might not get in but you shall never get out.

They had thanked their rescuers, who had watched them briefly with eyes bright with revolutionary fervor and who had then darted back to their posts to harry and slash and keep the forces of the King/Lord at bay. Trys had shaken his head and Roxyna had smiled proudly, and then they had begun the climb from floor to crazy floor.

Proof against all but the most severe of the earthquakes which had shaken the mountain and the Hold over the centuries, Hold Gate, nevertheless, had sustained its share of damage. However, Trys found himself hard pressed to discern just what architectural features had been caused by earthquakes and what had been designed by the seemingly mad minds of the ancient architects. Long and winding stairways led to blank walls. Corridors widened and narrowed even as their floors were frozen in static undulation. The edges of huge gaps in the floor were neatly finished off with brilliantly colored tiles.

Trys finally came to the conclusion that the earthquakes had caused damage which the architects had then incorporated into their overall design. Hold Gate had become a finely finished ruin which celebrated rather than attempted to cover up its flaws.

The revolution seemed to be in much the same state. They met men and women who cried out revolutionary slogans even as they charged through ill lit corridors toward they knew not what. And they came upon knots of people who huddled in oddly shaped chambers, nearly sobbing with despair at the course of the revolution as they saw it. Roxyna tried to slow down the one group and cheer up the other, but with little success in either endeavor. Trys could tell she was troubled by what she saw, but that she held on to her belief in the essence of the revolution.

And so, they made their way steadily, if erratically due to the nature of the corridors and stairways, toward the Hall of the Revolution. It had been their goal since they had set out from the causeway. There Lyrdahl waited for them. There resided the seat of the revolution.

The Hall had only recently taken on its revolutionary label. Its original use was lost amid the myriad uses to which it had been put since the Gate had been built. In recent memory, it had served as a banqueting hall, a hospital, and an armory. Now it contained the heart of the revolution.

As Trys consciously drew his attention away from the ancient, sunlit wall to consider the rest of the Hall, he was struck once again by the architectural melding of ruin and modern design. The proportions of the Hall were grand. Its red, black, and white tiled floor spread out for hundreds of yards in every direction from the doorway through which Trys and Roxyna had entered. It occupied nearly two thirds of the story of Hold Gate on which it was located.

However, its grandness was marred by the fact that the story above the one on which the Hall was located, literally intruded. Portions of the ceiling, which did rise to heights of thirty feet in most places, sagged to such depths that only about four feet of space remained between ceiling and floor in others. The center was the worst. It bulged downward in a huge bowl of sagging plaster and stone held together and supported by a cunning system of pillars. Trys could tell the pillars were a fairly recent addition, since they were devoid of embellishment and smoothly practical.

The sunlit wall lay to their right as they entered the Hall. Roxyna led Trys toward it and around the sagging center of the ceiling. The strange acoustics created by the bulge allowed Trys to hear a loud discussion being carried on across the Hall before he could actually see where it was coming from. A few shuffling feet were all he could catch a glimpse of from under the bowl of the ceiling.

They rounded the curve of the ceiling and stopped close to the ancient wall. Trys's attention was drawn from the yellow softness to the group of men and women who gathered in an area near the bulge where the ceiling and the floor had maintained their original orientation to each other.

The men and women were clustered about a chair which was set on what once must have been the pedestal for some large sculpture. The pedestal was close to the wall and the chair leaned against it for some extra support, which it needed since one of its legs was cracked and it swayed dangerously as its occupant leaned forward or sat back in it.

The occupant was Lyrdahl, the leader of the revolution. He was leaner than he had been during the riot in the square before Hold Gate. His features were sharper and his hands twitched about the ends of the arms of the rickety chair as he shifted back and forth in a pattern of feverish restlessness.

The group which milled about the pedestal, and on which he fixed his exhaustion sharpened attention, were a mixture of men and women in various stages of exhaustion themselves. A few looked fresh and even well dressed, while most were haggard from lack of sleep and disheveled from manning the barricades of Hold Gate. Splashes of drying blood and hastily tied bandages distinguished the ones who had been in the thick of the murderous battle which raged on all sides of the Gate.

Roxyna stopped Trys by putting her hand on his forearm. They paused by the sunlit wall.

"Trys, you must know there is trouble with the revolution. There is dissension about how it is being led and anxiety about the amount of pressure which is being applied from all sides. The attack of the Blood Guards on the causeway was not the first time they have attempted to take the lower part of the Gate. Ice Guards, in combination with Lord Grendyl's men, continually besiege the upper portions. It's the first time in centuries that Hold and Camp have worked together, so to speak," she ended wryly.

"And Lyrdahl?" asked Trys, glancing toward the pedestal and the man in the shaky chair.

"He is the revolution." She put a burst of her old energy into the slogan, but he saw her face crumble slightly as soon as she said it. "He believes in it fervently and will do all he can to make it succeed."

"What role do I play here?" asked Trys tentatively.

Roxyna turned to him with a spark of excitement in her eyes. "You offer promise in so many ways. You are the heir to the half throne. You are an Interpreter. You sympathize with the goals of the revolution. You could be our rallying point."

Trys winced at her enthusiasm. He had stumbled into his current position of potential heir and he was not certain how much of the revolution he really agreed with. He knew he would not be a suitable rallying point for anything. In fact, all of it, the politics of revolution and Hold and Camp, sickened him at that moment. He simply wanted to retreat from the swirl of events with which he had so little to do.

He glanced at the light softened wall next to him and noticed that the sun had risen higher in the distant sky. The blurred image upon the mural was lit at a higher angle and its outline was sharper but its intent still vague. For a moment, he focussed his thoughts upon the mystery of the unresolved image. It was like running his fingers around the curve of a prayer horn and allowing his mind to follow along. A shout snapped him out of his reverie.

"There is the revolution! Look, he has arrived!"

Roxyna stirred nervously and took Trys's hand in hers. She gave it a warm squeeze and led him toward the pedestal where Lyrdahl now stood and shouted his welcome.

"Do what you believe is best," she whispered to him.

He looked at her face, set in an expression of determination but softened by what he knew to be love.

"Thank you. I will do what I can to keep us both alive."

She nodded and strode purposefully toward the pedestal, towing him along by the hand.

Everyone turned to them. Trys saw expressions ranging from fervent hope to utter disbelief, and he thought to himself, if these are the faces of the revolution, then it is in trouble.

"Welcome," said Lyrdahl in a voice designed to carry across the Hall. "I have been waiting for you. The revolution has been waiting for you."

"I appreciate the welcome. It is nice not to have swords drawn when I enter a room. But I must decline the honor of being the revolution. I am nothing more than a novice Interpreter."

Lyrdahl scowled for the briefest of seconds and then carefully replaced that expression with one of magnanimous humor. He even managed a bluff laugh. "His modesty is charming, is it not?" said Lyrdahl as he swept his gaze about the room to include everyone in his address to Trys. "Charming but unnecessary here. You are home. After all, this is the Hall of the Revolution."

"Only recently renamed, I believe," observed Trys.

"Because the revolution is the event of the moment. It is happening even as we speak."

"Yes, I have seen how the revolution goes throughout Hold Gate. I must tell you that..."

"That it soars to unimaginable heights. That it pushes back the oppression on all sides. That it inhabits the souls of all who believe in it," interrupted Lyrdahl with a fierce intentness.

Everyone, except Roxyna, seemed to hang on Lyrdahl's words. Trys could see the man manipulating the crowd, bolstering the true believers and giving hope to the skeptical ones. He had to admit the man was good.

"What is my role in all of this?" Trys decided to ask the question bluntly, since his subtlety was only turned against him by the half mad, wholly fervent man before him.

Lyrdahl glanced once at the expectant crowd and then smiled slightly. "You are the rallying point of the revolution which I shall lead to victory. You are the potential heir to the half throne, it doesn't matter which one, and you are a former Interpreter who has become dissatisfied with the established order. You bridge the yawning gap between the way things are and the way things are meant to be. With you in the front rank, we will sweep on to victory."

"Being in the front rank is an honor, but one I must decline just now. You see, I don't know how much I believe in this revolution of yours."

Lyrdahl strode to the edge of the pedestal closest to Trys and leaned over tensely. "Forces are in motion which cannot be stopped easily or quickly. These forces may not be controlled but they can be directed. I will direct them where I see fit, and you will help me."

"Or else?"

Roxyna moved closer to Trys as Lyrdahl's head snapped back and his eyes narrowed. "He is merely being cautious, Lyrdahl. He has been through a lot."

"Silence! I can already see where your loyalties lie."

Roxyna bristled. "I am loyal to the revolution."

"But not to me," hissed Lyrdahl through clenched teeth.

Trys sighed. The time for fencing with words was over. "She is true to the revolution, Lyrdahl. You are trying to use it to gain power just for yourself."

"Silence," warned Lyrdahl.

"If I do have power, then I want all of you to listen to me," said Trys as he turned to include the men and women about the pedestal. "The battle for Hold Gate is not going well. The revolution is in trouble. I cannot say if the revolution is right or wrong. Like most things it contains a bit of both. But right here and now, it is faltering. The only sane thing to do is to get out while you still can. There must be passages out of the Gate which can get you to other sections of Low Hold. If there is no one to fight, the forces of the Hold and the Camp will have to fight with each other. That can work to the benefit of the revolution in the long run. And a revolution is all about the long run. Give it time. It has started. But if you are not careful it will be utterly crushed today. Live so the revolution may live again another day."

Even as he spoke, Trys was aware that Lyrdahl's anger was building. He could see his visions of glory evaporating and he was not about to let it happen without a fight.

With a bound, Lyrdahl leaped from the pedestal and landed close to Trys who took two steps back.

"I was wrong! You are not the revolution! You have come to kill the revolution! You have come to kill me!"

Not being armed himself, Lyrdahl spun and grabbed the blood blade from the back scabbard of a man next to him. He slashed the air with it and lunged toward Trys.

"Stop it!" screamed Roxyna.

"Shut up, you traitor!" he screamed back. Instead of finishing his lunge, he swung the edge of the blade at Roxyna's head.

Trys yanked out his own blade and charged forward. But Roxyna drew her dagger, deflected the blow, and slipped off to one side.

"Kill them! Kill both of them!" ordered Lyrdahl who waved the sword around but stepped back, now that the first flush of the killing madness had passed.

The warriors drew their blades and encircled Trys and Roxyna, but kept some distance from them. Roxyna moved to Trys and turned him around. He looked over his shoulder, wondering what she was doing. She put her back to his and held her dagger out steadily toward the men who faced her in the circle of death which surrounded them.

"I'm sorry," she said. She reached back with her left hand and patted his right side. He clamped his right elbow tightly against the hand for a moment even as he kept the blade of his own sword in a defensive posture.

"There's nothing to be sorry about. The man is mad but the

revolution might survive despite that, at least in the long run."

"I don't mean that, exactly, although I am sorry for that, too. I mean I'm sorry we never had a chance to make love."

Trys looked sharply back over his shoulder. Roxyna also darted a backward look. She smiled at him and then looked away. He reached back with his left hand and touched her hip. She swayed it out to meet his touch.

"Do it now!" screamed Lyrdahl.

The warriors attacked. There were nine in the circle. Five of them shuffled about to face Roxyna who they viewed as the easiest one to take out first. Two lunged at her. Trys swung his long blade out to drive back the four facing him and then spun to try to impale the one on Roxyna's left.

"Thanks. Just stay back," hissed out Roxyna as she twisted under his blade. In one sinuous motion, she managed to come up inside the guard of the man on her left, stab him directly through the heart, and swing back to her original position with her back against Trys's.

All of their attackers took a big step back. "I guess I won't worry so much about you," said Trys.

"That's right. I've protected myself for some time in Low Hold. I know all of the tricks of knife fighting," she answered with some pride.

"There are a lot of them, though," remarked Trys. "Sooner or later, they will probably get through our guard."

"Let's make it later."

And with they settled down into a defensive posture, watching the small movements of their opponents to try to gauge when one might be preparing to make a move.

A half hour passed and three men lay dead on the floor. Trys had sustained two minor cuts and Roxyna a shallow slash along her left arm. Lyrdahl watched it all intently from his pedestal. Trys could tell he was working himself up for another hysterical outburst, even as his warriors continued to keep their distance and prod gingerly at them with their blades.

"I've had enough of this!" began Lyrdahl in an ascending voice. "Finish them off! They are enemies of the revolution! Death is all they deserve!"

The circling warriors all nodded grimly and were about to make a final deadly rush, when a man ran around the bulge in the ceiling and up to the base of the pedestal. He was cut and bleeding from various wounds. He panted with exertion and weariness.

"Lyrdahl," he gasped out.

"What is it? I'm busy here."

"The Gate is falling."

"What do you mean?"

"Falling to the Ice Guards and the Blood Guards and Grendyl's men. And it's falling because of you."

"What drivel are you talking?" snapped Lyrdahl.

The man straightened up, even though the wince of pain showed it cost him dearly. "The others are winning because our own people are killing each other. Half of our officers have gone over to the other side, while the remaining half slavishly follow your orders to hold a given corridor at any cost. We command a hundred yards of a corridor while the invaders hold the rest. It is over. The revolution is nearly dead."

"Kill him, too." Lyrdahl pointed at the messenger.

"No." The single word murmured through the crowd about the pedestal and even reached the circle about Trys and Roxyna, which suddenly broke and left them alone, still back to back.

"It's over. You're over," said the messenger as he raised his blood stained blade which glowed with the warmth of the freshly spilled blood along his length.

"You will listen to me. You will obey me," said Lyrdahl, even as he moved to the back of the pedestal and close to the wall where the sunlight still glowed. "I am the revolution. I am the leader. You have to listen to me for it to succeed. We can still win. We can still kill them all. No one will be left. No one. Only the revolution. Only the revolution!"

On the last word they surged forward. Lyrdahl threw up his hands and then went down under the hacking blades. Trys looked away from the slaughter, while Roxyna watched with a determination to see this phase of the revolution to its bloody close.

When the killing was over, the men and women stepped back from what they had done. They looked at each other with a mixture of horror and satisfaction and confusion. With their leader gone, they had no idea what to do other than to survive. That notion seemed to strike all of them at the same moment and without a word of farewell, they left the Hall of the Revolution in all different directions.

Trys and Roxyna looked at each other.

"We've got to get out," murmured Trys.

"I can get us out. I know the Gate."

"Where?"

"Down to the River Ice. Down to the galleries there. You remember the galleries, don't you?" She smiled slightly.

"Yes. I remember them."

"Hold Gate will be taken over by Ice Guards or Blood Guards, or both. We can't go into Low Hold. That leaves..."

"The Waste," replied Trys with a sigh of relief. At that

moment, he wanted nothing more than to run to the Waste, to hide in the Waste, to cleanse himself in the Waste.

"Yes, I guess so. I've never been into the deep Waste," said Roxyna with a tremor of fear which seemed incongruous after the courageous battle she had just fought.

"It's good. And I'll be with you."

"Yes, you will be. Let's go."

They turned from the pedestal. As they did so, Trys noticed the blood from Lyrdahl's body had spattered over the wall which the sunlight was about to leave as it moved in its course through the distant sky. The splash of blood gave a bizarre definition to the picture seen so dimly before. The ascending line was an image of the Hold rising triumphantly from the ruins of the mountain. The Hold appeared like a clenched fist which had smashed the top of the mountain. Above the tumbled stones, it was being shaken in defiance at the softening rays of the sun.

Trys stopped for a moment to contemplate the scene of death. Part of the revolution had died there, that much he knew. But what he was not so certain of was what part still lived, within people like Roxyna and even himself. He wiped his hand across his eyes as if to clear them of the weariness he felt pressing down on him. Then he turned and walked quickly after Roxyna who waited at the door to the Hall of the Revolution. Together they went down and out of Hold Gate.

## XXIV

TRYS PAUSED by an opening in the outer skin of Hold Gate which had once been a high vaulted window. Only the extreme point of the arch remained to hint at its former grace. The rest of the opening was a broken jumble of stones and masonry which defied the viewer to imagine what it might have looked like, even as it allowed a panoramic view of the River Ice and the Waste beyond.

Trys sucked in a lungful of the frigid air and shook the drops of blood from his hot blade. They spattered a drift of snow just inside the opening and hissed. He had just dispatched two of their pursuers. They had been Ice Guards. Before that they had encountered Blood Guards and Lord Grendyl's men. Hold Gate swarmed with the enemies of the revolution and its defenders were only seen down obscure corridors fleeing for their lives.

Roxyna had been upset by how quickly the revolution had collapsed, but she had already made up her mind it was not completely dead, merely in retreat. Trys had agreed, both to comfort her and because he felt that something like the revolution, which had swelled up from the lowest layers of society, could never be entirely extinguished once it had begun.

He had sent Roxyna on ahead while he had fought the last rearguard action. She had protested, but he had insisted, wanting to find a safe haven in which to rest for even a short time. She had hurriedly told him the route to follow just before he had shoved her forward, and then turned to face the latest set of foes.

The two Ice Guards had been even more tired than he had been. Their defense had gotten sloppy and, with a burst of energy, he had been able to thrust one through the throat and then slash the edge of his blade across the chest of the other. The one with the throat wound had died quickly. The other one had not lingered long after that.

He shook his sword once more. The blood metal was hot enough to evaporate the small amount of blood left. No more drops of red darkened the snow drift.

It was then he realized he had shaken the blood from his blade without an invocation to the gods. He had done it as a practical matter; to clear the length of blood metal from annoying drips. It had been a long time since he had performed an act to propitiate the gods and he suddenly felt empty and unworthy. The Hold did strange things to people. Cyln had often told him that. Only now did he know how strange.

He turned from the opening and listened for any sounds of pursuit behind him. He heard nothing. Taking his blade in his left hand, he flexed the aching muscles of his right hand. He was not used to so much sustained swordplay. He shook his head at the thought and at his realization of his lapse of devotion. He then walked down the set of shallow steps near the opening. Roxyna had told him to keep to this corridor and keep moving down toward the River Ice.

Three sets of steps and four corridors later he found himself at the entrance to a chamber which seemed to beckon him in. Through the wide empty entranceway and the high windows across from it, he could see the moiling surface of the River Ice beyond and below the chamber. But it was not the River Ice which called him. It was a sense of familiarity about the space immediately in front of him.

He stepped through the entranceway and into a room which was high and vaulted and airy and, most importantly, sacred. The chamber had once been a place of worship. Both the design and the lingering sense of peace told him that. It was similar in design to places of worship and interpretation in the far North, only on a grander scale. The narrow length of the room was oriented along a north and south axis. The Northern end tapered to a point, like the tip of a blood blade. The Interpreter would stand in the alcove created by the curved walls as he shared his interpretation with the people gathered below him. There was no altar or dias, for all stood on the same level. The space was arranged to provide a sounding board so that even if the Interpreter spoke quietly, he could be heard in all parts of the chamber.

Trys walked in and down to the alcove. The unquiet surface of the River Ice was on his right hand and the solid mass of the mountain from which the chamber was carved was upon his left. He half closed his eyes as he moved reverently to the dusty point of the room. It had not been used for centuries, but the chamber still retained a sense of the sacred and Trys reveled in it.

He entered the alcove and found the traditional symbol of the ice laden sun worked in colored stones upon the floor. Here was where Mother Ice and Father Sun merged for a brief moment. Here was where the ultimate harmony of Winterhold was manifest.

Trys bowed his head for a second to gather his thoughts, and then raised it and turned to the open, empty space of the ruined chamber. He raised his hands, his left one still holding his blade, and intoned the opening Chant of Creation from the Chronicles of Blood. His voice filled the room and spilled out across the River Ice. He was sure the chamber quivered as he once again put it to the use for which it had been intended.

He completed the chant and lowered both hands and head. Staring down at the symbol beneath his feet, he suddenly realized he had not seen Roxyna. She should have reached this chamber, if she had come down the same way he had.

His head shot up and he scanned the distant corners of the sacred chamber. There was nothing but the debris of centuries of neglect. But then he heard a scuffling. Just as the space was designed to carry his voice outward, it also brought back to him sounds from the far corners. The scuffling came from a small doorway at the end opposite to that of the alcove.

Trys transferred his blade from his left to his right hand, but remained standing on the symbol upon the floor. It gave him strength, and he felt sure he would soon have need of that commodity.

The scuffling resolved itself into the sound of footsteps upon the dirty floor as a group of people emerged from the doorway. Six warriors entered first and took up positions in a line which spanned the width of the chamber. Roxyna was brought out next, each of her arms held tightly by a warrior. She walked stiffly but with little resistance. And finally, Lord Grendyl swept in, his blood blade drawn and his eyes blazing.

"Roxyna," whispered Trys, forgetting his voice would carry the length of the room.

"Yes, your sweet, rebellious Roxyna is my prisoner," said Grendyl. "And now, so are you."

"The revolution is over," said Trys as if that would explain and excuse everything.

"That may well be. I did find the dead and somewhat mutilated body of Lyrdahl in a large and ugly hall of Hold Gate. He was certainly one of the leaders of the rebellion. And now I have the other one."

Trys sighed. "I am not a leader of the revolution."

"Perhaps not a conscious leader. But you are a force which needs to be dealt with. You hold certain...power."

Grendyl had decided to enter Hold Gate and to find and remove Trys himself. His connection with the half throne was too strong to allow it to remain unbroken, either by a declaration of illegitimacy on the part of the Interpreters or by the elimination of the man from the equation altogether. As he had suspected, Dwilkon had refused to declare the claim null and void. The sneaky Interpreter had not wanted to get rid of a potential pawn without first being absolutely certain that the player held no value for him. Grendyl had threatened the gaunt High Interpreter, but had been summarily dismissed. Being as direct as he was, Grendyl had decided to deal with the threat to the half throne in the only way he knew how.

"You mean my birth mother and father? No Interpreter has given that any legitimacy. No one has recognized any claim to the half throne, and none has been made."

"I am here then to make sure that none is ever made," declared Grendyl who raised the length of his blade before his face. At first, he held the flat of the blade toward Trys. Then, he turned it so one edge faced Trys while the other faced him. It was the ancient challenge to a duel.

Trys took a deep breath and held it for a moment. He knew Lord Grendyl was accounted one of the best swordsmen in the Hold. His age did not diminish his ability. Indeed, his longer experience with the blade was said to have enhanced his skills.

Trys let out his breath and stepped off the symbol of the frozen sun and onto the main floor of the ruined chapel. He reached a point about ten feet from where Grendyl stood and stopped. He brought his blood blade up before his face and was about to repeat Grendyl's actions when Roxyna spoke up.

"Trys, you don't have to. Run. Run right now, and you can still escape. You can make the causeway before they can catch you and be in the Waste in no time," she said in a tone of voice intended to be commanding.

Grendyl looked back at the woman and then at Trys to see what effect her words would have. The blade held steady before his face.

"I love you, Trys," pleaded Roxyna. "Save yourself for my sake."

"I will save us both, and I will do that by staying," said Trys firmly.

Trys turned the blade in his hands so it appeared to him that Grendyl was split in two by the length of the sword. The challenge and acceptance were now complete.

They stepped forward and crossed blades. The high ping of blood metal on blood metal signalled the start of the duel.

Trys lunged once and then twice and was somewhat surprised to find Grendyl backing away from his energetic but not particularly skillful attacks. He was even more surprised when the First Lord shuffled forward, slid inside his guard, and casually pinked him on the left thigh as if to show him just how easy it would be for the old warrior to defeat the novice swordsman.

Trys slashed his blade to left and right furiously as he backed away from the unwavering point of his opponent. He reached down and touched the cut on his leg. His fingers came away slick with blood but also the knowledge that the wound was only superficial. He realized then he could not match Grendyl in skill with the blade.

The older man's experience with the blade precluded that. But perhaps he could overwhelm him with his youthful energy, as long as he stayed out of the deadly reach of the sword.

With that in mind, Trys went to work alternately battering at the defense of the First Lord and skipping back out of reach of the thrusting blade. Sweat beaded his brow and his arm was beginning to ache horribly when Trys noticed that the point of Grendyl's sword did not flash back to its defensive posture quite as quickly as it had after a series of slashes and a sliding but cautious thrust.

Grendyl's eyes narrowed when he realized his opponent had noticed the slight show of weakness. He gritted his teeth and brought his blade up viciously to send a thrust from Trys up and over his head. He then spun and kicked out with a booted foot. Trys easily avoided it, but took two steps back. They both paused and watched each other carefully as they panted and gathered their strength once again.

Roxyna struggled in the grip of her captors and one yanked hard on her arm. She cried out. Trys glared at the warrior who had hurt her. He had had enough of the sparring. Even if he did manage to kill the old warrior, he assumed he would have the rest of his men to deal with. After all, this was the Hold and rules which applied to challenges in the Waste were probably not honored here.

Trys carefully measured the distance from where he stood to where the two warriors held Roxyna. He had worked his way around to Grendyl's left and so was closer to the three than he had been at the beginning of the duel. He knew Grendyl was slowing and if he put on a burst of speed, he might be able to get past the old warrior and over to Roxyna before anyone knew what was happening.

He let his weight shift to his left foot and raised his blade, as if he were about to launch another attack at Grendyl. Instead, he turned and lunged for the warrior holding Roxyna. In two long bounds he reached the group. Before the warrior on Roxyna's left, the one who had hurt her, could draw his blade, he was staggering back with Trys's blade already sliding out of his pierced heart.

The other warrior let go of the woman and drew his blade. That gave Trys just enough time to grab Roxyna by the very arm which had been twisted and pull her back with him to the end of the chapel where the symbol of the frozen sun adorned the floor.

"That was foolish," said Roxyna as she stumbled and nearly fell. Trys kept her on her feet and squeezed her arm. She winced.

"Sorry."

"Oh, it was wonderful, just foolish," grinned Roxyna. "Watch out!"

Trys dropped into a crouch and spun about, his sword

swinging out in a low arc. The warrior who had held Roxyna had followed them. He tried to stop but was too late to avoid Trys's blade. It caught him just above the knees. He went down. Trys stepped in and thrust him once cleanly through the heart.

His blade pulsing with heat from the spilled blood along its length, Trys turned once again to face Lord Grendyl. He discovered the First Lord waiting patiently for him, as if the brief interlude of Roxyna's rescue had been an accepted part of the duel.

"You fight well," commented Grendyl.

"I make it up as I go along," replied Trys.

"Yes, I noticed that. I believe I have also noticed all of your weaknesses. I will have to end this little confrontation now. Especially since you have killed two of my men and rescued your lady, for the moment."

"I understand. And you will understand that I intend to prevent you from doing just that."

"Of course."

Without another word, Grendyl raised his blade and began a savage, slashing attack which drove Trys back toward the design on the floor where Roxyna waited. Trys could feel the old warrior testing his strength with each hard blow and looking for the slightest crack in his defense.

He found it. Trys had just cleared the point of Grendyl's blade from a probing lunge at his chest and was bringing his blade back to cover himself, when he realized the aching muscles of his arm would not respond as quickly as he needed them to. In a flash, Grendyl had cut past his slowly rising sword and fallen down on Trys's head.

Trys twisted to the left to try to escape the descending edge of the blade. He could not get completely out of the way. The blade caught him on the left side of his head, sliced down across his left ear, and cut into his shoulder.

A last desperate jerk of his body prevented the sword from biting deeply into his shoulder. It turned in Grendyl's hand and skimmed across the leather of the singlesuit, opening it up but not the skin beneath.

While Grendyl staggered forward with the power of his blow and then pulled himself upright, Trys danced back and swung his sword wildly to ward off any further blows. The blood from his head wound came in a gush and nearly blinded his left eye. A quick touch to his head and his left ear told him the scalp had probably been cut shallowly but that a portion of his left ear was missing.

Trys had no idea of how much blood he might lose nor how quickly. In an instant, he decided to use the adrenalin pumping through his veins and carry the attack to the First Lord.

He cut high, then low, then high again. The clang of blood metal on blood metal echoed from the gaping walls of the chapel and out across the River Ice below. Grendyl parried and then hesitated, seemingly stunned by the savagery of the attack.

In his heightened state of strength and awareness, that second of hesitation was all Trys needed. He stepped inside Grendyl's defense and brought his blade down hard. Lord Grendyl's sword was at the end of an outward swing. He did the only thing he could to save himself. He raised his left arm to block the blade.

The edge struck Grendyl's wrist and cut through it. With a cry of anguish, the First Lord sank to one knee, let go of his sword, and grasped the wound with his right hand.

Trys stopped. Before him knelt his opponent. His left hand was gone. Grendyl looked up. Trys clearly saw he expected the final cut and that he would take it like a warrior, unflinching and brave.

Instead, Trys raised his sword before his face. He turned it from the edge to the flat facing the First Lord. "The duel is over," he murmured.

Through gritted teeth, Grendyl said, "For now. Only for now. Go. You have won that right."

Lord Grendyl's men had begun to surge forward once they saw their leader grievously injured. They had nearly reached the spot where the two stood transfixed when Grendyl swung his head about and shook it at them. They stopped. Glares of anger and impatience were focussed on Trys.

Those glares were interrupted by a clamor from the doorway at the far end of the chapel. A group of seven men and three women burst into the chapel. They were revolutionaries in flight, but fully armed and obviously using their weapons to cut their way out. Trys could feel the warmth from their blades as it wafted across the open space of the chapel.

With a shout, the revolutionaries recognized the hated First Lord and charged at the small band which surrounded him. His men formed a tight circle about their wounded Lord and settled down to the grim business of fighting, glad to have someone to vent their frustration on.

For a second, Trys paused. He was not sure he should leave his worthy opponent in such a situation. But Roxyna tugged on his arm from behind and he spun about.

"Let's get out of here."

"But Grendyl..."

"Has his men to protect him. And you have a bad wound. You look like you should be the one on the floor."

Trys reached up to the side of his head. The blood had slowed but was still flowing down across his shoulder.

"I guess I did get a little cut..."

"It's a gash and I need to bind it up or you will soon collapse from loss of blood. Let's go."

"Which way?" Suddenly, Trys felt light headed and he blinked to clear his left eye of the blood which still trickled into it. He stared about him at the chapel and could not seem to decide in which direction lay safety.

"This way," urged Roxyna, who grabbed him firmly by the arm and led him at a lope for the crumbling wall whose tall windows looked down upon the River Ice.

She scrambled up the pile of loose stones beneath a window and Trys followed. His foot slipped just as he reached the top of the pile and he went down on one knee. As he picked himself up, he glanced back into the chapel. There he saw one of Grendyl's men putting the finishing touches on a makeshift bandage about the stump of his left arm. He then watched as the First Lord grabbed up his sword and stood to direct his men as they battled the fervent attack from the desperate revolutionaries.

Trys knew at that moment that the gods had gotten him through the fight and that perhaps they had some other use for him. He turned and slid down the scrye on the other side of the window. Just beyond the River Ice lay the Waste and, what he hoped was freedom from the deadly ways of the Hold.

## XXV

THE CAUSEWAY was littered with dead bodies, but empty of any live combatants. The Blood Guards had fallen back to the Camp after taking the lowest levels of Hold Gate and holding them for several days. The revolutionaries who had struck and disappeared, had disappeared for good with the final dissolution of the revolution. The Ice Guards still rummaged about within the Gate but ignored the causeway as a distant frontier, not worth possessing.

A light snow had fallen only an hour ago. It had laid a modest shroud of white over the fallen. Trys bent over a body and brushed the snow away from the torn chest. The head of the brum pike had smashed in most of the chest but had not damaged the Waste cloak of the dead warrior. With a grunt of satisfaction and then exertion, he yanked one arm free from the folds of the cloak, rolled the body over, and pulled the cloak off the other arm. He stood up and shook out the stiffly frozen leather. The miniature snowstorm he created sent out a fine mist of snow to mask the ugliness of death at his feet.

He turned to find Roxyna a little way off, poking her way amidst the carnage on the causeway. She paused, prodded a body with her toe, decided against it, and moved on. She had winced when he had first told her they must scavenge what they needed to move out into the Waste. They required Waste cloaks, weapons, and as many concentrated food supplies as they could comfortably carry. She had gritted her teeth and nodded. While she had never been out into the deep Waste, she had lived and thrived within the harsh environment of Low Hold. Survival meant doing distasteful things, but it was worth it.

She stopped again. Trys could tell she was estimating the size of the Waste cloak upon the body at her feet. A quick nod and an even quicker movement, and she had stripped the cloak from the body. She then walked rapidly toward him, shaking out the cloak as she came, keeping it as far from her body as her arms would allow.

"I've got one," she said, proud of the fact she had managed to acquire the cloak rather than being pleased with the quality of the cloak itself.

With a flourish, she gave the cloak a final shake and settled it about her shoulders. With only the hint of a squirm, she slid her arms into its folds and flipped up the hood. She pivoted to give Trys a good view of the cloak from all sides.

"Is this a good one?" she asked in a critical tone of voice. "I've worn Waste cloaks before but never for venturing out into the real Waste. The ones I've had were heavier on style than protection against the cold."

Trys looked it over as she turned again and smiled at the way she smiled bravely back. "That's a good one. It has several layers of hide sewn together. The number of layers are critical. Too few and you freeze, too many and you sweat and then freeze. That one looks like it has just the right number and it's well put together also."

Trys slipped into the cloak he had picked up and settled it about him. He did not flip up the hood since his head still ached from the wound inflicted by Grendyl and the left side of his head bulged with the bandage and herbs the Roxyna had improvised from bits of leather and cloth and supplies from the apothecary shop she had brought with her.

After she had completed her ministrations, she had stepped back and declared him quite jaunty looking with the swathe of the bandage sweeping down across one side of his head. He had lost a part of his ear and would have a scar on his forehead, but he assured himself it was better than the wounds he had given to the old First Lord.

They gathered together their supplies. They consisted of several pounds of concentrated food, which would last them a few weeks in the Waste as long as it was doled out in meager portions, a blood blade, dagger, and light brum pike for each of them, even though Roxyna protested she did not know how to use a pike to which Trys replied he would certainly teach her the use of the handy weapon and tool, two extra Waste cloaks, which could be arranged to form a commodious tent for two people, and, of course, a breather mask for each of them.

Trys bundled the supplies into the extra Waste cloaks and tied them expertly. They then strapped on their blades, slid on their breather masks, and took up their brum pikes. They were ready.

Without hesitation, Trys strode down off the causeway and into the Waste. He did not even look back, until he realized that Roxyna was not in back of him. He turned to find her poised on the crumbling edge of the ancient structure, as if afraid to take the plunge into the wild element before her.

He shoved up the snout of his loosely tied breather mask. "What's the matter?"

Roxyna ground the butt of her pike into the loose stone of the causeway. A chunk broke off and tumbled down into the snow where it sank from sight. "That's the problem." She pointed to the sunken stone with her chin.

"It's just a loose stone which fell into the snow," said Trys with a frown.

"I feel like that stone," she said quietly. "I feel like I'm coming loose from all I've known and I'll be swallowed up by the Waste."

Trys bowed his head in thought for a moment. He could see her point. She had only known Low Hold all of her life. The seemingly limitless expanse of the Waste was a daunting sight and it did require a set of survival skills entirely different from those which Roxyna had developed.

"I'm here to help you. You're tough and resourceful. You'll learn how to live in the Waste, and you'll discover how glorious the freedom is which exists out there." He held out his hand to her.

She nodded and hopped down from the causeway. She sank into the snow up to her knees but retained her balance. After plowing through the soft snow, she reached his side and took his hand in hers. He squeezed it. She squeezed back.

"Let's go," she said in a low but firm voice.

Hand in hand, they ascended the first snow dune and stopped at the peak to look back at Hold Gate. Wisps of smoke and tongues of fire were visible on several levels of the monolithic structure. But even as they watched some of the fires winked out and the smoke diminished.

"Much of the interior will be damaged," she remarked. "But the basic structure, that which makes Hold Gate, Hold Gate will remain. It will survive, and so will I."

"We may be back some day," suggested Trys, trying to encourage her.

"Perhaps. But I'm in no hurry. I grew up there, but I need to live out here now. Let me get that down right and then maybe I'll want to return."

"A true woman of the Waste," smiled Trys.

"I like that, a woman of the Waste." Roxyna smiled back.

Together they crested the dune and slid down the soft snow on the other side. Their feet dug in and their bodies leaned back to keep them from falling down the steep slope.

They reached the bottom in a swirl of powdery snow. When it settled, they found themselves standing on the true edge of the Waste, flat and white and limitless. A short distance off, they also discovered two figures swathed in Waste cloaks standing next to a light skimmer sled, its sail neatly furled and abundant supplies tied to its sides, fully equipped for travel.

Trys gripped the shaft of his brum pike in both hands. He nodded to Roxyna that they should approach the pair with caution. As they did so, the taller of the two figures took a step forward and threw back the hood of the cloak. There, smiling at them, was Cyln.

Trys cried out and ran forward. Roxyna followed more tentatively, not knowing who this woman was who so excited Trys.

Trys ran up to her and embraced her and Roxyna stopped dead in her tracks. He then turned to Roxyna and said, "This is Cyln, my good friend and mentor, Cyln. The bodyguard to the Queen/Lady."

The former statement reassured Roxyna, while the latter one put her on her guard immediately. Even though she knew Trys was the son of the Queen/Lady, she was not sure what sort of reception Trys might expect from the ruler. After all, Lord Grendyl, one of the Queen/Lady's chief supporters, had tried very hard to kill him only hours ago.

"Why are you here?" asked Trys.

"To meet you, of course," replied Cyln.

"How did you know we would be here?"

"I knew you would head back to the Waste. That is what I would have done. I also heard of your encounter with Lord Grendyl. He was rushed back to the Hold to have his wound tended to. He will live." She said this last with some regret but a certain amount of respect as well.

Trys touched the left side of his head. "He is a formidable opponent. I too will have a scar to remind me of the battle."

"I taught you well, I see."

"And, yes, we are headed North. I have had enough of the Hold. Roxyna goes with me." Trys turned at this to motion Roxyna closer.

She stepped forward with a determined stride, as if she had to show her pride before such a well known and respected figure within the Hold. She thrust out her hand and Cyln took it. They shook. A slight smile curled the ends of Cyln's mouth. Trys could tell she approved of the firm, honest clasp.

But the smile faded quickly as she recalled the other person still standing a few feet away. She looked first at Trys and then at the person and then back to Trys. Trys could tell the bodyguard wanted to say something but was uncertain how to do it.

A couple of more glances between the two of them and she threw up her hands. She blurted out, "Trys, do you still have the medallion?"

"Why, yes, I do."

"Then put it on and meet your birth mother before you leave for the North."

Cyln sighed with relief. She had finally said it. Roxyna tensed, the old revolutionary impulse of hatred for things royal warring with the realization that the woman standing close by was Trys's mother.

Trys stared hard at the woman still muffled in her Waste cloak. The last time they had met it had been as strangers. Now that he knew the truth of his birth, he was uncertain how the woman who had given him life would treat him. She was the Queen/Lady, after all, and in his experience that came before all else.

Alisande pushed back her hood to reveal her head with its gray hair streaked with black; hair which had once been all jet black. Both she and Trys suddenly moved forward. He wrapped his arms about her and crushed her to him. She returned the embrace with as much fervor.

After several moments, he eased up and let his arms slide from around her but continued to hold her hands in his. He moved back to see her face. Her eyes brimmed over with tears.

"I can see your father in you," she said in a voice husky with emotion, "as well as enough of myself to make me both proud and uncomfortable. I am sorry for the heritage I have given you."

"I would have no other," he replied in a hoarse whisper.

"I still can hardly believe you exist. I thought you had died at birth. And now to find you, to hold you."

"My life has been turned upside down also. My parents are suddenly my adoptive parents and you are my birth mother. A huge change occurred in a split second. But I will do my best to help you out where and when you need..."

Alisande gently placed her hand on his mouth. "Hush. Don't make promises just now. You are your own person. That is one benefit from all of this. You did not grow up entangled in the web of politics and hatred and greed. Perhaps you may even be the person who wipes away the rotting web. Don't try to be my son. Be yourself. I will love you all the more for that, just as I loved your father."

Trys nodded and squeezed her hands which he still held.

Cyln stirred uneasily behind them and then spoke up. "My Queen/Lady, I sincerely hate to cut short this reunion, but you must return soon to the Hold and Trys and Roxyna must get away before troops from either Hold or Camp track them down."

Alisande sighed raggedly. "I have just found my son and I have to leave him so soon. But, of course, I do understand. My life has been nothing but doing what must be done. Why should this be any different? Remember Trys, being a Queen/Lady forces one to learn all of the harsh lessons about sacrifice. I would advise you to stay as far away from the seats of power as possible if you want to live your own life in your own way. A small crumb of advice from a mother to her son."

Trys smiled and nodded, unable to frame a reply.

Alisande then turned to Roxyna who took a step back and appeared confused about whether or not she should bow to the sovereign before her. The Queen/Lady beckoned her to come closer. She shuffled to Trys's side.

"Roxyna, I want you to take care of my son, as I know he will take care of you."

Roxyna merely nodded, overwhelmed by the revelations of the past few minutes.

Alisande then took Trys's face in her hands and kissed him on both cheeks and the forehead. She lingered over the last kiss but finally dropped her hands and moved her lips away from contact with the skin of his face.

"I give you my blessing, my son." Her voice grew ragged as she said the words. She swallowed and then continued in a more practical tone. "For your own sake, you must never return to the Hold. Only death or imprisonment await you here."

"And my mother," replied Trys. "I cannot promise I will never return."

"I understand. I understand all too well," she said softly.

"Trys, help me to get the skimmer turned toward the Waste," said Cyln.

Reluctantly, Trys let his hands slide out of his mother's grasp. He then turned and walked stiffly and determinedly to where Cyln hauled on the skimmer sled to turn it. He shoved hard and it slewed about, grating on the rough snow beneath its runners. Cyln hopped up onto the sled and ran up the sail. A freshening breeze which blew away from the Hold and toward the Waste belled out the bryl hide.

Cyln motioned for Roxyna to get on. She ran to the sled. Cyln indicated she should sit in front of the sail. The bodyguard busied herself in showing Roxyna how to lash herself on securely and how to help Trys sail the skimmer.

Trys turned and walked back to Alisande one last time. He reached out and touched her cheek and smoothed her hair.

"Farewell, mother."

"Farewell, my son."

The skimmer was beginning to gather some speed when Cyln called out to Trys to hurry. He turned and ran for the slowly moving sled. He leaped on and grabbed the light tiller which allowed him to guide the skimmer over the snow.

Cyln grabbed his upper arm and squeezed it hard. She then slid off the sled and gave it a last push with her foot. A strong gust of wind sent it flashing forward over a low snow dune. It disappeared from sight for a moment and then rose again. Clear of the dunes, its sail snapped taut and it picked up speed. Trys did not even need to tack, but simply held the tiller straight and let the wind push them toward the heart of the Waste.

Cyln walked back to stand next to Alisande who strained upward to catch a last glimpse of the vanishing skimmer.

"I found him, only to lose him again."

"Now that you have found him, you can never truly lose him again, my Queen/Lady."

"Wisdom from the Waste, my dear Cyln?"

"I recall hearing that when I was young, a very, very long time ago." She was also about to say she did not think they had seen the last of Trys or Roxyna, but she stopped. Better to see what the gods disposed. Instead, she put on her official air and said, "We must get back into the Hold, my Queen/Lady."

"I know. And I can go now with a lighter heart, just knowing he is out there somewhere. And Cyln, dear Cyln, I want to thank you for saving him for me, the first time and all of the others."

Cyln grunted and helped her monarch ascend the slippery side of the snow dune with more than her usual display of concern. Alisande felt the strong, reassuring pressure of her fingers and smiled. She patted her bodyguard's hand where it held her. Cyln grunted again and they kept walking. They reached the top of the dune and slid down its other side.

The wind picked up. It moaned over the top of the dune and threw a fine scrim of snow over the now empty spot. All traces of the meeting were eradicated. The surface of the Waste was once again smooth and pristine. The wind moved on and left the snow and the silence behind.

~*~

## Stephen Almekinder

Stephen Almekinder has a variety of experience as a writer. He received a finalist certificate from the Writers of the Future Contest for one of his short stories. He wrote a radio play which was produced and aired. He adapted the science fiction novel Nova, by Samuel R. Delany, into a screenplay with the permission of the author. And one of his short stories was published in a science fiction/fantasy magazine, Once Upon A World, in 1997.

The Blood of Winterhold is a sequel to Winterhold. He plans to continue the saga, since there are many other stories yet to be told.